FRESH KILLS

A journalist and documentary film maker, Reggie Nadelson is a New Yorker who also makes her home in London. She is the author of six previous novels featuring the detective Artie Cohen ('the detective every woman would like to find in her bed' *Guardian*), most recently *Red Hook*. Her non-fiction book *Comrade Rockstar*, the story of the American who became the biggest rock star in the Soviet Union, is to be made into a film starring Tom Hanks.

ALSO BY REGGIE NADELSON

Bloody London
Skin Trade
Red Mercury Blues
Hot Poppies
Somebody Else
Comrade Rockstar
Disturbed Earth
Red Hook

REGGIE NADELSON

FRESH KILLS

arrow books

Published by Arrow Books, 2007

2 4 6 8 10 9 7 5 3 1

First published in Great Britain in 2006 by
William Heinemann

Arrow Books
Random House,
20 Vauxhall Bridge Road,
London SW1V 2SA

Addresses for companies within The Random House Group Limited can be found at:
www.randomhouse.co.uk

The Random House Group Limited Reg. No. 954009

A CIP catalogue record for this book
is available from the British Library

ISBN 9780099465690

The Random House Group Limited makes every effort to ensure that the papers
used in its books are made from trees that have been legally sourced from well-managed
and credibly certified forests. Our paper procurement policy can be found at:
www.randomhouse.co.uk/paper.htm

Typeset by SX Composing DTP, Rayleigh, Essex

Printed in the UK by CPI Bookmarque, Croydon, CR0 4TD

For Helena

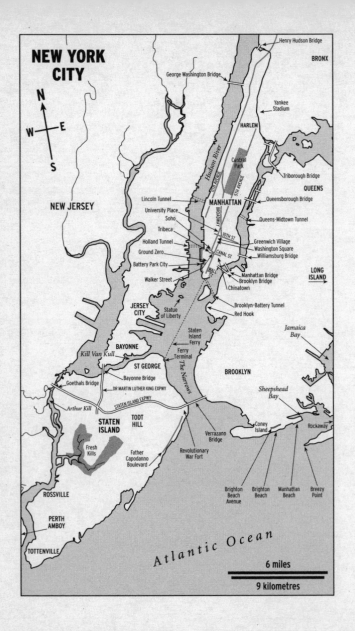

Part One

Tuesday July 5

1

The steady noise of the engine above me changed, I sat up, opened my eyes, squinted into the sun. The small sightseeing plane flying low over Coney Island stuttered across the sky and I held my breath, waiting for the crash. Next to me on the beach, my nephew Billy was stretched out. One hand holding a radio tuned to a Yankees game, his big adolescent feet in black sneakers, laces trailing, propped up on an empty pizza box from Totonno's.

The plane disappeared behind backlit clouds, probably heading for some airstrip nearby where tourists caught sightseeing flights.

It was Tuesday, a mild July day when only a few people, maybe a couple dozen, were stretched out on the sand near me catching some sun. Two old guys sat on low green plastic beach chairs and played gin rummy. A couple of women, their wives probably, wearing pull-on velour pants and matching windbreakers in pink and blue, sat near the men, reading Russian newspapers that rattled in the breeze. A Pakistani family ate lunch from metal containers, the compartments stacked up on each other, chatting in Urdu, probably Urdu, maybe imagining they were back home taking the afternoon off on some beach in Karachi. In Midwood, in the interior of Brooklyn around three miles from Coney Island, there was a big Pakistani community. I could smell the food. It made me hungry.

At the edge of the water, a chubby teenage girl with carrot-colored hair jogged heavily, her feet pulled down by damp sand. Two boys ran gracefully past her. An electric blue mermaid, also near the water, picked up her sequined blue tail, and scuttled up towards the boardwalk. The plane appeared again. Everyone on the beach looked up. No one moved now. Sun glinted off the mermaid's blue tail.

All this seemingly in slow motion, while music came from a boom box somewhere – Otis Redding's "Dock Of The Bay", which I'd always loved. I realized that the mermaid was one of the girls who dressed up every summer to march, if you could call it that, in the annual Coney Island Mermaid Parade.

The plane, out of control, zigzagged across the blue sky over the ocean, flew away from the beach, dipped down, one of its wings hanging loose, like a wounded insect. I got up, stumbled on the sand, found my phone in my jeans, called 911. It was too late. In a slow spiral, the plane lost altitude and then suddenly, snagged by gravity, fell.

In the windows I could see two faces looking down. Maybe they could see blue water coming up at them, Russians reading newspapers, a man running from Nathan's clutching a hot dog with a wiggly line of yellow mustard on the dog. I wondered if the people in the plane could see the mustard, and what they were thinking, or if there was time. Then the plane hit the sand and broke. People on the beach backed away, terrified, expecting an explosion, smoke, fire.

Next to me, Billy was already on his feet. Around us, people were grabbing their bags and towels, toys and cards, news-

4

papers, chairs, radios, coolers, looking up, running towards the boardwalk, then stopping, unsure which way to go.

Is it terrorists, I heard a woman say to her husband. An attack? The boom box kept playing; on it, the music changed, the Drifters singing "Up On The Roof".

The silvery plane lay near the edge of the water a couple of hundred yards away, crushed like a Coke can. The surf bubbled onto the beach and washed the pieces of the plane. I could just make out the bodies, half in, half out of it, including a little girl who was maybe three years old. She didn't move.

"Is anyone dead? Is the little girl dead?" Billy was staring at the plane, rigid with attention.

"Let's go," I said to Billy. "Come on."

He didn't move.

We had come out to Coney Island because Billy said the first thing he wanted when he got home to Brooklyn was to eat a pie from Totonno's. That and to sit in the sun and look at the ocean, and catch a few rays, he'd said, posing, his face up to the sky, hands on hips, like some guy in a TV commercial for suntan stuff.

"Now," I said.

Cars and trucks were screaming in the direction of the beach, driving onto the sand. Emergency crews were all over the wreck, pulling out the bodies, loading them into an ambulance. I thought I recognized a detective in a red jacket I'd met someplace. Smoke trailed upwards from the wreck. I grabbed for Billy's hand, he tossed his knapsack over his shoulder and we ran.

"Artie?"

"Are you OK?" I said to Billy. We were on the boardwalk, leaning against the railing, looking at the plane wreck, brushing sand off our clothes.

"This is really weird," he said. "I'm glad you're here."

"Let's get out of here."

"You think everyone's OK?"

A girl of about ten was standing near us with her mother, crying. Billy turned to her.

"It'll be OK," he said. "Hey – it's OK. It's over now. You all right?"

Billy Farone, who was my half sister's kid, was fourteen, lanky, broad shouldered, and nearly six feet tall already, as tall as me, almost. Last couple of days we'd been together, mostly he seemed to take things as they came. For an adolescent, he was pretty easy-going. He was interested in what people said and how they felt, and it was disarming. People liked him. He was a charming kid.

Thick black hair fell over Billy's forehead, his blue eyes lit up his face which, with the faint Slavic cast, cheekbones, chin, that kind of thing, reminded my of my father. Once in a while, hands shoved in his pockets, the big sneakers, the shoelaces undone, swaying a little side to side as if he was growing too fast to keep it all together, Billy was still a kid. Now, making sure the girl who'd been crying was OK, he seemed almost grown up. Black jeans, red T-shirt, a dark blue Yankees jacket, he leaned against the railing. He looked out at the water and the plane, worried.

"You think they're alive?" he said. "The people in the plane?"

"I don't know."

To change the subject, I told Billy how Charles Lindbergh opened Floyd Bennett Field a few miles away, one of the first airports in the country. 1923. Over by Dead Horse Bay, which was what they called it back then when the city's dead horses were boiled down for fat there and the stink was unbearable.

"Who's Charles Lindbergh?" Billy said, and I explained about the guy who first flew the Atlantic solo, took off from Roosevelt Field on Long Island by himself and how after that they called him Lucky Lindy. Billy was pretty interested in the story – he was a kid who mopped up information and paid attention to the answers when he asked you questions – but he made me stop when I him told how Lindbergh's baby was kidnapped. Case of the century, they had called it.

After a while, we went and sat on the boardwalk steps. Billy told me that he could tell right away from the arc of the plane that it hadn't been coming anyplace near us, and that he felt pretty crappy because he found himself waiting for the crash. He had wondered if it would spin, or just plunge nose down. He didn't want it to fall, but if it was going to, he wanted to see.

"It's the way people feel about car racing, right? Isn't it?" he asked me. "If it's going to happen, you want to see. Right Artie? I mean it was just crazy. You want some of my cucumbers?"

He took a plastic bag full of cucumber strips from the knapsack he carried over one shoulder. "God, I love cucumbers," said Billy and told me he liked the way the pale green flesh looked, the coolness and the crunch. In Florida, he added, cold cucumbers were great on a hot day. What did they say, cool as a cuke? Also, Billy said, he loved slicing them up, peeling the dark green skin with the red Swiss Army knife I had given him when he was younger. He held out the plastic bag.

People were all over the wreck of the plane. I stayed where I was; I figured no one needed an off-duty Manhattan detective like me messing up the scene.

"What?" Billy ate a piece of cucumber.

"Nothing."

"Come on, Artie, what?" He smiled. "What? Tell me. Please, please, please, please. I want to know what you're thinking."

I didn't answer him because I didn't want to lie. I was thinking how I couldn't believe that Billy was the same kid who had killed a man – been accused of killing a man – a couple of years back.

"Artie?"

"What?"

"You think we could go fishing tomorrow?"

"Sure."

"Awesome." He put the cucumbers back in his bag.

"You have any place in mind?"

"I was thinking out on the island, like Montauk? Any place, so long as it's you and me and we could fish, like before, the way we used to, you know?"

Before. Before Billy had been locked up in the place – they called it a therapeutic facility – in Florida. Before.

I nodded.

"I could make sandwiches for us," he said eagerly. "I'm really good at it. I can do those giant heroes with salami and cheese and ham and pepperoni and roasted peppers, and we can take sodas, and just hang together. I heard they got stripers running already. Blues. Guess what?"

"What?"

"Guess."

"Tell me."

"I even heard you can fly-fish in Central Park now," Billy threw his arm up and out in an arc as if he was fishing. "It sounds goofy, though, right?"

"We'll go to the island," I said. "You feel good and all?"

"Great." He put his hand on my sleeve, tentatively, wanting to hold on like a little kid, but too big for that now. His hand was as big as mine, the skin was rough and I knew he played ball without a glove.

"You know what?" he said.

"What's that?"

"You won't believe this. You'll laugh."

"Try me."

"I'm sort of hungry."

"You can't be hungry," I said. "We ate a whole pizza, and

some calzones, you ate cucumbers, we had waffles for breakfast, and bacon and about a quart of OJ."

"I'm a growing boy, right?" Deepening his voice, he mimicked some pompous pundit he'd heard on TV. He had the family knack for mimicry.

Again I thought how OK he was now. He was cured. Everything had finally fallen into place and he seemed like a normal New York kid who could talk a blue streak, fluent and funny, and sometimes pretty wry, and very observant. The sickness was gone. It was over.

"Artie?"

"Let's eat," I said. "Whatever you feel like."

"Something else." He was shy. "I need to ask you something."

"Whatever you want," I said, but my phone rang before he could answer.

"Where are you?" Sonny Lippert said on the phone when I answered it.

"On the beach," I said. "I'm busy."

"I have something I want you to do for me," said Lippert, my sometime boss. "A favor. I'm tied up in a shitty case and there's something I don't have time for, man, and I want you to do it."

"I'll call you tomorrow."

"Which beach?" Lippert said.

"What does it matter, I'm on the beach, I came to eat a pizza, whatever. I'll call you later. Hello?" I pretended the signal had gone.

Billy said, "Who was that?"

"It doesn't matter. Where do you want to eat? You want some hot dogs at Nathan's?"

"Let's go look at the plane."

"What about the hot dogs?" I said, but he had already started walking towards the wreck on the beach.

I said, "What?"

"What?"

"You were talking to yourself."

"No kidding? That's crazy." Billy was halfway down the beach, loping towards the wrecked plane. "Jeez, Art, I'm going to be like some young old guy, talking to myself. You never know, I could be drooling soon." He laughed as he imitated an old man stumbling along. Then he straightened up, and walked next to me.

"I'm almost as tall as you now," he said. "How old do I look? For real."

"Seventeen," I said.

There had been big tall men in my family in Russia when I was growing up there. My own father was tall, but my uncle Joe was a giant. He was almost seven feet tall with huge shoulders and a neck thick as a tree. He played basketball in school. Later on, because he thought he was a freak, he killed himself. I was fifteen when it happened but no one told me.

I got it out of my mother later on. Joe ran a vodka factory in Vladikavkaz near the river Volga. The peasants, shriveled and sickly from the war and malnutrition, were scared by Joe's size. They taunted him. Said he was a monster, that his size was the devil's work. Uncle Joe was forty-two when he shot himself.

"Hey, you wanted to ask me something," I said to Billy.

"It doesn't matter."

"Talk to me."

Billy stopped walking.

"Artie, can I come live with you for good? I can, right? I mean maybe not right now, but later, you know? I want to be like you so much. I think about it all the time. I could help you with cases and stuff, and we'd be together, like all the time."

I didn't know what to say. He was home on leave. He would go back to Florida in a couple of weeks. It would be a long time

10

until he was free. I didn't answer at first and then, because I wanted to see him happy, I said, "Sure."

"Hey, I'll race you," Billy said, and began running down to the water, kicking up sand with his black sneakers.

2

Until I saw Sonny Lippert coming towards us, I didn't think a whole lot about the fact that it was near this stretch of beach a jogger had found a heap of kid's clothing a couple of years back. It had been the dead of winter – a woman in a red fox fur coat walking her dogs on the snow-bleached boardwalk that day. More than two years. I remembered now. As soon as I saw Lippert, I remembered everything, and then I thought, so what? It didn't mean anything.

We were standing near the plane wreck. Billy had been trying to get up closer to it, but a guy in uniform asked him to step back, and he did it right away, politely, and nodded sagely as if he understood. Later he told me he was learning his way around cops, how they worked, imitating them, practicing their moves. He wasn't just playing around, he said. How old do I have to be to be a cop? he asked me. How long before I can start?

"Fuck you doing here, man?" The voice was Sonny Lippert's.

Sonny didn't shake my hand. Instead, he gave me one of those half hugs American guys go in for, then stepped back as if he'd startled himself by his own affection, and sank up to his ankles in the soft sand. With a neat wiry body, like a boy's, he was a little guy. He looked well, though. He looked like he was taking some care of himself. He patted his pockets.

"Where the fuck are my glasses?" said Sonny.

He wore a yellow shirt, black linen jacket, good chinos, and expensive loafers. His hair, a tight cap of black curls, was turning gray and I figured he had finally quit dyeing it. Sonny was about sixty-five, but his skin was tight and smooth. I didn't believe the rumors that he'd had work done on it.

"What am *I* doing?" I said. "What are *you* doing, Sonny?" I looked at his polished shoes. "You came out for some sun on the beach, wearing shoes that cost you four hundred bucks?"

"Don't break my balls, man," said Lippert. "You told me you were at the beach eating pizza, where else were you going to be except Coney? I need something from you," he added softly, as he surveyed the chaos on the beach. "You remember what happened on this particular beach, man? Two years ago already."

"I was trying to forget until you showed up."

Still looking for his glasses, Lippert went over to one of the guys who was close up to the wreck and asked him a couple of questions. The guy paid attention. You could see it impressed him that Sonny Lippert was asking his opinion. Everyone knew Lippert.

"So?" I said, when he came back.

"It's a fucking mess," Lippert said, gesturing at the wreck. "They don't know dick about what happened either, at least not yet. Ask me, I don't think it's terrorists, I mean what's the percentage in crashing a plane with a few people on a practically empty beach on a weekday? Probably some lousy tourist plane they put too many people in, they're too heavy and boom, ground coming up at you, you going down. So, Artie, man, you came out here to eat a pizza?"

"You called me, Sonny, remember? You got here pretty quick."

"I was in Brooklyn anyhow." He kicked aside a red flip-flop that lay upside down on the beach. "I hate it when there's only one shoe. I mean where the fuck is the other one?"

After his wife left him, after 9/11, Lippert had been next door to dead. Back then he was drinking a bottle of Scotch a day, sometimes two. He seemed better, sober, OK. After forty years in law enforcement, Sonny only worked special cases now, usually child crime. When he was working, he was sharp, honed, wound up tight as ever, maybe too tight, like a million-dollar clock that you always figured was about to bust.

"Sonny, what's going on?"

"An old case," he said. "Something's come up."

"What's that?"

Sonny looked around him. The beach had filled up with people, officials, tourists who had stopped to gape at the plane, kids down from the boardwalk.

People walking their dogs stopped and the dogs howled, maybe smelling something in the summer sun. Near me were the men who'd been playing cards on the beach and their wives, and they were discussing the crash in English with thick Russian accents.

"Terrorists," one man said. "For sure."

"Bastards," said another guy. "Foreign pricks."

"With you everything is terrorists," said one of the wives. "Maybe this is regular accident. Everything with you is aliens," she said and I wondered what kind of alien she meant, from Pakistan or Mars. It was New York. The argument went on.

"Not here," said Sonny. "Not now. I need to talk to you alone, man. Let's go."

"Can't do it," I said.

"So what are you really doing here, man, I mean, we going to play some kind of game?" Sonny glanced in Billy's direction.

"Who's the kid?" Finally, Sonny found his glasses in his jacket and put them on. "So?"

"Yeah, so, I came out here to catch a few rays and eat at Tolonno's, just like I told you."

"It's Tuesday, Artie. The holiday weekend is over. What's going on?"

"What do you care?"

"Say I care," he said. "Say I care because I want something from you."

Before Sonny could say anything else, the detective in the red jacket I thought I had recognized jogged over across the sand, and smiled at me.

"Artie, right?" she said.

"Yeah. How are you?"

She put out her hand, "Clara Fuentes from Red Hook."

"Sure," I said. "Yeah, hi, nice to see you."

On a case over in Red Hook the year before, I'd met Clara, a good-looking woman, dark hair in a ponytail. Mostly I remembered her by the bright red windbreaker. I recalled that she had asked me if I wanted to go to a big party she was working during the Republican Convention.

"How you doing, Clara?"

She held up her left hand to show me the gold ring and beamed. "I got married."

"Me, too," I said. "Last summer."

"Bunch of bourgeois pussies we are, right? You happy? What's her name?"

"Maxine," I said.

"Congratulations."

"You too."

"I'm gonna have a kid." Clara patted her stomach.

"Great."

She waved her hand at the plane. "What do you think?"

"I don't know."

No matter how deep the lull or how quiet the city felt or how complete the illusion that things were fine now, everything – a downed sightseeing plane, an overturned gas tanker that set off a fireball on Bruckner Boulevard, a freak Staten Island ferry crash – made me tense up. Me and every other cop in the city. I saw a couple of guys from the city's anti-terrorism squad on the beach. Unlike the Feds, these guys were good. Fast, too, like shit off a shovel.

Billy was talking to a guy in uniform, very serious, very interested, the two of them glancing over at the wreck. He stuck his hands in the pockets of his jeans, and pulled his jacket across him like he was cold. He waved at me and started in my direction. When he shambled up to us, I put my hand on his shoulder.

"This your boy?" Clara said.

"Hi, I'm Billy," he said.

Clara shook his hand, patted my arm, and walked away towards the wreck.

Lippert shifted his attention. "You going to introduce us, Art, man? What's your name?" he said to Billy.

Billy put out his hand to Lippert and said, "Billy Farone."

Lippert didn't move. His face looked gray. The muscles in his forehead twitched. I thought he was maybe having another heart attack. He just stood and stared at Billy, then suddenly moved back, maybe an inch. No one would have noticed, except me. Me and maybe Billy.

It unnerved me, the way Lippert looked, what he might do, the way he retreated from Billy, the way his eyes flickered.

Everything seemed to go quiet. The noise around us, Russians gabbing, the cops, the ambulances, the people on phones, the wind, all faded. It was as if the soundtrack on a movie had shut down. The three of us stood on the beach not talking. I could see that Lippert was literally shocked. He didn't say anything.

Maybe Lippert didn't know that Billy was temporarily on vacation from the facility in Florida. Maybe no one had told Lippert and he was pissed off because he was out of the loop. Maybe I should have called him. So we stood, Lippert unmoving, Billy smiling and holding out his hand.

I knew that Billy was cured. In the facility in Florida, school, juvenile center, prison, whatever the hell it was called, they had made him better. Kids could change. Billy was better. When I had picked him up in Florida a couple of days earlier, I'd met his shrink and his shrink said Billy was OK. He was funny and easy and charming and intelligent, like the little child he had been once a long time ago, before everything got screwed up. I saw it almost right away. It wasn't an imitation. It was for real.

"Hi," said Lippert finally. He shook Billy's hand, and tapped him on the shoulder, a weird gesture, not really a pat, more like a doctor testing your knee to see if your reflexes were good.

"Yeah, nice to meet you," Billy said.

"I'll call you," Sonny said to me.

"Fine," I said.

Lippert walked off with a backward wave of his hand, not saying anything, just walked away towards the crash site. He didn't say why he had wanted to see me. Maybe he didn't want to talk in front of Billy.

Two years ago, when I found Billy at the beach club at Breezy Point, Sonny had been there. More than two years. It had been the end of the trail that started with the pile of clothes on Coney Island beach. Sonny was there when I found Billy sitting by the body of a dead man.

3

"Who was that guy, the little skinny one on the beach?" Billy said when we were sitting in a cafe on the boardwalk in Brighton Beach about a mile from Coney Island. "He was like kind of weird with me. You think I did something wrong, Artie? He was looking me over like I was some kind of specimen. I don't think he liked me a lot."

"You were fine." I handed Billy a menu. "What do you feel like eating."

"But who was he?"

"His name is Sonny Lippert. He's sort of my boss. Don't worry about him. He's pretty strange some of the time, like people are when they get older, you know? You didn't recognize him?"

"Why should I?" said Billy.

"Are you OK?"

"Yeah, I'm so happy to be home, honest, but I'm like a little scared."

"What of?"

"You know, if people will be OK with me, if people don't want me around," he said. "Hey, so can I have the lamb, is that OK?" He looked over the menu at me and smiled.

It was early evening, the beach emptying, people beginning to arrive at the cafes and restaurants spread out along the boardwalk. Near us, tables filled up, people talking English and Russian, tourists gazing at the menu, locals ordering beer and vodka. Groups of musicians played on the boardwalk, a trio of girl violinists, some folkies.

"You know who Vladimir Vysotsky was?" I said to Billy.

"Who?"

"He was like a Russian Bob Dylan," I said and Billy nodded knowingly and we both watched as families crowded the boardwalk, women pushing strollers, men hoisting bottles of Baltika beer, others eating sunflower seeds from sacks and spitting the husks over the railing onto the sand. From loudspeakers at a cafe down the boardwalk pop music blared, the kind sung by mustachioed men with balalaikas for backing.

Old men sat on benches at the edge of the boardwalk; once they had talked about going home, but their home had disappeared. The Soviet Union had simply stopped existing. Like spacemen without a country to land in, they just sat here on the coast of America, staring at the ocean.

"Do you think I can have the lamb, Artie?" Billy said.

"You can have whatever you want, you know that, anything, you don't have to ask."

"Honest?"

"Honest," I said.

Billy ordered his dinner from the waitress in Russian. His accent wasn't bad though he stumbled some with vocabulary. The waitress, who wasn't more than twenty, blonde, pretty, with brown eyes, and a pair of very tight white jeans, looked at Billy as if he were a grown man she wanted. He asked for a Coke.

"Your Russian's really good," I said to Billy and ordered a beer.

"I worked on it," he said. "I wanted my Russian to be good, like yours." He took a piece of bread from the basket and ate some. "At home, it's so weird, my mom talking Russian half the time, my dad not really understanding anything. In any language, you know, I mean his English is funny, and he says stuff like 'ain't', doesn't he? I mean I love him, but he's not so smart, except with the restaurant. He does that really great, right?"

The waitress came back with the drinks.

"Your dad is really famous for his food," I said to Billy. "Johnny makes terrific food. He's a twenty-six in *Zagat*." I said. "You know what that means?"

"Sure, it's that restaurant guide thing. Course I know. Can I have a sip of your beer?"

I pushed the glass towards him, he tasted the beer and made a face, gave it back to me and drank some of his Coke.

"See, it's kind of hard with them," said Billy earnestly. "I'm not saying it's their fault, but my mom with her all her crazy Russian stuff, history, language, everything rattling around in her head like, I don't know, dried fish bones. She's scared they're going to send her back to Russia or something, then she gets scared we'll still be fighting in Iraq when I'm eighteen and I'll have to go. She is so screwed up, Artie, and she makes up for it buying clothes and going to psychics." Billy gulped down the rest of his soda. "My dad isn't like that but his family, you know, it's all religion, his mom wanting me to see priests. You know her? My grandma, Big Tina? The crazy one whose house smells of vanilla candles? I mean, who wouldn't be a nut job around them, right?"

"You're definitely not a nut job."

"Thanks," Billy said. "I don't want to seem spoiled, they're OK for parents, they give me nice stuff, I just kind of wish I could help my mom understand so she wouldn't be so totally upset all the time."

"Yeah, me too."

"They just can't read me at all," he said. "They don't have any, what's that word? Empathy. My mom and dad, they can't see how I feel, they never could, you know, so if I seemed different from other kids, they got scared I wasn't just an ordinarily weird kid, but beyond strange."

"So talk to me," I said.

Billy took a deep breath, picked some ice out of his Coke glass and put it in his mouth, crunched it up, swallowed.

"When I was a little kid, I thought everything had feelings, including the fish in my aquarium," he said. "I gave them names, I got them little plastic castles to live in." He stopped suddenly. "I'm talking too much."

"Go on," I said to Billy.

The waitress appeared and put down two plates of grilled lamb kebabs and rice pilaf. We ate. Billy ate like a kid who never got enough. At his age I'd been the same way, my mother joking around, telling me I probably had tapeworm. In the late 60s, there had been plenty of food in Moscow; for breakfast, along with boiled eggs, my mother served up caviar, red, black, whatever I wanted. At school I ate big plates of stew. All winter long I ate ice cream on my way home. Even now I could taste the sour vanilla flavor of Russian ice cream.

Finishing his last forkful of rice and green peppers, Billy sat back slightly and yawned.

"Tired?"

"Yeah, a little. I get sleepy a lot. In Florida, you have to get up for school early, and I always think how I wish I could just have five more minutes. I can sleep absolutely anywhere, anytime. It's like I never get enough."

"Maybe it's growing pains."

"You think? Sometimes I think I can hear myself getting taller."

"Billy?"

"Yeah?"

"How come you wanted to go to Coney Island as soon as we got back to the city? I mean, was there a reason, except for going to the beach?"

"Like I said, it was for the pizza."

"And?"

"I don't know, see places I used to like," said Billy, yawning again. "I thought maybe we could go over to my house. There's stuff I want to pick up. See my fish. I don't know if mom kept my aquarium going. Do you know? You think the fish are all dead? Do you think anyone took care of them? I wrote and wrote and wrote, lots of e-mails and even some letters saying what to do with the fish. I told my mom what fish food to buy and how she should put the lights on at certain times. I just wanted to come and hang out and maybe take a swim. See my fish, like I said. Did I say that? Get a whiff of the ocean."

"You don't swim in Florida? They don't have a beach?"

"Do you think the fish are all dead?" he asked again. "What? Oh, I'm sorry, you asked me about swimming. They don't take us to swim," he said. "Except in the pool inside the school, which is plenty far away from everything including a beach. You get told it's rural so the kids can fool around out of doors, but what they mean is we can't run away. You see, Artie? And like who can blame them, I mean there's a lot of very bizarre kids in there. Dumb, and seriously strange. There's this kid who was a habitual shoplifter – that's a good word, habitual, right? Anyway, he only ever shoplifted major amounts of school supplies. What kind of kid wants school supplies, unless he's selling them cheap? He's nuts. He does a lot of weed, and he gets punished plenty. Can we not talk about it right now?" Looking at me, Billy shrugged his shoulders apologetically.

"Of course."

"I'm sorry," he said very softly. "I don't mean to like shut you out or anything, it's just too soon. I just need to forget about it for a little while."

"That bad?"

"No," he said. "It's fine, I just don't want to think about it right now."

"You want dessert?"

"Can we maybe go get some cones? There's this place that has the best mint chocolate chip."

"Sure."

Billy didn't move.

"What is it?"

"That man, Artie. Look."

I turned around. A fat guy on the boardwalk was staring at us, but as soon as I got up, he walked away. I put some money on the table and looked around for the waitress. Billy was on his feet.

"Can we go, Artie? Please?"

After we left the cafe, we walked along Brighton Beach Avenue, under the elevated train tracks that made a metal canopy over the street. Calmer now, Billy looked for the ice cream store he remembered. I asked him why the man on the boardwalk had scared him, but Billy shook his head. Said he was OK. It was nothing.

In the store windows, the banks, the restaurants, most of the signs were Russian. Laid out in a deli window were fish – gilded chubs, oily succulent sturgeon, orange smoked salmon. Alongside them were heavy black breads, Russian cookies and tubs of pickles swimming in brine.

You heard Russian on the street, but some of the people

looked Asian; immigrants from remote republics, which had been part of the USSR, had begun replacing people from Moscow and Odessa. Pakistanis, Hispanics, Chinese were moving in, too; Brighton Beach was layered now like an anthropological dig. A lot of younger Russkis had gone, moved out, to other parts of Brooklyn, Staten Island, Jersey or Long Island.

A few elderly Jews still sat on fold-up stools along the sidewalk and gossiped in Yiddish. Their parents had settled here in the early part of the twentieth century when Brighton Beach was the end of the streetcar line.

Waiting for a red light to change, an old woman glanced at us suspiciously. No one I knew, no one Billy knew, just a Russian woman with a headscarf and broken shoes.

Billy kept close to me. I put my arm around his shoulders for a second, then took it away. I didn't want him feeling I was nervous. Whenever I came to Brighton Beach, though, and I didn't come if I could help it, I always got a toxic whiff of the Soviet Union. Toxic for me, anyway; it smelled like fear and boiled potatoes.

Ugly clothing, angora sweaters in turquoise with big shoulders and gold sequins, fox fur stoles, leather pants, fancy china, was set out in store windows along the avenue. Inside I could see women trying on the clothes and examining the black and gold porcelain. Tourists bought overly salted caviar in the shops and ate pirogi at Cafe Arbat. They went to The National or Rasputin, the fancy nightclubs where vodka flowed and the floorshow included flame eaters, jugglers and long-legged showgirls. Hookers worked the side streets. But the Russian mob, having extracted what they could out here, had moved on. Crime was down.

"You're pretty quiet," I said to Billy after a while. "What's the matter?"

"I can't find the ice cream place." He sounded fretful. "I just can't find it."

"Artemy!" A voice called out from a doorway a block further down the avenue.

Emerging from the door of his bookstore was Dubi Petrovsky. Lovingly he patted the big Dutch bicycle, custom made he had told me, that was chained up outside.

"Come on," I said to Billy. "You'll like this place. Dubi might know where the ice cream store has gone."

"You still riding your bike, Artie?" said Dubi, who swept us both inside his shop.

Tall, with a handsome beaky face like a big mournful bird, Dubi had the best bookshop in Brooklyn. He was born in Odessa, but he spoke English without much of an accent, also Russian, French and Yiddish. Dubi was about fifty, but he looked ageless. If you invited him to your house for dinner, he showed up with a bag of groceries, usually a cheesecake, paté and salami minimum. I knew that Dubi got up mornings around five to work out at the gym. The rest of the day he spent in his shop where books lined shelves from floor to ceiling; first editions were kept behind glass in an old mahogany cabinet.

Dubi shook my hand, said hello to Billy, and you could tell he was great with kids, not condescending, but interested.

"Take a look around," he said. "See if you can find something which interests you."

Billy looked first at a rack of newspapers and magazines, Russian, Ukrainian, English, French, Arabic, Spanish, Urdu. From the time he was a little kid, Billy had always been a compulsive reader. He read everything he got his hands on, adventure stories, sci-fi, grown-up novels, history.

"You interested in newspapers?" Dubi asked him.

"Yeah," said Billy softly. "Wow, can I look at some of these?"

"Of course," Dubi said.

"I love reading them, I really do. I like to read about stuff, you know, so I buy the papers. They don't let me do it that much down in Florida, but I get stuff on the net."

"Enjoy yourself," Dubi said to Billy who was already lost in the racks of papers. "So, you're good, Artemy? Maxine is good? You put on a few pounds, I see, so marriage agrees with you?"

"Yeah," I said. "Maxine's out in San Diego with her girls, visiting their cousins, they have zoos and shit out there, and theme parks and pizza with pineapple."

"Very nice," said Dubi.

On Dubi's makeshift desk, heaped with books, was a small TV; on it Paul McCartney was singing "Yesterday", his old boy's face crinkled up with delight. The camera pulled back. McCartney was in Red Square.

Following my gaze, Dubi said, "A Beatle in Mosow. I would kill to have been there. I never ever dreamed there would be Beatles in Moscow, not even one Beatle. It is like a dream. I sold my book by the way," he added. "I'm going to be published."

"No kidding. That's great, Dubi. Terrific, man."

"History of Beatles in the USSR, a real publisher in Manhattan, too."

"Congratulations."

"It's only the first volume."

"There're others?"

"Sure. Beatles is everything. Beatles is history of the entire world since 1961. In USSR, everybody is Beatles fan. Even Foreign Minister Ivanov says he learned English as a kid listening to Beatles. About this creep, Putin, I am not so sure, however. He's a very bad man, Artemy. Bad but the West sucks up to him. For natural gas, for diamonds, oil. No one gives a shit except for this."

"You said it."

To Billy, Dubi said, "When I was your age, I was in love with the Beatles. Bitles. We pronounce it Bitles because we have no way of knowing. And it's still best band in world, Stones are OK, but no one makes melody like McCartney."

"You know about the Beatles?" I said to Billy.

Billy made a comic face. "Sure I do, course, you think I don't know anything about anything before 50 Cent? Pulease!"

Dubi gave him a thumbs-up, reached across to his desk and presented Billy with the album that McCartney had recorded in Moscow. It had a red star on the cover.

"Vinyl! How cool is that! Thank you so so much," said Billy. "That's really crazy. Thanks a lot. I already like the Beatles, I'm sure this will be really good. Artie, look!

"Your Uncle Artie thinks all Russkis who live out here in Brighton Beach are thugs or crass ladies with fur coats, you know?" said Dubi. "Tell me what you like reading best, Billy."

They went into a huddle, a book lovers' crouch as they inspected books starting on the bottom shelf. Dubi retrieved books, handed them to Billy; together they pored over pages, discussed plots, characters, writing styles. A slim hardback caught Billy's attention.

"What's that?" I said.

Billy got up to show me, a memoir about fly-fishing in Montana. Nimble as a kid, Dubi jumped up and looked over his shoulder.

"I'll buy it for you," I said.

Dubi interrupted. "It is a present. So bring your nephew over for dinner soon, Artie."

We all shook hands. Billy was halfway out of the shop, but Dubi pulled me back and said, "Great kid, Artyom. I like very much."

Billy turned back from the doorway. "Who's that man? Look, over there, in the street?"

A few yards away, an old man whose skin was broiled purple

by the sun and who had an immense mustache was glad-handing a couple of tourists.

"Rabbi Abraham Abraham," Dubi said. "Always says he was already in Brighton Beach when there were still chickens on the streets. Must be over eighty. Likes to say he's King of Brighton Beach. I once saw him walking into the ocean with the Coney Island Ice Breakers, the club that likes to swim dead of winter. You want to meet him, Billy?"

I said, "I think we'll pass."

"Well guys, nice to see you. Nice to meet you, Billy. I heard so much about you. I heard you were coming home."

"How did you hear?" I said. "Who told you, Dubi?"

But Dubi had disappeared into the back room of his shop where the phone was ringing.

The sun was going down fast now.

"Should I call you Uncle Artie?" Billy said.

"What do you think?"

"I never did. I just always called you Artie."

"So that's good," I said.

"I asked Dubi about the ice cream place," Billy said.

"And?"

"He told me he doesn't like American ice cream. I have to find it, you know," said Billy. "It has to be there. It's the best stuff I ever ate, ice cream wise, I thought about getting some all the time I was in Florida. I used to go there with my dad when I was a kid."

Not finding the ice cream upset Billy.

"I can't remember," he said. "I don't know if it's gone or I forgot where it was."

While Billy was worrying about ice cream, I realized a car was keeping pace with us. A shabby maroon Lincoln Town car. A couple of yards separated us from the car. I couldn't see who was driving, but I knew someone in the car was watching me.

Or Billy. Was it Billy they were watching? Was someone checking on him? Someone aware he was out on vacation, away from Florida, someone who had an interest?

"Watch it, asshole," an angry voice said. I had bumped into a woman with big blonde hair, stonewashed jeans and a skintight halter-neck top under her purple denim jacket that was studded with shiny gold beads. "Watch it," she said again.

I kept my mouth shut and put my hand on Billy's arm.

"We can get ice cream somewhere else."

"I feel so bad that I can't find it, Artie."

"You mean the ice cream place?"

"Anything," Billy said. "I can't find things. I don't remember. I can't tell if they're gone, or if it's me."

"What things?"

"Places. A place I got sneakers once. Like that. The knish stand."

The car was still there.

"Let's just go." I got out my cell phone, which had started ringing.

It was Sonny Lippert. He told me to meet him at Peter Luger's, where he was eating dinner. I told him I couldn't. He said he needed me.

"I would have talked to you at Coney Island, but it wasn't the time or place, man," said Sonny.

"I'll call you later."

Billy pulled the sleeve of my jacket. "If you have to go, I'm OK, I'm not going to be an asshole about an ice cream cone. I want to go to my house anyway and check on my fish, and get my things. I'll meet you after. I have the keys. I kept my set of keys. You trust me, right?"

"I'll go with you."

"Can't you trust me? I'm fourteen, Artie. Please? Otherwise it's just like being locked up."

"Then stop for a minute. Talk to me."

Billy stopped and leaned against the wall of a bank.

"I just need to go home," he said.

We walked towards my car silently, me pretending to look in shop windows where all I really saw was Billy's reflection. His head was down, eyes on the pavement. He had given up on the ice cream. When he looked up at me, his face was sad.

After a while he said, "So can we really go fishing?"

"Yeah. You pick a place, we'll go."

"Like I said, any place would be fine."

"You're really cool, you know that? I mean I'm so impressed the way you deal with stuff."

"You are?" Billy flushed with embarrassment or because he was happy, or both. "I learned," he said. "I think this is me, Artie, I think this is how I am, and something bad happened, like you read people get brain tumors and it makes them weird, I think something like that. Maybe I got a brain tumor, or that cerebral hemorrhage thing, and it went away, or there was this one nice doctor, he was really really good, and I think he cured me. You know? So I need to go to my house," he said. "I need to see my fish."

"Come on," I said when we got to my car. "Let's go."

"Did you see that car that was following us?" said Billy. "Big ugly car, sort of purple? I saw you watching. I saw you and I figured it was following us for some reason."

"Yeah, but I don't think so. I don't think it was anything."

"Where are we going?"

"Your house."

I drove the mile or so to Manhattan Beach where the Farones lived. It was dark now. Lights were on in the suburban houses, which were always freshly painted, lawns trim as wall-to-wall carpet, with plaster statues of nymphs and goddesses. The tidy blocks ran up to the beaches, which were private around here. In the rear-view mirrors I looked for the maroon car but it was gone. Just paranoia, I told myself. I was nervous for Billy. Wanted him safe.

My old red Caddy made me easy to spot. I knew I should trade it in for something else, but I loved the car, and anyhow Maxine always said, "I didn't marry you so I could drive around in a beige minivan. You're my access to glamor, honey, keep the car, no matter how often it has to go into the shop." I looked at my watch to check the date. July 5. Tuesday. Maxine would be home Sunday and I was glad. I missed her.

In front of the Farone house, I pulled up. Billy pushed open the car door, jumped out, ran up the walk, and spun around twice and waved like crazy. He was home. Already he had his keys out.

The phone rang again; it was Lippert.

"Don't bring the kid with you, either," he said.

I got out and followed Billy up to the front door.

"My keys don't work," he said.

I got a set of keys from my pocket.

"Here," I said. "Your mom gave me these."

"She changed the locks?"

"I guess."

Billy looked defeated. "They didn't want me here, you think that's why they did it?"

"I'm sure it's not why. Look, you go see your fish, whatever, and I'll pick you up in a couple of hours. If I leave you, you won't go out, right? I'm not supposed to leave you alone, and I don't like even asking if you'll stay at the house, but I have to."

Billy lit up like a bulb. "I promise. You can phone me every two minutes, or anything, it would just be so great to know that you could trust me. Thank you," said Billy. "Thanks."

"I trust you."

He leaned over and kissed my cheek, then drew back and blushed.

"Thanks, Artie."

"I'll be back in two hours."

"Good. OK." Billy started laughing.

"What's so funny?"

"Nothing. I'm just laughing. I'm just like happy."

Billy sauntered up the walk to his house, arms swinging, hands flapping, skipping every other step, whistling "Yesterday" loud and off-key. Whistling and skipping at the same time, then turning to wave at me as if he felt free.

4

A week earlier, Genia Farone had stood on her new back patio – made of imported fieldstone, she told me – looking at her swimming pool, which was oval and deep blue; gold mosaic fish sparkled on the bottom. Real gold leaf, Genia said.

Genia had called me that morning sounding desperate. I went over and asked what was wrong, but she was reluctant to talk. Instead, in a kind of ritual I was used to now, she showed me around her house.

Fancy loungers with blue and white striped cushions were positioned near the pool, for conversation and cocktails, Gen said, as if expecting a stylish crowd to appear poolside. In her mind were pictures of old Hollywood gatherings and she'd had a bar built with a white leather top and stools to match, and there was a fancy stainless steel barbecue, glass-topped tables and big terracotta pots of white orchids. Plucking a few dead leaves off a plant, Genia smiled faintly, satisfied.

From inside the house came voices of workers putting new shelves in the kitchen. Power saws buzzed. A quartet of movers grunted as they dragged in furniture bound in thick cloth and duct tape, like mummies. The house was Genia's obsession. It was as if all the stuff somehow added up to a life, as if the material goods were ballast that kept her from drifting away.

I felt for her. Stuck with Johnny Farone, Genia believed she owed him because he had married her and made her an American citizen, got her the house and furniture, the Range Rover, the clothes, and because they had Billy.

"What do you need?" I said.

"They're letting him out for two weeks," Genia said in Russian. "Billy, I mean, Artyom. I was going to go down to Florida to pick him up, but Johnny's getting some kind of award in London for the restaurant. We heard Billy was getting out, but we'd already planned this trip for ages. I talked to Billy's doctor in Florida, his shrink. I talked to the administrator. They said it's fine. You're his godfather, Artyom, you're his guardian if anything happens to us. You're on all his paperwork. If he is good, there can be some more time off, or whatever they call it, at some point, not now, but later they'll let him out. This is too much to ask of you, I know." Genia sat down on the edge of a lounger, got a pack of Dunhill's from her jacket pocket and unpeeled the cellophane from the red and gold box.

I sat beside her.

"You don't want to go." It wasn't a question.

She lit up, sucked in the smoke, blew it out and said, "I'm scared."

Genia seemed distant, affectless. All the Botox meant her face barely moved and you couldn't tell what she was feeling. Toned from the gym, her body was hard. She crossed her legs, flexed her tanned right foot in its silver snakeskin sandal – she told me she went to a tanning salon regularly – and the muscles on her calf showed. She wore black linen Capri pants and a white silk jacket. Her expensive clothes – Gen never failed to tell me where she got her outfits – were like costumes.

"I'm a design whore," she had said once, a rare night when we went out drinking together, the bar at the Four Seasons Hotel where she loved going, and she got drunk enough to laugh at herself. Mostly, she seemed too thin, too brittle.

"Have you seen him at all?" I said.

"Who?"

"Billy," I said. "Your son."

"Don't be mad with me, Artyom. Yes, once I saw him," said Genia. "Johnny goes to see him. You think I'm bad person, bad mother? It scared me very much this place they put Billy. It reminds me."

Our father, Genia's and mine, had been in the KGB. When she was born, he was already married to my mother. Genia said he forced her mother to give her up for adoption. He didn't want her around. According to Genia, he never made any effort to see her.

Once, when Genia was a young woman, she had waited outside his office and followed him on the street. She told him who she was. He greeted her politely, but that was all. The USSR was a prudish country. An illegitimate baby would have wrecked his career.

In the Soviet Union Genia had been scared all the time, because she was illegitimate, because my father – our father – was in the KGB, because later he lost his job. In Brooklyn, she was still scared. The business with Billy had involved cops and the legal system and an institution in Florida. I knew Genia thought it was the kind of place they sent crazy bad kids from poor families.

Even after almost twenty years in America, fear still claimed her. Genia was scared of governments, of the law, scared that she would be sent back to Russia because of our father, because of her history, because of her son. In her mind, deported to Russia, she would be locked up. This kind of fear was the real fallout, the garbage that was left over from the Soviet Union, and it made people sick. Genia had never believed in her own life, not the bad luck or the good.

"Will you go?" She took another drag on her cigarette. "Please."

"I'll go."

"You will? Oh, Artyom, thank you."

"What about when you get home from London and Billy's still here?"

"I don't know." Sitting on a blue and white striped cushion near her pool behind her big house, Genia tried to work out how she should feel about her son. "Maybe will be OK then."

"Where should I pick him up?"

"I'll write everything down, Artyom. I'll make all the calls. We'll be away only four, five days. When I am home, I will see him. I'll try. He'll come here to be with us at home. I promise." Genia smashed the butt of her cigarette in a heavy glass ashtray on the table next to her. "I swear to you."

She reached into her jacket pocket again and gave me a set of keys. "Here, I give you keys to my house, in case you want to stay here with Billy. Use the pool. Enjoy." Everything had been arranged.

"Artie?"

"What?"

"It is allowed for me to go to London?" Genia spoke in her formal English with a thick accent. "They let me back?"

"You're an American," I said as she got up to go inside and tell Johnny about the plans. I followed her and thought, poor Genia. She was an American citizen, but she would die an immigrant.

In the living room, Johnny Farone was asleep on a white suede sofa, his feet tangled in a black cashmere blanket. Genia tugged at his arm. He opened his eyes and sat up.

"Hey, Johnny, how's it going?" I said because I couldn't think of anything else.

He hauled himself up to a sitting position. Johnny was fat. His skin, what with gout, diabetes and liver problems, was a strange mouse color. Leaning forward so he could see his swollen feet over his stomach, he tried to jam them into stiff sandals that lay on the floor, then gave up.

"John, Artie is going to pick Billy up in Florida," Genia said. "Please say thank you."

"Thanks man." Johnny pulled his orange polo shirt down over his plaid Bermuda shorts. "Thanks a lot. That's great. I was really looking forward to taking Genia to London, you know? We planned this trip long before we heard Billy was coming home."

"Yeah."

"It'll be nice for him, Artie, you know? I mean you understand the kid and he loves you so much, and all the stuff you guys did together, baseball and fishing and stuff." Johnny reached for a bowl of chocolate truffles on the coffee table and popped one into his mouth. "And we'll be back and then he can be with us. God, I miss him a lot," said Johnny, who was a good sweet man who loved his kid.

"How's the restaurant, Johnny?"

"Did I tell you I'm opening a new place over in Staten, brand new, waterfront, seafood, marina, everything," Johnny said. "There's a lot of money out there now, rich Russkis, everything. Guess what I'm calling it."

"What?"

"The Staten Island Fishing Club," said Johnny, triumph in his voice. "You like that? You like it? I mean, the way you and Billy like going fishing and all. It will all be for Billy some day," he said, as if nothing at all had happened to his son.

Johnny Farone had made it big with Farone's, the restaurant he owned in Brooklyn, and he had worked like a dog for it. He had started from nowhere, a fat guy who owned an auto parts shop originally and didn't expect much. Success made Johnny generous and loyal – he couldn't believe his luck. After he was diagnosed with diabetes, he tried to keep off the cream sauces and big Barolos and sweet liqueurs and red meat, the things he loved most next to his wife and kid, but what else was there for him, he asked. I liked Johnny.

I headed for the stairs.

"Where are you going?" Genia caught hold of my sleeve.

"Billy's room," I said. "See if there's anything I should take with me."

"You should ask me first," she said. "You should ask, Artyom."

"I'm sorry. Let's go up together."

Genia hustled me out of the living room and through the front door.

"I need a cigarette, Artyom, come outside."

On the front steps, she lit up, and I said, "You can't smoke in your own house?"

"Makes furniture stinky." Genia sat down on the front steps and I sat beside her, reached for her cigarette and took a couple of drags.

"I thought you quit," she said.

"I'm trying. When are they letting Billy out?"

"Saturday."

"I'll start early Thursday, make sure there's plenty of time."

"Thank you, Artyom," Genia said in Russian. "Thank you. So I will go to London with Johnny for a few days, OK? I don't like going on planes, but he begs me, he says, Gen, they're giving me this big award for restaurants in New York, they honor me, important magazine, please, you'll like it. So you see, I am like all American wives now." She gestured at the house. "I redecorate. I go shopping. I accompany husband on his business trip."

Again I reached for her cigarette.

"Keep it," said Genia and lit up another one. "First time, I went to Florida, Billy was in locked ward, Artemy. Locked ward. Locks on doors." Genia wrapped her arms around herself. "His room is very nice, very comfortable, and corridors so warm and fuzzy, clouds painted on nice sky-blue walls, pictures by children, like hospital for children, but there are locked doors. All I can think about is wards for crazy people in Soviet Union. I can't go back."

I kissed her cheek. "I hear you."

"I will owe you," she said.

"You don't have to owe me. It will be fine. I'll take Billy's fishing stuff with me in the car," I said. "He'll like that."

"I don't know where it is."

5

"You want steak?" Sonny Lippert said when I arrived at Peter Luger's in Williamsburg, where he had a regular table and a house credit card. It was the only way you could pay there except with cash, and they didn't give those cards to a lot of people. After I had dropped Billy at his parents' house, it only took me twenty minutes to get to the restaurant.

"I ate." I was still a little pissed off the way Sonny treated Billy on the beach.

"With the kid? You ate with the kid?"

"My nephew, OK? Billy."

"Yeah, yeah. Sit down, man," Lippert said. "Come on, at least have a drink."

"I'm driving."

"Ha ha ha." He picked up his wine glass and sipped at it. "It's a nice Cabernet. California stuff, I forget the fucking names of these things. Trouble with drinking wine is wine bores come out of the woodwork. Pour some for him," he told the waiter. After his heart attack, Sonny gave up Scotch for wine.

The restaurant was busy. Big men, their bellies shoved under the edge of the tables, chowed down on the best steak in

New York, along with hash browns, double-fried fries and creamed spinach. Most of the guys, their jackets hanging over the backs of their chairs, had tassels on their loafers. A lot of expensive red wine got passed around. A man in a monogrammed shirt, voice booming, counted his table. Seven guys, he announced, meant seven bottles. Each of the bottles probably cost a grand.

At his corner table, Lippert cut a piece of the rare porterhouse, dripping blood and butter, ate it slowly, swallowed, and drank a little more wine.

"How did you know where I was, Sonny? You came out to the beach because you knew I was there? Yeah, I know, you came because I said I was eating pizza on the beach and you knew it was Coney Island. So what else? So, I'm here, Sonny. What?"

"Like I said, I was going to tell you out by the beach, but with the plane crash, it wasn't the time. Tell the truth, I was looking for you to invite you to dinner, all of you, Maxine, the kids, and then you said you were out by the beach, so I figured I'd take a stroll on the boardwalk." He put his fork down.

"That's what you wanted? To invite us to dinner?"

"Where's Maxine?".

"In California with the girls."

"You taking good care of her, man?"

"Please. Skip the domestic lecture, OK?"

Maxine, who I got married to the summer before, always said we were like two old guys, Sonny and me. He had given me his signed Jackie Robinson baseball for a wedding present, his most prized possession. He had always thought I was a jerk about women, and he wasn't wrong, but that I finally got it right with Max.

"I need you to do something for me. I would do it myself, but I have a case that's getting to me, man," Sonny said and put his fork down.

"I'm busy," I said.

Mostly these days I was working paper cases. Someone in the department had asked around for a Russian speaker, which is how I ended up at a desk where I read faxes from Moscow and ate too many candy bars.

The stuff that rolled off the fax machine was pretty worthless. The only interesting thing I'd come across was money filtered through a bank in Chechnya from Pakistan and onto London, and some money, also from Chechnya, laundered through second-hand car dealers near Detroit. Anti-terrorism guys took all of it over from me. Most of what I was left with were bad bank accounts and corrupt real estate deals.

It was fine except that I missed the noise of the station house and the sound of the guys swearing, and the bang of the locker doors and the late-night stink of stale Chinese food. But I didn't work nights or weekends; I didn't feel like I was getting ulcers from looking at dead people, I worked nine to five; it was a life. I could take a few days off when I needed to. It was how I'd managed to get the time to pick up Billy in Florida.

The waiter, who was paying plenty of attention to Sonny, brought me the Scotch I had ordered and I drank it down, and then looked at my watch.

"When I was a kid, it was like big old guys ate here, you know?" Sonny said. "I remember we would hang around and watch the cars and the men in big alpaca coats and hats, like they were Rod Steiger in *On the Waterfront*, you know what I'm talking about, man?"

I could tell Sonny was starting to wander, and I didn't know even now if it was a tactic or if half his brain was permanently pickled from all the Scotch he'd drunk. Even now, he spent a lot of time drifting backwards into his childhood, his adolescence in Brooklyn which was inhabited by a huge cast of people, his parents who read Marx to him at bedtime, gangsters, union guys, politicos, prizefighters, ball players, Floyd Patterson, Jackie Robinson, Julius and Ethel Rosenberg;

in the same past lived the musicians he loved like Dizzy Gillespie and Charlie Parker, and Sonny counted himself an original hipster which was why he said "man" in every sentence. I had stopped beating him up for it. I never knew how much of it was true, but for Sonny it was so real, it didn't matter.

At the next table, a foursome was talking loud French. I half listened. It was business talk.

Sonny turned to look. "You understand them, man?"

"Yeah pretty much."

"How come?"

"You know I can talk French, Sonny. What do you need from me?"

"Your mother, she's who made you learn, right? Isn't that it? I fucking hate the language, also they talk so frigging loud, you know?" Sonny said. "Their food's OK, they write great. You want to know why I hate the language? Not because of the shrub – you know President George Bush. You like that, shrub for Bush Jr?"

"I heard it before."

"I hate their superiority and their anti-Semitism and most of all their language because I didn't learn it right. I should have done languages, like you, and then I could have read the good stuff in the original. Balzac. Victor Hugo. Flaubert. Shit."

"Sonny, I have to go."

"I had this French teacher at my high school and I was the smallest kid in the class, and he liked to pick on me. Mr Driscoll was his name and he'd say, 'Sonny, *comment allez vous?*' And I'd freeze. I knew the right answer, but I'd fucking freeze, man, and if I didn't know the right answer, Driscoll would turn to the other boys in the class – it was an all boys' school – and he'd say in this weird sinister drawl, 'Give him the treatment boys. Give him the treatment.' So all the boys would beat the shit out of me. I ever tell you about him? Or about the shower teacher, Mr Castro, the one who taught us how to soap ourselves? Jesus. I could have read Zola, in the original, you know, if it wasn't for that pig Driscoll. Man, I could have even read Proust, though not my thing, not all that fancy society stuff, not really, too many fucking countesses and tea cookies, man, but the writing! I could have really read it all, except for Driscoll. Give him the treatment boys. I got to go to the bathroom, Artie."

Lippert got up. He reached in his pocket and tossed a Polaroid onto the table, turned and headed for the men's room. I knew he wanted to leave me hanging, make me wonder what the big-deal case was. I wasn't going to budge. I looked at my watch and figured it was time to get back to Billy. Then I picked up the photograph. It was a picture of a baby doll. One of its feet was missing.

"What the hell is this?" I said to Sonny, when he came back to the table. "What's this fucking picture?"

"It's a doll," he said. "With its foot cut off."

"I can see that, Sonny."

"Listen to me, you remember those cold cases, the kid on Long Island, the other one out in Rockaway where they found the bodies with limbs cut off? Years back."

"I remember. Yeah."

"In the hospital, when I was sick, I did some reading, and afterwards, at home, I had some time. There were more. One possible upstate. Now I got a fresh one. Jersey. Near Bayonne. Same kind of deal, Artie. Little girl, man. They chopped off her feet."

I didn't say anything.

"What's it mean, man? So she couldn't run away? So why kill her?"

"I don't know." I still had the photograph in my hand and Sonny snatched it away.

"This is her doll, man. No ID. Just Jane Doe, her and her

doll. She had her dolly with her, Artie, man." He knocked back what was left of his wine. "Who does these things to kids, man?"

I'd heard him say it before, over and over: Who does this to kids? Lippert had been obsessed a long time; even after he retired, he worked as a consultant with a unit he set up to look at child crime. I felt for him, but I couldn't help him, not now, not with Billy in town.

"I have to go, Sonny."

"You want to see a picture of the girl?" Sonny said. "She was raped, too, the one in Jersey was raped."

"I'm sorry."

"Look, I'm not asking you to come on this with me," he said. "I'm just asking a favor for something where I don't have time now. Just free me up to pay attention to Jersey. It's for Rhonda, OK?"

Rhonda Fisher, who had been Lippert's assistant for about thirty years, and was always in love with him since way back, finally got her chance when he had the heart attack and she went to the hospital and was there every day. He didn't marry her or let her move in permanent, but she cooked for him and once in a while he took her somewhere nice for dinner.

If Sonny still talked like a 50s hipster, or tried to, and if he was still wound up tight, he was a lot lighter of spirit since he'd been with Rhonda. She listened to the music he liked with him. She took care of him. Since he let her through his door, he drank less and ate better.

Instead of picking on a sandwich – tongue and Swiss, usually – or just drinking dinner when he was out, now he seemed to like food. I watched him cut another piece of steak. It was the first time I'd seen him eat like he actually cared what was on his plate.

"What?" I said.

A friend of a cousin, or maybe a cousin of a cousin, but someone related to Rhonda anyway, was in trouble, he said. Russians, probably low class. "They need help. Think of it as a good deed, man, help keep you from coming back a cockroach."

"Rhonda's Russian?"

"Her grandparents. Both sides," Sonny said. "Russian Jews."

"They're on Staten Island?"

"Dead. They're dead. But there's some cousins came over in the 80s, and listen, it won't take long. A couple hours is absolutely all I'm asking."

"I don't know anything about Staten Island."

"I'm asking you because of Rhonda. The woman called and asked Rhonda if her boyfriend, meaning me, I guess, had someone who could talk Russian. Look, she sounds like a nice woman. She wakes up one night, the way Rhonda heard it, there's a burglar, and the husband runs downstairs after the creep and disappears. He doesn't come back."

"Maybe he didn't like her."

"Just go talk to the woman is all I ask."

"Who did you say she was?"

"Jesus, man, I told you, some kind of relative of Rhonda's who Rhonda feels like she never did anything for and now she's alone, and no one understands what the hell she's saying. She said, OK, maybe I know someone." Sonny ate some more of his steak. "This is good."

"Who said?"

"Rhonda."

"How did the woman know you could get someone?"

"Rhonda's always talking about me, man, you know that." Sonny grinned faintly, a lugubrious, defensive, diffident grin I had never seen before and I realized he really loved Rhonda.

"The woman knew about me?"

"How the hell should I know? Yes. Probably. Not by name

maybe. What difference does it make? Maybe Rhonda brags about you, too," he said. "No kidding. She's your number one fan. I mean, just give it a couple hours, right?"

"No."

"Excuse me?"

"I'm off this week and I'm busy."

"With the boy? You want to talk about that?"

I didn't want to talk about Billy. I kept my mouth shut. Sonny waited.

"Yeah, OK," I said finally. "I'll go."

"Tomorrow would be good," said Sonny.

"No. When I can."

"I'm not asking you to change your life, man. I'm just asking you to take a run over to Staten Island."

"I said I'd go. For Rhonda, I'll do it. I'll take a run out there," I said to shut him up. "I'll go talk to the woman once, if you want, when I get some time, OK? I'll do that if you want me to. What's her name?"

From his jacket pocket, Lippert took a piece of paper with a name and address.

"Here's the deal over there on Staten island," Sonny said. "You ever been over there? People in Staten Island are strange, like they barely live in New York, man. I mean there's boroughs and boroughs, you know? I get Brooklyn, the Bronx, even fucking Queens. But Staten Island, I mean it's like some parallel universe, like you're already in New Jersey."

"How come you know so much about it?"

"I taught a course at the college out there once, a million years ago, I got a part-time job, I was shacked up with some girl. It was wild. Borough president, name of Albert Manascalo," he said, beginning to sink into his past. "Al to his friends. He had so much power he could make a Jew an honorary Italian if he wanted. The place was full of rage and religion, man, you hear me? Redemption if you got lucky.

Dark stuff. You ever really get into Dostoevsky? It's like all there."

"Staten Island is like Dostoevsky?" I said. "You're losing me."

"Pretty much, man. Her name, the lady you got to go see, get this, man, is Gorbachev."

"You're fucking with me."

"Yeah, like Gorby. No relation. Or maybe there is, maybe there's a branch of them over on Staten Island. First name Vera."

"I'll take a piece of steak," I said.

6

Little kids rode skateboards in the dark up and down the Brooklyn streets, weaving in and out, like bumper cars in an amusement park. Streetlights picked them up as they darted out from behind buildings, swerved onto the sidewalk, smashed into the street, chasing cars, daring cars, hanging on to a rear bumper for a ride, before they swooped away into dark shadows behind buildings.

I was on my way across Brooklyn after seeing Sonny and I'd probably had more to drink than I should have, and I was driving too fast when the kids got in my way. This part of Brooklyn a few miles from the ocean was low-lying, ramshackle and poor. Immigrants – Pakistanis, some Chinese, some Jews – shared the space uneasily with local gangs.

On one street out front of a bodega, I saw two boys, huge kids, who resembled grown men, with cans of beer in their hands. Younger boys begged beers from them and swaggered into the stores with false IDs, trying to buy smokes. No one asked a lot of questions around here.

"Fucking watch it," yelled a white boy, maybe sixteen and mean-looking – who appeared in front of me out of nowhere on his skateboard and forced me to slam on my brakes.

The kid danced his skateboard into the middle of the road, rocked on it, danced it up close to my car, reached his hand out and touched the hood of my car, grinning, laughing, taunting me. He had his baseball cap on backwards, pants hanging low on his hips. He was playing to me. In my headlights I could see his face. I felt like ramming the creep. Instead I leaned out of the window and told him to fuck off, but he made a face, gave me the finger and started whistling. A couple of his pals, waiting on the curb, jumped their boards into the street. White boys, maybe Hispanic. I leaned on my horn.

I kept honking. Flashed my brights. In the hard white flashing light, the boys looked like clowns, and one of them wasn't any older than Billy. Then, without warning, all three swerved up to the car window, laughing.

I leaned on the horn some more. Told them to fuck off. Warned them. Rolled up the window, stepped on the gas, forced the boys back. I was pissed off and a little scared and I didn't really care — just for a second — if I hit them. In the rear-view mirror, I saw two of them follow me to the corner, where I turned fast, doing sixty, maybe more.

The side street was almost empty. In the mirror, I saw the maroon car coming up behind me. I was sweating now, and feeling crazy, wondering if the guys on skateboards had forced me into this one-way street on purpose, if it was all a set-up, if the kids were connected with the maroon car somehow. I didn't believe it. It didn't mean anything, never did, not most of the time.

I drove past some Hasidic men in eighteenth-century outfits who were discussing God or the price of diamonds. Kept going towards the ocean, to the beach, past broken streets that were empty, the car still on my tail. I cut across a gas station that was shut. I could see patches of rust on it and bumper stickers. The driver looked fat, with a big head.

Then I lost him. Like that. It made it worse, him appearing, then just disappearing. It was as if he wanted me unnerved, off balance, more than he wanted to close in. I was probably drunker than I knew. The guy in the car made me feel hunted. I thought I saw him again in the rear-view, and wondered if I was hallucinating, or just scared.

I cut over to Manhattan Beach and the Farone house as fast as I could without crashing into anything.

No one was on the steeet except for a teenage girl on a bike. I recognized her as the chubby kid who had been running earlier at Coney Island where the plane crashed. I parked and got out of my car near the Farones'. For a few seconds I stood on the street, listening for other cars, but all I heard was the whispery sound of the ocean on a calm night.

The door was unlocked. No lights in the house, just the door left open. I knew I should never have left Billy alone.

"Billy?"

Except for a light coming from the second floor, the house was dark. I heard a very faint noise. I couldn't track it. I kept my hand on my gun. Where was he?

"Billy?"

I felt like a dope, my voice bouncing off the walls. Pushing through the dread that I felt thickening around me, I went upstairs to the landing outside Billy's room. I pushed the door cautiously. The smell of turpentine hit me.

There was no one inside. On the walls, paint samples — pink, orange, rose — were streaked in horizontal lines. A drop cloth, stiff with paint, lay on the floor. Rolls of wallpaper were stacked in a corner near a ladder that lay on its side. A rough work table made of a couple of boards held a radio, a couple of paint cans, a box from Dunkin' Donuts, and paint brushes stuck in a glass Mason jar half full of dirty water. Three blue and white cardboard coffee cups were on the table too, one of them half full; in it floated a cigarette butt.

Billy's things were gone. His bed, books, desk, clothes, posters, computer, all gone. The room where he'd lived since he was a little boy had vanished. Even the shelves were gone. It was as if he'd been cancelled out.

Standing in the room, the conditioning off, it was hot. A single yellow light was on out back and from the window, though it was dark now, I could just see the patio, the blue pool, the striped loungers, the white orchids that were ghostly at night. A bug zapper was on in the yard. The sprinkler sprayed water in irregular patterns across the grass.

The noise like a mouse was coming from the garage underneath Billy's room. It got louder, moving, into the kitchen, up the stairs, then muffled by the carpet. An animal, I thought. A dog. The Farones didn't have a dog. I waited.

"You saw?" Billy was standing in the doorway of his empty room, his face somber. It was Billy who had come softly up the stairs. He was barefoot.

I wanted to put my arms around him, but I wasn't sure how he'd take it so I just said, "Are you OK?"

"I'm OK."

"What about the fish?"

"I can't find them, not the fish or the tank. I just hope they're not dead," he said, voice wavering at first like a little boy, then growing steady. "Look, I have to figure my dad took them to the restaurant so they could be fed. He would do that kind of thing. He probably has them on some pasta Alfredo or something."

"It must have been lousy, finding your room like this," I said.

"I'm OK," Billy said. "Honest."

"The front door was open."

"I left it like that for you. I didn't go out. I promised you I wouldn't. I went into the yard was all, and the garage. They put my stuff there."

"I didn't see any lights."

"I just put a little one on in the garage."

Billy set off back down the stairs and I followed him to the kitchen and through a side door into the garage. Genia's green Range Rover was in its usual spot, so was a long table with power tools she had bought for Johnny that he never used. His silver Porsche, which had cost him a bundle and which he could barely get into now he was so fat, wasn't there. I figured maybe he'd left it at the restaurant. Stacked against the wall were blue plastic storage crates and next to them Billy's fishing gear, his bike and his computer.

On one of the crates was a stack of school books. With a Russian's snobbish love for anything intellectual, Genia made Johnny buy fancy editions of Russian novels, Tolstoy, Pushkin, Dostoevsky, in expensive leather bindings with gilt writing, but she kept them behind glass in her living room. Did Genia buy them from Dubi Petrovsky? Was that how Dubi knew Billy was coming home?

Genia was scared of Billy being at home. Redecorating his room was a way of making him disappear. I was furious with her. I had left a message in London to tell her I'd picked Billy up in Florida; she didn't return it. I thought about calling again, but what would I say? That she was a lousy mother?

"Artie?" Billy was holding up a dark blue hoodie he'd taken from one of the crates. "My stuff doesn't fit me. You think that's why they put it here? You think that? I went into my room and there wasn't anything at all, Artie, they took away my stuff, and put it in these boxes." He put the hoodie down and picked up a pair of jeans and looked at them. "Do you think they planned on giving my stuff away, Artie?" He sounded a hell of a lot calmer than I would have been. "You think they figured I wasn't coming back? You think they didn't want me to come back?"

"Maybe they just thought you outgrew a lot of your clothes." I said. "You brought some things back up from Florida, right?"

"Sure, yeah, I left my bag over at your place, remember? I guess I was thinking I'd like to have my old clothes. You think it's like a metaphor or something? Old things not fitting? I'd like that."

I pulled the lid off of one of the blue boxes. Inside were more books. Billy inspected the titles. It gave me the creeps, him standing there with his childhood packed into plastic boxes in his parents' garage.

"Maybe your mom was planning on redoing your room."

"The wallpaper has ladies on it from olden times and gold borders and there's pink paint. You think that's for me? It's better if we tell the truth, at least to each other," said Billy. "I'm OK with what my mom did, honest, I really am." Pulling a thick white sweater from one of the open boxes, Billy put it on. His arms stuck out six inches from the cuffs and he started laughing, and then I laughed.

"How about we go shopping tomorrow for some new stuff?"

"Sure," Billy said. "We could give my stuff to some poor kids, right? My grandma, Big Tina, always gave shit to the church, you know. I could drop it off with her." He looked at me. "Except she's too weird. They're all weird on the Farone side except my grandpa and no one gives him a break except me. It's just old clothes. I really don't care. I'm with you, I'm good, I really am." He put up his hand to give me a high five, then grinned at the corniness of doing it.

"Let's get a soda or something," I said, and my voice bounced off the cinderblock walls of the garage and sounded faraway and thin.

*

In the kitchen, I turned on a light. Billy got some Frescas from the fridge.

Scrubbed down clean as a hospital ward, the kitchen was all fancy Italian glass cabinets and granite counters. The fridge motor turned over.

I took a long swallow of the Fresca and said, "I'm sorry I took so long earlier."

"Where were you?"

"Something to do with work," I said. I'd been with Sonny Lippert two hours if you counted going and coming.

"I got used to it, being by myself, when I was a kid," Billy said thoughtfully, as if he'd thought about the business of being alone a lot. "Down there, in Florida, it's like there're almost too many people. You have to share a room. You have to eat with everyone. You never have any time. There's usually some shrink hanging around and stuff. It's great to have some time alone now, I mean sit around and read or just chill."

"Is it hard?" I sat down at the counter, and Billy climbed up on a stool opposite me.

"It's OK. It's boring sometimes," he said, pushing his hair off his forehead. "There're a couple of really good teachers. I mean most of the kids are like practically illiterate, you know? They made me a tutor in English. I get to tutor younger kids. I like that. They're so like weirdly grateful just to have someone not treat them like idiots."

"That's good."

"Artie?"

"What's that, sweetheart?"

He rolled his eyes.

"What?"

"You can't call me sweetheart," Billy said. "It's way too weird. I'm fourteen."

"I could call you buddy. Or pal."

"I don't think so!"

"Why not?"

"On you that's even more weird, I mean you're not the type."

"What type is that?"

"Bubba-type guy."

"Got it."

"I have something I probably need to tell you," said Billy, pushing his hair away nervously, looking a little shifty now.

"What's that?"

"It's pretty awful." He drank his soda and rolled the can between his hands.

"Come on."

"OK. It's like I smoke. I'm trying to quit, but once in a while, I can't help it and I don't think I can make it through two weeks without one. Also, I don't want to lie to you. I really don't. Are you mad at me?"

"What about in Florida?"

"We sneak them. They know. They figure we're all so screwed up, not to mention that there are kids there who did a lot of drugs on the outside, a cigarette isn't the worst thing." Billy dug a pack out of his pocket.

"I should give you the lecture, right?" I said. "It is a lousy thing. It really does suck. You end up with some crap disease and wheezing and coughing. You smoke, then you die."

"You quit?" Billy said.

"I'm trying."

"Can I have just one?"

"You don't need to ask me."

"Let's go outside so I don't stink up Mom's house," said Billy. "She doesn't like that. Even she goes outside when she smokes."

"I know."

"You do?"

"Yeah," I said and we went outside together.

On the patio by the pool in the half dark, the only light coming from the kitchen, Billy lit up. He didn't smoke like a kid play-acting. He smoked like an adult with a habit.

I was dying to join him but I thought I should try to be some kind of role model.

"Let's go home. My place," I said. "Tomorrow we'll go fishing, and maybe buy you some cool new stuff."

"Am I making you nuts, smoking?" Billy said. "I'm so happy you quit. I want you to be around forever. I'm really going to try." He crushed the cigarette in an ashtray on one of the glass tables.

From inside the house, the phone rang.

"I'll get it," I said.

Through the kitchen window, I saw Billy carefully pull off his clothes. From behind he looked like a man. He jumped in the pool. Water splashed over the edge. From the street came the sound of a garbage truck, grinding trash in its maw.

Holding the receiver, in the second before I heard the voice on the phone, I knew something was wrong. Maybe it was only afterwards that I knew. When I replayed the incident, me picking up the phone, Billy jumping in the pool, the crude voice on the phone, felt like I knew all along.

"Get him out of here," the voice said.

"Who the hell is this?"

"We don't want that kid in Brooklyn, you got that?"

"Who the fuck is this?"

"What's the difference? I know exactly who the fuck you are. You're that Russki cop, right, who's related to Johnny Farone's wife? So you listen, you take him back or we'll do it for you. You understand? He did plenty of bad shit already and he ain't going do to nothing again like that, so I want him out, you get him the fuck out of here."

I kept my mouth shut. I wanted to make sure I remembered the creep's voice.

"The kid is garbage," said the voice on the end of the phone. "You don't leave garbage around the house. You don't bring it into the neighborhood. I don't want none in mine, so get him the fuck out."

I told him to work it up his ass and hung up, but I was scared. I knew who it was. It was Stanley Shank, the brother of Heshey, the guy that died, the guy they said Billy killed.

I thought about Shank's tone. He had expected me to answer the Farone phone. He wasn't surprised. He knew where I was. He knew Billy was with me. The maroon car that had followed me belonged to Shank. Why the hell didn't I talk to Shank on the phone? I should have calmed him down instead of telling him to shove it. He was a crazy, volatile guy who would stick a knife in you if he got mad.

Shank was a big fat ugly man, with a head like a cantaloupe between soft heavy shoulders like mashed potatoes, but he was solid. Mean. He used to run a fishing boat out of Sheepshead Bay, docked it the other side of the inlet from Manhattan Beach where the Farone house was. Half a mile away, not more. Shank knew his way around fishing knives, the kind he kept on board.

I'd seen Shank clean fish on the dock one time. He worked fast with the knife, his face full of concentrated glee. I'd also seen the kind of damage he could do to people with it.

Someone had told me Shank went bust and had to sell the boat to rich Russians and that it made him more pissed off than ever.

I didn't think Shank would do physical harm to Billy – it was too easy to trace it – but what sacred me was he'd call the tabloids and tell them Billy was out. Shank would make Billy seem like a freak, a kid who only got out on vacation because he was connected. After that, there'd be no place for Billy to go except back to the institution in Florida. Maybe not even there if Shank wanted to press the case that Billy should have been in a real prison all along.

I wanted Billy out of Brooklyn.

From the kitchen, I watched as he emerged from the pool, dripping, wrapped a blue towel around himself, dried off, then he put his clothes back on. He glanced at a large rectangular object that stood against the back of the house. It was neatly covered with a heavy black plastic sheet. Billy pulled it off carefully and stood, not moving. I couldn't see what was under the plastic.

I pushed open the patio door.

"What are you looking at?" I said.

Billy turned around. "My aquarium. The tank's empty. There are no fish left in it, Artie. It's empty and cleaned out and put away like I would never want it again. You think my dad really took the fish to his restaurant?"

"We can call, if you want."

"I don't think so," said Billy. "No, let's not do that, Artie."

"How come?"

"I'm pretty sure the fish are dead."

"So let's go back to the city,"

Billy told me he was ready.

"Can I drive?" he asked. "Can I?"

On the way up from Florida, I let Billy drive some of the time. I picked him up on the Saturday of the July 4 weekend, and we drove home together, him and me, me driving mostly, up from the swampy heat, me wanting to stop at Cape Canaveral and see where they launched the shuttle. Instead, because he was restless and wanted to get to New York, we kept driving.

When we hit a stretch of empty road, I let him take the wheel. Billy said I'd taught him how and that he remembered sitting on phone books and I let him drive around empty streets in Brooklyn early in the morning.

He was a good driver. Tall enough to drive without the phone books now, he drove gracefully, one arm resting on the window ledge, both hands on the wheel, looking ahead, never distracted by the radio.

In small towns where we stopped to pick up food or eat at some diner, American flags sprouted from houses and lawns. In one dusty town the lamp posts and stop lights were hung with pictures of soldiers fighting in Iraq. Hispanic guys most of them, women too. They were young, nineteen, twenty. Some were dead, others waiting. For a mile, as far out as the strip malls, the pictures fluttered along with limp yellow ribbons.

Once, we hit a parade coming up the block, a fire engine decked out with bunting, a few old guys in World War Two uniforms walking behind the engine, and little kids tagging along. It was like a movie.

"July 4 is on Monday. My independence day," Billy said. "Right?"

I had picked Billy up at old man Farone's house — Johnny's father, John Sr — in a development in Florida where a lot of Italians from New York had retired. The streets were named for romantic Italian towns: Pisa, Bellagio, Siena. The houses all had cheap stucco fronts, red tile roofs, mangy front lawns.

Donna Farone, one of Johnny's sisters, lived with the old man. Her name was Maria LaDonna, but everyone called her Donna. It was because of her Billy was allowed to see his grandfather. He had always liked the old man who took him fishing, like I did, when he was little.

John Sr had moved to Florida when his wife threw him out of the house after forty-seven years; she said he liked little girls. No one ever proved exactly what the old man did, and anyhow, after he got to Florida, he'd had a stroke. Most of the time he sat in a wheelchair in the house and tried to form words.

When I got there, Billy was sitting outside on the steps. Next to him was a young guy who turned out to be a shrink. He got up and introduced himself – Andy Swiller, nice to meet you – and the two of us walked a couple yards from the house.

A tall skinny guy in chinos and a short-sleeved green plaid shirt, he said he was a doctor doing some of his training at the facility – a lot of interns came to spend a year. Behaviorists, genetics, psych; we got all kinds of modalities. That's what he called it.

I asked him what Billy had. He told me it wasn't Asperger's. It wasn't some other form of autism. It wasn't one thing or the other. There were co-morbid diagnoses when one didn't fit. Shrinks start talking co-morbid, I get crazy.

"So what is it?" I said.

"You can't always slot the kids in," said Swiller, said it wasn't the time to talk about it, said he was hoping Billy could eventually come out whole and have a real life. There were kids like that, he said. Told me he liked Billy a lot; they got along great, both being from Brooklyn and Yankees fans.

I tried pushing him. "How is he?"

"You want my professional opinion or just how I feel?"

"I figured in your business they're the same thing."

"Fair enough," Swiller said, "I think he's good. I think he's better."

"Cured?"

"Make sure he gets a good pastrami sandwich when he's in New York," said Swiller, and scribbled his name and numbers on a card that he handed me. He wished me luck and shook Billy's hand, told me to call him any time and got in his car.

"Ready?" I said to Billy.

"Am I ever!"

Through the screen door of the house, I could see Donna

Farone. I could see an elderly man in a wheelchair. Old man Farone, I figured.

"Everything OK out there, Billy boy?" he yelled out. He could talk after all.

It was around four a.m. at a motel somewhere in Virginia when Billy woke up screaming. He sat up in bed, sweat pouring off his forehead, and told me about the dreams in which he's executed. Taken to a death chamber, stuck with the needle, killed.

It started a few days after he got there. He had never been away from home except for one night on a sleepover with a boy down the street in Brooklyn. He had always had his own room. He didn't know about other kids, especially not the kind of kids in the facility who could barely read and write. He felt surrounded. People watched him. The dreams began.

It happens every night in Florida, Billy said. Every night, while the noise of other boys he shares a room with creeps into his sleep, and he can't tell if he's still awake or dreaming. The night noises of the boys, coughing, snoring, sneezing, yelling, reminds him of the noise of his mother's refrigerator at home: first a steady hum, the whir of the motor, then, suddenly, the clunk of machinery before it turns over and settles back into a steady drone.

Waking up those nights in Florida – and he wakes up every few hours, he says – he turns over, looking for quiet. His feet are cold. The blanket is too short for him and leaves his big feet uncovered, as he tumbles down into sleep again. For a while there's nothing, just the hole of sleep.

Then the dreams. Walls moving in. Crowds of boys taunting him. Billy himself in the locked ward, doors at the end of the corridors bolted shut. He feels trapped like a boy caught in a net, like a fish on a hook, and he thrashes around and can't get free.

Gangs of boys chasing him to the end of a long hall, all the boys whirring, clunking, sucking, snoring. They're running after him to the death chamber, which is when the screaming starts. He can't tell if it's a real death chamber or a video game, but it's him and they will stick a needle in his arm and make him die. Every morning, his sheets are soaked with sweat.

Billy has read the books, seen the movies, knows how people will watch him die through a little window. This is the worst part, people watching while he's tied down flat as a board, and they stick the needle in.

Inside his dreams, Billy wakes up screaming. No one comes. He reaches for a word, can't grab it, it hangs in front of him, letters made of ice that begin to drip, just beyond his grasp in the dream world of unremembered phone numbers and lost names, and he reaches harder because it's the only thing that can save him, can make him safe. The background noise gets louder, boys closing in on him.

Every night. Billy hates going to bed. He can't fend off the dreams. He refuses. Is punished. They take away some of his books. He can't sleep. He can't get hold of the word.

That night in the motel on the way back to New York from Florida, I finally got Billy to lie down in bed. I sat with him all night. As it got light outside, he drifted into a light sleep.

And then everything seemed better. We kept driving. I thought maybe Billy's worst time was over. On the road, we talked and laughed and ate potato chips out of huge bags and peanuts in the shell and by the time we got to the Holland Tunnel, the car was a mess. I had almost convinced myself that the newspapers had been right: all Billy had done where Heshey Shank was concerned was defend himself. Or else he had been nuts, had been out of his mind when he killed Heshey.

On the Manhattan side of the tunnel, I turned east on Canal

Street. Billy put his head out of the window, pulled it back, and started laughing.

"What's up?"

"I'm happy," Billy said.

"How come?"

"New York," he said. "We're home."

7

"I'll lock the door," said Billy as we left the Farone house.

He locked up carefully, maybe showing me how careful he was, while I went ahead of him towards the street and my car. Most of the houses on the block were lit up and there were street lights every few yards that made pools of yellow on the sidewalk.

Did I smell it before I saw it? The sewage smell of rotten garbage hit me first. On the edge of the front lawn where Genia had planted pink roses – the neighbors appreciated these elegant touches, she had said – was a pile of trash. Wet garbage – cold, half-eaten burgers, banana skins, egg shells that gleamed weirdly white in the night light – had been dumped along with beer cans and wet newspaper and what looked like diapers. You could smell the shit.

I looked for the garbage cans and couldn't see any and remembered the plastic bins that belonged to the house had been placed neatly near the garage. Someone had trucked the garbage in and dumped it.

"Let's get out of here," I called to Billy. "Now."

"What's the matter?" he said, coming down the steps of the house.

"Get in the car."

"OK, sure," said Billy and then he saw the garbage. "Garbage men are all fucking idiots."

"Some guy probably just trying to dump stuff into the truck missed," I was running my mouth, making stuff up, trying to reassure Billy.

"It's OK, Artie. I'm OK. I think we should clean this mess up."

"Just get in the car," I said. "Please. Let's go."

From the car, I put in a call to a young cop I knew in Brighton Beach. Bobo – his real name was Boris Borisovitch Levin, the parents were Russian immigrants – was a good guy I'd helped train on the job. He still lived with his parents, and he knew everything that went on around Brighton Beach. I asked him to get someone to clean up the lawn at the Farones. I also asked him to drive over and make sure everything was OK.

On the way into the city, Billy slept. The radio was on, but he didn't hear it, his breathing deep and even. Asleep, he looked sweet, like a little boy. I knew the doctor in Florida was right. Billy could come out whole. The sickness was gone. "He's good," the shrink had said. In the city at my place, he'd be safe.

I looked in the rearview mirror. I wanted Billy out of Brooklyn, away from Stanley Shank and his crude phone calls and the creeps who were Shank's friends.

Looking at Billy, I knew I had never cared about anyone more than this kid. He felt like my own; he always had.

By the time we got to the bridge, the weather guy on 1010 was predicting a couple of dry days. The sports guy said the Yankees were doing lousy. On the news was an item about the plane crash in Coney Island and something about a little kid found dead in a vacant lot in Midwood. Battered with his skateboard, the kid was only eight. It could have been one of the boys I'd seen earlier. It could have been Billy who got beat up.

I drove over the bridge, and watched Manhattan's lights come towards me, and I was feeling a lot better when my phone rang.

"I went by that house like you asked me," said Bobo Levin, the young cop from Brooklyn. "I cleaned up the garbage myself for you, Artie. What bastard did that?"

"You see anything else?"

"Not much. There's a few scratches on the mailbox, and the garbage thing. Looked to me like somebody wanted the Farones, is that their name, to know they'd been around. I checked the doors and windows," said Bobo anxiously, wanting to impress me. "Is that OK with you, Art? Anyone living there? The pool was full of water."

"Yeah, it's OK, thanks, man," I said. "The people who live there are away for a couple days. Business trip, something like that. London. I'll get in touch with them; you don't have to bother about it. You did great, Bobo. I owe you."

"You don't owe me, Artie. You don't want me to write it up?"

"Maybe not. That good with you?"

"Sure, man, sure, of course," Bobo said. "Friends of yours?"

"Relatives."

"Jeez, you've got family that sure lives nice," he said, not envious, just appreciative. "One weird thing."

"What's that?"

"I almost killed myself when I tripped over some hunks of glass in the back yard. I mean I had to do a little breaking and entering, but I figured you wanted me to take a good look around the house, right Artie?"

"Right," I said to Bobo. "Go on."

"There's like a lot of broken glass there, heavy stuff, you

have any idea what it could be? I almost cut off my hand on it. Bastards who do this, I'd like to kill them," said Bobo. "You know?"

"I know."

"Is it a problem?" he said. "You want me to go back?"

"You think the glass could have been an aquarium?"

"A what?" he said.

"Like a tank for fish. A fish tank?"

"Sure, could have been."

"What did you do with it?"

"I put it in with the other garbage. Is that OK?"

"Yeah."

"Which kind of bastard did this, Artie?"

"I don't know," I said. I didn't want Bobo raising an alarm, so I added, "Maybe just some garbage man that was a slob, you know?"

"Yeah, Artie, that sounds like what it was." He was eager to please me. "One other weird little thing."

"Yeah?"

"Near the glass I found this plastic, I don't know, like a toy castle or something. That's what it was, come to think of it, Artie, it was like this little toy castle with turrets and all."

Later that night, when Billy was fast asleep, I wandered around the apartment feeling restless. I turned the TV on, then turned it off, sick of the news. I put on a Stan Getz album called *Spring Is Here* that always made me feel better. Over the speakers was the photograph of Getz by Herman Leonard. Sid McKay had given it to me when I got married. Poor, dead Sid.

Music still playing, I went and took a hot shower, made coffee. I wondered if I should take a trip out to Brooklyn to confront Stan Shank and knew it was a stupid idea. I had no real evidence it had been Shank who threw garbage on the Farones' lawn.

Let it go, I told myself. Leave it be. All I wanted was to protect Billy and he was safe now in the city, in my apartment, mine and Maxine's and the twins'. I went and checked on him in Millie's room where he was sleeping. He didn't stir.

There was plenty of space for him here. The girls could double up for a while. If things went OK while Billy was out of the facility in Florida, they might parole him. It was a fantasy, it wouldn't happen, but I hated for him to go back to the place where he had nightmares about dying.

I had called Maxine when I went to Florida to get Billy. I knew she didn't like the idea of him and wouldn't want him in the apartment, but she didn't say it, assuming he'd be with his parents in Brooklyn. I didn't mention he was with me. He'd go to Brooklyn Friday when Johnny and Genia got back. Maxine wasn't due in until Sunday. Anyhow, maybe she'd change her mind when she met Billy.

I wanted a drink, but there was no Scotch left and I didn't feel like a beer. Being in the apartment without Max and the girls and the noise they made depressed me. I had hated leaving my loft for this apartment, but Maxie wanted it so bad. It was a condo with her name on the deed, a view of the river, a good school close by, a bedroom for each of the twins. She could walk to work, something she had never done in her whole life, she told me. She had always taken the train, sometimes two subways and a bus.

I pretended to like it. She didn't seem to notice – or maybe she didn't mind – the thin walls, the cheap burgundy carpet in the hallways, the noise of the couple upstairs screaming at each other. To her, it was the best place she'd ever lived, and just coming home at night to Battery Park City and our apartment in a brand new high rise lit her up. I loved her loving it and I wanted to feel the same way. I tried.

I went out onto the little balcony where, if I leaned over, I could see the river, the bike path along the Hudson, the young trees and grass that reminded me of the suburbs. Leaning against the railing, a boy and girl, maybe nineteen, twenty, were locked together munching on each other. I felt old. I went into the kitchen and poured myself a glass of wine. I went back into Billy's room. In the living room I changed the music, then switched it off. Maybe it was OK if I went out for an hour. I needed some company.

Downstairs in the lobby, I gave Jorge, the doorman, twenty bucks and asked him to check on Billy in half an hour. Jorge was a nice guy. Reliable. Billy was fourteen. What could happen? I went out, turned back, made sure Jorge had my cell number. He told me not to worry.

Zipping up my jacket, I headed east. Halfway there, I thought I should turn back, that I shouldn't have left Billy, but I kept walking. I should have done a lot of stuff, but I kept going, which was what I usually did. If you stopped moving, you started thinking, and for now things were OK, I told myself, so what was the point?

8

There was nothing small about Tolya Sverdloff, not his size, or
his style, or the way he greeted you – happy, sad, pissed off,
depending on his mood – and as soon as he saw me walk into
the bar, he called out over the noise, "Artyom, darling,
sweetheart, I'm so glad to see you, have some drinks. Come.
Have something to drink. Many drinks. Champagne! Good
stuff!"

The sleeves of his black silk shirt rolled up, a huge apron tied
around his waist, Sverdloff, who towered over everyone, was
behind the bar. Six-six, three hundred pounds, he was a big
man with a face like an Easter Island statue and dimples the size
of a baby's fist. His hair – it was turning gray, I suddenly saw
– fell over the high forehead. He was leaning across the bar,
talking to an English guy and he introduced us and we shook
hands.

Turned out the guy, whose name I didn't catch, owned
some restaurants in downtown Manhattan, including the place
we were in and which Tolya wanted to buy. Good-looking
guy, too, brush-cut hair, soft spoken, he was talking earnestly
to Tolya about early Soviet film – Eisenstein or something,

though it was hard to hear — while Tolya tried to get a price out of him for the bar.

Tolya extracted a bottle of champagne from a wine fridge, picked up a couple of glasses, relinquished his job to the real bartender, and came around the other side where he poured the champagne out and offered me a glass.

"You want?" he said to me. "What the matter with you?"

"Nothing," I said. "Yeah, I want a drink. With a Scotch for a chaser."

"Don't be an idiot. It's Krug, Artyom, this is nectar from paradise. You can't drink Scotch with it. Some of the time, I think you are still provincial Russian boy," he said. "You look lousy."

"What provincial? I grew up in Moscow, I live in New York, so fuck you," I tasted the champagne, which was delicious.

"You too," Tolya laughed, and added something really filthy in Russian. With me he talked a mix of Russian and English, and his English was sometimes perfect, if he felt like it.

Tolya spoke five languages, he could quote poetry in all of them, he knew his way around art and wine and music, but when he was pissed off, or maybe when he wanted to get back at his parents — both had been famous Moscow actors and intellectuals — he hunched his huge shoulders, stuck the butt of a cohiba in his mouth, and put on a silk shirt that cost a grand, strutted around and dropped his articles so he sounded like a peasant or a hood. It made me nuts. I'd given up harassing him about it.

The champagne cheered me up. So did seeing Tolya, who considered good booze, food and great-looking women staples of a decent life.

"Just give me a minute, Artyom. I want him to sell to me," said Tolya and gestured with one huge hand at both the guy he had been talking to and the bar. "I want bar of my own. Bar named Pravda should, truthfully, be possessed by Russian fellow, right? Would be so nice. I fix up, I serve caviar, I serve Krug and caviar, and maybe I become modern-style DJ." He aped a guy spinning platters with both his enormous hands. "Maybe not."

While he returned to his negotiations with the English guy, I sipped the wine and leaned on the bar next to a pretty girl wearing a thin white T-shirt and no bra.

Tolya Sverdloff had once worked in Moscow as a DJ, broadcasting news of Russian rock to the Chinese in Chinese when it was all the poor bastards in China could get. It was after I had left Moscow, but I knew Tolya had done risky stuff, had gone to jail back when the Soviet assholes still called rock music "musical AIDS". Another age.

I said, "What the hell are you talking about?"

"Pravda, good Russian name, I keep name. Excellent name, which is absolute truth." Tolya laughed at his own joke. "I want to smoke. Let's go," he said, shook hands with the English guy and made his way through the crowd and out towards the street where I followed him.

It was Tuesday night but it was summer and people were in the streets. Gangs of great-looking girls in tiny skirts and tight T-shirts, midriffs bare, paraded up and down the street in flip-flops and backless heels, making a sexy little noise against the pavement. Tolya leaned against the building and poured some more champagne into the glass I still held, then passed me the bottle.

From his gold cigar case with a cigar engraved on it, a huge ruby for the burning tip, he took a cohiba and stuck it in his mouth. From time to time, he smiled at girls in the street and occasionally one of them waved back and called out his name. Tolya knew a lot of people.

"I love the summer," said Tolya, removing his cigar from his mouth. "I love this time when girls come out in little skirts and tiny tops and everything is showing. This can drive a man crazy, of course, all of them bouncing around, so lovely and delicious." We had been friends, him and me, for ten years, more even, back since he saved my ass from some hoods on the Brighton Beach boardwalk.

"You got the message I was back?" Tolya said. "I left this on your machine, also where I am regularly drinking at night."

"How do you think I knew where you'd be?"

"Then what took you so long? I got back last week."

"I'm sorry. I'm really sorry. How the hell are you?"

Almost a year earlier, in the middle of the night, I had driven Tolya to the airport. I wasn't sure where he was going. He left New York in a hurry and I didn't know if it was because of real estate deals that went bad or something worse.

Over the months, we'd talked a few times. I knew he was in Havana, then in Moscow, which scared the shit out of me. You did bad deals in real estate there they killed you. Also, if you survived, there was Putin to lock you up. Putin didn't like rich people he couldn't control. Far as I knew, Tolya didn't have oligarch dough, but he had plenty and he liked to play the part. Once, when he was on the phone, I'd heard him call Abramovich by his first name. Tolya was back in the New York, and I was glad as hell.

"I was away last week," I said. "So I'm here now. You're OK?"

"I'm very fine." Tolya switched to Russian. "I'm through with business. I sold everything; all my property I sold except I kept one nice little apartment in Moscow, one in New York, a little house at the beach, something in Havana. This is all. I give up all business because, Artemy Maximovich, business is crap. Commies were right. Mr Karl Marx was definitely the man. Maybe he didn't exactly lay down a great plan for the future, maybe he didn't want to live that way, especially since he liked his wife wearing nice clothes, maybe his plan wasn't so hot in all details – fucking workers are more

74

conservative than fucking bosses, you know – but he certainly knew how things would be, and what kind of shit capitalism would turn into, Artyom. I plan to see my kids, read books, learn about wine. Become wine master. Listen to important music."

"Your rock days are over? You're moving into old age? What?"

"You, Artyom, have no taste in music at all. You listen to white-boy jazz, you think this is music?"

"This from a man who once considered Boris Gribenshikov a prince of rock. Hey, I saw Dubi Petrovsky today, he found a publisher for his book on the Beatles."

"I like Dubi," Tolya said. "Perhaps, Artyom, I will buy one small vineyard." He was mildly drunk and in a very good mood. I admired his black linen jacket. Brioni, Tolya said.

Tolya, who could not resist one more suit, one more silk shirt, for whom the word Brioni was like a term of endearment, and who possessed at last count – his last count – forty-six pairs of custom made Gucci loafers with eighteen carat gold buckles – took the champagne bottle from me and held it up like a trophy.

"Nineteen-ninety, Krug," he said. "My favorite year. Year everything happens, grapes grow good, Commie assholes losing grip. A very good year." He hummed a little of the Sinatra tune and I told him to shut up, and we laughed and he said, "You want to eat something?"

"I'd rather drink."

"Over there." Tolya gestured at a bench where we went and sat. The unlit cigar was still in his mouth and he got out his heavy gold lighter and lit it slowly.

"So, like two old guys we're sitting on a bench and I'm wondering what's going on with Artyom. Why doesn't he call? Why doesn't he say anything now, except for small talk about the Beatles. What's going on?"

I didn't want to talk to Tolya about Billy. I had seen the look on Sonny Lippert's face on the beach, and I didn't want any grief from Tolya about it. I looked at my watch. I felt restless again. I got up.

"I should go home."

"Artyom, please, sit down. I see in your face there's shit in your life." Tolya was no longer switching back and forth between languages, but speaking Russian; for him Russian was for serious talk, the literate purring Russian that made me feel my soul was being fingered. It made me think of my father and Uncle Joe, the giant, who spoke the most beautiful Russian of them all. When Joe came to visit us in Moscow from his miserable job in the south, my mother, who had a crush on him because of the way he spoke, made him read aloud from Pushkin.

Tolya poured more champagne into our glasses and set the bottle on the sidewalk near our bench.

"What's with you?" he said. "Talk to me."

"I'm fine."

"You don't want to talk?"

"I don't know."

"You want to eat?"

"You asked already. I said no. How's Valentina?"

"Good."

"The girlfriend?"

"What?"

"Your girlfriend, the nice one, the Russian, the one you felt you could be with permanent?"

"I don't know." Tolya was lousy at choosing women — normally, he liked strippers and hookers, except for the time he wound up with a dour little architect who made him miserable. He avoided my question about the nice Russian and drank some more.

"This is lovely wine." Tolya gazed at the liquid in his glass

76

like he would a gorgeous woman. "But did you ever taste Clos de Menil? Better than money, or women." He smiled. "Maybe not women."

"We're going to discuss wine? Tolya? I don't give a shit, I don't know dick, it comes in red or white."

"I love you when you pretend to be a philistine," he said, still talking Russian. "You think it makes you more American, this posing as dumb and dumber. So talk about other stuff. You're the one who doesn't answer questions, you're the one hiding some shit or other."

"I need to smoke."

He offered me the cigar case, put it away, found a crumpled box of cigarettes in his pocket.

"I make club for smoking," Tolya said in English now. "I call this place 'Yes Smoking'. Maxine is OK?" he said. "She's pregnant, maybe?"

"She's in California with her girls."

The cigarette tasted great.

Tolya leaned his elbows on his knees and contemplated his cigar. "It's the Farone boy, isn't it? Something's wrong with Billy Farone."

The skin on my arms felt cold.

"How the fuck did you know that?"

"I'm a genius."

"I don't believe you. Tell me how you knew?"

"Calm down. I just know you. What's wrong with him? He's sick? What?"

"No."

"You saw him?"

I nodded.

"In the place in Florida where they sent him, the one Sid McKay helped you fix?"

"So maybe I saw Billy," I said.

"How is he?"

"He's fine."

We sat in silence. I needed to talk. I needed to tell him.

"So, the way you felt about your girls when they were young, you'd do anything to protect them, right?"

"I kill for them," he said in English without melodrama, the way he might say he'd get them a glass of water. "When they were little, also now."

"I feel like that about Billy. I love Maxine's twins, and your Valentina, but this boy, he's like mine. I can't explain."

"He's your blood."

"I don't believe in all that crap. I don't believe all that sentimental Russian garbage."

"Believe, don't believe," said Tolya with a dismissive gesture. "It doesn't make any difference what you believe, or what you think, Artemy, it is what it is. You cannot change this. Billy is your family."

"I saw him." I threw away my cigarette. "He's OK, I mean he's better, I think he's cured, or maybe he just outgrew the bad stuff. His doctor told me it could happen. Billy is smart and handsome and funny and he talks a lot and he notices stuff, and he can be really focused on whatever interests him, baseball or books or fishing, Christ, you don't think I've become like some weird pedophile?" I could only say it to Tolya, and when he burst out laughing, I felt better.

"Artyom, this is how people feel about their children. You're not a pedophile, you don't want to sleep with the kid, you want to take care of him. I remember when my girls were little, I'd sit and stare at them and think how beautiful was their soft skin, and I would give them baths," Tolya said. "I have a nephew, you don't know him, in Moscow, and it was like that with him also, when he was just before being a man and still a boy and had first little hairs on upper lip and I kiss him good night and I would think how wonderful he is. I didn't want to have sex. It doesn't mean that. Is OK. Is fine," Tolya said. "That's not all, is it? I mean, you want to tell me, or I can just go back in the bar."

"He's here."

"Where?"

"At my place."

"How come?"

"You said it was OK to take care of him."

"Yes, it's OK, but not to bring him here to New York to stay in your apartment. What happened? Where's his mother? Billy ran away?"

"They let him out for a couple of weeks. His parents are in London. I said I would take him just until Friday, and then he'll go to them. Billy's different now."

"I believe you. You don't have to keep saying it. I believe."

"You'll meet him, you'll see. I want you to meet him."

"I'd like that," Tolya said softly.

"Why were you worried he was at my place?"

"Because of his mother. Because of your half sister, Genia, who might be mad at you for stealing her boy. Her, or his father, Fat Johnny Farone."

"I didn't steal him."

"I mean metaphorically. That Billy loves you more than his own parents. I've met the parents," Tolya said. "Even I would prefer you."

"Thanks."

"It's what you had to do," he said. "It was the right thing, being with him. I just don't want you to have trouble with the parents, OK? That's all. So bring Billy to my place tomorrow, we'll make a New York brunch."

"Thank you."

"What is all this 'thank you' bullshit? You're my friend."

"I needed you to believe me," I said to Tolya in Russian.

"I believe."

"I'm scared someone wants Billy gone."

"Serious?"

"I don't know."

"You want to talk about it?"

"Not yet."

"So go home and take care of him. And come to my place tomorrow."

"I told him we'd go fishing tomorrow."

"So come first," said Tolya. "I have great smoked salmon, best wild Norwegian that you can't get anywhere else. I have smuggled it in," he added triumphantly as if it would taste better being illegal.

"I have to go." I got up and looked for a cab. Tolya kissed me Russian style on the cheek three times.

"You're going to your apartment?"

"Yeah."

"Good, this is good, you shouldn't leave him alone."

"What's wrong with that?"

"Don't get mad with me," Tolya said. "Billy has been away, he needs time to get used to being home with you and to the city, you said someone doesn't like him being here, so he needs you. Just take care of him."

9

After the champagne I felt almost mellow, and when I found Sonny Lippert waiting for me near my apartment building by the river, I was OK with it.

It was going on midnight. Sonny wanted to talk about the case in Jersey, the kid who got killed and got her feet cut off, and the way it reminded him of the cold cases he could never forget. He was focused on a serial type thing, sure there was a string of murders dating back a decade.

We were neighbors, Sonny and me. He had moved to a building in Battery Park City first, before Maxine and I moved into ours a few blocks away. We didn't run into each other much, so I was surprised when I saw him.

With the Hudson behind us, we leaned against the railing. Sonny looked up at the apartment buildings clustered here, a few blocks west of what had been the World Trade Center and was now a hole in the ground.

"Listen, Art, man, I'm so sorry I was hounding you earlier. I'm fucked up with this case. I was waiting out here, hoping you'd come by, you know, so I could apologize. I get into that drift, you know, I get so fucked up with my past, thinking about the old days, my parents, I dream about them, I dream about falling between the crack in their beds like I did when I was a kid, only I keep on falling, and there are these other little kids only they're missing limbs. Never mind. You think I'm fucking nuts, right?"

"Sonny, it's fine. Look, I'll come over one night and we can listen to some music, right? What do you need from me?"

"So I was waiting 'cause I wanted to apologize for the way I was with Billy Farone, I was just surprised to see him, you know, and also to ask you again if you could maybe help me out on Staten Island. This is for real, not to divert you from whatever you need to do or anything. It's just for Rhonda. She feels lousy that she didn't help these people, and there's nothing she can do and she's kind of obsessed with it. She already went and took food and money. The woman talks some English, but she needs someone who can speak the lingo. I don't even mind riding out with you, like tomorrow morning, for instance. I have someone I need to see anyhow. I could do that, Art. I know the lay of the land out there in Staten, if you want me to come."

"So why don't you do it?"

"I can't get involved with Rhonda's personal stuff while I'm on the job."

"OK," I said. "Sure. I owe Rhonda."

"You don't owe her."

The champagne had warmed me up. "Yeah, I do. I owe her for taking care of you when you were fucking dying in the hospital, and her sleeping over in your room every night and busting their ass at St Vincent's if they didn't do the right stuff for you."

"Thanks."

"You're welcome." I said goodnight and set off for home, then I turned back.

"You hear anything about the plane crash earlier?" I said.

Sonny told me that the people in the smashed-up plane on the beach were a Russian family. Only the father survived along with the pilot, and the father was still critical.

Lippert didn't think them being Russian meant anything, just figured he'd pass it on to me. Didn't think any of it meant a thing, except that people who took little kids up in planes like that were idiots. The plane had come from a place over in Jersey.

"I talked to someone who talked to Cohen and I think we can forget it being anything except a sightseeing plane," said Sonny. "The *other* Cohen, that is, man." David Cohen was the city's anti-terrorist czar and Sonny had a line to him like he had to everyone in town. "It was like they said on TV, it was an accident, the plane was a piece of crap and it broke up. And it doesn't mean dick, you know, that kills me, man."

"Sure."

"You think they'll ever put a building up where the fucking Twin Towers were, man?"

"I don't know, Sonny."

"They been fighting over that space like dogs over a bone. Jesus."

"Yeah, sure. Now they're telling us the towers were never built to withstand a bad attack. Poor bastards died in it, maybe for no reason. You believe that?"

Sonny looked up at the buildings again and then he laughed, a short snort of a laugh.

"You remember how after 9/11 they said Bernie Kerik took an apartment where he could see right into the pit?" Lippert said.

"Yeah, I remember."

"Our beloved police chief, Christ, he was something. They said he used to pass out plaster busts of himself to people. They said he liked to go out on the balcony with his girlfriend, what was her name, Judith something, the publishing one, and she would lean over the railing with him behind her and they'd do it looking down at the pit. After all, 9/11 was what made him a hero, and he liked that, so that's where he liked doing it with his girlfriend." Lippert laughed. "You think it's just urban legend?"

"Who knows?" I said.

"Artie?"

"Yeah?"

"Where's Billy?"

I gestured towards my building. "Upstairs. Asleep."

"Take him home to his parents, Art, man, as soon as possible, to avoid any trouble. I won't say any more."

"What kind of trouble, Sonny? What do you mean?"

"You know, man, keep the boy safe."

"Everything's fine," I said.

"You probably know what you're doing, man."

"You sucking up to me?"

"In your dreams, man." Sonny said. "But you told Maxine you have the boy with you in the apartment, right? You should tell her. Go home and get some sleep. I got to go, too. I got some calls to make. I'm going to get the bastards who did the little girl in Jersey and all the others. I'm going to break whoever it is. See you tomorrow."

As soon as I opened the door to the apartment, I knew something was different. Couldn't describe it. A smell. A feeling. I'd been snooping around apartments a long time and it just came to me. Maybe I was wrong. Maybe I was drunker than I knew. Some of my CDs were on the table and I couldn't remember if I'd left them there, but so what? So what if Billy got up and played some music? But what if someone else had been here?

When I checked on Billy he was still asleep in the room where I'd left him – I'd never seen anyone conk out so completely – blanket over his head, feet sticking out at the bottom.

In my bedroom, the shirt I'd taken off when I changed was on the bed where I left it, but it was folded differently, I thought. Maybe not. My head was fuzzy and I got undressed, then I put my pants back on and went downstairs to look for Jorge, the doorman, who was out front smoking.

Jorge said that Billy had not come down from the apartment at all. He said he also went up to check on him once. Yeah, Jorge said he had been in the lobby the whole time, except for going to the bathroom once and out on his dinner break for like ten minutes. Just to pick up a breakfast burrito even though it was his dinner because he liked the burritos, homemade, he said, at the corner deli. Good coffee, too. A black and white cookie was what he had for dessert, though some of the time he went for an oatmeal raisin cookie or, if it was hot, maybe a Haagen Dazs chocolate-covered ice cream bar. Like everyone in New York, Jorge's every meal was a complicated story.

I didn't think Jorge was lying about Billy, but his dinner break made me uneasy. I took the elevator back up and the woman in it stared at me because I wasn't wearing a shirt. I couldn't tell if she was disgusted or interested. I really was pretty drunk.

"Tell Maxine," Sonny had said.

I didn't want to lie to Max. I didn't want to make a mess of things this time. We were married, I loved her, and we were friends. She wasn't going to fall apart because I had Billy in the house for a few days. Why would she?

Maxine was plenty tough. She was a 9/11 widow, and she had worked forensics in the days when they were bringing in pieces of the firemen who died; her husband had been one of them. They never found him, not even a little piece of finger, she always said. Not even a finger.

I looked at my watch. It was one in the morning. Ten in San Diego. I dialed Maxie's cell and waited.

"Hi," she said. "Hi!"

"Where are you? Did I call too late?"

"We're on a dinner cruise in the harbor. It is so entirely gorgeous here, honey, I so wish that you were with us, it's just beautiful. San Diego is so clean! The girls adore it, and they like their cousins, and wait a sec, no, never mind, they're up on the deck. I think maybe I had a few too many glasses of wine, so if you think I sound silly, blame the vino. Also, I can't believe this, but we met a retired guy who lives around here, he was sitting near us on the boat for a while, he says he actually designed the first space buggy, the thing they rode around in on the moon, this real American inventor type of guy. Back when. Said in those days he slept on a waterbed. He was reminiscing, don't think they were connected. It's so cool how people out here just talk to you. What's up?"

Max was exuberant, and I could picture her, long limbs stretched out, a glass of wine in her hand, engaged, chatty, charming everyone she met, including some guy who told her he designed the space buggy. At forty, Maxine looked ten years younger. She was smart and practical and she loved me. I didn't want to lie to her. Still, I was nervous about Billy.

I said, "Hey, are you smoking? Did I hear you exhale?"

"I had one. I couldn't help it. You?"

"Me too," I said. "I'm trying, but I had a drink with Tolya and I cheated. He wants to buy a wine bar."

"Jeez," said Maxine.

"I miss you."

"Me too. A lot."

"I have something I have to tell you," I said.

"You won the lottery?"

"I wish."

"You won the lottery and you lost the ticket, but I love you anyway. Do you care that we're always sort of broke?" Maxine said. "Do you wish you'd married some rich girl?"

"Don't be an idiot."

"OK, I'm a knucklehead as my uncles would have said. You could have married a rich one," said Maxine. "You were hot when I met you."

Glad to avoid what I had to tell her, I said, "What do you mean 'were' hot?"

"You're married now."

"So it's fun out there?"

"Oh, Artie, honey, it's amazing, the sun shines, the beaches are great, the zoo was fantastic, the girls are in heaven, I just so totally wish you were here. What is it? What were you going to tell me?"

I told her. I said that I had picked up Billy Farone in Florida, like I'd told her, because his parents were away. I also told her he was here with me for a few days until they came back.

What for, Maxine asked me, her voice crisp now. What did you do that for, she said. They should never have let the kid out. She told me she knew how I felt about Billy but it wasn't my job to take care of him. Billy has parents, she said.

"Listen to me," said Maxine. "He killed a man."

I didn't answer her.

"Artie? You there?"

"It was complicated," I said.

"No."

"He's different now. You'll see. He's fine."

"I don't want to see," she said. "I don't want him anywhere near where my girls are, or our apartment, not now, or later. I don't want anyone knowing he's there. It makes us a target," Maxine added. "If he's there, then take him someplace else. I don't want him around, and I don't want to talk about it either."

"Wow, that's tough."

"I'm sorry if you think so."

"You'll see how different he is," I said.

"No," she said. "I don't want to see."

In bed, I spent a lot of the night staring at the ceiling. It was Wednesday morning now. There wasn't much noise, not even a garbage truck, just the distant hoot of a tug on the river. I saw the clock at three, again at four, and all I could think about was Maxine's chilly tone when she refused to discuss Billy with me.

I didn't remember falling asleep. In the morning my head was killing me from a hangover. I reached for the phone to call Maxine, but it was five a.m. in California. There wasn't much to talk about anyway. She didn't want Billy here.

Part Two

Wednesday July 6

10

"Wake up, Artie." Billy was standing over me with a glass of orange juice in his hand. He was wearing faded jeans, a denim shirt and his black sneakers. He was fine. It was morning.

I swung my legs over the bed, took the orange juice, drank some, realized I was naked and Billy was looking at me. I got back under the covers and finished the juice, not knowing why it made me uncomfortable, him seeing me like that.

"Thanks," I said. "That was great."

"Service with a smile," he cracked. "You want me to make breakfast for you? I'm a pretty good cook. Mom taught me."

"What time is it?"

"Almost nine."

"Shit," I said. "It's late."

"For what?"

"We're going out for breakfast. You feel like making coffee, though? You know how?"

"Artie, I'm fourteen." He left the room and I went and took a shower, got dressed and went into the kitchen where Billy was making coffee. He poured some into a mug. I drank it.

"Good. Thanks," I said. "You like music, Billy?"

"Course. How come you're asking?"

"I was just wondering."

"I like it a lot, all kinds of stuff, I even like to listen to classical music, like Ellie plays." Elena, his older half sister, Genia's daughter by her first husband, played the flute with an orchestra in Seattle. "I looked at some of your CDs," Billy said. "Was that OK?"

"Sure," I said. Come on. We have to stop by my loft. You remember? The place I lived before Max and I got married. We're going to stay there, you and me, so I need you to get packed."

"I guess Maxine doesn't want me here," said Billy and I wondered if he'd been listening in to our conversation and tried to remember if I had called Max on my cell or on the land line. Land line, I thought. Had there been a click? Stop it, I thought to myself. Stop.

I didn't lie to him either.

"She doesn't know you yet."

"It's OK, Artie. I understand," he said. "I'd like to stay at your loft. I always loved it there when I was little."

"We'll be there together."

"You mean you and me?"

"Yes. Billy?"

"What?"

"Did you go out at all last night?"

"No way." He said, stuffed his hands in his pockets. "I wouldn't go out without telling you. I got up and you weren't around, so I had a cigarette, I'm really sorry I did that, Artie, I'm so totally sorry, and I went back to bed. I know you have like a life, I want that for you, and I just figured you went out to get a drink, or something. But maybe you could let me know next time, 'cause I was sort of worried, which is dumb."

I felt bad. I had accused him of something I'd done, and I

said, "You're right. I'm sorry." I gestured at the newspapers piled on the couch. "You were reading?"

"You don't believe me, or what?" His tone was soft, a little disappointed, but not hostile. "About going out?"

"I believe you. So what do you read first in the papers?"

"When I'm away, when I'm down there, you know, in the place in Florida, I like reading stories about New York. Sometimes I can't remember myself when I was younger and living at home, I can't feel it, and reading stuff about New York helps me."

"I feel like that sometimes, the thing about remembering myself in the past."

"You do?"

"Yeah."

"Do you think they felt anything?"

"Who?"

"The people in the plane?" he said.

"Probably not."

"I wish I knew how they felt."

"Why?"

"To understand more. Who are we having breakfast with?"

"After we drop your stuff at my loft, we're going over to a friend's, Tolya Sverdloff, who has a place in the Meat Packing District. He's pretty crazy and he was a famous rock star in the Soviet Union. Also, his Russian's a lot better than mine, so you could practice with him if you want."

"I'll get my stuff."

Billy went into the bedroom and came back quickly with his duffel bag and fishing gear. We left the apartment together, and I got my car and we rode over to Walker Street where my loft was, left his things, then headed for Tolya's.

"So, listen. I have to check something out today," I said. "It'll only take me a couple of hours. You think you could maybe hang out with Tolya? Then I could pick you up and we could go fishing."

"Can't I go with you?"

"Not this time," I said. "You have any cigarettes left?"

"You're worse than me," said Billy and started laughing, which made me laugh, too, and he got out his pack of cigarettes. There was only one left.

For the first time since yesterday I didn't look over my shoulder. We shared the cigarette, Billy and me, like kids smoking in secret, passing the smoke back and forth, still giggling.

"Surprise! Surprise, surprise." We were barely through the door, when Valentina Sverdloff, Tolya's daughter, was all over me, kissing my cheek, greeting Billy, introducing us to the little girl who grasped her hand as if for life support and whose name was Luda.

Val had brought Luda back from Russia and she barely spoke English. In Russian Val told Luda I was her dad's friend and like family and she should call me Uncle Artie. Then I introduced Billy. He couldn't keep from staring at Val, who was beautiful and then, when she kissed him, he turned red and looked at his feet.

"I wanted to completely surprise you, Artie, darling, you didn't know I was home, did you? I made Daddy promise to absolutely not tell you. Should I still call you Uncle Artie too?" said Val, letting go of the little girl who climbed into a red egg-shaped chair where she dangled her feet over the edge.

Luda was about nine, with a solemn Slavic face, big eyes, and thin blonde hair in pigtails fastened with floppy pink satin bows. She wore pink shorts, shirt and sandals. In front of her was a large plasma screen that hung on the wall and on it, encouraged by Val, she watched *The Incredibles*. Every few seconds, she glanced away from the TV and at Valentina as if to make sure she was still there.

"Billy, could you sit with Luda a little while?" Val put her arm around his shoulder. "I think she'd like that."

"Billy speaks good Russian," I said.

"Yeah, sure," said Billy who went and sat on the floor near Luda's chair.

"He's terrific, and very handsome. Who is he?" Val said.

"Billy's my nephew.

"Wow."

"I think he's in love with you already."

"Yeah, yeah."

"When did you get back?"

"I got back from Moscow yesterday," Val said. "I brought Luda with me."

"Where's your dad?"

"Out getting bagels. He said he had to go to Murray's for them because other bagels are not up to his standard."

Billy was chattering to the little girl and she was beaming at him. I sat next to Val on the huge cream leather sofa and said, "You look great. Different."

Six-one and gorgeous, Valentina was just out of her teens. Last time I'd seen her, she'd had a platinum crew cut, but her hair, long now, was heavy and dark, pulled back into a ponytail. She wore tight black jeans and a sleeveless black turtleneck. Her feet were bare. She was beautiful enough you couldn't look at her without staring. Her face trapped you like a magnet.

"Do you think I'm beautiful?" she had said to me the last time we met, before she left New York for Russia.

Val could see herself through other people and it made her nervous. I was always a little ashamed of how easy it would have been to fall for her, but she was half my age, and she was Tolya's daughter. He would have killed me.

"What's Moscow like now?" I said.

"Let's have a Bloody Mary or something," said Val.

I looked at Billy and Luda, who were still in front of the TV.

"They'll be fine," Val said and I followed her into Tolya's immense stainless steel kitchen where he was smoking a little cigar and scooping caviar out of a blue can onto plates that held warm blini. He was wearing big linen shorts and a linen shirt and a pair of cream suede Guccis, no socks.

"You're admiring my legs, Artyom? I have very nice legs," said Tolya.

"I thought you went out for bagels," I said.

He pointed to a bag that must have contained two dozen. "I went. I return." He gestured to a door. "Kitchen door goes out to the stairs. My Valentina looks wonderful, yes?"

Years earlier, when Val was a child, some hood in Moscow who wanted to hurt Tolya kidnapped her and cut off one of her fingers. Tolya took his then wife, Val's mother, and Val and her twin sister, Masha, to Miami. The girls grew up American. No accent, no mannerisms, nothing to remind them of home except for Val's finger which was only a little stub of flesh.

"Yes," I said. "She looks terrific."

Val got a pitcher of Bloody Mary out of the fridge and poured it into heavy squat glasses and we sat at the table while Tolya finished fixing breakfast, heaping bagels onto a platter, unpacking the salmon he claimed to have smuggled in.

"How was Russia?" I said to Val.

She sipped her drink and it left a red mustache on her lip.

"I went to Moscow," she said. "I went to the small cities, I traveled a lot, I even went to Chernobyl, and the towns near by in the Zone of Exclusion, like a dead Soviet world, which of course made daddy completely freak out. I met children. No one gives a shit, Artie. People talk all kinds of intellectual bullshit about the post-Soviet world, but it's the kids who have cancer from leaking nuke plants, and the kids who got it worst

96

in the siege at Beslan and the Moscow theater. Others get dirty
needles used on them in hospitals where the nurses sell the
clean ones to addicts. Some kids are just plain vanilla regular
victims of poverty." Val knocked back her drink; it made her
choke slightly and she put it down. "I drank that too fast. I
drink too much."

"What about Luda? Who is she?"

"She's nice, isn't she?" said Val. "She's a sweet girl. I brought
her here for a vacation. They allow you to do that. She was at
this orphanage. Her father is dead. Her mother can't support
her and she's dying anyway from cancer. Don't look at me like
that, I'm not trying to save the world," she said. "I just want
Luda to have a nice time once in her life."

"Artie?"

It was Billy. He'd been standing in the doorway that led
from the living room to the kitchen, listening.

"What's up?"

"I think Luda is hungry or something. She's crying. I like
didn't know what to say. I'm sorry."

"I'll go," Val said.

"Did I do something wrong?" Billy said anxiously.

"No, sweetheart, no," said Val. "You're just great."

"Let's eat," Tolya said. Val returned with Luda's hand in hers,
and we all sat down at the kitchen table.

"Is Luda OK?" said Billy to Val in English.

"She's fine," Val said.

The table was loaded with food, the salmon, blinis and
caviar and a bowl of sour cream and one of crème fraiche,
white fish, sable and chubs and smoked sturgeon. There was
chopped herring and three kinds of cream cheese – scallion,
caviar, vegetable – mountains of bagels – onion, raisin, sesame
– and sticky buns and croissants. I was hungry.

"I forgot the juice," Tolya said.

Half a bagel in his hand, Billy jumped up from his chair. "I'll get it."

He opened one of the doors of the huge restaurant-style fridge, a massive hulking stainless steel giant with clear glass doors and a motor that purred. It was like an enormous animal in the corner of the kitchen. Carefully, Billy extracted a pitcher of orange juice.

"That's like so huge, that refrigerator," said Billy to Tolya. "You could climb inside if there wasn't so much food. You could like chill out." He laughed at his joke. "Did you know we saw a plane crash on the beach yesterday? Me and Artie. We were on the beach at Coney Island and we saw it come down. Did you see that on TV? It was everywhere. It was in the newspapers. I saw it for real.

"I saw," Val said briefly. "Let's eat."

Billy went on talking about the plane crash.

"Maybe we could talk about it later," Val said while Luda examined a croissant, and Billy, realizing he had said something wrong, and not knowing what, inspected his bagel.

"Should I like apologize?" he whispered to me.

"Don't worry."

We talked in English and Russian, Russian for the little girl, Luda. Val, who had a sixth sense about people, knew Billy was hurt by her refusing to listen to his story of the plane crash and she moved her chair closer to his and talked privately to him and tickled his chin with a daisy she took out of a vase on the table. Far as I could tell, Billy was in heaven.

After we made pretty good inroads into the food, Luda whispered something to Val who took her back to the living room to watch TV. Billy, asking if he could help, went after them, trailing Val like a puppy. When Val came back, she sat down next to me. Tolya was out on the terrace, smoking and talking on the phone.

"Billy's watching baseball on TV with Luda and explaining it all to her," said Val. "Is he cute or what? So, Artyom, Uncle Artie, so." She leaned back, stretched her bare arms towards the ceiling, her sweater pulled tight across her breasts.

"You like my perfume, Uncle Artie?" Val put one arm along the back of my chair.

"Don't flirt with me."

"I'm such a bad girl," she said. "You have no idea."

"Bad how?"

"I don't want to do like other rich girls," said Val. "I don't want to get married, I don't want to be a bridezilla, you know, with the million-dollar wedding, and the Vera Wang dress and the perfect diamond chic-let for a ring, the little square-cut diamond that costs minimum a hundred grand and no one's even planning on staying married for long. It's not me, and it never will be, and oh, my poor mommy in Florida, it's all she wants, so I say why don't you remarry, Mom? She has the guy with the yachting cap and the real gold buttons on his blazer and the country club. She doesn't want to, so my sister will have to do it because Masha is the good one," Val added. "Also, since you asked, I like sleeping around. I like feeling I can do what I want."

"You're still a kid."

"That's the one thing I'm not," she said. "Never was a kid, except for having a crush on you."

"Stop it."

"I'm serious," she said. "Well, a little bit serious. How's your love life?"

"I'm a married man."

"Sure."

"Cut it out. Tell me about you."

"Me, you know, a sailor in every port like they used to say." Lowering her voice, she added, "You want to talk to me about Billy, your nephew? How come I never met him? I don't remember him being at your wedding last year."

I wasn't sure how much Val knew about Billy. She hadn't been in New York when it happened, the business out at the beach club at Breezy Point. By the time I got married, Billy was already in Florida.

"Not right now," I said.

Val played with the little gold cross that hung on a thin chain around her neck. "I'm going back, Artie."

"Being in Russia, it made you happy?"

"I felt useful. I'm not religious, not in that way, Artie, darling, but I believe in something or other. I'm Russian, right? You're Russian, you either believe in something or you're fucked up, unless you're sixteen and playing tennis at Wimbledon or something and then you're really a mess." She laughed. "Poor little Russian girl tennis players. You should see them, seven years old, they arrive in Miami or some place, with nothing at all. Just hoping."

I reached for the coffee pot.

"In Russia I could help," Val said. "I could listen to some of the children and maybe get a doctor for them."

"You'd be good at it."

"I don't like her being there," Tolya said, coming back into the kitchen. "These places where she goes, places with terrorists, nuclear shit, people with AIDS, now she stays home."

"Pop! Nothing happened to me. I was really safe, and everyone looked out for me. I swear."

"I can't win, can I?" Tolya said. "I want to show you something." He reached for a box of cigars on a shelf, which he opened. The smell was delicious.

"We share, one each," he said, extracting a cigar. "Something very special, partegas series D, factory in Cuba no one goes there, not for tourists, hard to get, very amazing, Artemy. I invest."

"How much?"

"What how much? How much for perfection?" Tolya inquired, beginning the ritual of lighting his cigar.

"I thought you were through with business."

He handed me the stogie so I could sample it.

"This is pleasure, Artyom."

"My dad is like a child. Humor him," said Val, carrying dishes to the dishwasher.

"Listen Tolya, can I leave Billy here for a few hours?" I said.

"Is your home, too, if you want," he said. "Of course. Yes. We are here all day."

My phone rang, and I didn't recognize the number, so I went out on the terrace that overlooked the meat market and the river and the city. It was a warm morning, but not hot, and I could see little waves in the Hudson. The cigar in my hand made a wisp of smoke. I took a puff. Normally I didn't like cigars much, but this was different and delicious and for a second it diverted me from the phone.

"You there?" a voice said. It was the same ugly voice.

"Who is this?"

"You take him away. The boy. I don't want him nowhere in this city, you understand?"

"Shank?" I said. "Shank? Fuck you, you stay off my phone." I cut him off.

Shank – or whoever kept calling – had called too often. The threats were too thin. He was pretty much all hot air, I told myself. I turned off my phone and stuck it in my pocket.

"Who was that, Artyom?"

I turned around and saw Tolya behind me.

"No one," I didn't want any advice about Billy now, or anything else. "Nothing. OK?"

"Whatever you say."

The ash on my cigar fell off and I watched it drift away towards the river. I put the cigar out and dropped it in the garbage can in the kitchen.

"I have to go now," I said to Billy who was still in Tolya's living room watching the TV with Luda. I called him over to the other side of the room. "You OK with me going?"

"Sure. We already talked about that," he said. "You still feel like going fishing?"

"We'll go this afternoon."

"I'm fine. I promise," said Billy, then leaned over and whispered conspiratorially in my ear, "The Russian kid, Luda, is really cute, but between us, it's like she's so totally needy."

"Yeah?"

He made a face. "She just tugs at my clothes and chatters to me, she says she just likes talking, and I don't know what to say back to her. I mean I don't understand half of it, she talks this weird Russian, and some of it's like baby talk. I should be nicer, but it's, like, jeez. Then she says she loves me because I'm her family now. Weird. I'm so trying, though. I am. I mean it's nice for Val if I do it, right?"

"You like Val?"

"Please."

"You're in love with Val?"

"Artie!"

"So, listen, Luda's had a tough time," I said. "Just be nice like you're doing, but you don't have to take care of her. It's not your job. Hey, I meant to ask, did you call your parents in London? You have the number?"

"God, I forgot. I am such a total dope. Can I do it from here?"

"Tolya and Val, they're like family. Like you and me, the same thing. You can do anything."

"But you're not related to them," said Billy.

"Sometimes it's the same thing."

"But you and me, we're really related, right?"

"Yes."

"Don't stay away too long, OK?"

"Promise."

"I'll go make nice with the kid," Billy said. "She's had a lousy time. I don't mind hanging out with her, you know, she's a good kid even if she never shuts up, right?"

"You know anything about Russia, about how lousy it is?"

"I was only in Florida, you know. I wasn't like on some foreign planet. They have TVs. I know you like to take care of me, Artie, I do, and I like it the way you ask if I'm OK all the time, but I'm not a baby, I could be nice to Luda, it won't kill me." Billy hugged me briefly, then pulled away, probably embarrassed. It reminded me of when he was little and hugged me a lot, reminded me of the heavy warmth.

"Remind me where you're going?" he said.

"Staten Island."

"On a case, right?"

"Right."

"Will you tell me all about it later?"

"Sure," I said.

On my way out of the apartment, I looked back to see Billy and Luda, playing pick-up sticks. Billy was completely focused on her and she was looking up at him with an expression of pure rapture, or maybe that was the wrong word; it was more like devotion, as if she'd do anything in the world for him in return for the attention.

11

I took the Verrazano Bridge to Staten Island. It seemed made out of spun metal, a broad span hung by elegant threads over the Narrows, which connected the Hudson to the Atlantic Ocean. In the middle of the bridge you were high up, forty stories over the city, Brooklyn behind you and to the right, the Statue of Liberty and the tip of Manhattan and the curve of the harbor ahead. To the left, the passage out to the Atlantic Ocean was interrupted by Coney Island where I could see the old parachute jump in the amusement park like a broken toy.

I loved the bridge, the way it connected Brooklyn to Staten Island, the way it seemed to throw itself off the coast to the huge remote island that was the fifth borough, three times as big as Manhattan, but empty. I loved the way the watery city was spread out, the New York archipelago. Up here I felt like I could breathe. Billy was safe with Tolya. No one was following me. I hadn't been sure if the call this morning really was Shank. Maybe I'd just been paranoid.

Next to me, in the passenger seat, arms folded across his chest, Sonny Lippert dozed. I had called him earlier and he was already up, working, but he said he'd ride out with me like he promised, maybe visit a guy he knew. I could drop him and he'd get a radio car to take him back to the city.

Staten Island was almost as remote to me as Iowa. I didn't think I'd been out here more than four, five times in my life — a few times to see my old partner, Hank Provone, once to visit Maxine back when we were just friends and her first husband Mark was alive and they threw a barbecue where they lived near the Arthur Kill, the far side of Staten Island opposite New Jersey.

One time I went over and back on the ferry with Lily Hanes when we were still together. We'd sat out on the deck of the ferry, drinking beer and watching the Manhattan skyline, the lights. Lily's red hair, long in those days, blew all over the place in the breeze off the river. Later we watched the moon, hanging low and yellow, was reflected in the water, and I felt happy.

I drove off the bridge past an old Revolutionary War fort and into the suburban sprawl of Staten Island. It looked huge, and unknown, big as Queens. A Sheryl Crow CD Maxine had given me was playing.

"Can we change the music, man?" Lippert opened his eyes. "I must have dozed off some."

I put on a Clifford Brown album that I knew Sonny loved. A few minutes later, he said, "Listen, pull over, yeah there, La Rocca's, that was always a place I liked. Good pizza. Good ices. A slice and an ice, they used to say. Also I need the bathroom. Getting old, Art, man."

I parked and we went into the pizza place where the owner remembered Sonny, or said he did, and offered us espresso. Sonny accepted, and ordered a small white Sicilian-style pie, ricotta and mozzarella.

"I didn't have breakfast," said Sonny. "Let's sit outside, Art. You'll have a slice."

After Sonny used the bathroom, we carried the coffee and the pie onto the deck at the side of the restaurant and sat down. Lippert munched some pizza. "Take a slice, Art."

"Can't," I said. "I just ate. You want to talk to me about your case, the little girl in Jersey with the doll?"

"You feeling magnanimous, man?" He glanced across the road at the neat rows of houses, most of them sprouting American flags, neat lawns, sprinklers, stuff like that.

"Sure."

"Not now," Sonny said. "I was up all night thinking about the bastards who did this, that they're out there, man, maybe in Jersey, maybe looking for more little girls."

A large black guy emerged from an SUV that had pulled up in front of La Rocca's and went inside. You could hear him through the open door laughing with the owner.

Lippert turned his head. "Times must have changed over here. You know Staten Island was the only place above the Mason-Dixon line to side with the South during the Civil War, man? So the Italians who lived here did not like the you-know-who coming over from Brooklyn and they figured when the Verazzano Bridge opened in '63, the 'outsiders', which to them meant black people, would just overrun the place. No one said it but they figured Staten Island was for white people, Irish was OK, but the other kind, I'm putting it a lot more polite than they did."

"I caught that, Sonny."

"Instead, more Italians arrived and the bridge became known as the 'Guinea Gangplank'. The two local growth industries were real estate and garbage, and I remember, yeah, man, I do, the strategy for real estate was to find a place with trees and then, in the middle of the night, cut them all down. Next morning, it was no big deal to get the zoning board to agree to let them build houses there – to reduce the erosion that came from cutting down all the trees, which was Italian logic." Deep in his storytelling, Sonny snorted with laughter. "There was a wooded hill next to this college where I taught for a while. One morning all the old-growth forest had gone. There was just mud. The zoning commissioners were there before the mud dried, and permission was given to build thirty 'Mother-Daughters'. You know what those are? Like semi-attached houses, one part up, one down, where the daughter starts in the basement. As mamma declines – check the ankles, man – she moves down to the basement, and the daughter and whatever of her family remain – the husband is now mostly with the girlfriend spending nights in the Holiday Inn – take over the upper two floors. Gotta think about the gene pool, man. So long as it's white. Russians been moving in now. White Russians, you could say."

"Yeah, fine, Sonny. So thanks for the history, you want to go? I ought to see this Gorbachev woman or whatever she's called, Rhonda's relative, because I have to get back to the city."

Sonny wasn't ready to go. He had moved into one of his riffs and, like a musician high on music or drugs, he was impervious to anything else. It had taken me years to understand it was Sonny's displacement activity, the way he kept the horror at bay: when he was working an ugly case, Sonny escaped into his past. Once, in the middle of a story about his childhood, he had suddenly turned to me and said, completely lucid, "Suspends all thoughts of death, man. My stories. You know?"

Now Sonny finished his slice and said, "Once upon a time, Artie, Staten Island was a place where people went to hang out in the summer, rich people in mansions, working people in fishing huts along Raritan Bay or the Atlantic shore. Even before the bridge, before the ferry. Staten Island ferry's a hundred this year, you know that man?"

"No, Sonny."

"And then someone thought about garbage. It's garbage,

man, don't you see? Garbage is a perfect metaphor for economic mobility, for the wasteful economy of the US of A. Every one of us makes ten tons of garbage a year. Garbage is disgusting. It smells. No one wants to take it away after it's put out onto the streets by building supers in New York. To solve the problem, we transmuted garbage men into sanitation men, gave them decent wages, great health care, and allowed them to retire on more than full salary after twenty years, or sooner if they could manage to develop a work-related disabling injury, which most of them are naturally able to arrange. Man, we produce so much garbage. But then we thought, what the fuck do we do with it after the sanitation men collect it? This is all about transportation and real estate, especially in places such as New York where property is so valuable, you get my drift?"

"I really have to get going," I said and Sonny finally followed me to my car, where he kept talking.

"How many Jews want to get involved in garbage?" said Sonny.

I turned the key in the ignition. "What is this, a Jewish Princess joke?"

"Real estate to us Jews is the Seagram's Building or four thousand square feet on the water in Great Neck."

"Where are we going?" I said.

"Or we figure education is another way up and out if you don't do real estate. But if your people, like those good Italian Catholic people, are suspicious of education and the subversive things that might even be slipped into a vocational school curriculum, like literature, you know, the way up is through transportation. And garbage," said Sonny triumphantly. "Like Staten Island. They already had the real estate. So they think, how do you lure someone to live in a place with a name like Fresh Kills? You can't.

"I mean if you're Italian, it's enough already with the kills, you want safety and cannoli. A few of them start thinking, because they're not stupid, let's put the garbage in Fresh Kills. And voila, the world's largest urban landfill site. Did you know that it's so big, man, it's one of the objects you can see from space along with the Luxor Hotel in Vegas. Cute, huh? Take a right there, yeah, where that sign is."

"Very cute."

"It all added up. Who owned the land in Fresh Kills that the City bought for top dollar? Which zoning board did the City have to deal with? Which social club was hovering over it all? This is not a trick question," Sonny said. "Who managed to get their hands on the private land that was really public, and take over the 'carting' business, and what was this 'carting' thing anyway? I mean it was schlepping garbage, right? I was there, I'm telling you. There were a few beach huts and swamps and stuff and now there was this huge fucking landfill. The stink was something." Sonny laughed. "But you want to know the real thing about this place, it's where most people settled to nurture their lives and express rage. I mean it. Take another right."

"You're sure this is the way to Rhonda's cousin?"

"You're going to drop me first. I'll show you where to go, man, and then you drop me."

"You're not coming with me?"

"It wouldn't be seemly, Art, man. I mean, what the hell would a senior law enforcement guy like me be doing sniffing around some minor Russian thing in Staten Island for his girlfriend? I'll show you where, though. Also, like I said, there's someone I need to see on my Jersey case."

"Fine." I was feeling faintly irritable – all of Staten Island looked the same to me and it seemed to go on forever.

"There, over there, make the left turn," said Sonny. "I knew someone said the water got so polluted around Staten Island, you walked in for a swim, man, you came out without feet."

*

On the way to Sonny's friends who lived somewhere called Todt Hill, there were plenty of Italian eateries. In the small front yards of the bungalows were plaster statues of St Anthony and all-year Christmas decorations. On one screen door was a marines poster and the words "Standing Tall". On other doors and walls and in windows were pictures of firemen who had died on 9/11.

Here on Staten Island you still felt some of the anxiety about it all. Flags were everywhere, flags, slogans, red white and blue. The back of a porch swing I saw was covered with a laminated flag. Every other street was named for a dead firefighter. Staten Island had had more dead firefighters than any other place. I used to laugh at the outer boroughs' way of naming streets – Father Cappucino Boulevard, stuff like that. Then 9/11.

Maxine got upset when they named a street for her dead husband. " I don't need that," she'd said. They did it anyway and she had to go there and cut a ribbon. I went along with her and felt like a jerk because I was alive.

The rest of the city might have calmed down some – there were days I felt we were over it, or at least in a kind of benign stupor – but on Staten Island, you felt people were just waiting for the next attack, waiting for the next shoe to drop, so to speak. I looked at my watch to check the date. It was July 6; in two months it would be four years since 9/11; four years, no shoe, not yet.

"Nice, huh?" Sonny said as we started up a hilly area with plenty of trees, and some good-looking houses.

"Where's the house, Sonny?"

"Keep going straight," he said. "You know I said people came out here to nurture their rage?"

"Yeah, right, rage," There was no point trying to stop him.

I half listened, half looked out of the window. Porticos, columns, vast lawns, topiaries eight feet high, up here some of the houses resembled the White House, others looked like mafia palaces, which was probably what they were.

"You know something, Art, man, the weapons they're using in the so-called Culture Wars, they were field-tested on Staten Island," Sonny said. "I'm not kidding. The War was for the hearts and minds of the kids. Everyone around here was asking would the government or schools take over from parents? Or that big-time most important thing, the church, and who would pass on the culture, the family values, and sex stuff and the truth about creationism and God. It's nothing new, man," Sonny said, "I taught a course, you know, at the college, and you got mostly girls, because boys went to work. Girls got a little time in the subversive world of education before they became a nurse or secretary, or just got married and had babies, and the faculty, who mostly wished they were in the city, were shagging the students and the students were pretending they were hip, and it was OK. I knew a nice girl there. Never mind.

"Anyway, you'd hear how these girls went home and their fathers and boyfriends would rage around about Evil on the nightly news. There would be warfare at home. Mom would hover with platters of pasta, and the girl would say something like, what if Vietnam is wrong, at least they said that back then, probably now they say, so what if there were no weapons of mass destruction or what's so wrong about Janet Jackson at the Super Bowl, or I'm thinking of going to law school or, worst of all, I want to live in Manhattan for a while. That was like saying you wanted to spend a few years in hell. Make a left at the corner, Art," said Sonny." You know what I did?"

"What, Sonny?"

"I was an idiot, so I organized an evening where students could bring their boyfriends and fathers so they could learn about what was happening at the college, and we ordered in drinks and snacks to show hospitality. I get up and welcome them and talk about the curriculum, leaving out the shagging, natch. And suddenly, there's this beefy boyfriend up from his seat, crawling across the conference table where we're all sitting and sipping warm white wine from plastic cups and he's screaming about how the 'spics and niggers' are ruining Staten Island. The door opens and framed in it is this guy named Lloyd Stevens, and he's like an extra large black man.

"He enters as the other guy utters the N-word. Everyone freezes. Lloyd fills up the entire doorway and the light behind him makes him appear even darker, and Lloyd, who runs the college veterans program, says in his softest, calmest voice, 'I was in my office across the hall and I heard more sounds than usual coming from here and thought I should come by to see if my help might be needed.'

"Lloyd is big and handsome, like Sidney Poitier in *The Heat of the Night*, and he turns to the crazed Italian guy who's sprawled on the table, yelling about spics and niggers, and Lloyd holds out his hand and says, 'Hello, I'm Lloyd Stevens, can I help you get to the coffee?' I mean, Call me Mr Tibbs, right, Art man?" Sonny was laughing so hard at his own story now that tears ran down his face. "Oh, man, those were the days. That's the house. You can pull up there."

Tires crunching over the gravel, I stopped alongside a Porsche and a couple of Mercedes. Before Sonny got out, he said, "You think you'll be OK?"

"I'll be fine," I said.

"So thanks, Art. Anyway, I filled you in on Staten Island, right? Just remember, they came here to nurture their rage."

"I'm out of here," I said. "Her name is Vera Gorbachev, right?"

12

A woman poked her head out of the front door of the Gorbachev house the second I parked in front of it, as if she'd been waiting by the window, watching for me. Before I could get up the front steps, she retreated, shut the door on me. There weren't any cops in sight but the alleged crime was a few weeks old so I wasn't surprised. I hit the bell, which played the theme to *Dr Zhivago*, and waited.

The house wasn't far from the Fresh Kills landfill and it had three American flags out front, one on the door, another hanging from a pole, the third stuck in sand in a cement pot. Another pot held purple geraniums that matched the paint on the door. There were six kinds of siding.

You could write a book about the siding on New York houses out here in the boroughs. In the same row as the Gorbachevs' were houses whose siding included shingle, fieldstone, brick in several colors, wainscoting, clapboard, limestone, brownstone, granite and marble – green, black, gray – some fake, some real. The Gorbachev house itself had fieldstone running up a chimney and something that passed for pink granite on the front. The faux mahogany door had an oval piece of stained glass, featuring some saint, a brass knocker in the shape of an eagle, and a set of wind chimes that tinkled in the breeze. In front, the lawn was perfect, like carpeting, little rows of red, white and blue flowers neatly arranged.

At the side of the house, I could see sticks for tomato plants, a baby blue Ford Escort, maybe eight, nine years old, a garbage can turned upside down and a kid's tricycle.

"Hello?" a voice said, and I jumped as the door opened again and the woman I'd seen before emerged onto the front steps. "Who are you?" She had a heavy Russian accent.

I showed her my badge, asked in Russian if she was Mrs Gorbachev and told her I had come because Rhonda Fisher had asked me to. She said yes, she was Gorbacheva, but in America everyone said Gorbachev even for ladies, no one bothered with the feminine version. She said I was welcome and I should just call her Vera.

She was different from what I had expected. Her English was lousy, but her Russian was educated. She was tiny, not more than five feet tall even in the backless gold sandals with high heels that went tippy-tap, tippy-tap on the stone steps. I was guessing she was around fifty.

Blonde hair pushed up onto her head, a pencil stuck through it, she was pretty in a faded Slavic way. The air was chilly for July, and she clutched a white jeans jacket around her. Under it she wore a stretchy black skintight top and light blue spandex stirrup pants which, as I saw when she turned and led me into the house, showed off her ass.

In the kitchen, fussing with fancy coffee cups and saucers she took from a cupboard, Vera told me her husband, who had disappeared the night of the burglary, was Italian and his name was Al Laporello, but that she didn't take his name when they got married. She pointed at a chair. I sat down. There were cookies on the table.

Vera started making coffee in a red espresso machine that

stood on the fake marble counter. A radio was tuned to a Russian pop station and Vera left it on so the songs – the kind you heard on the boardwalk at Brighton Beach – infiltrated the room along with the smell of coffee. Then Alla Pugacheva began to sing, which made Vera smile.

"So good," she said.

Al was older, Vera said. He supervised garbage company where she had worked. She'd been trained as a chemist before she came to America. In Kiev, she added. She said she was half Ukrainian, but considered herself fully Ukrainian because it was superior to Russian. Ukrainians were closer to European.

She lit a cigarette, then left it on the edge of the counter while she poured the coffee into the gold and black cups. Somehow I didn't get the feeling Vera Gorbachev was in real despair about the disappearance of her husband.

"You're here about the robbery?" Vera put two cups and saucers of aromatic coffee on the table, picked up her cigarette and sat down. "Please take cookies."

I turned the cookies down. "Yes. Your cousin Rhonda asked me to come," I said.

"Not my cousin, cousin of my aunt's husband's daughter. I think. Nice lady, Mrs Fisher. She brought me lox and bagels, even pastrami." Vera blew out the smoke. "Rye bread also."

"She said you wanted to talk to someone who knew Russian."

"Cops around Staten Island do not speak Russian. My English is lousy. Sometimes people help only because they hear my name, Gorbachev, and they think, oh, maybe she is relative. They ask me, you are related to Gorby?"

"What do you tell them?"

"I say, sure."

"How long have you been here?"

"Long time," said Vera. "I never bother to learn English well. Enough for my job, nothing more." She went to the fridge and got out cheese and crackers, heavy cream for the coffee, salami and a jar of red caviar. She put it all on the table. You could die of a heart attack eating cake and drinking coffee on Russian cases. No self-respecting Russki who let you in their house let you out before they fed you to death. Or maybe it was their revenge on cops.

I reached for a wedge of Brie. "Thank you."

"Yes. You are welcome. Please help yourself to everything."

"Would you like to tell me what happened?"

"Yes, of course."

Sitting on the edge of her chair, Vera Gorbachev put her cigarette in an ashtray on the table, picked up a cookie from the plate and began extracting the chocolate chips, which she ate one at time.

"I keep talking in Russian, OK?"

"That's why I'm here."

"So we are asleep, two weeks ago this is. I sleep very well," she said. "My husband, he is older, he gets up often in the night, you understand, to use the bathroom. On this night I heard him. I went out to the top of the stairs and saw my husband wearing his underpants, yelling at a man in the living room."

"You saw the guy?"

She shook her head. "Not really. My husband is screaming at him and screaming at me to go back to our room and also because I left the front door open, so it was my fault. I did not. He said I did, but it was not true. The guy is trying to get out of the front door and then I yelled out for my husband to let him go, but no, he can't leave it, he can't leave anything, so he follows the man out of the door."

"How could you see this?"

"You can see the living room from the stairs. I'll show you. Come," Vera said.

I followed her out of the kitchen through the living room,

past a huge plasma screen TV that hung on the wall. A yellow leather couch faced the TV, there was a furry white rug and a long black glass dining table, a milky blue vase of silk roses on it and a stack of kids' games.

"You and your husband have children?" I said.

"Not now," she said, then added hastily as if my question made her nervous, "Yes, I mean they are nieces. From my sister's family who is married to a man so rich – Russian man – she leaves toys for her kids at her house, my house. Both. Easier, she says."

"Where does she live?"

"Staten Island also, over near water where there are many big fancy houses for Russians who pay cash. These are rich people, and very nice," said Vera. "My sister is nice, her husband is so nice, a Russian. They have a big house with chandeliers, but we look out for each other. She gave me TV. I talk too much," she said with a stagey laugh as she started up the flight of stairs. On the landing, she called down, "Here, look, stand here."

I went up and stood next to her. She had been telling the truth: everything in the living room was visible from the stairs.

"After you saw him yelling at the guy, then what?" I tried not to crowd her. The landing where we stood was small, but she didn't seem to mind and she didn't move. I inched away from her.

"I yell to my husband to leave him alone, this guy who broke in. He is waving gun, but he doesn't do anything, just waves his gun and then runs out of the door and my husband, who is an idiot, follows him."

"You called the cops? You dialed 911?"

"I could see nothing important was missing, TVs, and my jewelry was upstairs. I thought he would come right back, he was just showing me he was a big tough man," Vera said.

"Your husband."

"Yes."

"You waited how long?"

"Five minutes, ten minutes. I got nervous. I put on clothes and went outside. No one is there. I called his cell phone, but it was dead. I call my sister and her husband goes to look. Afterwards, I called the cops. I don't like cops."

"Why's that?"

"I grew up in Kiev," said Vera, as if it explained everything.

"You talked to the police?" I said, heading down the stairs to the living room.

Following me, she raised her shoulders in a little gesture of despair. "What is the use of this? I don't speak very good English, and they are not interested. They take notes in little notebooks, but nothing happens. Nobody finds my husband's body, nothing happens."

"You think he's dead?"

"I don't believe this, no. I don't feel this."

"So you called Rhonda."

"I knew her boyfriend is a top gun in law enforcement, you can say this, top gun?"

"Sure." I thought about Sonny Lippert. "Definitely top gun."

Vera sat on the yellow leather couch. I asked for a cigarette because I figured it would count as work, this collegial smoking ritual. Also, I was dying for a smoke.

With a red Bic lighter, Vera lit it for me and it tasted great. I didn't think she was telling me everything, so I sat on the edge of a blue chair that felt like suede and tried conversation.

"Ukraine, right? Kiev."

"Yes," she said. "Where did you learn your Russian?"

"Growing up."

"In New York?"

"In Moscow."

Vera played coy. She was also a snob. I started feeling like a jerk, like I'd come on a pointless errand. I started worrying about Billy. Billy had been fine at Tolya's, he had charmed everyone, had seemed easy with Tol and Val and Luda, the little girl. People responded to Billy, I'd seen it with Luda, the way she had looked at him, so attentive and happy.

Had it been Stan Shank for sure on the phone? Someone else? There had been cops who didn't like the way we handled Billy's case. Parents of kids who knew Billy had been freaked out.

"Anything else you want to tell me?" I said to Vera Gorbachev.

"So you're from Russia," Vera said. "You sound so American, but you probably learned English when you were a child."

I nodded, thinking of Birdie, my mother's friend who had taught me English in her one-room apartment on the outskirts of Moscow.

"I've been here a long time," I said. "You?"

"Fifteen years," Vera said. "Was good times then. I had boyfriend who says glasnost means we will travel all over the world. I don't know where he went. I am in Staten Island. You like to travel?"

"Sure."

"Me too. Especially I like Florida, which is so nice and warm," she said. "You like it there?"

"You married your husband when you arrived in this country?"

"Yes. Why? You think I married him for my green card?"

"Did you?"

"Yes," she said. "But he's OK. Al Laporello is nice Italian man, except Italians look down on Russians. We're above black people, but we are immigrants."

"Your husband is much older?"

"Yes. Fourteen years."

"Go on."

"Nice, sure, for a garbage man," said Vera whose voice was

tinged with disdain. "Garbage is disgusting, garbage stinks, nobody wants to take care of moving garbage or getting rid of garbage. Except Italians."

"You don't like Italians?"

"We're all Americans, right?" She was sarcastic.

"How come you don't like to speak English?"

"I speak OK, but I ask Rhonda to send someone Russian like you so I can tell you all the details in the right way."

I suspected her English was a lot better than she let on; she was going in circles and I wasn't sure why. I didn't really care. It wasn't my case.

"It is better on Staten Island now than ten years ago," said Vera. "Many Russians leave Brighton Beach, they move to Staten Island, which they say is the new Brooklyn."

"What's the new Staten Island?"

"New Jersey. Here you can buy Russian groceries, candies, caviar, bread, smoked fish, even imported cookies, newspapers, and beauty salon my brother-in-law's sister owns that has name of Queen of Hearts. Very intellectual," she said. "Good hair cutting, for guys, too. I can give you address."

"Thank you."

"No problem, like they say."

"You don't seem so worried about your husband."

"I worried," said Vera. "I worried and worried, then I decide it's like last time when he also disappeared for a few weeks. He came back. I worried almost to death first, and then I thought I couldn't worry any more."

"Can I see the rest of the house?" I said.

"You want to see the bedroom?" Vera stood up and stretched. She was a sexy woman. She was coming on to me. I was getting too old for this shit. "Fifty coming up," Tolya had said to me. "You first."

"Yeah, yeah, yeah," I'd said. "Not for a few more years."

"I could use some more coffee," I said to Vera.

"OK," she said.

While Vera was in the kitchen, I ran upstairs and looked around the master bedroom, a guest room and a bathroom, which was tiled completely in black marble. Nothing looked out of place. A picture of Al Laporello and Vera Gorbachev at their wedding was on a dresser. In his tux with a frilly shirt, Laporello was pear-shaped and balding, but he looked happy.

Downstairs, Vera was waiting with two cups of fresh coffee. She had taken off her jeans jacket and through the stretchy fabric of her top I could see her breasts, the nipples sticking up through the thin material. I drank my coffee and ignored her.

"Nobody is around," she said. "You want to make completely wasted trip to Staten Island? You could imagine I am a lonely housewife waiting for milkman," Vera giggled.

I felt embarrassed for her.

"This would be one time, for only this thing, for hell of it, like when we were young. You never did it like that?" she said.

"Forget it," I said.

"No?"

"No."

"Well, bye-bye, Artie."

"You can call me if you think of anything about the case," I said.

"I will tell cousin Rhonda thank you for sending me Artie who speaks such lovely Russian," said Vera sarcastically.

I said goodbye, and I beat it. I had done what Sonny Lippert had asked. I'd tell him I thought things were a little strange at the Gorbachev house on Staten Island, and that Vera wasn't exactly desperate about her husband, but that it was nothing the local cops couldn't handle.

Staten Island detectives would find Al Laporello and the creep who broke into the house. I could only hope that when

121

they found Laporello, he was still alive. Nothing to do with me now; I was done here.

In my car, I looked in the rear-view mirror, then at the Gorbachev house. The street was empty. I shut the door and drove away. Back to the city. Back to Billy.

On the way home, I got lost.

In the glove compartment I found a map and tried to read it while I drove. On the map, Staten Island was huge, suspended between Manhattan and Brooklyn and Jersey. On the Jersey side were tanker ports and oil depots. Around the fringes of the island were inlets, bird sanctuaries, water meadows, creeks, islands I'd never heard of. I passed boarded-up factories, abandoned industrial parks, rotted docks, piers, wharves. The watery edges of New York were tough to work; people could disappear without trace here.

I called Tolya to make sure Billy was OK, but the phone was busy.

About a mile from the Gorbachev house, I turned left and ended up in a dead end where there was beach grass and tall weeds and a few crappy mobile homes. A sign pointed to a correctional facility. I turned the car around, looked at the map, and cut down towards the water.

A second sign pointed to Fresh Kills. I had been out to the dump once or twice. It went on forever, a mountain, a sea, an endless vista of garbage, huge quivering cliffs of garbage, seagulls pecking at it, the stink unbearable. People said it woke them up at night; like dirty diapers boiling in the sun, they said, it made you want to vomit. Why had I been to Fresh Kills the first time? I couldn't remember. The second time had been after 9/11 when they reopened the dump.

The shattered remains of the Twin Towers – paper from copying machines, sheetrock walls, plastic chunks of computer, metal filing cabinets were shipped over to Fresh Kills by barge. It became a desolate crime scene where detectives and forensics people sifted through every item from the attack, some you didn't want to name. I went over once to visit a friend who was working there. I didn't go back.

Halfway back over the Verrazano, admiring the blue of the water in the summer light, I started wondering what the hell Vera Gorbachev really wanted. I still couldn't get through to Billy – my cell was running out of juice – and I was plenty anxious now. I felt pulled in too many directions – keep Billy safe, give him some space, satisfy Sonny Lippert. The Gorbachev thing didn't feel right. I tried Billy a third time at Tolya's, the phone rang, but no one answered.

13

Eating a mint chocolate chip ice cream cone, looking nonchalant, Billy was leaning against my door when I got home. I lost it. I'd driven back from Staten Island, gone to Tolya's, discovered Billy wasn't there, lost my temper. Tolya told me he let him go out because Billy wanted ice cream and to look at some clothes, wanted some new jeans. I went nuts. Then Billy phoned me and said he was standing outside my place.

When I saw him, wearing black jeans and a green T-shirt, completely involved in a complicated method of licking the ice cream cone, oblivious to anything else, I felt really pissed off — mostly because I'd been so scared.

"Hey, Artie."

"What the hell happened to you?"

He looked at me worriedly. "I'm fine. Don't be mad. Please. Here, you can have the rest." He held out the cone. "Come on, Artie. Take a bite. It's really good."

"No thanks." I got out my keys, went through the door, Billy following me, picked up mail from my box and then got into the elevator and went upstairs.

"Artie?"

By the time we were in my loft, I had cooled off.

"Try it," he said, holding out the ice cream again like an offering.

I ate some ice cream.

"Good, right?"

"Yeah."

"How good?"

"It's pretty good."

"You have a green mustache."

I wiped my mouth.

"You're OK?" Billy asked.

"You asked me not to go out without telling you, so could you do me a favor in future and tell me where you're going and when?"

"I promise. But you could always just call me."

"What on?"

"I have a phone. I'll give you the number," Billy said. "I thought I gave you the number.

"They let you have a phone in Florida?'

"What is this, a police interrogation?" he said, but he laughed nervously. "Come on, Artie. It's funny."

"Yeah yeah."

"When I was coming up here, they let me have a phone so they could find me," said Billy. "I mean so they could keep in touch. Come on, please, please don't be mad. Artie? I'll make you lunch. Hey, I'll share a cigarette with you. You want to watch a game?"

"Maybe."

"Artie?"

"What?"

"It makes me scared when you get nervous about me. I mean, there was the garbage at my house and stuff, is everything OK? Is someone going to hurt me?"

"No," I said. "No one's going to hurt you. How about we watch the game?"

"You'll watch with me?"

"Sure."

He turned on the TV, then threw himself on my couch, and continued eating his way through the ice cream and the sugar cone and I thought to myself: get over it. I pushed Billy's feet to one side of the couch and sat down. The phone rang.

"You found him?" It was Tolya.

"Yeah."

"So if he wants to go out for ice cream you let him go," Tolya said. "You can't stand guard over him his whole life, Artemy, are you listening to me? I know about this stuff. I have two girls. I spent my life watching over them, then I had to let go. It was you who told me I had to let go of Valentina. You have to do that. I met Billy. You told me he's fine, then he's fine."

"You liked him?"

"Yes. Also, Luda is in love with him. He's very nice with this little girl, very sweet. This makes my Valentina happy. Also, I'm calling so you'll come tonight to Luda's birthday party."

"Sure," I said. "Where?"

"I buy entire toy store for one night for little Luda," said Tolya. "Is called slumber party."

"What time?"

"Six, seven. Billy of course comes also. Party for kids, OK, then we go to East Hampton, for vacation. Come with us. Big house I rent for summer, ocean in front, pool, tennis court, butterfly trees. You ever see butterfly trees?"

"I think Billy's probably too old for a girls' party at a toy store."

"So next week, I rent Madison Square so he can play basketball, for now he comes to Luda's party. I see them together, Artyom, they are like brother and sister, both children with sad times."

For once, though I'd pretty much stopped paying attention, Tolya's crazy English got to me.

"Speak to me in English. Or Russian. But for chrissake cut the crap," I said. "Do me a favor. My head hurts."

"So take an aspirin," Tolya said. "See you later."

"Yeah, I'll think about it."

"You took care of something on Staten Island? Something that upset you?" said Tolya. "You reported in to Sonny Lippert like a good boy?" There was no love lost between Tolya and Sonny Lippert.

"I called Sonny. I did what I had to. I saw the woman on Staten Island whose name, you'll love this, is Gorbachev. Fucking Russians."

"Like us?" He grinned. "Oh, I forgot, you're an American. God bless America," Tolya said and started to sing, then switched to the "Internationale". He had a terrific voice and though I wouldn't have admitted it to anyone on earth, it made the hairs on the back of my neck stand up.

"Is there anything on Staten Island except garbage?" Tolya asked.

"Fucking beats me."

Later on, a smear of green ice cream still on his mouth, and stretched out on the couch in my loft, Billy watched the opening of the Yankees game, sipped at a can of Coke and looked about as content as a kid could look.

I went into my bedroom to change my clothes and put on the radio. Along with the weather and stock market report, there was news about some homeless guy attacked over on Mott Street. It only caught my attention because Mott was a few blocks from me.

In Chinatown, the streets were always jammed. People bought bok choy and lychees and haggled over fake Vuitton bags and Prada wallets. Among the crowd and the hagglers, it was easy to miss a homeless guy lying on the sidewalk, no one noticed he was bleeding. Mostly people picked their way around the homeless, now there were so many of them on the streets again. Eventually, a cop noticed the guy.

I listened to the rest of the news, went to the closet where I still kept a few things, found some clean chinos and a new black polo shirt I'd picked up on sale, and put them on.

While I was changing, I noticed that an old denim jacket of mine had slipped off the hanger onto the floor. I hadn't worn that crummy jacket in years. I hung it back up.

"Hey." Billy smiled up from the couch.

It was the same seductive smile my father had always used when he wanted something, wanted me to work harder in school, wanted my mother not to worry if he took me away fishing for a weekend; probably it was the same smile he used as a KGB guy on those occasions when smiling got results. I knew I had it, too, and I didn't like it about myself much; not so much the smile, but the ability to make people talk. It seemed like a kind of con, ingratiating, disingenuous, cunning.

But my father was dead and my mother could no longer speak. She had talked plenty when we were still in the USSR. She got in trouble for telling the truth about the system, and my father lost his job because of her being a noisy Jew. But now in the nursing home in Haifa, she was so deep in the fog of Alzheimer's that no one could reach her at all. I had gone over to see her after I got married. Maxine wanted to come but I could see how nervous she got every time there was a report of a suicide bombing on TV. I went by myself.

In a chair by a window, my mother sat. I leaned down close to her to show her my wedding pictures.

Ma?

There was no response. All that was there was the form of a woman who resembled my mother sitting in a low armchair by a window. Now, I sat on the edge of the couch and ruffled Billy's hair.

"Wow." Billy was watching clips from an old Yankees-Red Sox game. "That pitch was like so insanely crazy."

"You can't say that about the Sox. They're the enemy. Didn't I teach you anything?"

"Why?"

"History," I said.

"That's not fair," he said with a kid's sense of the rightness of things. "They did it good, isn't it fair to say it was good?"

"You want to be a real New Yorker, you have to harbor a grudge against the Red Sox," I said. "That's how it is."

He looked confused.

"I was joking," I said. "Sort of."

"They teach us not to get mad," said Billy earnestly. "They teach us to be rational. I like it, being rational. I do. One of my therapists told me, you feel upset or something, talk to yourself. It's like intelligent people can make themselves better."

"How many therapists do you have?"

"Never mind, Artie. Just come and watch the game. It's just starting."

"Who's playing today?"

"Yanks and Orioles," he said.

"I'm sorry about the fishing, but we'll go tomorrow for sure."

"How was Staten Island?"

"Weird."

"Could we fish there?" Excited, Billly bent one arm, miming the way he held his fishing pole.

"Sure."

"If you have a case to work on there I could help you."

"You want me to be straight with you?"

Billy nodded.

"I can't ever take you along on cases."

"I see."

"I'm sorry."

"If you have to go back to Staten Island, I could always like wait in the car," Billy said. "I can go with you and wait or you could leave me at some diner or something. Then we'd go fishing. Can I use your computer? I want to look up places to fish there just in case you have to go again. Artie?"

"Go use the computer if you want."'

He scrambled up to a sitting position, crossed his legs, leaned forward, excited.

"I have a better idea," said Billy. "I just had a wild idea, like could we maybe catch the last few innings of the game? We could get the subway. What do you think? Remember how you took me after 9/11 to the stadium and got me the Yanks jacket, and everyone was singing?"

"You remember?"

"Course I remember," Billy said. "I remember everything we ever did together because they were the best times in my whole entire life."

"I promised Tolya Sverdloff we'd go to a birthday party later for Luda, the Russian kid. We could probably go to the game and get something to eat after and still make the party."

"Please," Billy said. "Please please please please."

"OK, OK."

"You know, I was thinking they should keep Luda in America."

"Why's that?"

"'Cause she's so full of rage," he said. "Maybe over here in America someone can help her."

"I don't understand exactly."

"I mean, those little kids like Luda who are orphans in Russia, they live a horrible life, they're orphans, no one gives a shit or anything, and there's terrorists everywhere," said Billy. "Luda told me people take children hostage and kill them. Everything they see is bad and I bet those kids are getting ready for some kind of revenge the rest of their lives."

"When did you get so smart?" I said.

"Yeah, you think?" Billy was beaming. "Do you ever feel like . . . never mind."

"What?"

"Do you ever feel I'm your own kid?"

"Sure I do. Let's get ready or we'll miss the game."

"Honest?"

"Yeah, you know that."

I went to the kitchen where I kept spare keys in a jar. I gave them to Billy.

"This way you don't have to hang around downstairs waiting for me again. Just in case."

"Thanks," Billy said, beaming. "For like trusting me," he added, putting the keys in his pocket. "I'm glad we're here. I don't mind one bit that Maxine didn't want me at your other apartment. I like this better."

The loft was a mess. Scaffolding was up near one of the big industrial windows. The walls needed painting. I had moved most of my things and some of my furniture to our apartment, Maxine's and mine, and the loft looked bare. My plan had been to renovate, first for Maxine and the girls and me. When I realized she was too happy in the apartment near the river ever to leave, I figured I could rent out the loft and make some dough. I told myself I planned to rent it out.

On his way to the bedroom, Billy turned and said, "This is your real place, isn't it?"

He knew me. The way some kids do, Billy instinctively got how I felt. For now, I didn't want to think about Maxine coming home and me taking Billy back to his parents who wouldn't know what the hell to do with him. I didn't want him going back to Florida. I resisted thinking about any of it. Something would work out.

I switched off the TV. I went to my bedroom to get some money from a stash I kept in the closet. From the doorway, I saw Billy. His back was to me. He was standing in front of my open closet, looking at himself in the mirror that hung on the door. I could see him reflected in it. He was wearing my old jacket, the one that had fallen off the hanger.

The homeless guy who got beat up on the sidewalk in Chinatown died that afternoon while we were at the Stadium cheering for the Yankees who wiped out the Orioles 12–3.

We ate hot dogs heaped with sauerkraut, drenched in mustard and ketchup and Billy put mayo on his, too, until we felt like bursting. Then we had Cracker Jacks. We joined in all the yelling and cheering with the family next to us. There were five kids, four of them girls, decked to the nines in Yankees gear. One of them was around Billy's age and I noticed they spent a lot of time laughing together.

The sky was murky, but no one cared so long as it didn't pour, and everyone was lit up because the Yanks were finally doing something right, so we yelled some more and clapped until we were hoarse and our hands hurt.

"Artie, look at the woman selling cotton candy, she has like a Louis Vuitton do-rag on her head, that is so New York." He nudged me. "God, I'm happy to be home."

"I see Florida didn't exactly crush your New York attitude."

"If you had a mom with an entire closet of Louis Vuitton everything, including a dog carrier when we don't have a dog, you'd spot all of it. I could be a designer birdwatcher, like one of those people who hang around the park with little books looking for different species. Weird, right? I can do Vuitton,

Armani, Chanel. My mom so like talks about it all the time. God, look, did you see Derek catch that?" He stood up in his seat.

The only seats I could get at the last minute that didn't cost a fortune were high up. Billy, who was so excited he couldn't sit still, got up, sat down, then hung so far over the railing that for a minute I got nervous, but he said he only wanted a better look at Randy Johnson. Sitting down, Billy discussed if Randy's pitching could bail the Yankees out with a man sitting on his other side.

"I still love Derek," he said. "I think I love him best. I think. I know all Derek's stats, you want me to tell you? Or Mariano. He's pretty cool. He reminds me of Gary Cooper in *High Noon*."

"You know a lot of stuff."

"Well, duh. You keep saying that, of course I know stuff. I'm taking film history in school."

"Everyone loves Derek," I said, as Jeter singled in the fourth.

Billy said, "So where's this thing? The birthday party for Luda."

"A toy store," I said. "Big one. Midtown. I'm sure your mom took you there sometime, right?"

"You think we should get Luda a present, or something?"

"You think?"

"We could get her some Yankees things, like a jacket and a cap or whatever," said Billy.

"Fine."

"Is the party going to be mostly little girls?"

"Probably," I said. "Yeah. But Val will be there."

"Right," he said, rolled his eyes, gave this big wicked grin he had started using when he was pleased, and stole the last sip of my beer.

*

We were leaving the Stadium, making our way with a huge crowd towards the subway, when a pair of Chevrolet Suburbans screeched up the curb. Sirens blazing, lights on, the drivers jammed on their brakes. We were near enough to the edge of the crowd that I got us, Billy and me, onto the sidewalk.

The vans had blacked-out windows. The doors flew open. Four guys, Kevlar vests, helmets, holding their M4s like they were marines getting ready to hit the beach in a movie, jumped out. The crowd still pouring out of the Stadium stopped, froze.

Next to Billy and me, a clutch of Japanese tourists in short-sleeved shirts, probably here to see Hideki Matsui hit a couple homers, looked frantic. I heard voices from the crowd, people wondering if there was a terrorist attack. Maybe it was a movie, someone said. From the Stadium you could still hear Sinatra singing "New York, New York" over the speakers, which they always played when we won a game – Liza Minnelli sang it when we lost – and Billy looked up at me.

I held up my hand for everyone around me, the Japs, Billy, other fans, to stay still. The guys in the Suburban were a Hercules team, part of the city's street-level anti-terrorist operation. They showed up places around town at random, for practice, and to let people know they were a presence. These guys were good. They were fast. A dog one of them held on a lead sniffed the ground.

Was there an attack? Was this practice? Real? Voices rose out of the crowd.

"We are here to protect you," I heard one of the Hercules guys say to a woman who was arguing with him because she couldn't cross the street.

"What about my civil rights?" she said, in a thick Bronx accent.

"Lady, shut the fuck up," said a man nearby.

134

"This is like the fascists," the woman said, furious.

"Listen, you might be old, but you're not a vegetable and if you don't put a sock in it, I'm going help you do that," a man in a Yankees shirt said.

"You think it's a bomb-sniffing dog?" Billy whispered to me, while one of the officers explained to a tourist from Baltimore that protecting people was their job.

"It's not an attack," someone yelled.

"Idiot," someone else said.

For a couple of minutes, the huge crowd tensed up, waiting, and then it let go. It was an exercise. It was OK. For now. People set off for the subway again.

No one in the city believed the Feds could do much if there was another attack. The city's own anti-terrorist operation was getting ready. Intelligence people sat in an unmarked warehouse down in Tribeca near my place. Other units inhabited facilities in every borough.

The sight of the bulked-up Hercules guys with guns made me feel, for an instant, something bad was coming again, but I got hold of Billy's arm and we got over to the Yankees shop to buy a present for Luda.

"You OK, Artie?" Billy said.

"Yeah," I said, when my phone rang. It was Sonny Lippert. His voice was excited.

"I got a lead, Artie, man." Lippert said loudly. "I'm closing in on a couple of suspects for the creep that killed the little girl in Jersey."

"Good, that's good," I said, watching Billy comb the aisles of the Yankees shop.

"Listen, I'm not going ask you to work this Jane Doe with me, I'm not, you did plenty going out to Rhonda's relative and taking that off my hands, but I want to ask if you still have any notes from that case out by Sheepshead Bay a couple years back."

"I could look. I probably turned my stuff in."

"But maybe you kept something? Maybe you remember something you didn't want people to know?"

"I don't know what you mean, Sonny. I could look. You want to spell this out?"

"You're alone?"

I glanced out at the heaving crowd coming out of the ballpark, trying to get to the subway.

"Not exactly," I said. "I'm at the Stadium."

"You remember how it turned out to be some crackhead?"

"So?"

"I'm not so sure anymore, Artie, man. That's what I'm calling about. We're gonna try to get some DNA on this Jane Doe and match it up with some others."

"How come?"

"They way the little girls looked. The kind of knives somebody used on them."

"I'll look for the notes, Sonny."

"Thanks, man. You remember her name, right?" said Sonny, and I knew he'd been stringing me along, that he remembered her name fine, but he wanted me to say it.

"I remember her name."

"Yeah?"

"Her name was May Luca, Sonny, you knew that already. I have to go."

"So how come you're so defensive, man, I mean, be happy about this, right. One more thing."

"What?" I knew what was coming, I didn't want to know. "I'm getting on the train, Sonny, OK, I'm losing the signal."

"So May Luca, man, the little girl that was killed over by Sheepshead Bay? Wasn't she friends with Billy Farone? Back when? Didn't they attend some school or other together, man? Weren't May and Billy friends?"

"What's that supposed to mean?"

"Nothing, man, I just thought the kid might recall something about May. You with him now?"

"Yeah, Sonny."

"Good. That's good." Lippert's tone softened. "Be with him. I wish I was with my kids."

"I'll try to get you the notes," I said and hung up.

"What do you think?" Billy was holding up the presents he had chosen for Luda; a miniature version of his own dark blue satin Yankees jacket was in one hand and in the other, a bobble-headed Derek Jeter doll. "You think she'll like these? I mean if I get her one the same as mine?"

I told him I was sure Luda would like the presents he had chosen and I paid for them, we left the store, climbed the stairs to the subway platform – the train ran out of doors from an elevated platform up here in the Bronx – and waited. My heart was racing. I was out of shape, I told myself; running up the subway stairs had winded me. I checked my watch. It was twenty after six. July 6.

14

"Welcome, welcome," said the girl in harlequin hot pants, a purple chiffon bow around her red-white-and-blue curls, and a yellow fur jacket that could have been dyed bunny. "I am Miss Jelly Bean, and I hear you'll be spending the night with us here at Toy Heaven. Have some candy, please," she added, plucking jelly beans and fruit-colored Lifesavers from the emerald green tutu she wore over the hot pants.

From a waist-high container built to resemble a large see-through purple jelly bean, Miss Jelly Bean pulled cell phones, all of them pink and purple with soft covers painted with flowers. One was handed to each little girl who stopped by. The ring tone played the Barbie song.

Behind Miss Jelly Bean were more enormous see-through containers of candy – jellybeans, red hots, Good and Plenty, nonpareils, raisinettes, M&Ms, red Swedish fish, Gummy Bears, in a dozen colors, including pink. The kids, all girls, all around nine or ten, the same age as Luda, yakked excitedly to each other as they ran all over the place, some munching on slices of pink pizza, others running into a photo booth to get their pictures taken, some having their faces painted or their arms temporarily tattooed.

There must have been twenty little girls. A couple of them, shooting the breeze about their outfits, candy and sodas in their hands, resembled miniature Manhattan ladies at a cocktail party. Overhead, on a trapeze hooked up to the ceiling, an acrobat did terrifying stunts while the little girls looked up and screamed. Pink balloons also hung from the ceiling. Silver and pink mirror balls hung among the balloons and on every shelf available were giant pink lava lamps.

"Jeez, Artie," Billy said. "How insanely weird is this?"

"Think of it as a sociological study," I whispered. "You know what I mean?"

"I know what sociology is." He helped himself to a scoop of M&Ms. "Also anthropology." He looked at the girls. "Did you know there are places in Africa where they send all the boys away to live together when they're around fourteen, and they don't let them out until they grow up and become OK people? So what I want to know is, what about the girls? I mean, Artie, look at them. Jeez. Talk about hormones."

From behind some shelves piled eight feet high with stuffed animals, including two life-size gorillas made out of some kind of mink-colored plush, Tolya appeared. I had half expected him to show up in clown clothes, but he wore a black silk shirt, bright red silk pants and red loafers made of some sort of rare skin. In one ear was the big emerald he sometimes wore. Beside him Valentina, who was wearing a short pink silk dress, held Luda's hand and looked at her father's shoes affectionately.

"Not exactly your regular American daddy," she said to me. "Imagine how many reptiles died for my dad's shoes. You think I'll inherit them?"

"So nice birthday party for Luda," Tolya said. "I buy whole store for tonight. Billy, I apologize that is mostly little girls."

"That's OK. It's her party."

"I have car for you, though, and video games. You want to see? Downstairs. One girl has brought her brother, about same age as you, so we should go downstairs." He had fallen into his hood's English.

"Wow," said Billy turning to grin at me. "Sure. Thanks. I'd like that a lot." He hesitated.

"What is it?" I said.

"What should I call you?" he asked Tolya.

"You could call me Uncle Anatoly, if you want. But Tolya's OK."

With Billy in tow, Tolya started for the escalator and the two made their way between shelves of lime green stuffed frogs, yellow plush snakes and kangaroos bulging with baby kangaroos all in blues and purples and other colors not really known in nature.

In the background, music from a karaoke stand played and a tiny girl in tight pink shorts and a halter-top, a miniature Streisand in the making, belted out "People". Four "Village People", all of them little girls, followed her and performed "YMCA". The kids knew all the moves.

"God, they've been playing that at kids' parties since I was a kid," said someone standing near me.

Half a dozen adults moved among the children, introducing themselves as guides and gurus. One of them, a guy who looked like he was in some chorus line on Broadway on other nights, introduced himself to me as the guru Heathbarishi whose mantra included good things about the Heath Bar. There were a couple of hobbits, and an Incredible who looked a lot like an out of work Arnold Schwarzenegger. All of them carried huge pink knapsacks out of which they produced presents for the kids — watches that sang, digital cameras, an assortment of clothing, bags of candy, and real money; the coins were colored pink.

Standing near me and holding Val's hand, Luda jumped up

and down, chattering in Russian, unable to stand still. Her hair was braided with glittery pink beads. Her purple dress matched high-heeled shoes, which were covered in glitter.

Part of the store had been turned into a designer boutique, and the girls selected what they wanted and changed into their new party clothes in a dressing room screened off by a pink velvet curtain.

"Stella McCartney," said one midget fashionista emerging from behind the curtain.

"Galliano," said another, adjusting her skirt. It was part of the deal, she said to me casually, and added she had attended quite a few of these parties. "At one we got very nice little mink jackets," she cooed.

Luda plucked at my sleeve, and said in Russian, "Look, over there."

"What?"

My sleeve still in her tiny hand, she steered me towards an area where a sign read: NURSERY.

In white nurse costumes, young women tended fake babies in this make-believe hospital nursery. The nurses picked up the babies and burped them. They fed them with real bottles. The babies came in white, black and Asian and could be special-ordered in "other", which, the nurse informed me, included Native American. Another of the nurses who, given her body and the way she moved, probably worked most nights as a pole dancer on Eleventh Avenue, put a doll in my arms.

"Real lifelike, right?" she said. "The little girls love them. We keep running out, the mothers come in and go crazy. It's the hot item, I mean we can't keep them, I heard there's people selling them off the back of trucks, on the black market, they get double, triple even. Nuts, right?"

Swaddled in real baby clothes and a blanket, wearing a cloth diaper, the thing I held was four or five pounds and had the flesh of an almost real baby. I gave it back to the nurse fast.

Ponytails jiggling with effort, two of the little partygoers were taking lessons in tending babies from the woman who looked like a pole dancer. One of the girls rocked the fake baby in her arms knowingly. "These are not like dolls for little girls, you know," she said. "These are like real babies." She was very certain.

The nurse held one of the dolls out to Luda who recoiled from the feel of the rubbery flesh and pushed it back at the nurse. She was distracted by a row of computer screens across the aisle.

Face red, she climbed onto a stool in front of one of the screens.

"What is it?" Luda said to me.

A young guy with a digital camera tried to take her picture, explaining that he would put it in the computer and she could then choose hair and eye color. Then a doll, looking just like Luda would be produced.

I didn't know if Luda understood any of the English, but she was too high on sugar and excitement to care. I translated; I told her about the lookalike dolls; and she started crying.

"I don't like this," Val said. "It's creepy. Come on Luda, darling, let's go dance."

Silently, Luda cried; obediently she followed Val towards a dance floor that had been set up in an open space and the two of them jiggled around to the music from the karaoke.

"POS," someone whispered as I glanced at a trio of girls smearing make-up on their faces.

"What?"

"Parent Over Shoulder," whispered the girl who wore a white bunny jacket as she spoke into the pink cell phone, which she dropped because her hands were greasy from eating pink potato chips. The phone bounced, its case made of something pink, thick and rubbery, the girl picked it up and began giggling into it again. POS, she said again, meaning me.

"Hey."

I turned around. It was Billy, who wanted me to see the radio-controlled car pit downstairs, and I started after him but I got sidetracked by Luda who was calling my name from the dance floor.

"I'll meet you down there," I said to Billy.

He shrugged, and turned away.

"Wait," I said, but he was already gone.

"He's a really great-looking boy," a voice said. It was Lily Hanes.

"Thanks."

"It's Billy Farone, right?" She leaned lightly against a rack of rag dolls with yellow hair.

"Yeah."

"Beth is here." Lily waved an arm in the direction of a gang of girls dancing; the tallest one with the black hair was Lily's adopted daughter.

"I can see. She looks terrific. She's going to be tall, like you."

"Can't be the genes," Lily smiled. "How are you, Artie? I've missed you."

I said I was fine and tried to ignore the effect her words had on my gut.

Lily looked good. Her red hair was pulled back from her face and she was wearing a green silk shirt and black jeans. I didn't know she was back from London.

The last time she'd been in New York for a while, I had seen her a couple of times. I went to her apartment to visit Beth who I had helped her adopt. I felt connected to Beth and sometimes I took her to the movies and then home. On those occasions, Lily and me, we were polite, like divorced people who had made their peace. I never drank with her. I never even sat down at her place. A while back I'd heard she and Beth had both gone back to London.

I said, "You're in the city for good?"

"I hope it's for good."

"On Tenth Street?"

"Yes. Always. I only ever sublet my place."

"Alone?"

She smiled. "Should I assume you mean, is Beth living with me?"

"She looks great."

"She'll go back to London next week."

"She's going to be with what's his name, Ted, Ned, Fred, the one you married?"

Lily said, "He already had a family from a previous marriage and it's good for Beth when she's there, all the kids, the house with the garden. She wants to spend the summer there, maybe stay for part of the school year."

"You OK with that?"

"I don't know. She adores her school. I don't mind her getting some of her education in London. I go over. She comes here. We'll see. It makes me sad when I'm not with her."

"Not sad enough to stay married to what's his name?"

She changed the subject, "I came to see you last summer. I went to your place. I waited outside."

It wasn't long after Maxine and I got married and I had seen Lily waiting outside my building. From my car, I had seen her standing in the rain and I had driven away.

"You didn't answer my calls, either," she said.

"I'm sorry," I said and realized there wasn't any tension between Lily and me now; maybe after all the years we could be friends.

Lily looked around her.

"I hate this kind of shit, spending like this for a kid's party, but it's what people do now," she said. "They give parties for one-year-olds at the Four Seasons that cost thousands. I heard about a woman who turned her apartment into a zoo and brought in animals. I mean it's insane, talk about fiddling while Rome burned. You want to talk about Billy? You want to tell me?"

"You think there's any booze in this place?"

"If Tolya's giving a party, there will be booze," she said and I followed her as she made her way towards a soda fountain in the middle of the room.

Everywhere were security guys; Tolya had his people out in force, Russians made of muscle and tattoos. Although dressed in red and white striped shirts, they still looked like weight-lifters, their huge arms like slabs of meat.

Suddenly, a clown jumped in front of me and made faces. I pulled back. I always hated clowns. Hated them even when I was little and a trip to the Moscow Circus was the only entertainment going. My mother took me to it and I cried all the way home, she said. I was five.

We got to the soda fountain and Lily climbed onto a high stool and I got on the one next to her.

"Hello," said a milkmaid in a ruffled apron. "We have grown-up pop for the grown-ups," she said and pulled a bottle of pink champagne from a miniature fridge behind a soda fountain.

Reaching across the soda fountain for a bowl of Red Hots, Lily began tossing them in the air; she caught each one in her mouth, and then downed them with the champagne. "Hey, this is good stuff," she said.

"How long do they let the kids stay?"

"All night," said Lily. "It's a slumber party."

"Christ."

"So tell me about Billy."

"Yeah, well, he did really great in the place in Florida, and they said he could have a couple weeks at home. I went down to get him because Genia — you remember Genia? — she went pretty nuts when they sent Billy away. She wanted him to go to one of those hotsy-totsy schools for kids with problems, kind of school that costs ninety grand. The judge didn't agree with the idea."

"Artie darling, you know judges put kids in those schools when they're emotionally fucked up and have maybe a brush with the law, shoplifting, selling weed. Not like Billy."

"I know. But when I saw him and talked to his shrink, and having been with him, I know he's OK. You think it can happen like that?"

She looked at me with the pale gray eyes, and I knew she'd tell me the truth. Lily Hanes, who I'd been with on and off for more than ten years, was never coy, never smuggled messages, didn't lie.

She put her hand on my arm. "Yes," she said. "I have to believe that."

"Thanks."

"I'm not just telling you what you want to hear. I'm a fucked up old leftie, and I believe in nurture, and if Billy had a screwy childhood, but someone in Florida got hold of him and got him to understand himself, why couldn't he be better, and if you don't believe that, what's the point? There's always some fucking fashion in head cases, you know? So they discover Asperger's syndrome, that's supposed to be a way to describe variations of autism, but now everybody has it. You're a guy and you're a self-centered prick and your wife turns fifty and she realizes you've been focused only on your work, so she says, you know he's kind of Aspergerish. So many brilliant guys are now supposed to have some version that they call it Geek Disease. The dumb ones they label Fragile fucking X Syndrome."

"Billy doesn't have that stuff. I talked to his shrink. What's Fragile X?"

"Genetic shit, mostly boys, they did a lot of criminal studies over at Riker's, inmates, a lot of them have it," said Lily. "Like

I said, I have to believe a lot of this genetic stuff is bullshit, and if you fall for it it's like being some kind of fucking Calvinist or something, no free will, everything's wired into you pre-birth, you might as well stop trying. Christ, I could sure use a cigarette. You want to go out on the street for five minutes?"

"Thank you."

"You're not going to get weepy on me, like some old Russian who's thinking of home and the silver birch trees, are you?" She smiled. "Come on."

I wanted to go out on the street for a cigarette with her. I wanted everything with her.

"It's just nice to see you," I said. "Do you remember that time we rode the Staten Island Ferry at night for hours?"

"Don't," Lily said.

As we looked for an exit sign, I spotted Tolya. Surrounded by ten-year-old girls sitting on the floor in a circle, he was playing a guitar and singing a Russian love song to them. No band, no bass, no backing of the kind he'd had when he was a rocker, Tolya's voice was pure. Standing at the back of the circle of children was Billy. For a moment he stood and listened and then turned and walked away.

"Did you know Tolya could do that?" I said to Lily.

She nodded. "He used to sing to Beth when she was little. Lullabies, too."

"Now you're crying."

"Don't be silly," she said.

At the back of the circle of girls listening to Tolya I found Valentina who was sitting cross-legged, her arms around Luda. She got up off the floor.

"Do you know where Billy is?"

"He's fine, downstairs, playing with cars and video games. He said he'd come back up for the birthday cake. I'm Valentina," she added, holding out her hand to Lily. "Tolya's kid."

"This is Lily Hanes," I said.

"I know that," Val said. "I'm really happy to meet you. Gosh. Hi. My dad talks about you all, and I mean *all*, the time!"

"Hi," Lily said. "I need a cigarette."

Val looked at both of us and said, "Go on. Go."

It was midnight. The streets were empty. The air was cold, the sky clear and we stood outside the toy store. Lily's cigarette smelled good. She passed it to me and I took a deep drag.

After a while, she started laughing. She laughed hard, like she always laughed in my dream – I dreamed about her more than I wanted to admit. It was infectious and for a while we stood on the empty street, and laughed.

"What?" I said, catching my breath.

"It was so completely hilarious," she said. "The store. The toys, Tolya in those red pants, you and me trying to party with ten-year-old girls who look like they're going on thirty, and the fake babies, and the milkmaid."

Lily's shoulder was touching mine and right then I knew it would never be any good without her. Standing alongside her, it was as if I could breathe again.

I thought about Maxine and the girls, about the apartment, about everything. I would stick with it, best I could. I wouldn't sleep with Lily, either. I had to talk to her, though; I had to see her.

"It's no good," she said. "Is it?"

"No."

"No good with us apart, I mean."

"I know that was what you meant," I said.

"What should we do?"

"What do you think?"

"I don't know. Nothing, probably." Lily took my hand and leaned her head against mine. "I feel better. Seeing you," she said, then she tossed the butt of her cigarette into the curb where it landed in a tiny puddle and floated, like a miniscule boat. "I can feel OK so long as we can see each other once in a while. We should go back in," Lily said. "Artie?"

"Yeah?"

"It'll be OK with Billy, you'll see. It'll be good."

The screams were shrill and compulsive and seemed to go on forever, the sound of a small girl screaming so that you figured her lungs would explode. It was like a car alarm going off in the night except it was terrified and terrifying.

In the crumpled purple dress and dirty pink tutu, Luda was huddled on the floor of the toy store, Val crouched next to holding her as best she could. Next to them, also on his knees, his arms around Luda's shoulders, was Billy. Head down, he was whispering to her.

Lily had taken Beth home. Tolya had the rest of the kids at the soda fountain and was singing Beatles songs with them while the milkmaid dished up ice cream to keep them distracted.

Luda gave another horrifying scream and Billy suddenly jumped up, his face blank, then turned and ran across the floor, and down the stairs. I started after him. Tolya saw me and caught my arm.

"Let him be for a minute. I'll send one of my guys down to make sure he's OK. Her screaming scared him."

"What happened?" I said.

"The dolls." He tossed me a pack of cigarettes. I didn't care what store policy was. I lit up.

"What?"

"Look, I better keep these kids quiet until we can get them home. It was the dolls they make to look like the children," said Tolya, pointing to a shelf with a row of dolls that had Luda's face.

"Why did you make so many?" I said to the woman running the computers.

"I thought she said she wanted six to take home. I didn't understand. The boy said that's what she wanted, he translated."

"Which boy?"

"The tall one with the dark hair."

"Hey, wait." It was Miss Jelly Bean calling me, but I was already running for the stairs. When I got to the lower level, I asked one of Tolya's muscle guys where Billy was and he told me in his crude Russian that the boy had slipped past him.

Where is he? Where is he? I asked everyone I saw. All the way back up to the main floor, out to the street, past the glass cases where Barbies smiled and modeled ball gowns and astronaut suits, beyond stuffed teddy bears, past model trains, and toy pianos and drum kits and shelves of brightly colored books, electronic games that lit up and made noise, and from somewhere the sound of rap music, and me, running. I ran, sweat running down my sides, until I got to the street. I didn't see Billy there, either, but I could still hear Luda screaming.

Part Three

Thursday July 7

15

It was Thursday, early, a few hours after I got home from the party at the toy store when Vera Gorbachev called, crying and yelling stuff at me in Russian.

"Come. Please," she said. "Now."

I told her to call 911 if there was a problem, then hung up. I felt heavy as lead. Didn't get much sleep the previous night. I fumbled for a pack of cigarettes and some matches I'd left on the floor after I got home from the party, half out of my mind about Billy, and found him fast asleep on my couch.

I'd already promised him we'd go fishing. For a while I lay in bed, smoking and trying to clear my head. Taking Billy to the party had been a stupid idea. I'd promised him time with me, fishing, baseball, guy stuff, and then I made him go to a party for little girls.

Luda's screams had scared the shit out of him. He took off after he tried comforting her and she kept on bawling. He'd just wanted out and he had walked away from the store and come back to my loft.

I didn't want to leave him alone again, and anyhow I didn't believe Vera Gorbachev was in any kind of real trouble — she gave off the scent of a woman who wanted a lot of attention. I didn't like her. The way she also gave off a faint smell of malice, along with her neediness – not malice exactly, but some kind of aggression – she reminded me of Big Tina Farone, Billy's grandmother.

Finally, I got out of bed, got dressed, made coffee and woke Billy up. He told me he was sorry he'd left the toy store without saying anything to me. He'd left a message, though. Two messages.

Wearing blue and white striped pajamas that were too small for him, his wrists and ankles sticking out, Billy sat at the kitchen counter and drank a glass of milk. He kept growing out of his clothes, he said. I made toast. Billy asked for jelly.

After he ate, he told me he could laugh about the toy store business now, and he was kind of chagrined – it was his word – that he had been freaked out. The toys, the little girls, the crazy amount of sugar everyone had been eating, him included, and then baby dolls that felt like real flesh – it just got to him. I said it was fine, just to tell me in person when he was taking off. He looked tired. I felt bad for him.

"It's OK, Artie," said Billy. "It was probably the craziness of it, and the crowd and, if I'm like honest, some of the video games we got to play downstairs were kind of violent." He rubbed his fists in his eyes. "I'll be fine," he said. "So you want me to like tell you the actual truth? You won't be mad?"

"You can tell me anything."

"So this kid they brought along for me, one of the girls' brothers, he was downstairs and we were playing video games and with the electric scooters and cars and stuff, and this kid had some weed. We smoked a little. I didn't feel so good afterwards. I already ate hot dogs and stuff at the game, and then candy, and I was like in the bathroom puking, and I'm like really sorry." Billy looked like a little boy. "I'm a jerk."

"Go get a shower," I said.

"Thanks."

"For what?"

"Not yelling at me," said Billy, heading for the bathroom.

"Billy?"

"Yeah?"

"If you want that old denim jacket of mine that's in the closet, you can have it."

Turning, he beamed at me. "Honest?"

"Sure."

"That's like so crazy. Thank you. Can I wear it today?"

Couldn't stop thinking about Sonny Lippert's call, the case he was on, the dead girl in Jersey, no name, no ID, just a small, three-year-old Jane Doe, and her killer somehow connected back to May Luca in Sheepshead Bay. May Luca, who had been friends with Billy.

I wanted to ask him about May Luca, see if he recalled anything that might help Lippert on the little Jane Doe in Jersey, but I figured I'd wait. I heard the shower run. Going to Staten Island to see Vera Gorbachev was about the last thing on earth I wanted to do. By the time Billy and I left the loft, I heard the phone ringing; I didn't bother turning back.

Most of the way to Staten Island, Billy was quiet. My old denim jacket was big on him, but he seemed pretty pleased to have it. In his lap was the book about fly-fishing we got at Dubi Petrovsky's shop, and he read while I drove.

When we got to the Verrazano Bridge, Billy looked up from the book and said, "I like your Lily. I think I met her before when I was real little, didn't I? I remember a woman with red hair."

"She's not mine," I said. I had been thinking about Lily a lot since the night before.

"Oh, sorry, yeah."

"Where did you go last night after you left the toy store?"

"Nowhere," said Billy. "I went to your loft and fell asleep."

"I tried your phone."

"I probably forgot to charge it. There's not that many people I can call, so sometimes I forget. But you like Lily, right?"

"I'm married to Maxine. You OK, Billy? I'm not so good with you smoking dope, I'm not."

"Me either," he said. "They might send me back or something. Also I felt so horrible, you don't have to worry."

"I'm not."

"What I'm like worried about is Luda. I tried to talk to her but she just kept crying. I like her. She's a really cute kid."

"Yeah, she is."

"But I like Val better," he said, awkwardly.

I tried to keep from smiling.

"Luda will be fine," I said. "Val and Tolya will take her out to Long Island and she'll be fine. Hey, you feel like talking to me about Florida at all?"

"Not really. Is that OK?" He reached for the radio.

"Is the school any good?"

"It's OK, it's fine, honest," said Billy, settling on a station playing some crap by Eminem. He picked up his fishing book.

"But you don't want to talk about it?"

"Not right now."

"Is there anything that scares you?"

"What do you mean?"

"I don't know. Being away from home, stuff like that? Being with those other kids?"

"The thing I get scared of is hurricanes," Billy said. "Last year, you know there were all those storms in Florida and once they evacuated us, and we had to go in buses on the road and there were millions of people in cars, bumper to bumper. No one told us exactly where we were going. I didn't think they really knew, either, it was just like let's go. People were getting crazy. So, yeah, hurricanes scare me a whole lot. Who are we going to see on Staten Island?"

"A Russian woman. It won't take long. I just have to talk to her."

"Is there a map?"

"Glove compartment," I said. "Why?"

Billy got the Staten Island map and spread the stiff paper on his knees. "I like maps," he said. "I like thinking about places I could go some day."

"Like where?"

"Anywhere. Everywhere. Maybe Russia some time. Hey, you don't have to worry about me, Artie. I'm having a great time. I know sometimes I get like a little strange, but I'm just sort of not used to, I don't know, a lot of stuff, I mean just being able to decide what I want to eat. I probably missed out on some stuff normal kids know about while I was away. You want gum?" He pulled some Juicy Fruit from his bag and offered me a stick. "Florida's OK because I have a lot of time to read."

"You want to talk about what you've been reading?"

"Nah, not right now. I don't want to end up like a geek, you know?" Billy said. "So I listen to the kind of music other kids like. Between us, I think rap is so boring. I like classical, and your kind of jazz, but if I told people my age they'd think I was beyond geeky."

I looked in the rear-view mirror before I put the gum in my mouth.

"You checking to see if that car's there again?" Billy said.

"Just checking on traffic," I said and folded up the gum.

We chewed and the sugary yellow smell of the gum stank up the car. There wasn't much traffic, Billy fell asleep, and I pressed a button on the radio and got a station playing an old Erroll Garner tune and felt content for a minute.

*

A young cop in uniform was leaning against a patrol car on Vera Gorbachev's block, and when I parked in front of her house he sauntered over. I showed him my badge. He was there, he said, to keep an eye on things.

"Nobody was here yesterday," I said.

"I don't know about yesterday, all I know is I got the word this morning, keep an eye on the house, the block, that's what they told me, so here I am." He went back to his car where he picked up a comic book off the hood where he'd left it.

Now there was a cop on the Gorbachev's block, I could probably get away a lot faster. I told Billy, who had been waiting in my car, I'd be back fast

"Am I allowed to take a walk or something?" he said.

"Sure, you're allowed. Just don't go far."

He didn't answer.

"So humor me," I said. "I want you close by, I want to talk to this woman, and then I want to have breakfast with you and go fishing and forget everything else. Deal?"

"You said it!"

Slumped on her leather sofa, hands holding the sides of her head, Vera Gorbachev was still in the same blue spandex pants as yesterday; shredded Kleenex covered her lap. Even when she talked, mumbling in Russian, she kept crying. Hard to understand. Hard to believe this was the same woman who had come on to me the day before.

"Tell me what happened," I said.

Through the window I saw Billy; he was leaning against my car, smoking a cigarette. He saw me, made a face; I smiled back.

"Please, try to stop crying," I said to Vera. "I can't understand what you're saying."

Dragging one of her hands across her eyes, she left a black smear of mascara. "They threaten me," she said.

"Who threatens you?"

"Who, I don't know. They make my husband disappear and then last night calls start," said Vera. "They tell me to shut up about everything or they come for me too, and I don't know who they are."

"Who? Look, I can't help you if you don't tell me, or try to tell me." I tried to figure out a way to make her stop blubbing. "Could I get a cup of coffee?"

"You think this is Starbucks?" she asked.

"In that case, I'll take a vanilla caramel grande latte cappuccino with a cherry on top," I said because I couldn't think of anything else. It made her laugh some.

Vera stood up. "I'll make tea."

"Then make tea."

In the kitchen, she put water on to boil. I sat at the table. Again she told me how she had been awakened one night a few weeks earlier, how her husband heard the noise, went down and found a burglar, ran after him, then nothing. Repeated the story exactly as if someone had coached her. Footprints near a swampy area about a mile from the house had been found, said Vera, but kids used the place at night to drink and smoke in crappy boats tied up to a landing there.

"What else?"

The water boiled, Vera made tea. From the fridge she took a plate with a chocolate cake on it.

"No cake," I said. "Thank you."

Ignoring me, she began slicing up the cake, got plates, put everything on the table, waited while I drank some tea.

"Tell me," she said. "How does he run, tell me this?"

"What?" I ate a piece of cake. "Who?"

"One of feet missing. Hard for him to run, even with good fake foot and shoes."

"Who?"

"My husband. Al."

"You mean one of his shoes is missing?"

"Feet."

"They cut off his feet?" I said.

Eating cake, Vera began to cry again.

The husband had a couple missing toes was all, but it took me a while to work it out. Turned out that Al Laporello lost them from frostbite during a visit to Russia when he was a young American guy on an exchange program. Apparently Laporello was a space nut and somehow he managed a visit to Yuri Gagarin's house. It was the dead of winter when Al visited the town of Gagarin, and he stayed out so long, he got frostbite. His missing toes had nothing to do with the little girl in Jersey whose feet were cut off, just coincidence; it didn't mean anything.

Yuri Gagarin, hero of Soviet space, was the thing that had made us superior to the Americans. In school, teachers talked about Gagarin and his face was everywhere, on posters, on plastic bags. He was what passed for a rock star. His face, the space suit, the helmet were imprinted on my brain forever.

Stuff like that stayed tucked in a crease in your mind, the kind of useless information that silted up your brain and filled your hard drive until it crashed and then you were old, and crazy, overrun by some kind of dementia.

I had never been to Gagarin, but Vera Gorbachev's husband, Al Laporello, an Italian American from Staten Island, had gone.

"On the phone, did you recognize any of the voices?" I asked Vera.

"I'm not sure they are really Russian, these guys have accents."

"Guys?"

"Yes," she said.

"More than one?"

"I don't know."

"How many calls?"

"Six in last two days."

"Why didn't you mention it yesterday?"

The tears ran down her face again. "I forgot."

"What kind of voice?"

"Not so old," Vera said. "Middle-aged is possible. Young is possible. Also like someone who learns Russian. Accent."

"What kind?"

"I don't know. More tea?"

"No thanks."

"Don't go away."

What Vera wanted, I realized, was company. She was rattled. She was needy. Her husband had disappeared and it had probably occurred to her that he was looking for an excuse to dump her and beat it. She didn't say, and I didn't offer the idea. Or maybe Al was just dead.

I went outside where the young cop held up the comic book he was reading.

"Japanese," he said. "It's good, this stuff, you know? I mean it's not just for kids."

"You talk any Russian?"

"You kidding me? I'm Irish."

"Is there anyone who can stay with Mrs Gorbachev? Answer the phone for her, make her feel safe?"

"I don't know. They told me to keep an eye on the block. It's all I can do," he said and returned to his comic.

Through the screen door of her house, Vera Gorbachev had been watching, and when I went back inside her house, she said, "Who's the kid?"

"What?"

"In your car. I saw him earlier when you got here. Great-looking boy, tall, dark, yours?"

"I have to go."

"I don't want to be alone," said Vera.

"There's a cop outside, if anyone calls, tell him. Call a neighbor. I'm sorry about your husband, but I have to go. Unless you have more to tell me."

Standing just inside the door, Vera said, "So maybe my husband got involved in some small deals, you know, garbage stuff, I mean literally, out here, garbage was big business, but now, since they closed the dump at Fresh Kills, people are fighting over pieces of it. My Al was OK, but he was pretty square guy," she laughed. "Before he got into garbage, he was a plumber."

"So he fucked up someone's toilet and they kidnapped him?"

"He had some new ideas about garbage. Maybe someone didn't like that. There're people around here don't like Russians that much, you know? So my husband has a Russian wife and someone doesn't like. Why don't you tell your kid to come inside?"

I turned and saw Billy on the steps.

Vera opened the door and said to Billy, "Come on. He speaks Russian?"

It seemed to cheer Vera up, Billy talking to her in Russian, and we all went into her kitchen where she put out plates of cheese and cold cuts for him. Billy piled up ham and cheese on bread and started eating, and I went out into the backyard to take a call from Maxine.

I told Max about Billy because I had to. I told her I had taken him to my place.

"Your place?" she said. "I thought we had a place together."

I walked across Vera's yard and looked at a kids' blue plastic wading pool.

"You know what I mean," I said into the phone. "My loft. You didn't want him in our apartment, so I took him there. What else could I do, Max? What did you want me to do? His parents are in London. Come on, tell me." I was pissed off now and she heard it.

"Never mind." Max hung up the phone, something she never did. Maxine didn't hang up on you. I felt lousy.

From where I stood, I could see Vera and Billy through the kitchen window. He could have passed for eighteen. She had her head close to his and they were laughing and it looked like she was coming on to him and he was liking it, or maybe I was seeing things. A couple drops of rain fell on my head. I ran inside. I should have called Maxine back, but I was pissed off at her.

At the kitchen table, Billy – flushed, smiling – was busy extracting an ice cube from a glass of orange juice. He put it in his mouth and crunched it around.

"We should go," I said.

"It's starting to rain."

"Yeah, well, you won't melt." I knew I sounded sarcastic but I was upset over Max.

Billy stood up, arms hanging down at his sides, head bowed, staring at his sneakers.

"Just go get in the car," I said. "Please."

He went, and I said to Vera, "You have my number. There's a cop on your block now. You'll be OK. If you get any more calls, let him know."

There was nothing much I could do for her. Either she knew who had threatened her and wouldn't tell me, or she didn't know. I was done here.

"The boy, his name is Farone?" Vera called out when I had started for the door. "He said Billy Farone."

I turned around. "Yeah. So?" I tried not to let her see my surprise.

"I know the parents," said Vera.

It made me edgy, her calling me back for this. I didn't know what the hell Vera Gorbachev wanted; I kept thinking it: what do you want?

"Sure, Johnny Farone, the husband, has restaurant Brighton Beach," said Vera. "Everyone knows them, sure, and Evgenia, the wife, always around, saying hello. I heard the son is away in some boarding school. So it is this Billy you brought? He was away? Another boy?" she asked, in a wheedling tone.

Vera Gorbachev knew the Farones, but so what? Maybe she'd heard gossip about Billy. Something wasn't right about the Gorbachev business and I couldn't put my finger on it. Lippert had asked me to go talk to Vera because she was related to Rhonda Fisher, his girlfriend. Vera Gorbachev was a lot less worried about her husband than she should have been. People with funny accents were calling her. I wasn't sure if she was telling the truth. I beat it.

We were on our way to a pond Billy had read about. Told me it was a good place to fish. The phone rang. It was Sonny Lippert.

"I talked to Rhonda's relative again. I can't do any more," I said. "I'm leaving there now."

"I'm not calling about that, man, I want you here in the city."

The line broke up and I couldn't hear him. He called back.

"Just get to the city," Sonny said. "Is the boy with you?"

"Yeah, so what?"

"I told you, I want to talk to him about May Luca. He could really help me on this thing."

"Can't hear you, Sonny, there's no signal," I said, lying, and when the phone rang again, I didn't answer it.

"You have to go to the city?" Billy said.

"Let's go fishing."

"Really?"

"You bet."

"Come on!" Billy put his feet contentedly on the dashboard

and another piece of gum in his mouth. "I'm so happy," he said. "Let's get donuts. Chocolate ones."

"You're hungry?"

"Maybe I'm addicted."

"You're a funny kid."

"Am I? I mean is that good?"

"It's really good."

16

"Holy shit," I heard someone say when we got to Hank Provone's big house over near Tottenville. Holy shit. The phrase twanged me back to 9/11 as fast as a picture of the planes crashing the Twin Towers, but why? Why that phrase, I kept thinking as we walked, Billy and me, to the back patio of Hank's house where a crowd had gathered around a portable TV.

"What's going on?"

Hank looked up at me. "Jesus, Artie, don't you know?"

"Know what?"

"London. This morning. Christ, it's happening all over again."

Hank Provone had been my partner for years, best I ever had. He was retired now and lived on Staten Island in a big house near the water. He was a good guy and I felt sad I didn't see him more. We used to call him Provolone because of his name and because he liked cheese on everything. Meat and cheese, any kind, was Hank's idea of a feast.

I'd been fishing for a couple of hours with Billy, we didn't catch anything, but we laughed a lot. I'd brought him over to Hank's to say hello. Now, Billy beside me, I stared at the TV.

Three bombs, maybe more, had gone off that morning in the London subway. Another bomb ripped open a red double-decker bus like a can of sardines. Streets jammed with cars, ambulances, and police were filled with people streaming past; on the curb, others sat, faces smeared with dirt, clutching silver shock blankets.

I started looking for Johnny and Genia in the terrified crowd on the screen three thousand miles away.

My God, I thought and reached for Billy's hand.

Hank saw it and said softly so the others couldn't hear, "You have someone over there?"

"Billy's parents," I said.

"Come on," said Hank, moving us away from the crowd to the edge of the patio where the water began and a few sailboats bobbed. "You OK, Billy?"

"I'm not sure," he said, "I don't know what's happening over there."

"I left your dad's phone number at home. You know where your parents are staying?"

Johnny and Genia wouldn't ride the subways, would they? Genia never set foot in a subway as far as I knew, not in New York anyhow. But she was in London and she hadn't called me. If they were dead, would that mean Billy was mine forever? I was his legal guardian. For a second, my back prickled with a kind of strange restless feeling, like something buggy creeping across it.

Billy recited his father's cell number, adding, "My dad's phone, he says it's like tri-band and it works every place. He brags about it like he invented the phone. You think they're OK?" said Billy, looking distracted, worried, scared.

While I tried to get through to London, Billy stayed close to me, me wanting to hold on to him, both of us straining to hear the TV. I put the phone on redial.

"Lines are probably jammed up," I said. "I know they're OK, your mom and dad, I just feel that."

"Me too," said Billy who sat down on a chair suddenly.

"What's that?" I said, squatting next to him.

"I'm scared."

"I'm here."

"If something happened to them, would I be able to stay with you?"

"Nothing happened to them."

"But like if?"

"Nothing happened. I'll get the name of the hotel," I said.

Hank, who had been standing quietly near us, said, "Hey, Billy, I'm gonna get on the landline and see if I can get through to a friend of mine that's a cop in London, OK?" Hank ran a hand through his wild curly graying hair which he tried – and failed – to tame into a crew cut. "Meanwhile let me get you a soda or something. Billy? You think you're up to meeting a few people, hang out a while with the other kids, maybe help us devour some barbecue? Ribs, burgers, steaks, some dogs. I make a mean guacamole, too."

Billy said OK, nodding shyly. Hank gave him a high five. Except for Sonny Lippert, Hank was the only guy I'd told about Billy – told the whole thing – back when the bad stuff was happening. Billy had been accused of murdering Heshey Shank out at Breezy Point. People wanted him tried as an adult. I had needed help when we made the case for him as a juvenile, and set up the newspapers to report it was self-defense. Hank Provone came with me. He stood up for me. Otherwise, he kept his mouth shut and I loved him for it. I suddenly felt glad to be here.

People on Staten Island were tight with their communities; they identified themselves as being from Tottenville or Rossville, not from some outer borough of New York. In Rossville, which was still open countryside in the nineteenth century, whole Sicilian villages settled together. Before the landfill opened, before the stink of garbage permeated the place and people sealed their windows with duct tape during the worst times.

I'd let things drift with Hank and me, didn't know why. Now I was with Maxine, I'd spend more time here. She would understand, she had lived on Staten Island with her first husband.

With his belly straining to get free from his faded Springsteen T-shirt, Hank didn't look much older than when we last worked together, ten, eleven years back. He had retired after 9/11.

"I can't even think of the right words for the bastards who put bombs in London, we should cut their nuts off first, and then fry them," said Hank. "The Brits are such pussies, they just lock them up for a few years, me I'd stick a needle in them. People thought it was over. We knew. So, hey, Artie, you missed me? Come and say hello."

Hank pulled me back towards the group in front of the TV. "Everybody, it's Artie."

Folded up on a chair a little way from the TV set was a woman I recognized from some of Hank's parties. She had lost her son on 9/11, and sat now, tears coming out of her eyes but not making any noise.

At the other end of the yard was a group of teenagers who sat on the edge of the pool, kicked their feet in the water and stared into their soda cans. A couple of older boys held beer bottles. From somewhere in the house Springsteen played on a stereo. Hank never played anything else.

"This London thing sucks, man, right? Jesus Christ," Hank said. "Fucking terrorists. I'm like yelling holy shit over and over when I saw it because it was like it was all happening again."

So I remembered; the first words on the first piece of video I saw as the first plane hit the south tower that morning, a New York voice crying out: "Holy shit."

"Nobody wants to fucking talk about it, so people who are

hurting are so grateful you even remember them it breaks your heart," said Hank. "One 9/11 fireman's widow, I still go over and take her a bottle of wine or just sit and talk and last time I was there she was like god blessing me and so on and so forth. Jesus, Artie, you remember the sound of the locators?"

I remembered. The day after the attack, when we were working non-stop on the smoking pile of shit at Ground Zero, there had been an eerie noise like cicadas, something in the woods, hundreds of them. It was the locators firemen wear so they can be found in the smoke. They were still beeping on dead fireman in the rubble for days afterwards.

"Take it easy." I put my hand on Hank's arm. "Where's Mary?"

"She's in the kitchen cooking where a woman belongs." Hank laughed.

The Provones had five kids – Hank was only twenty-one when they started – and the house was always filled with them and their children and cousins, and uncles and aunts, Italian, Polish, Irish, Greek. "We're the fucking UN of Staten Island," Hank used to say.

"Hey, Artie," a voice called. It was Stellene Anastasiades, Mary Provone's niece. We had dated for a while. I had been crazy about her. She was a great-looking woman, now pregnant with her fourth kid.

She waddled in my direction, still gorgeous, blonde hair pinned up on top of her head, belly sticking out, gold flip-flops crunching the gravel underfoot. In my hand was my phone. Come on, Johnny. Just call me, I kept thinking: call me!

"Artie." Stellene kissed me, and tapped her belly. "Say hello to the new boys."

"Boys?"

"Triplets. Can you fucking believe it? I got three boys, I said to Stas, let's try for a girl, and we get, hello, triplets, boys. I'll name one for you."

"I'd really like that."

"Come on," Stellene said to Billy. "You should meet some of the other kids," and before he could protest, she had his arm and was steering him towards the pool, Stellene like a blonde Greek cruise ship, Billy in tow.

From a distance, I watched him with a couple of other boys about his age. A few girls in those "wife-beater" undershirts you saw everywhere, their boobs hanging out, circled around Billy. He accepted a hot dog from one of them and bit into it. He seemed a little awkward, but he joined in and before long he was swept up in the teenage action.

"Artie, let me get you a beer or something," Hank said, heading for the table that was covered with food, meat ready for the barbecue, bowls of potato salad and potato chips, boxes of pastry, rows of beers and sodas.

From the cooler I took a bottle of Corona and it was wet and cold against my hand. I was thirsty. The crowd in front of the TV dispersed, some of the women peeling off towards the house, maybe to go fix stuff in the kitchen, a few of the guys settling in at table with a pack of cards. One of them was a black guy I didn't know. He got up from his chair.

"I can't stand watching this stuff," he said. "I'm going inside to catch a game."

I thought about the black guy I'd seen at the pizza place with Sonny Lippert.

Hank, who saw me look, said, "Yeah, yeah, we got everyone out here now. A cop's a cop, right? We're very PC these days. And me, I never gave a shit what color anyone was." He nodded towards the house where the black guy had gone. "Dave Green's a good guy, he's from Guyana, they got a whole community out here and they're real smart." Hank pulled down his T-shirt. "The old men are dying off, them and their stupid racist rage with them. I remember when my pop used to sing me a song about the Latin from Staten Island with his guile and his smile, can you believe it? American is American, I told my grandfather, and we were all immigrants. My grandpa is ninety-two and all he wants is to suck on his rage." Hank looked back at the TV.

"Bastard sons of bitches terrorists," he said. "I'm thinking of offering to go over to London, see if I can help or something. We know what it fucking feels like. We look at that fucking hole in the skyline every day. Seventy-eight firefighters we lost, you want to call that a holocaust you could do that. We got 9/11 widows, we got 9/11 kids, look at Stellene's nephew on her husband's side that lost his uncle who was a fire captain, and saw his own dad jump out of a window. They ID'd him in some photograph as a 'jumper'. That's going to take a generation to fix. How's your Maxine?"

"Good," I said. "She's out in California for a few days."

"You guys should come out more often, now you got a life, man. We're so happy for you that you and her got married, you know. Me and Mary both."

My cell phone was ringing and I saw that Sonny Lippert had called four times. He was leaving messages, saying it was urgent for me to get my ass into the city. Urgent, he said. Make it fast.

"I should probably go," I said to Hank. "Lippert's been calling me on something. I don't want Billy getting upset, with his parents being in London."

"Lippert said it's urgent?"

"Yeah, it's probably nothing, I mean Lippert sometimes calls when he wants advice on taking a piss or because he heard someone speaking Russian. Other times it matters. He calls four times, I try to pay attention. You know."

"I know," Hank said. "So Billy will stay here," Hank added. "We'd love to have him. Like I said, I'll get on the phone if you want. I have plenty of favors I can call in. I know this guy in Scotland Yard, how cool is that? I know him pretty good."

"Nobody knows anything about Billy, about that stuff back when, you know," I said. "I mean the whole story, only you and me."

"And Lippert," Hank said.

"Yeah."

"Billy looks fine to me," said Hank. "Look at him; the girls are loving him being here, guys too. Billy seems like a real nice boy."

"Thanks. Hey, you didn't hear anything about some Italian guy a couple miles from here over by Fresh Kills that just disappeared like that, walked out of the house and nothing?"

"Laporello, something like that? Married to a Russian woman?"

"Yeah."

"I think I heard something. Why?"

"I got asked to take a run at it by Sonny Lippert. It doesn't matter."

"I mean Staten Island is still pretty small town when it comes to gossip," Hank said. "I feel like I remember the whole deal was somehow connected to a beauty parlor where they thought somebody was laundering some cash or something, ring any bells with what you heard? Queen of something, the beauty parlor, one of those cockamamie family businesses. The Gorbachev woman's brother-in-law's sister owned the place and someone said Gorbachev was sleeping with the sister's husband. I didn't pay attention. You want me to find out?"

"Only if it's easy."

"You want to eat something."

"Later. You think we're going to get hit again, I mean the London thing?"

"I don't know," Hank said. "I wouldn't go in the fucking subways if you gave them to me, you know, but that's just me, I'm a fat old cop, and what do I know? I missed you, buddy."

"You know any good places to fish around here, Hank? I told

173

Billy we'd go later, we tried one place, but it was pretty lousy fishing."

"Plenty," said Hank. "I'll write them down. Wait a sec." Hank went into the house, came back, handed me a piece of paper with some addresses and a set of keys.

"I got a rental property out at the north end of Staten, up almost opposite Jersey, end of Fresh Kills, I started buying after they closed the dump," he said. "House is empty next couple of weeks, the new tenants don't move in until then, in case you want to get away from the city, with the boy, whatever. You could always use it. It's close to the beach, everything you need."

"I probably won't need it," I said.

Hank pressed the keys into my hand. "So return the keys. That way I get to see you again. OK?"

Hank Provone was one of those guys who was not formally educated but whose instincts were stainless steel. He had a built-in emotional compass. I thanked him and again I looked over at Billy.

He was talking to a girl with long brown hair. She was wearing a flouncy white skirt, and a red shirt tied up at her waist. She was about fourteen, like him, and she reminded me of someone. She kicked the toe of her sandal against a cracked paving stone, talking to Billy as they stood together near the edge of the swimming pool, holding their soda cans and eyeing the booze set out for the grown-ups on a table near by.

"Who's the girl?" I said to Hank.

"That's Katie, my youngest," he said. "Don't you remember?"

"She's grown up a lot."

"Yeah, they do that." He looked at the two of them. "They seem good together, don't you think, my Katie, your Billy. They look good together, Artie."

"You getting ready to walk her down the aisle already, Hank?" said Stellene, who was listening.

"I'm not talking marriage, for chrissake. Katie's only fourteen," Hank said. "I'm talking in general. It's just nice, seeing them like that."

I saw Katie twist a strand of hair around her finger, and Billy looking at her, and the two of them shifting from foot to foot. He moved closer to her, and she didn't pull back. I thought I saw Billy smile.

I waved at him, and he whispered something to Katie and walked across the patio.

"Hey."

"Yeah, Artie," said Billy.

"You having a nice time?"

He nodded.

"Is it OK if I leave you here for an hour or so? I have to go into the city and you can come, but we'll just have to turn around and come back if we're going fishing some place later. What do you think?"

"Did you ever notice how people are always leaving kids or parking them or dropping them off like sacks of laundry, or garbage for recycling or something?" said Billy. "Hey, it's fine. I'm joking. Don't get so worried. I'm having fun and it keeps my mind off London. You don't have to watch me like I'm an egg about to hatch. Go away. Go."

"So you like Katie?"

"Artie, pulease!"

He punched my arm lightly, and without looking back, sauntered over to the kids near the pool.

I said goodbye to Hank and made for my car when I heard someone on the gravel behind me.

"Hi," Billy said.

"You changed your mind about staying?"

"No."

"What?"

"Nothing, never mind."

"What?"

"I love you," Billy said.

Before I went home, I stopped by the mall where the Queen of Hearts beauty salon was. Filled up the car at a gas pump there, then went over to the salon.

In the window, along with a price list for various beauty treatments, were pictures of Russian pop stars. Inside were two guys — I could see them through the window — getting their hair cut. Three women sat under dryers, one of them getting her nails done. I went in. I tried to remember how it felt not just to talk Russian but also to feel like one.

The girl behind the desk who was reading a copy of a Russian magazine, and eating candy out of a glass dish, glanced up at me as I came in, ran her hand through her platinum hair, and looked bored.

I asked if I could make an appointment to get my hair cut.

Slowly she put down the magazine, and finished chewing on her candy, then opened a large appointment book and slowly looked through the pages. It took me back to Moscow, the girl's sullen expression, her chipped nails, her disdain.

In the background was the buzz of women yakking loudly in Russian at each other over the hairdryers. I didn't know what I expected to find, but Vera Gorbachev had mentioned the beauty salon; so had Hank Provone.

On a shelf over the desk in the salon was a TV. On it were pictures of London, the bombings, the dazed people, cops, medics.

I made an appointment for a haircut for the next week, then asked if I could use the bathroom. The girl pointed towards a curtain at the back of the shop. Behind it were two doors, one partly open. It led to a small room, table, some chairs, a couple of men sitting in them, talking, smoking. The room was filled with smoke. One guy looked up, saw me, and closed the door. Nothing else. I used the bathroom.

An older woman was coming through the front door as I was leaving, a young guy, maybe fifteen, sixteen following her. He caught your attention. Very slim, very blond, he wore some kind of Latin shirt, with puffy sleeves, and tight black satin pants.

The woman introduced herself to me as the owner of the salon, admired my shirt – to her I was a potential customer – and introduced the boy as her son. She said he was a champion ballroom dancer, especially in the cha-cha and salsa, and he had been away to dance camp, but was back to help out in the studio she and her husband owned. It was very popular with Russians, she said, and gave me a card with a coupon so my wife and I could attend a class.

In Russian, I thanked her and told her I'd just moved to Staten Island and had heard about Queen of Hearts from Vera Gorbachev. She didn't say anything, just went out to the street and beckoned me to follow her.

"Gorbacheva, she's a friend of yours?" the woman asked.

"Not really. An acquaintance."

"She's trouble. She messes in people's business, she does favors for not so nice people, you understand? Don't get involved, OK? I mean, my advice, not my business to stick my two cents in, but just my advice."

I thanked her, and we shook hands again, and I kept her card. I didn't think I was going dancing any time soon, but maybe I'd get my hair cut after all. I ran my hand through it. It was probably too long.

On the way home, I tried Johnny again on my phone. No answer. Circuits jammed. As I got near the city, I glanced up automatically at the empty space where the Trade Center towers had been. A silver airplane flew through the gap.

17

"Sonny Lippert's looking for you. Call me." I picked up Lily's message from my answering machine even before I got home from Hank Provone's place. Lily's voice was tense and in the background I could hear the TV and the news coming in from London. Sonny Lippert had called her. Said to pass me a message. Why was he calling Lily?

At Lily's building on Tenth Street, the doorman was off. I buzzed the intercom and went up to her apartment.

"Is Beth here?"

"She's out on Long Island with friends," said Lily. "I didn't want her in the city after last night and the business at the toy store." She looked at the TV. "Now this. Is it starting all over again, Artie?"

"I hope to God not."

The scene from London played over and over on the screen: bombs in the subway; people smashed from one train into another; the red bus ripped open; London in gridlock first, then empty; weeping people; flowers in cellophane cones, letters, teddy bears on the street to mark the dead.

Bastards, I thought and put my arms around Lily. London

was her second home. She had lived there on and off for decades. It was the city she loved most of all.

"You talked to everyone you know over there?"

"Yes," she said.

Awkwardly, I let go of Lily and sat on the arm of her couch. She was wearing cut-off jeans and an old black T-shirt, her red hair was stuck on top of her hat and she was barefoot. She looked worn; the skin under her eyes looked bruised. On the wooden coffee table, among the piles of books and magazines, was an ashtray full of butts and an empty wine glass stained red from the dregs.

"What about what's his name?"

"You mean the guy I married briefly?"

"Yeah. Him. The one with the little designer car. I'm sorry, honey, I shouldn't joke."

"Yeah you should. It's the only thing to do. He's fine. He called me. He's fine and I'm sure his car is fine." She smiled. "He'll have theories already about what happened. He'll have the politics of it all nailed down. Shit, Artie, I don't know anything anymore. How did I ever feel so certain? What kind of fucking arrogance was that? Where's Billy?"

"I left him with Hank Provone over on Staten Island. You remember Hank? Big guy who was my partner?"

"I always liked him. I used to fantasize we could live an ordinary life like Hank and Mary."

"You did?"

"Yeah."

"Hank said hello. Listen, Billy's parents are in London and I can't get through, so I'm feeling a little fucked up about it. I don't want to lay it on you, but I can't talk to anyone else."

"I'm so sorry."

"I think they're probably fine."

"You tried the hotel?"

"I got the number from Johnny's restaurant and I called, but

I can't get through anywhere," I said and now it hit me, suddenly, like a ton of bricks, hit me that maybe Johnny and Genia were dead. Could be dead. Weren't coming back. I'd thought about it earlier, but not seriously. It was too improbable. Only around fifty people had died, the reports said.

"Take it easy," said Lily. "You want me to try some people in London?"

"Yes."

"Give me the Farones' cell phone, or their hotel. Artie?" She disappeared into the kitchen and came back with a bottle of Scotch and two glasses, poured a couple of drinks and handed me one.

"Thanks. What the hell did Lippert want, calling you?"

"He just said he was looking for you. He was calling around. Said to call him."

"He sound crazy?" Already I could feel myself getting dragged into Sonny Lippert's case, not the Gorbachev woman, but the dead girl in Jersey.

"A little crazy. Drink up."

"I like it when you baby me," I knocked back half the Scotch.

"Let me make some calls," said Lily, took the number I gave her, went to her desk, opened a fat address book and picked up the phone.

For a while, I drank the Scotch, Lily called London, the TV played. I thought about Billy and what I'd do if Johnny and Genia were dead. After a while, Lily turned around.

"I didn't get them, but I got the concierge at their hotel who saw them this morning early, before anything happened, and they were asking about directions for Sloane Street because the woman – it must have been Genia – wanted to go to Armani there. He said she had red hair and sounded Russian and I asked was the husband fat and American, I didn't know how else to put it, and he said yeah. They asked if he could get them a reservation at the River Cafe for lunch after they went shopping," said Lily. "I mean that's totally in the wrong direction from any of the attacks Artie. I made him ask the doorman if they went out after that, and the doorman was Russian, or Serb or something, and had talked to Genia, and they did go out, really early before all the shit started coming down. So probably they got stuck in Hammersmith. I'm rambling."

"Where?"

"Hammersmith, where the River Cafe is, miles from anywhere."

"You love London, don't you?" I said.

"Yes."

"Only you could get everyone in a hotel helping you."

"I mean it's not definite because no one knows if they actually went to those places, and I called the River Cafe and they never showed up, but the whole city was gridlocked, so it doesn't mean anything. I just think it's OK. I made friends with the concierge and he said he'd really try to find out what he could."

"You're wonderful. Thank you."

Weirdly, for Lily, she blushed. "Yeah yeah. No big deal. It's nothing."

"You're embarrassed."

Lily got up from her desk, took off her glasses, and came over to sit near me on the couch.

"Artie, darling."

I put my arms around her, and she leaned against me.

For a while we sat together and watched TV, not talking. I knew I should get over to meet Sonny Lippert. I knew I should go. I'd go soon. For now, I couldn't. I couldn't leave her. All I could do was sit by Lily and hold her and try not to let her see I wanted to cry.

"You might have some competition," said Lily softly against my ear, but I knew from her voice she was only joking.

"Who?"

"I'm teasing you," said Lily. "Valentina, Tolya's daughter, has been calling me endlessly, asks my advice, talks to me about her work. She took me out to breakfast this morning. She's an adorable girl. She has what I think the kids call a woman-crush on me."

"I don't blame her. I have one of those."

"You're not a woman, idiot." Lily reached for a black and red lacquered Russian box I once gave her. It was empty when she opened it. She wanted to smoke, she said.

"I don't have any cigarettes." I said. "I'm trying not to. You want me to go out for some?" I stood up and when I looked back down at Lily, she was crying.

"What's the matter?"

"I don't know what to do without you." She fumbled with the empty box.

For a moment I stayed standing, not because I wanted to leave her, but because I didn't, and what might happen scared me. I thought back over all the times we'd been together: the night I met her when my uncle Gennadi was dying in the hospital; when she adopted Beth in China; in London when it never stopped raining and she went away with someone else.

It felt as if everything I'd done, good, bad, anything that mattered, Lily had shared. She knew all about the Soviet Union because she had worked there as a reporter, and she understood the strange place I had grown up. Somebody asked me once what the most important thing that had happened to me in the last ten years was. I didn't answer, but what I thought was: meeting Lily.

I could talk to her. People always think that with guys it's the sex, and it was that, too, with Lily. But the talking mattered. Even when she made me crazy, I knew that she got it, got me. She loved the music I loved.

The first time we went out it was to Bradley's on University Place, long time ago, before it shut down. A good trio had been playing – I couldn't remember the name. Lily had liked my music, the musicians I liked, even before she met me. I looked at the TV and saw more pictures of a terrorized London. If the world was cracking up again, I wanted to be with Lily. I'd stick with Maxine, but I had to see Lily. Talk to her.

She got up slowly, said, "I need a shower," and left the room. I could hear the water through the bathroom door. I sat and waited for her. Sonny Lippert could wait.

I listened to the shower and thought about going in and getting under the water with her and other stuff, but that would have made everything impossible. Instead, I went into the kitchen. I couldn't find the coffee. Lily had fixed it up, everything was different and there were new wood cabinets and appliances.

"Hi."

Hair plastered to her scalp from the shower, Lily came in wearing a starched white shirt, sleeves rolled up, and black jeans. She put her bag on the kitchen counter.

"You changed it. The kitchen, I mean."

"Yeah, you like it?" said Lily.

"A lot."

"I made them keep the pipe. Look." She touched a piece of old steam pipe that ran up the kitchen wall. "I said they had to keep it. The contractor thought I was nuts."

"What did you keep it for?"

"You don't remember?" Lily reached up and pointed to a faint mark on the pipe, which was painted creamy yellow like the rest of the room. "One of the first times we went out together, we were going to hear music at the Village Vanguard, I think it was, you came to pick me up, and you had a gun in an ankle thing. You took it off and you got your handcuffs, which I guess you had in your pocket. Anyhow, you handcuffed the gun to the steam pipe. You guessed I didn't like guns, and you just did it."

"I forgot."

"I always remembered you doing that," she said. "You seemed very cool."

"Then you found out the truth."

"I liked you even better when I found out you were as big a mess as the rest of us."

"The kitchen looks really nice now."

"I finally earned some money for a change," Lily said. "I sold out. I did some work for a PR firm, that kind of thing. I just got bored with politics, monitoring everyone's behavior, especially mine. God, was I righteous. So I'll be on the PC shit list, I can live with that. I think it was when I was working for some NGO, you know, and I realized they were a lot more interested in gender politics in the office than actually getting something done in Africa. They bored me. I bored myself."

"You don't bore me."

"I was glad Sonny Lippert called me, I had an excuse to call you."

"I would have called you anyway."

"They played 'Someone To Watch Over Me' that time we went to Bradley's, didn't they?"

"Don't."

"Darling, maybe you should call Lippert now," said Lily.

"In a minute."

"Maybe I got you over here on false pretenses," she said. "I just wanted to talk to you first."

"First?"

"Before Sonny gets you involved in another case. Before you have to take Billy back to Florida."

"Why would I take him back now?"

In the living room, we sat on the worn gray couch, and Lily played with the blue and red kilim that was thrown over the back of it.

"What's wrong?" I said.

"I shouldn't say it."

"You can say."

"I don't get why we're not together," said Lily. "I mean I get it, I was a jerk, you married Maxine, and who could blame you? I mean in the bigger way, I don't get why it was so fucked up. Why I fucked it up. Never mind. I just mean that I miss you."

"It will be OK."

"How?"

"It just will. Somehow."

"You have such an optimistic streak," she said. "It's like you're still an immigrant who thinks he's lucky to be here and somewhere the streets are actually paved with gold."

I laughed. "I do?"

"Yeah."

"I should go."

"I'm going with you," Lily said.

"Did Sonny Lippert tell you what he was calling about?"

"He just said he wanted you, and there was some kind of tip-off about something, but he started rambling about something from his childhood, so I wasn't sure."

"Did it sound bad?"

"Call him."

"Yeah. It's probably just him ranting about something he read in Tolstoy or remembered from his childhood in Brooklyn, he probably just wants me to listen. I'll call."

After a couple of tries I got Sonny on the phone. He was terse. Not rambling. Told me where to meet him. Now, he said, coldly. Where the hell were you, Artie? I've been calling you.

Lily put on her sweater, and shifted her bag onto her shoulder, took my hand, and said. "You should call Billy before we go."

"Why?"

"For the same reason you left him safe with Hank on Staten Island," Lily said. "You don't need me to spell it out. Make sure he's safe."

"What did you mean before when you said I'd have to take Billy back?"

"I didn't mean anything. I meant at some point. Let's go, Artie."

I meant at some point. I thought about the maroon car and Stan Shank's ugly voice on the phone warning me to get Billy out of Brooklyn. Was that what Lily meant? Did she know something? She was half out the door, busy with her keys and then the elevator button.

She kissed me. "It doesn't matter anymore if you're married to Maxine, or anything, even if we can only be friends, so long as we can see each other, as long as we can talk."

"Yes," I said and the elevator doors opened and we went out into the street together.

Lily had a new black Honda, and we sat in it, not talking.

"You have a car now?"

"Go on, torture me about my lack of commitment to the environment. It's OK. I'm getting old, I need a car. It's just easier when Beth's here, I can take her places. The truth is I like having it," she said, her eyes on the road, turning left on Broadway, driving faster. Lily was a lousy driver.

"Call Billy," she said, wobbling between a couple of trucks and a taxi. "You'll feel better if you know he's safe."

"Watch the cab," I said. "Did Lippert say something about Billy to you?"

"Call."

I got out my cell and dialed Billy, and he answered right away. He told me he hadn't heard from his parents. He said he was fine. He was sure everything was OK. I asked if Hank wanted to talk to me.

"He's cooking steaks," Billy said. "He's wearing a big apron and a silly hat, and he's outside grilling steaks as big as my head," he added. "I'm watching the game, Artie, and we're all hanging out. The weather isn't so great. I'm really OK with hanging out here until you come. We can fish later, right? Or tomorrow, we have time, right?"

"You like her, Hank's daughter, Katie?"

"Artie! Stop asking me. It's none of your business. Yeah," he said. "I kind of like her. Mr Provone said we could go to a movie or something."

"Alone?"

"He said he'd drive us if we wanted, I mean later."

"Do you want to?"

"Maybe," Billy said. "Sure. I don't know. When are you coming back?"

"Soon as I can. So about Katie."

"Don't even go there," he said, laughing. "I don't need dating advice, for God sake, I'm just going to a movie."

"I'll be there as soon as I can," I said. "Can I talk to Hank?"

"I think he's kind of busy, I can see him outside running around like crazy because one of his steaks just caught fire."

"So what movie are you going to see?"

"*War of the Worlds* probably," Billy said. "It sounds pretty cool."

I had seen it with Maxine the week before, and I said, "I don't think that's such a great idea," but he had already hung up.

"Make a left," I said to Lily just as my phone rang, and it was Sonny Lippert. He sounded shaky. I said I was five minutes away from the address he had given me. It was in Chinatown. A tip-off, he said. Anonymous.

"Bad?" I said. "The Jersey thing?"

"Where've you been, man?"

"I was on my way."

"You didn't hear me say it was urgent."

"So it's about the Jane Doe from Jersey?"

"Something else," said Sonny. "We're just getting ready to go in."

I heard something in his voice that made me say, "You have a bad feeling?"

"Yeah," he said.

18

Rotting vegetables and fruit and other garbage overflowed the garbage cans onto the streets on the fringes of Chinatown, where we found Sonny Lippert outside a ramshackle warehouse.

Lily parked half in half out of a tight space on the narrow street. Most of the street was a building site – the buildings would be fancy condos soon – but a few produce warehouses remained, the kind where wholesalers delivered produce the local vendors picked up at dawn to sell from their stalls. I used to buy lichees in season down here.

"Hi," Lippert said to Lily, which was pretty friendly for him. "Thanks for passing the message."

"Hi, Sonny," she said.

I said, to him, "What's going on?"

"I'm not sure."

"You're not sure so you called me at Lily Hanes'? You're not sure and you wanted me to bring Billy with me? You were afraid for me to leave him alone? I thought you were in Jersey on the Jane Doe."

"I was in Brooklyn," he said. "Turns out the little girl, the

Jane Doe, was only visiting in Jersey when the creeps killed her. Her own parents live over by Sheepshead Bay. Same as May Luca. Same area."

I looked at the warehouse. "You think this is related?"

"I don't think this is related," said Lippert. "But anyone calls me with a tip, I pay attention. This time they gave me three fucking locations. Nothing else. First two, we got nothing, nada, a hoax. This is the last. I got a feeling. But it was a Russian voice, so I called you, man."

"Let's get this over with," I said.

Sonny Lippert told a cop in uniform to open the warehouse door and we went in. It was cold and dank.

In the gloomy interior a few people – the cop in uniform, a detective, a couple of people who worked the warehouse – were huddled together in the frigid air for warmth or comfort, like penguins in their Antarctic breeding ground. I didn't see any news people. I knew Lippert must have put a lid on the story. He was silent, which was not a good sign. When things were really bad, he kept his mouth shut.

Lily's hand in mine, we followed Lippert past empty wooden crates, which were stacked along the walls. Leafy greens stuck out through the slats. There was another door in the far wall.

In those few seconds, with Lily, and Lippert, and the others, knowing that something bad was the other side of the door, when the air seemed thick, almost solid with horror to come, I slipped on some rotten vegetables on the cement floor, fell on my knees, fumbled for balance in the dark, got up, and knew I was going to quit. I didn't want to be doing this for the rest of my life.

I didn't want to be going into warehouses and apartments where dead people waited. Didn't want to look at children with their limbs cut off. Didn't want to get beat up by creeps or cut deals with them to solve a case. Didn't even want to sit at a desk working paper trails when I knew the Russian money guys would always get off.

I'd had it. The thing I had loved best about being a cop, the camaraderie, the feeling part of something, was gone, and the rest was making me feel lousy.

The kind of adrenalin that used to wire me up at times like this, the sense that maybe I was doing something useful, was gone. I was flat. As if she sensed what I felt, Lily gripped my hand tighter.

Behind the second door was a room that was cold as hell and smelled sour and metallic, the way air conditioning sometimes does in a room where the ventilation's bad or something's wrong with the chemicals. I was creeped out by the place, the bad smell of rotten vegetables and the lousy air. What bothered me most, though, was I didn't feel much; I couldn't care much anymore.

"Artie, man?"

I headed towards Lippert whose face was colorless like a man in a black and white movie. There was hardly any light.

"I'm coming," I said.

In the corner of the second, smaller room, one of the uniformed cops pulled a dirty cloth off a large high rectangular structure. It was a restaurant refrigerator, stainless steel, with glass doors.

The motor whirred steadily, then coughed and turned over, and then began to whir again. No one said anything. It was quiet. Lily leaned closer to me.

Somewhere in the room food must have been stored because I could smell cucumbers. Squinting, I moved forward and peered through the dark and wondered why someone didn't turn on the lights, but maybe there was only the single busted bulb that hung from a string.

The cop turned on his flashlight and shone it at the refrigerator. Instinctively I tried to push Lily behind me. She stayed next to me. I forced myself to look in the direction of the beam from the flashlight.

Through the glass of the refrigerator doors you could see the shapes, four in a row. Lily saw, too; I felt her shudder. The cop moved the flashlight closer. I saw what was inside better. Couldn't make out exactly how old the babies were. A few weeks. Tiny. Dead. I couldn't look away; all I felt was Lily's hand and a smell of rotted cucumbers in my nose.

In the dark cold room we listened to the clunk of the motor on the fridge. No one said anything. Everything suspended, except my own breathing; all I could hear was my own breathing. I listened to it.

"Do it," Lippert said.

The guy in uniform broke the padlock on the fridge door with bolt cutters. The detective snapped on latex gloves. The sound startled me. He reached in the refrigerator and pulled out one of the bodies, then turned around. He was a huge mountain of a guy. His face was a faint green color. He cradled the baby in his arms like it was alive.

The cop seemed paralyzed. Lippert told him to take the other babies out. Do it. The guy just stood there holding the tiny baby. "Not real," I thought I heard him say.

Afterwards, in the street, everything seemed too bright. Lily, who had been holding my hand, let go of it, her knees buckled, she sat down hard on the curb. Feet in the gutter, she put her head down on her knees.

People – more cops, forensics – milled around. Lippert was on his phone trying to fend off news crews, but one from Fox was already on the street. Sonny, furious, seemed as sane as he had been in the twenty years I'd known him.

"Fucking fakes," said Sonny.

"What are you talking about?" I said. "What fakes?"

"The babies. In the icebox."

"I don't get it."

"Then fucking pay attention," said Sonny. "They're dolls, man. Dolls. Baby dolls. That little girls play with."

Still confused, I thought about the party at the toy store the night before and the nursery with the fleshy toy baby dolls.

"Where from?"

"Where from? From a store, from a factory, from China, from some fucking shithole of a city in China, Artie, where everything comes from these days. You want to see one up close? You want to hold it? I can arrange that."

"How come you're getting at me on this, Sonny?"

"I'm sorry. I am, man, I'm sorry. I just take it out on you, because, like who the fuck else except family can you take things out on?"

He motioned to the big cop who brought the doll over and held it out for me the way you would a newborn. Except it was fake.

The doll's flesh felt almost real, like it did at the toy store, except now it felt sticky. Maybe it was the warm humid afternoon, or my own sweat; I was sweating and the sweat got on the baby and made it feel real. Its blanket was pink and so was the little cap on its head.

"Who does this kind of thing, Sonny?"

"There was a similar case in Germany, except over there it was real babies which is what freaks me out, man. I just don't want this on the front page of the *Post*. Four newborns, toy babies, stuffed in a freezer, I don't get it, I don't even begin to get it, man, I don't."

"The little girl in Jersey, you showed me a picture of her doll that had its foot cut off. What kind of doll?"

"Fuck. You're right, man," said Sonny. "Oh shit."

"Take it." I gave the doll to a cop in uniform. "Just take it."

Lily was still on the curb, head on her knees. I sat next to her.

"Can you make it home?"

"Yes," said Lily. "I'll be at home if you need me."

"Yes," I said, and she kissed my cheek and, Sonny Lippert watching, walked to the street and got into her car.

"You got any smokes, man?" said Sonny. "I can't get rid of the stink."

"What stink?"

"Everything."

"Listen, Sonny, I'll help you out on this, I'll do what you need, but I have to go get Billy. I left him over on Staten Island."

"So that's good," said Sonny. "I mean he'll be around Hank's kids, people his age. He'll like that, right? I mean he was with you all morning, right?"

"I thought you wanted me to bring him in so you could talk to him about May Luca."

"I'm glad you didn't, man. Who'd fucking want a kid to see all this?" He pointed at the warehouse. "You gotta help me clear up this doll thing, Artie, man, I mean who called this in sounded Russian. I got to get at this before the copycats start in. I appreciate you helping me out."

"What about Rhonda's cousin on Staten Island?" I said.

"Fuck it," he said. "This is a lot bigger."

"You willing to spend some money?"

"What for?"

"So I can get some information for you?"

"How much is someone going to cost me?"

"How much you got?"

"For this thing?" Sonny waved his hand towards the warehouse. "Whatever. I'll get the department to stump up. You pay what you have to."

"Only money?"

"Anything," said Sonny. "Just do any fucking thing you need to. I don't want to open another door and find out there's real babies in the icebox, you understand me, man? You know? This is the kind of thing copycat junkies love, they love being the first, they want this, creeps who pick through the news looking for it. Go see your guy, pay the slimebag. Pay him whatever. What's his name?"

"You want to know?"

"Yeah, share with me."

"Samson Britz."

"Jesus."

"You know him?"

"Kind of guy after you do business with you want to take a bath. I met him once. He's a shitbag, but I don't care."

19

Missing. Has anyone seen this man, this woman, this young girl, missing, it hit you in the stomach, watching the news from London. Missing. Missing. Missing, young woman, man, went to work, last heard from on a cell phone, called at 8.39, to say I'm on my way, has two cell phones, neither one answering, took the bus, did he, or the Tube? The news from London played across the channels, the networks, the local stations, in the newspapers.

It was surreal, seeing Rudy Giuliani in London on a TV in an electronics store in Chinatown as I ran home, and me trying not to feel Rudy somehow got lucky being in London when it happened. Must have been Rudy's idea of a great trip abroad — relive his one great moment of redemption. But it was the missing posters, and leaflets and flyers, and the people clutching them that made me feel lousy.

It surprised me how many of them were foreigners — African, Russian, Pakistani; at a mosque in London an old man told a reporter how his granddaughter had gone to work at a bank and had not come back, and he tried to say how he had held her as a baby — his son held up her picture and she was a gorgeous girl – while he, the grand-father, wept.

After 9/11, New York had been plastered in pictures of the missing, on fences, on hospitals, on church walls; this wallpaper of the missing became part of the street scene. Months later it had remained, pictures tattered, wet from rain, pictures of people no one ever found.

It was the reason I didn't want Billy seeing *War of the Worlds* at the movies. There were scenes in it of people running away from attacking aliens and holding up signs that read: Missing. Anyone seen this man, this woman, this child? Maxine had had to leave the theater during the scene. I had followed her out onto Thirteenth Street. "I can't go back in," she said.

The news from London was like the far edge of a tsunami: little wavelets of fear reached New York, and made us nervous.

Already I'd had a couple of calls from my own office, telling me to be on stand by, that I might have to go back to work; already they were putting out feelers for who could help and there were plans to put cops in the subway and armed guards back on the streets. All of us thinking about the poor bastards stuck in a tunnel in London who were blown apart, blown into pieces, smashed into dust. Missing.

I ran into my building, still reeling from what I'd seen in the Chinatown warehouse. It worried me plenty that the kid who was killed in Jersey lived in Brooklyn and might be connected to dolls and to the old May Luca case. In the hallway, I stumbled past a woman carrying an empty stroller into the elevator.

I stared at her.

She was new in the building, the kind of self-obsessed yuppie type that had been moving in lately, and I barely recognized her.

"Something wrong?" she said, a little bit aggressive.

"I'm sorry," I introduced myself, and inquired about her baby to make conversation, but she just looked at me as if she was suspicious of the question, folded up the stroller and rode the elevator facing forward.

By the time I got upstairs and called Hank Provone, he told me that Billy had already gone to the movies.

Alone? I asked, and Hank told me to calm down, a couple of the older cousins were with them. Who? I asked. Two of them, he said, a girl and a boy. Responsible kids, Hank said. And Katie, his own girl. It would be fine.

"Hank?"

"Yeah, Artie."

"Do me a favor. I mean another one."

"Anything."

"Go pick the kids up from the movies yourself, could you?"

Being Hank, he didn't ask why, just said, "Sure, I will. Sure. Are you OK?"

In my loft, I put on a clean shirt because I had sweated through the one I was wearing. I looked around to see if anyone had been in the place. I folded the blankets Billy had used and put them away. I picked up a sweater he'd left on the couch. His duffel bag was on the floor of my bedroom. Instead of putting the sweater away, I unzipped the dark blue canvas bag and the rasp of the zipper seemed loud in my silent apartment.

From the bag, I lifted out T-shirts and jeans, shorts, a pair of green high top sneakers, a stack of underpants, some red swim trunks. Genia bought him nice things, mostly from Brooks Brothers, as if Billy attended a fancy boarding school.

At the bottom of the bag were a pair of brown loafers, a Yankees cap and fleece shirt, and books, which included a fishing guide, an unread copy of a Harry Potter book, short stories in Russian, a Russian dictionary, some schoolbooks and *David Copperfield*. A book about Charles Lindbergh, with pictures of Lindbergh and the airplane he made his solo Atlantic flight in, was untouched, still in the bookstore bag.

A thick plastic wallet fell out of the pocket of Billy's plaid jacket. It was full of photographs of the two of us: fishing on a party boat; at a Yankees game; at Billy's sixth birthday party. There was one of him at his First Communion, all dressed up in a white satin suit and white shoes with Johnny Farone looking fat, and me looking glum.

The Farones were Catholic and Genia went along with it. In one of the pictures, Johnny Farone stood in the background, like a distant relative and I, standing up close, looked like Billy's real father.

Thinking about how I'd found Billy trying on my jacket – I didn't think it meant much, but it bugged me, him wanting to look like me – I went through the clothes in his bag again.

The phone rang in the other room and I ran for it, and it was a guy I knew who I'd figured could help on tracking down Genia and Johnny in London. He said he didn't have anything on people named Farone. He'd keep trying. He'd call back. Sorry, Artie, he said. They're still missing.

It was Thursday. Maxine was due home on Sunday. I didn't know what the hell I'd do with Billy if she got back and the Farones were still in London. Or dead. I turned on the news.

What if they were dead? What if, I asked myself over and over while I got ready to go look for Samson Britz.

Consuming Diet Cokes one after the other, Britz was in his usual hangout, a bar in Chinatown near the waterfront and the old fish market that was gone now. Not far from the warehouse where the dolls had been stuffed in the refrigerator.

Britz was in the back, like he always was, where it was dimly lit; drinking his sodas, non-stop, pouring one, downing it, picking up another, he used the stuff like a junkie used heroin. At the other tables, a few elderly Chinese men sipped beers slowly and played cards. Above their heads, a TV screen was covered with news from London. Missing.

When Sonny Lippert told me I could spend money on Britz, I knew Sonny was plenty worried about the doll thing – really worried, not just spouting off – and the potential for copycats.

Samson Britz had been a cop, and he was a creep, a man who accounted for every favor and made sure he was always in the black. He called himself a private investigator, but what he was, was a man who retailed information and did it – sold it, one way or the other – to anyone who paid him.

What Sonny Lippert didn't really get was that Britz preferred information to money. He squirreled it away. You never saw him write anything down, but you could see his eyeballs turn back into his head, like beads on an abacus, click click, click, one for you, two for me. Three.

I only used Britz when I was desperate. Sonny had been right about him: you wanted to take a shower after you'd been with him because of the moral stink.

Always snappily dressed, even when it was hot, Britz wore a blue and white seersucker jacket, and sharp cotton pants, pink shirt, a pink and white polka-dot bow tie. He watched me come through the door of the gloomy bar and walk towards his table.

"Detective Cohen," said Britz, whose small talk sounded like a cop show he'd seen on TV. "Detective Cohen, long time no see."

I sat down and ordered a beer and when it came I drank half of it down in one gulp.

"So, you want to know something that I know?" Britz asked. "Would you like a freebee? I'm in the mood," he said, making my desire for information sound obscene, like some kind of vice he'd be happy to service.

"Sure."

"The sightseeing plane that crashed over Coney Island, that someone had fooled with the propeller when it was serviced, that's what I heard," he said.

"Who?"

"That costs more."

"I don't have time right now," I said. "Tell me something I can't hear on the news."

"So maybe you're here about the babies?" said Britz. "You don't mean to say you think I hadn't heard about the poor baby dolls in the freezer? Four blocks from here it happened. This is not news. Everyone knows. Everybody knows that they were fakes. So we wait for the copycats, the real babies, is that right? Isn't that why you're here, looking for Sammy Britz?"

"How does everyone know?"

"The movement of gossip in New York City," he said, holding up an auction catalogue on the table in front of him. Art sales were a regular preoccupation with Britz who figured he could make real money trading in art. Told me once he got the idea from some Japanese gangsters who worked the fine arts business. Along with being a creep, Britz could be a pompous asshole.

"Do you like the German Expressionists? I think they're really fucking depressing, but valuable," Britz said.

"Knock it off. What about the dolls?"

Britz raised his glass. "Everyone knows about it, which doesn't mean anyone knows how it happened. Grim stuff, right? Gruesome. Who the fuck does something like that unless it's a warning."

"What kind of warning?"

Drinking more Coke, Britz fussed with his seersucker jacket with a prissy gesture.

"I could make a guess," he said.

"Guess."

"Somebody who wants you to know that there's worse coming, that the baby dolls are advertising for the thing that's coming next. Somebody, for example, who kills a little girl in Jersey and cuts her feet off and leaves her little dolly with her. You know that part of Jersey, over by the Bayonne Bridge, opposite Staten Island?"

"Yeah, some."

"How come? You been to Staten Island recently?"

"How the fuck did you know that?"

"I didn't. Just asking. So I guessed right?" Britz said.

"What do you mean, someone wants me to know there's worse coming?" I said.

"I think I'm in the black now, Artie. I think you owe me now, isn't that right?"

"How much?"

"I'll see what I can find out. I'll let you know the price."

"Then tell me what the fuck kind of warning you mean, who from?"

"That would be 'from whom', wouldn't it?"

"Fuck you."

"If I knew that I'd be fucking rich, Artie," said Britz. "So, I hear your little nephew Billy Farone is out, they let him out of the nuthouse on vacation, isn't that right? Is he with you? Is he with his mom and dad, no, they're in London. I forgot. I hope they're OK." Britz looked up at the TV set and the pictures of the red bus and of people looking for their relatives. Missing. "They'll hit us again soon. Fucking Homeland Security couldn't protect us from a summer storm." He picked up a fresh Diet Coke and drank it, watching the TV without much expression.

How the fuck did he know about Billy? About Billy's parents?

Sweat poured down the back of my neck into my collar.

"What's the matter, Detective? You need another beer or

something?" Britz was getting anxious. "You going to say something or just sit there or what?"

I had remembered. Remembered when I had last seen Britz. Remembered him telling me, in this same bar where we were sitting, that he knew John Farone, Sr; Johnny's father, Billy's grandfather, was someone Britz knew, and Britz knew Stan Shank who had been Farone's partner. I remembered Britz talking about Shank. A crazy bastard, he had said. Something like that. "The Keyster," they called Shank.

Shank'd see a big fancy car, and if it was holding up the traffic or something, or waiting for someone to come out of a store, he'd stand nearby and wait for it to pull away, hold out a key, scratch the car or limo the whole length. He was famous for it.

I kept my mouth shut. I drank beer. Got some passing pleasure from the confused look on Britz's face and because I'd remembered about Shank. So far I didn't owe Britz anything. I tossed my card on the table.

"Call me," I said. "If you have anything I could get interested in on the dolls. I mean something worthwhile."

"Wait," he said.

"Yeah?"

"I could get you something else. For a price."

"What price?"

"I'll let you know." Britz picked up my card without looking at it, and then tore it into little pieces. "I have your number," he said.

20

I left the bar and Britz, found a newsstand and bought a copy of the *Post*. There was a headline that read COLD DOLLS. A report — if you could call anyone who worked for the *Post* a reporter — made connections between the dolls and the fact that the guy kicked to death in Chinatown was only fourteen, a boy with a cardboard sign proclaiming he was homeless and had AIDS. Child abuse was epidemic all over again, just like 2003, the piece in the paper said. Violence on TV and the movies to blame, was the conclusion. I threw the paper in the garbage can.

On my way home, crossing the Bowery, I saw a couple of cops with AKs on the corner. The city was getting edgy. A young guy who looked Arab crossed the street away from the cops, who glanced at him twice. Later I read that on one bus uptown some cop got on and gave the passengers a free lecture on how to spot a terrorist.

Some asshole in a van was honking, and at first I didn't hear my cell go off in my pocket. I dug it out, and called back. When Johnny Farone answered, I was so surprised I must have sounded really pissed off, instead of relieved, and I said, "Why the hell didn't you call me before?"

"Didn't Billy tell you I called him, Artie?" said Johnny, who was always sounding apologetic. "Jesus, I'm so sorry. I called Billy hours ago and told him, call Artie. I couldn't get you. Your phone was always tied up, you probably trying me."

"You're OK? How's Genia doing? When are you coming home?"

"She's going crazy. I can't talk that much. I'm in the hallway outside our room. She keeps watching the news on TV. We were on the street and she saw a couple of people who had been near the bombed-out bus, and one was bleeding a little and she went crazy."

"What were you doing there?"

"Genia was looking for some stupid antique store," Johnny said. "You know how she is about shopping."

"When are you coming home?" I said again.

Johnny's voice wavered. "Fuck knows. I mean fucking fuck, Artie, the airports are closed and Genia says she's not getting on any plane ever. She thinks the terrorists gonna get us. She wants to take a boat, for chrissake. I feel so bad for her, Artie and I don't know fucking what to do. I gotta go," he said. "I'll call you. You just take care of my Billy boy, OK? You gotta promise me, Art." Johnny was weeping into the phone now.

I was going to ask him about his father, old man Farone, and Stan Shank, but the line went dead.

I tried to feel angry at Billy for not calling to say his parents were alive, but I knew he'd been having a good time with Katie Provone; soon he'd be too busy with girls to go fishing with me. For the first time in a while, I laughed, mostly at myself, the way I was acting: protective, anxious, jealous; I was turning into a parent. I went home and got my car.

I wanted Shank. I wanted to nail him. I wanted him to leave us alone. It was Shank who had followed Billy and me around Brighton Beach on Tuesday afternoon and forced me down an empty street the same night, and Shank who kept calling to threaten me, and I was betting it was Shank who called in the so-called tips on the dolls in the refrigerator; Shank using a Russian accent, or maybe a friendly Russki.

For all I knew, Shank was involved with the dolls and the girl who died in Jersey. The more I thought, the more it seemed right, and I figured if I got something, I could make it stick. Get Shank picked up at least, get him out of circulation for a few days.

I knew if I went to Shank's place, he'd slam the door on me if I was lucky, or stick a knife in my neck. I needed a line through to him. Farone Sr in Florida was Shank's friend, which left Farone's daughters, Johnny's sisters. Donna lived with the old man and I didn't trust her any more than I trusted him. There was another sister named Tina, like the mother. She lived on Long Island some place – Rockville Center, somewhere like that.

Tina was listed under her own name. I was pretty surprised when a girl answered, said she was Tina's daughter, Sara; she recognized my name and gave me her mother's cell. She sounded nice, a nice kid with a sweet voice, and it came like a kind of balm, the mood I was in, the things that were happening. Finally, I got lucky.

Tina Farone – they used to call her Little Tina because it was also her mother's name – was at Johnny's restaurant in Brooklyn having cocktails with some girlfriends when she answered my call and she said she'd wait for me and we could have a cup of coffee or something.

She was as sweet as her daughter had been on the phone, voice, face, demeanor, everything. Sitting opposite me at Johnny Farone's restaurant, sipping a mojito, Tina answered my questions easily. Smiled easily. I'd never met anyone with less guile.

Younger than Johnny, she was blonde and blue-eyed, and wearing a sky blue cotton summer dress. She was probably in her late thirties, maybe early forties, and I'd met her a few times at family affairs – the last time had been Billy's First Communion – but I'd never really talked to her. I ordered a beer. The waiter brought it and brought Tina another drink.

"I don't even like these things that much," said Tina holding up her mojito. "They're supposed to be cool. How can I help, Artie?"

"You talked to your brother? He's OK, you know. Safe."

"Yeah, I didn't even know Johnny had gone to London until he called me. I try to stay in touch, but we don't see each other much, hardly ever, truthfully speaking. It makes me sad, Artie."

"You don't have to explain," I said. "Poor bastard. Genia's hysterical about London, and she says she's not getting on a plane."

"You want to know what I think, I think Genia's hysterical because Billy boy's in New York and she's scared of seeing him," Tina said. "She was always so crazy about that boy that when the thing happened, it made her nuts. I don't mean to say anything bad about Gen, so I mean like off balance, you know?"

"You knew Billy was here?"

"Johnny told me."

"Billy's good. He's with me."

"I'm so glad," Tina said. "But something's wrong, which is why you called me, is that right? Anything, Artie. Really."

I leaned forward. "You know the Shank family at all? Stan Shank."

"I knew them," said Tina. "My father and mother were all tied up with them back when, very pally. You met my mother?"

I nodded.

"I try not to feel bitter," Tina said. "My mom had me very

late in her life and it was a bad birth and she didn't want me at all, even though they named me for her, which I also hated because they called me Little Tina. You remember? They called Johnny 'Junior', and me Little Tina and we hated how we were named for our parents.

"I knew my ma didn't want me from an early age, I used to hear her yell at my dad, but they were Catholics, you know, she got pregnant, in those days what could they do? When I was fourteen, I just thought to myself, get over it, Tina. Just get over hating your family, and I got myself accepted at a boarding school, it was Catholic but I had worked out that it had a kind of liberal faculty, which my parents didn't know existed. All I said was it was Catholic and some of the teachers were nuns, so everybody was like oh, this is great, Little Tina is a good girl, maybe she'll become a nun or something." Tina picked up a glass of water on the table and drank it in a few gulps.

"I left home and that was it," she said. "In college I met a boy from out west. For a while I wanted to be like a rodeo rider, I swear to God, don't laugh, and I went and worked out west, and wore stupid hats, and great outfits with chaps and spangles. I wasn't bad but every time I opened my mouth, they knew I was from Brooklyn, and it didn't play that great, even if I looked pretty good in the hats. They tried making it work calling me The Bucking Brooklyn Babe. No one bought it." She laughed.

"What about the boy?"

"We got married, we got divorced. I'm married to a great guy now, who is not from the west. Mack's a dentist on Long Island, and he's a nice Jewish man who's happy for me to keep my own name which my mother never forgave me for, the Jewish part, and I have a great daughter – you talked to Sara – but yeah, I knew the Shanks some."

"What do you know?"

"I knew that Stan Shank and my old man were tight, they'd been cops together," said Tina. "They did business together, not entirely kosher, I'm pretty sure of that; they ran things in this part of Brooklyn. They weren't real players, they did little deals, electronics, toys, stuff they said fell off the back of a truck, stuff like that, and they could be harsh if someone got in their way. Cops that didn't play ball with them. Black people who had the temerity to show up over in Howard Beach to do business. It was the Russians they hated, though, because the Russians moved into Brooklyn, and they were smarter than my dad and Shank." Tina clasped her hands together on the table.

"So they took it out on their own women. My mom is half Polish, which my father claimed was the same as Russian, and Shank's stepmother was Russian, she's dead now, and her and his pop, who is also dead, thank Christ, had Herschel. They called him Heshey."

"Go on."

"Weird thing is Stan Shank also married a Russian. It was some kind of bond with those men, they married Russians and they got off on making fun of them and the women took it because they were immigrants and they thought, what else could they do, you know? My old man's in Florida. Shank's retired. Thank God. There were others."

"Shank had kids?"

"A boy that died, and a girl. Debbie. It made him crazy the boy died. God knows why, the boy had Down's syndrome and no one ever talked about it."

"You knew her? You knew Debbie?"

"Yes. She was OK, younger than me; I used to babysit her back when. I heard after she finished high school, she beat it. Went to live in Italy or something."

"You kept in touch?"

"I'll see if I can get a number."

"Anything else about your father?"

"Son of a bitch just sits in Florida and drools." Tina looked at her water glass. "What's going on, Artie, honey? Is this about Billy?"

"If you can get that number, that'd be great. Tina, how come they let Billy visit with your old man in Florida?"

She looked into her glass, then picked up her purse, extracted a lipstick and a compact and began fixing her mouth.

"It was never little boys they wanted, you know? They didn't touch the boys," said Tina softly. "My father adored Billy and Billy was crazy for him. They went fishing and stuff, he was a great cuddly granddad for the kid. You knew my mother threw my pop out of the house after forty-seven years because he was supposedly feeling up little girls?"

"I knew."

"I don't think him and the others had sex with kids or whatever, I just think they liked looking, maybe they felt them up if they got a chance," Tina said. "Which was plenty bad enough. Those men thought they were like little dolls, you know. I heard they figured if they were tender with them, or whatever, if they didn't hurt them, or what they figured was hurting them, it didn't matter. It was like they were playing with them in their old man's fucked-up view."

"How do you know?"

"Like I said, I heard. I picked up stuff my mother told me. I put stuff together. I knew about those little girls."

"Including you?"

"Not me. Never. Thank God."

"Your sister, Donna?"

"I don't think about it. Donna, who should have been a nun or a saint, took the old man on when my mother threw him out."

"What about Shank's daughter?"

"Yeah, I'm pretty sure the men got to Debbie," said Tina.

"She was only a little kid. I should have done something. Is Billy in trouble?"

"I don't know for sure. Someone doesn't like it that he's home for a while," I said, then wished I'd kept my mouth shut.

"I think I know how to reach Debbie Shank. Give me your numbers, Artie," Tina gathered up her purse, rose, hugged me and started for the door slowly, all the brightness gone. I went with her.

"Where is Billy now?" she said. "Maybe you should be with him. Artie, I don't want to alarm you and I don't know anything, but I would be with him all the time, at least until Johnny gets back from London, you know? Shank's a bastard. He made his half brother Heshey's death into a cause."

"Billy's safe on Staten Island with friends."

We went out to the parking lot and as Tina got into her car, I wondered if I should have told her anything about Billy at all. I called out but Tina was already pulling away in her SUV and she didn't hear me or pretended not to.

I got in my car and for a few blocks I followed Tina, wondering who she talked to. She was the only person I ever heard call Billy "Billy boy". Except for her father in Florida.

21

The deserted dead-end street on Staten Island, which seemed to be full of dead-end streets, was where I got lost after I took a wrong turn not far from Hank Provone's place. I wanted to see Billy. I didn't like the way Tina Farone had called him "Billy boy", and I wanted him with me. Wanted to take him back to the city with me. Keep him safe. My car was making crazy noises and I hit the brakes and got out.

My head under the hood, me poking around in the engine – pointless, but I figured I'd give it a shot – someone kicked the backs of my knees so hard my legs buckled and I folded up on the ground and lay there. It was sudden. It came out of no place and for a split second I wondered if I was dead before I blacked out.

While I was lying on my side, he kicked me again. Kidneys, I thought, and I went out again. There was nothing, no threat, no dread, no anticipation, just a sudden overwhelming, blinding pain, and another blow, and then the feeling that my guts had wrenched themselves loose, and I was falling and then nothing. I seemed to spin down into a black hole.

I didn't know if I was out for sixty seconds or an hour, I

didn't know if I was bleeding inside. My hand reached out for something to hold on to, and I managed to grasp the fender of my car. I didn't have the strength to hang on, my hand fell back, my whole body trembled, burning, bruised, the worst pain I'd ever felt. When I opened my eyes, I was lying next to my car, the pain so intense I had to close them again.

Where was I? In a way I didn't really care because my whereabouts seemed a lot less interesting than a way to ease the pain. I tried to roll over and tears poured out of my eyes. I waited. I smelled the faint, green smell of fresh-cut grass. It was drizzling, and the rain and tears ran down my face. When I opened my eyes again, I didn't know if I was asleep or not, or unconscious, but the only thing I thought about, the only person I wanted, was Lily.

Where the hell was Billy? I was hallucinating now, or was I? I couldn't remember where I had left him, and I didn't know if he was alone or if someone had snatched him off the street. The panic made it hard to breath. My stomach clenched up like I was going to vomit.

The rain that fell was erratic and thin, as if God, like an old man, got up in the night to piss on me. It was getting dark. My head hurt, and I couldn't concentrate, and I thought about believing in God, and wished I could. Somehow I crawled into my car. When I tried to turn the key my hand was shaking too hard. I waited.

In the glove compartment I found a half-empty bottle of Poland Spring and a plastic jar of Advil and I took four of them, figuring it would ease the pain enough so I could drive. I managed to start the car up.

I backed out carefully as I could, turned the car around, tried to get my bearings, tried to figure out if it was one of Stan Shank's creeps who kicked the crap out of me, when I knew what was happening: Shank's plan wasn't to hurt Billy; it was to set Billy up. Shank wanted to prove Billy was bad, get Billy arrested, sent away for good, maybe to avenge Shank's half brother Heshey, maybe because Shank was a vicious bastard.

Little Tina Farone or her old friend Debbie Shank might give me something I could use against Shank, though I wasn't sure about Tina at all now. Shank and his crowd wanted Billy gone or dead and they'd do anything, hurt anyone to make sure it happened. And that included me. Mainly me. Billy wasn't safe without me. He wasn't safe with me.

"He's not here," said Mary Provone, who was standing at her sink, rinsing dishes, chatting with Stellene who was at the kitchen table. "You look like shit, Artie, sit down for God's sake. Stellene, get him a glass of water and some coffee, or maybe you should lie down. I'm gonna call a doctor, honey, we have a friend a couple blocks over who's a good guy, good doctor, he'll come over if I call unless you want to go to the ER. Artie, you listening to me? Sit down."

"What do you mean not here?" I said.

Stellene poured me a glass of water. I drank it all and asked for more right away.

"What else do you need?" she said.

"Something for pain."

Stellene found some Percoset in the kitchen table drawer and handed me one.

"I could use two,"

"One's enough. You take too much of this stuff, you get crazy. I mean really like hallucinogenic. What's so funny?"

"I'd love to be hallucinogenic," I said. "Never mind. Why did Hank take Billy to the city?"

"I'm not sure," she said. "I guess Billy wanted to go back. He seemed anxious. You heard from his parents?"

"They're OK. That's not everything is it?"

Mary was silent.

"Where are the kids?"

"They went out for burgers," said Mary, putting down the dish she was holding. "They always go to eat after the movies."

"Katie too?"

"Yes."

"Tell me what happened."

"Artie, sweetheart, I think you should go home," said Mary. "They'll be waiting for you."

"They?"

"Hank wouldn't leave the boy alone, not after you asked him not to. Maybe the movie freaked him out," Mary said. "Maybe it was the bombings in London. Everyone's a little on edge around here, it reminds us," she added. "There was a lot of watching news and talk. You want someone to drive with you? One of the boys could drive you if you're feeling bad. What happened to you?"

"Mary?"

"What's that, honey?"

"What do you mean, the movie freaked Billy out?"

"Nothing. Forget it."

"You ever meet a woman named Tina Farone?" I said.

"Related to Billy? To Johnny? The one they called Little Tina because her mom was Big Tina?"

"Yeah."

"Sure. I knew her a little bit," Mary said. "We used to be sort of friends, but we don't see that much of each other anymore. We used to take our kids for horse-riding lessons together, Teen was good, she could ride a horse, and I would say, where'd you learn to ride a horse growing up in Brooklyn, and she'd laugh, I remember, and show me pictures of herself as a cowgirl or a rodeo rider or some cockamamie thing. Outfits with spangles, little bolero jackets, big hats. I don't see her now, though, not really. I think she moved out to Long Island. I used to run into her at the mall here some of the time. Why?"

"She lived around here?"

"Yes."

"And?"

"Her old man, John Sr, when he stayed with her, used to come around and shoot the breeze with Hank, and he made Hank feel it was like his duty to hang out with him because he had been a cop. I didn't like him. Hank tried to keep him away, but he felt dutiful, you know Hank, and John Sr wouldn't leave, he just sat around the back yard and drank beer and ate peanuts in the shell that he carried around in a paper bag, and sometimes I saw him throw the shells on the patio and Hank would pick them up. I was OK with the peanuts, but there was other stuff."

"What kind of stuff?"

"He used to stare at Katie when she was in her bathing suit, and once he made her sit on his lap. Finally I told Teen I didn't want him here, and that kind of broke it up with us, you know? John Sr, he'd be Billy's grandfather, isn't that right?"

"Yes."

"Hank took Billy to the city is all I know," Mary said. "Let me get a doctor for you."

"I have to go home."

Out front of the Provones I was getting in my car when Stellene came out of the house.

"What is it?" I said.

"Artie, listen, Billy should be at his school or whatever, or at least with his parents," she said. "Where are they, the parents?"

"In London. His mother is scared to get on a plane after the shit in the subways over there."

"Jesus," Stellene said. "Then you need to take him back to his school or just be with him."

"Why?"

216

"I think he's scared of something. Katie told me," she said. "We're close. I'm Katie's godmother, and she talks to me, and she said she really really liked Billy, I could tell anyway, she had that look, you know, like her mother, they have that thin skin and when they're happy it turns bright pink. So they sat together at the movies, and she said Billy was very polite. Maybe she was kind of miffed he didn't try to kiss her or anything. Afterwards, they all came out of the movie, and Hank was waiting to bring them home. Billy wasn't there. Katie said he just wandered off as soon as the movie ended. It took them half an hour to find him.

"Hank found him across the street at a diner by himself, eating a chocolate donut with colored sprinkles like nothing happened. He said he had felt hungry. Maybe it doesn't mean anything, and I asked Katie if she had the impression Billy was scared, and she said yes, even on the way to the movie, he was watching the cars that passed like he was looking for someone."

"I'm going," I said. "Call if you need me. You sure *you* should drive like that?"

"Yeah," said Stellene, patting her belly. "Triplets. Can you imagine? So go home and be with Billy. He needs you."

"But you like him, right?'

"Sure, Artie. I like him a lot. He was cute about me being so pregnant, asking me when I was having the babies and stuff. Go home."

22

"Is Billy OK? What happened? Where's Hank?" I said to Lily who was waiting for me when I got home.

"Calm down," she said.

Legs tucked up underneath her, a book in her lap, Lily sat on the couch with Billy beside her; his head on her shoulder, one arm flung over the back of the couch, he was fast asleep.

Untangling herself, Lily got up, pulled a blanket over Billy and said, "Everything's fine." She was wearing a yellow cotton skirt and a sleeveless black T-shirt. Little diamond earrings I had given her a long time ago were in her ears. It was the first time I'd seen them in years.

"Where's Hank," I said and fell onto a chair.

Stuffed with Percoset and Advil, I'd been nuts to drive myself home; weaving crazily through traffic, all I had heard were horns honking and drivers screaming at me.

"I'm taking you to the ER," said Lily.

"No. Tell me about Hank. Where the fuck is he? Mary said he brought Billy home." My hands were shaking.

"Hank said he had to go home," Lily said. "I called here a while ago, I can't remember exactly when, looking for you and

Hank picked up the phone. He told me he was here with Billy, he brought him back because Billy said he had to go home, and he had keys you gave him so it was OK. Hank promised you he wouldn't leave him alone. Hank asked me where you were and I didn't know and he said could I come over for a while and stay with Billy. He sounded pretty desperate to get back to Staten Island. I remembered you always said Hank Provone was a good guy, so I came."

"Mary didn't say anything about Hank needing to get home."

"Who?"

"Mary Provone, Hank's wife."

"I don't know about that," said Lily. "By the time I got here, Billy said he was tired. I felt bad for him. He said you thought he needed someone babysitting him all the time. I said I didn't do babysitting and I was only here because I liked him and also I was hungry, so we laughed and I made some salami sandwiches — it was pretty much all you had in the fridge — and he passed out before we finished. I covered him up on the couch, and that was it. I tried you like a million times," she said.

I looked at my phone. "The battery's dead. I think the phone is fucked. Someone kicked me in the general area where I had it in a pocket."

"You really need a doctor, darling," Lily put her hand on my forehead.

"That feels good."

It was late now, dark out. I was so sore I could barely move. If I went to some emergency room, they'd leave me lying on a gurney half the night, and I didn't think the guy who beat me up ruptured anything essential. They might not let Lily stay with me, and I wasn't leaving her, not now.

A hot bath would be just as good. I went into the bathroom and turned on the taps.

"You want a drink?" Lily called from the other room like she had a million times before.

"Yeah," I said, and I heard the clink of ice, and then the sound of Bill Evans playing "I Should Care", a track from the *Town Hall* album I loved. Both of us loved it.

Lily brought the drink into the bathroom, sat on the edge of the tub while I drank it, her face damp from steam. Then I sank into the water and stopped thinking.

Later, sitting on one of the kitchen stools, Lily held a glass of red wine, not drinking it, just staring into the liquid. She put the glass on a table and got up, stretched and looked for her bag, which she found on the floor. She put it on her shoulder and turned towards the door.

"I should get going," she said. "It's late."

"Don't go," I said. "Please. I need you. I'm scared."

She leaned her hip against my kitchen counter, and picked up an orange and rolled it between her hands.

"What of, darling, what are you scared of? Was it the dolls?"

I shook my head and sat down on one of the stools at the counter near Lily.

"No."

"What, then?"

"Myself. Billy. People like Stan Shank who want him dead."

"Who?"

"It doesn't matter. A creep."

"What else?"

"Maxine doesn't want Billy around," I said.

"She has children, it makes you irrational," Lily said. "I understand that."

"Even Billy's mother doesn't really want him."

"So, there's only you."

"You like him. Lily?"

220

"I like Billy a lot," she said.

"I just keep thinking about the dolls in that refrigerator in the warehouse, and how they looked like the dolls at the toy store. I couldn't say it before, not even to myself."

"Go on."

"I'm afraid of what people believe Billy did. That someone wants to set him up."

"And how much you care about him? That, too?"

"I don't know." I picked up the bottle of Scotch Lily had left on the counter and poured some for both of us.

"They made him well in Florida, didn't they?" said Lily, sipping her drink.

"You really believe that's possible?"

"You asked me before and I told you, yes. I have to believe it. Otherwise it's just some kind of Stalinist hell we're living in where everything is determined. But you have to take care of him, either way. You love him, so you'll look after him. That's it."

"That simple?"

"Yes."

"That's what Tolya said."

"Tolya has wonderful emotional intelligence," Lily said. "You wouldn't always think it, not the way he acts like a hood and his business deals, but he has perfect pitch for what matters. I thought that the first time I met him." She smiled. "In spite of his outfits."

"Sometimes I get jealous of you and Tolya. I mean sometimes I think you love him."

"I do love him. Don't be jealous, though." Lily patted my hand awkwardly, then pulled her hand away, picked up her glass, finished the drink. "I ought to go, Artie. I promised you, remember? When you got married to Maxine, I promised that I'd leave you be, I'd be good. I think I keep saying that, don't I?" said Lily. "It was me that fucked things up with us, Artie, darling, it was me that ran away and married a man in London with a small designer car," she smiled.

"It was all my fault. Do you remember when you took me up on the ferris wheel in London that New Year's Eve, the London Eye, you remember? You had a ring and everything and I just told you to forget it? It was a long time ago and I was a jerk. Listen, we had ten years together and then I ran away, and you found Maxine, and I don't want to screw things up for you anymore, so I should go. I seem to be saying that a lot. I'm trying."

For a while, we sat side by side, Lily and me, leaning on the counter, listening to Bill Evans, not looking at each other.

"Please stay," I said. "Please."

Lily got up, went to where Billy slept on the couch and looked down at him.

"He looks so much like you."

"You see that?"

"Yes," Lily said. "I'll stay a while."

She kicked off her sandals and settled into the big sloppy armchair where I sat sometimes and watched games on TV.

I went over to her.

"Not here," I said. "Please."

Lily lay beside me, sleeping. Wide awake, I listened to her breathing. It was raining. I could hear the rain hitting the windows, and all I could think was that the windows needed washing, and maybe the rain would clean off some of the dirt and dust. I reached over and touched Lily's long smooth back, but I let her sleep.

For a while, a few minutes, or hours, I didn't know because I didn't look at my watch, I felt OK, and I knew I felt OK for the first time in a long time, since Lily left me. It was a kind of contentment.

My father had never liked America. It wasn't because of the

politics. In the KGB, he had admired the opposition's tactics back during the Cold War. I wished he could have come to New York.

What he didn't like was the idea of America, the obsession with happiness. It made people into idiots, he said, and what the hell was it? Contentment was the thing you wanted, he used to tell me. Happiness passed, he always said; happiness was fleeting, like Dynamo scoring a goal in the last second of the match.

I don't know, but I felt content. And happy. With Lily next to me, and Billy in the other room, I felt deeply happy. It was as if this was my real family.

With Maxine, who was my wife, and her children, who were my stepdaughters, and who I cared for a lot, I sometimes felt restless. I had to try too hard, felt I was living the life I ought to want, the fantasy of a life other people thought I should have, the life they lived.

That night in my loft with Lily and Billy, it all felt real.

I thought it and then I began feeling lousy. I was a fuck-up. Maxine and the girls went out of town, and I was in bed with Lily. Tolya Sverdloff had been right when he told me once that I could never be happy without Lily. It had stayed with me. You'll never give her up, Tolya had said. You'll end up one of those sad old men who can't stay with one woman.

Part Four

Friday July 8

23

By the time a smudgy gray light showed in the window, Lily was gone. I must have fallen back asleep, and while I was sleeping she got up and went home. I felt better because she had been there, and empty now she was gone.

My bruises were killing me, and there were purple patches on my legs where the bastard had kicked me. I swung my legs over the edge of the bed, and reached for a pack of cigarettes I kept hidden from myself under the mattress. When I couldn't find them, still naked, I went into the other room hoping Billy had a pack.

"Billy?"

The sheets and blankets he'd used were neatly folded at the end of the couch. It was freezing in the big room with its high ceilings, and I went and turned off the air conditioner. Under the unit, Billy had plugged his cell phone into the wall to charge it. I picked it up.

He had been taking pictures with it. There was a picture of me, and one of Lily – she looked very pretty in it – that I was staring at when I heard a key in the door. I scrambled to plug the phone back into the socket, then I ran into the bedroom, climbed into a pair of jeans and grabbed a gun I kept in my sock drawer.

"Artie?"

I dropped the gun, and went into the living room where Billy was standing, keys in one hand, in the other a cardboard tray that held coffee cups. Under his arm was a bag. He set the tray on the kitchen counter and unpacked the bag.

"I went over to your friend's coffee shop across the street, I got us some breakfast," said Billy placing food from the bag alongside the coffee. "Coffee the way you like it, the guy, Mr Rizzi, told me, and toasted bagels, cinnamon raisin for me, and poppy seed for you, and plain for Lily – I hope that's OK for her – and I also got a couple of jelly donuts, and Mr Rizzi gave me a slice of blueberry pie to eat while I was waiting. Is that OK?" He was anxious as he arranged the food. "Where's Lily?"

From his perch on a kitchen stool, Billy watched me carefully, his face pinched with concern.

"It's great," I said. "I really needed some coffee, come on," I climbed up next to him. I pulled the lip off the coffee carton; the steam felt good on my face.

"Where is she?"

"Lily had to go home."

"She's so incredibly cool," said Billy. "She came over, and she made us sandwiches, and she gave me all kinds of books." He scooped some books up off a stool. "Look." He put them out on the counter. "Baseball books," he said, showing me *The Boys of Summer* and *The Natural*. "Stuff about fishing, an old-time one called *The Compleat Angler*. Also *Lord of the Flies*, which I read for English class, but I wanted to read over. Another one by Joseph Conrad. Lily's so awesome. I think she actually likes me, not just because she's your friend. She's funny, Artie. She made me laugh so much. What's the matter? You look weird."

"How come you didn't tell me your parents called from London to say they were OK?"

"Didn't my dad call you?"

"It took a while."

"My dad said he was calling you as soon as we got off the phone, honest to God, Artie, you know I would have called you, but he said he couldn't stay on because he wanted to talk to you," Billy said. "My mom is freaking out."

A glass of juice in his hand, Billy seemed distracted. He got off the stool and went to the couch. He dug his hands into the cushions, got down on his knees, searching for something, and then looked up, panic running across the handsome features.

"What is it?" I said, drinking the good coffee and starting on a donut. "What's wrong?"

"I can't find my phone."

"You plugged it in the wall to charge, didn't you? I mean you probably did," I said. "Right?"

Billy went to the socket underneath the middle window.

"How did you know?" He looked up.

"I just figured it made sense."

"I'm sorry about not telling you my dad called sooner." Billy's tone was cool, as he unplugged his phone and headed towards the bathroom.

"You OK?"

He didn't answer.

"What's wrong?"

"It's nothing, Artie, OK? Nothing." He was holding his cell phone. "I'm just going to take a shower, is that all right?"

On TV that morning there was a story about a two-year-old boy who almost got caught in a garbage truck somewhere in the boroughs; I didn't catch which borough, though it looked like Queens or Staten Island.

The house had a medium-size lawn out front, and the distraught garbage collector was on the screen. The boy was in his mother's arms, and she looked afraid to let him go.

The boy had crawled into a green canvas duffel bag that got tossed into a black garbage bag, and then a big garbage can lying near the front of the house. The garbage man picked up the bag and tossed it into the truck, turned on the motor; the compactor started grinding.

"I hear a scream," says the garbage man in his accented English – he might have been from somewhere in the Balkans – to the camera. "I hear terrible scream and I run to turn off the compactor, and I see his little hands and arms coming up out of the garbage bag, struggling to get out." He nods. "Yes. Three, four, ten seconds maybe before he is crushed. I get him free."

Cross-legged on the floor, holding his phone in both hands, Billy watched the TV attentively.

It was raining out, a dull, crummy kind of day, and I knew he was disappointed because he'd counted on us going fishing. He was mad because he knew I'd looked at his phone. An irritating flicker of tension snapped around the room, like an insect you can't kill.

I stayed at the kitchen counter, drinking coffee and working out what the hell to do. I had to nail Stan Shank.

For the first time since I picked Billy up in Florida, he seemed restless, like he wanted to get away, or maybe he was just plain mad. He watched some more TV. Got up. Got a donut and ate half of it. Went to the bathroom. Washed his face. He was jumpy and so was I.

When he came back from the bathroom, he fooled around with an electric scooter Tolya got him at the toy store. He didn't want to talk. He thought I was treating him like a little boy. I told him I was thinking Johnny and Genia would be back the next day. "Fine," said Billy. Nothing else.

"What did you think of the movie yesterday?" I said.

"It was OK."

"I thought some of the scenes where the people were

fleeing, you know, were really pretty good," I said. "Even if the creatures, the tripods, were kind of silly. Tripods, is that what they call them?" My own words sounded hollow to me.

"Whatever," Billy said.

"The end was ridiculous, really sentimental."

"Same as in the book," said Billy. "Same as HG Wells. I mean if it followed the book why was it ridiculous? I think it was great."

"You read the book?"

He turned back to the TV.

"What's eating you, man?" I said finally.

"Nothing."

"Come on."

"Please, Artie, I just need to sit for a while, OK?" Billy picked up a book and started reading.

I went into the bedroom and I was changing my shirt when Billy came in.

"I'm sorry, Artie."

I turned around. Billy stared at me.

"You're all banged up."

"It doesn't matter."

Panic in his voice, he said, "Shouldn't you go to some doctor or something? Are you going to be all right?"

I pulled the shirt over my head.

"I'm sorry," said Billy. "I really am. I just feel sort of weirded out, I mean being with those people yesterday, and I know some of them, at least Mr Provone, know all about me, know what happened before, and then the movie and not knowing about my parents. I'm just a little strange today, it's OK, but I shouldn't be mean to you, you're the last person on earth I want to upset. I'm sorry."

"Hey. You're allowed. You want to talk at all?"

He sat on the edge of my bed.

"I'm scared, Artie. I know some of what's been going on,

like that car following us, and people calling and you being worried about me, and I know someone wants me back in Florida or maybe not around at all. You think I'm nuts?" Billy said. "Sometimes I believe what people said, that I'm wacko or I'm some kind of bad, what do you call it, bad seed, or evil, or something, and then I think, what would I do if it's true? Where would I go?"

I hadn't seen Billy cry before; sitting on my bed, his eyes teared up and he rubbed his fists in them like a little boy.

"You're not nuts. You're not bad. Shit really does happen is all," I said.

He wrapped his arms around himself and I sat down next to him and said, "It'll be OK. I'll make sure it's OK. You believe me?"

"I believe you," he said. "I don't want to make trouble for you, I hate that idea, I think people could hurt you because of me, I don't want that." He sat up straight, rubbed his eyes dry and said, "I'm good now. I'm fine."

"I really need your help."

Billy lit up. "You mean I can really help you on a case?"

"Yes."

"Wow. Great. I'll do anything. Tell me."

"I'm going to really trust you."

"You can trust me, I swear."

"I have to go out, and I'm not going to get someone to stay with you, so you know I trust you, OK?"

"Yes. For sure."

"I need you to be here and pay attention to anything that happens. I need you to listen for any calls. I need you to write down the names of anyone who calls and any messages. If anyone delivers anything, I want you to tell them to leave it downstairs near the mail boxes. I need you to watch from the window and see what's happening on the street. Make notes. Take pictures. You can use your phone. Your phone has a camera?"

"You already know it does."

"Can you do all that?"

"Sure," he said, but he was disappointed.

Billy knew I had fabricated work for him when he wanted to work a real case with me. I saw it in his eyes. Not for the first time, I saw my father's cool blue eyes in Billy's. Maybe the intensity was genetic, too, except I didn't believe in the bullshit genetics that made you a creature of your ancestors.

"Artie?"

There was something different about Billy now, a tiny change in the way he looked at me. Knowing I had half made up work for him, he felt betrayed.

He returned the high five I gave him. He made a joke about Sherlock Holmes. But when I went downstairs and looked up, he was in the window, leaning on the wide sill. He waved a yellow pad and a pen, but he didn't smile.

Pain shot up my arm as I closed the heavy front door to my loft building. I didn't have time to see a doctor. It was Friday already and Max was coming with the twins on Sunday. She didn't want Billy around. I had to figure out what to do with him.

I got Johnny Farone on the first try. He promised he'd get a flight the next day, come hell or high water. He said it, come hell or high water, Artie; if I have to leave Genia in London, I'll get a plane. Saturday. For sure. I want to see my boy, he said. I told Johnny that I'd seen his sister, Tina, and he asked about her mournfully and told me he didn't get to see her much.

"I love Little Tina," said Johnny. "Her and Gen doesn't get along that good," he added. "I wish I was at home, Artie. I mean I just want to be home, you know. I don't even understand half what they're saying over here."

"Yeah, well have a safe trip."

I crossed the street to Mike Rizzi's coffee shop where I sat at the counter. Nobody else was in the place. I held up a pack of cigarettes, Mike nodded and I lit up.

"Friday, thank Christ," Mike said. "I'm tired."

Friday. If I could pin the business with the dolls in the warehouse on Stan Shank, or at least implicate him or his creeps for attacking me, if I could convince Sonny Lippert to pick him up, maybe I could keep Billy safe from Shank for a while.

I drank a cup of coffee and accepted a piece of cherry pie that Mike said was a new recipe, which included lemon zest. The *Times* had written him up for his pies. On the wall, framed in gold, the article hung next to the 9/11 memorial portrait of dead firemen in heaven. Beside it on a shelf was a small TV, which Mike had tuned in to Fox News, which was showing the attacks in London. I thought about how many times I had sat here, smoking, eating pie, looking at disaster on that TV.

Mike, tanned from his vacation in Greece, glanced up, and shook his head, and went back to reading a pie magazine. I was already on the phone, calling Lippert, then Britz, trying to find some information on the dolls. Stan Shank had been a cop, so his fingerprints would be available for a match. I closed my phone.

"You want to talk, Artie?" Mike Rizzi asked, looking up from *Pie Annual*.

"I don't know," I said."

"Good pie, right? Fresh cherries, man, this is the best season I ever seen, red, white, every kind of cherries, big as marbles, bigger. You have to use fresh, you can't freeze them like blueberries, I got ten quarts of blueberries out in my freezer out back in the alley, but I put them in Ziploc bags, two cups each makes a perfect pie, but I'm saving them for fall when there's only apples and pears, you know? I use a little brown sugar," said Mike. "I thought about getting rid of that fucking freezer, some months I don't even use it, but what the fuck."

"What?"

"Never mind. I'm just in a mood," said Mike. "Stuff in London got to me."

"I have to go, Mike. Can you do me a favor?" I could ask Mike pretty much anything. He kept an eye on everyone on the block, it was his turf, and I'd known him since I moved in.

"Sure."

"My nephew, you know, Billy?"

"Yeah, he was in the other day, wanted some ice cream, right, came in for breakfast this morning."

"Could you keep an eye on him. I mean you have my keys, could you run up in a couple hours, just make sure he's OK, bring him some donuts, something, so he doesn't think I told you."

"Yeah, Artie," said Mike. "Sure. Billy seems like a good kid, except when he was here earlier, he wanted to take a picture of me and when he realized he had left his phone upstairs, he got kind of, I don't know, worried. I guess maybe he figured he'd get punished for losing something like that. But sure, I'll go up later."

"Thanks."

I was halfway out of the door when Mike called me back.

"What's that?"

"How's Maxine?"

Over my shoulder, I said, "She'll be back Sunday. Day after tomorrow."

"Hey."

Outside the forensics unit downtown where I knew they'd taken the dolls, I bumped into Clara Fuentes, the detective I'd seen on the beach at Coney Island when the plane crashed. With one hand, she was holding a newspaper over her head against the drizzle, the other hand she held over her belly, though you couldn't tell she was pregnant yet. You saw that a lot with pregnant women, the way they held their hands — protect the baby, let the world know.

"Hey, Artie, isn't it?" she said for the second time. "What's up? You look upset."

Turned out that she had stopped in to gossip with a girlfriend in the department. I told her what I needed and she led me back into the building where she left me in a hallway.

A few minutes later Clara returned, and told me that the type of doll in the Chinatown fridge was made in China and was sold at the toy store uptown where the party for Luda had been. Problem was a lot of other upmarket stores sold them. I asked her about prints.

"Wait for me," she said. She went back in to her friend. I sat on a bench in the hallway. I waited. The tension built up so bad, I felt crazy waiting. Finally Clara reappeared.

"Artie? Hello?"

I jumped up. "Sorry. I'm sorry. I was thinking about something else."

"You ever heard of a guy name of Stanley Shank? Used to be a cop?" said Clara. "Sergeant out in Brooklyn."

"I heard of him."

"So all city employees get fingerprinted, right, cops, teachers, all of us, right?"

"Yeah, sure."

"Well, for some crazy reason, they turned up prints on one of the dolls from this Shank guy who's been retired for years. They make them in China, like I said, and people really dig them because they feel like real babies. Seems like people are paying way over the regular price 'cause every little girl has to have one. People are too fucking weird. Is there anything else I can do for you?"

"Nobody else? No other prints?"

Clara shook her head. "You were looking for somebody in particular?"

"I don't know. Listen, you did plenty." I noticed for the first time that, under her red jacket, Clara was in uniform.

"I pulled a shift on the subways, can you believe it, I get to search backpacks and shopping bags and pray to God no one files some kind of suit against me for being a racist bitch for profiling because I tell some hippity-hop Hispanic kid with pants down around his crotch to open his backpack instead of getting an old white lady to show me what's in her Coach bag," she said. "Jesus H Christ, because of London they want a cop in every fucking station. I make detective, they put me back in uniform and I get to hang in the subway with some rookie cop who doesn't know shit from shinola as my old man used to say. Anyway, you keep my number, in case?" Clara pulled a card from her pocket, brushed back her thick brown ponytail.

"Thanks a lot," I said.

She hesitated.

"You don't look so good," said Clara. "Did I tell you that I'm, like, pregnant. I probably did. I tell everyone."

"Congratulations," I said. "I mean it."

"Go," she said. "Go on. Nice seeing you, Art. Call if you want."

On my way to Brooklyn again – I felt I'd been shuttling back and forth between the boroughs endlessly, like a subway train gone off the rails – I stopped myself from doubling back home to check on Billy. It would cost me what was left of his trust. I had asked him to keep an eye on things. I kept going, calling Max while I drove to Brooklyn.

"Hi, it's me."

"Artie?"

"Hi, Max."

"Hi, Max, that's it?" She was irritated, and probably hurt, and I felt bad and didn't know what to say.

"Is it still nice out there? Is the weather good?" I said and heard the inane words echo off the distance between us.

"Very nice," said Maxine.

"When are you coming home?"

"Sunday, like we planned, but I'm going to try to get an earlier flight," Maxine said. "Jet Blue lets you change, and the girls are anxious to get home. So am I. I miss you, Artie," she said, very straight, very plain. "I miss you."

"Me too," I said. "I miss you. What time does the plane get in?"

"Five," she said. "I'll confirm it. I'll leave you a message if you're not home, or do you want me to leave the message at your loft?"

"Just call me on my cell. I'll keep it on. I'll pick you all up," I said, and she said OK, and hung up. Didn't ask where I was or what I was doing.

The rain was slashing down; it was hard to see out of the front window of my car. I had been a jerk, talking to Tina Farone without knowing what her loyalties really were; worse, I'd asked her to find Debbie Shank.

I called Tolya Sverdloff, left a message, called him in East Hampton and left another message. I was reluctant because I didn't want Tolya near Stan Shank. Helping me out a couple of years earlier, Tolya had ended up next door to dead at stinking Coney Island Hospital thanks to Shank. I just wanted him to know where I was.

If Shank beat me up, or worse – and better me than Billy – I'd make sure I left a trail a mile wide so people would come after him. I called Hank Provone. I left a message on Lily's phone.

Tolya called me back, said he had picked up my message, and offered to come in from Long Island.

"I can get a helicopter," said Tolya when I told him where I was going.

"Not now," I said.

"I'm always here, Valentina too."

"I know."

"Artyom, you know I swear, you know this is like brothers, this is my soul, your soul, you know I will do anything for you or your family, this isn't kidding. Do you understand me? This is not American-style friendship where everybody is analyzing everybody and counting up credits," said Tolya, who thought American life was superficial and existed only in the moment and that people had disposable emotions. He was wrong, but I thanked him, and he said it again solemnly in Russian.

I thought about calling Maxine, but figured it was better that she didn't know where I was going. She knew as well as I did, because we always talked about cases, how much Stan Shank liked using knives.

24

Gerritsen Beach was a small community, on the coast of Brooklyn beyond Brighton Beach, and it was mostly white, Italian, Irish, small houses, plenty of American flags, a lot of them soaked and dripping with rain. You felt people in Gerritsen Beach didn't like outsiders. There was no subway stop, only a single bus line. Under a greasy sky, it seemed inward-turning, apart from the rest of the city, almost sullen in its isolation.

I found Shank's house, and the woman who answered the door looked blank when I told her my name. She was Russian. The one time I'd been at Shank's house, I hadn't seen her, or couldn't remember her. She didn't react to me, but maybe she was covering it up.

Her hair tied up in a scarf, holding a dishtowel, Mrs Shank – she said she was Mrs Shank – told me Stan wasn't in. But she held open the door and I went in. Mrs Shank was friendly enough, which made me wary. She asked me to wait while she went in the kitchen and found the name of the bar where Stan was catching a game with some of his pals. She closed the door to the kitchen behind her, and I could hear the faint sound of her talking into the phone, very low, very intense.

In the living room where I waited was an expensive flat screen fifty-four-inch TV that hung on the wall, and silky covers on the furniture that stood on a deep pile emerald green nylon carpet. Over the mantelpiece was a fancy photographic portrait of Heshey Shank.

A row of candles under the portrait made it look like a shrine. Close up, I could see poor Heshey Shank's thick face and the uncomprehending eyes; he had been slightly retarded. A guy in a pizza place, looking for the term mongoloid, had come out with mongoose instead and poor Heshey got stuck with it.

A large crucifix made of gold metal was propped up next to the picture of Heshey. An ornate little vase, painted gold, held a few silk roses. There was a framed card from a funeral mass next to the flowers.

Stan Shank had told me once he only took in his younger half brother, Heshey, because he, Stan, was a good Christian, nothing else; now Heshey was a household saint and there were photographs of him everywhere. In Shank's eyes, Billy Farone was the Antichrist who had killed Heshey.

"Why don't you drop over and say hello to Stan, talk to him yourself," said Mrs Shank coming out of the kitchen, a fixed smile on her face, leaving the door propped open so a warm blast of meat and onions came from the kitchen. "I was just getting supper ready," she added, but I knew she had been talking to Stan. She handed me a scrap of paper. "Here is address. Tell him be home for supper, OK?" she said as if we were involved together in making ordinary domestic arrangements.

In front of the door, I almost tripped over a toy stroller still wrapped in plastic.

"We get it for our little granddaughter, Debbie's girl," Mrs Shank said.

I didn't stop. Clutching the address of the bar, I bolted for my car, skidded on the broken step of the house, fell on my knees like I was a hundred years old, yelled with pain, stumbled to my feet and got into the car.

Debbie's youngest? Debbie Shank? Tina Farone told me Debbie never saw the parents, that she had gone away to Italy to get her kids away from her own father.

Stanley Shank was drinking coffee out of a thick cup at a table with two other men at a cafe over near Sheepshead Bay, a few blocks from Johnny Farone's restaurant. Also at the table with Shank was Samson Britz, a can of Diet Coke in front of him.

As soon as they saw Shank look up at me, the two men went to another table and I couldn't tell if Shank had indicated that they should move. He didn't look surprised to see me. I knew his wife had called to say I was on my way.

A small-time hood, Shank wrapped himself up in moral righteousness from his religion and his fury about the way things were, foreigners moving in, blacks moving up, Shank himself going nowhere. He had a beef against the whole world.

No one invited me to sit, but I sat down on one of the empty chairs at Shank's table and tried to keep myself from hitting him.

"You want to apologize for sending your goons to beat the shit out of me over on Staten Island?" I said to Shank. "Or not. Maybe you don't want to offer an apology."

"I don't know what the fuck you're talking about."

"I accept," I said now that I'd set the tone.

It was the only way to deal with Shank. He was very fat. Making inroads on a meatball sandwich, with a side of spaghetti, he looked like he enjoyed hurting people even more than eating meatballs and red sauce.

The Samovar Cafe still looked like the Italian joint it once was, and there were plenty of red-sauce dishes on the menu along with chicken Kiev and borscht. A large samovar made out of painted tin metal stood on a table and a couple of old pictures of Russian athletes – including Oksana Baiul, the year she won the Olympics in figure skating – were on the wall behind the bar along with an oil painting of birch trees with snow on them.

It was the kind of place locals met to complain about the world and drink and play cards. You took one look at the Russian decor; you saw half a century of Italian just under the surface like an archaeological dig.

My shirt was wet from the rain – I got caught between my car and the door of the cafe – and the air conditioner dried it so it stuck to me. Shank was fat and Sammy Britz was small, and they were both a lot older than me, but I was glad I'd brought a weapon anyway.

"Accept what?" Shank said.

"Like I said, your apology for having my kidneys punched."

"Fuck you," he said.

"Listen, why don't you two just calm down, and we can talk it over," Britz said in an unctuous tone.

"Shut up," Shank said.

"I agree," I said.

Shank gave me half a smile.

"Your wife was very helpful," I said, just to get his goat. "I'm glad you're married to a good Russian woman, Stan. Very nice."

He ignored this and said, "It wasn't any goon of mine that beat you up, whatever the fuck you think I don't got no interest in beating you up, you hear me? What do you want?"

I held back on the dolls. I was saving it up, the fact that Shank's prints had been on the dolls in the Chinatown warehouse.

"I want you to leave me the fuck alone," I said. "Get off my back, Shank. Stop following me. Stop calling."

"You want me to forget what happened to my brother, Heshey? Well, fuck you."

"Half brother."

"My own blood," Shank said. "I had him confirmed, too. He was a good Catholic."

"It was your car following me around Tuesday. Ugly maroon job."

He lifted his enormous shoulders. "Whatever," he said.

I was going to ask Shank how he knew Billy was back in New York as early as Tuesday, the day he started following us. I was going to ask, when he said, "I have to take a leak" and left the table.

"Take it easy with Shank," Britz said to me, looking at his empty Coke can. "You listening?"

I didn't answer. It had occurred to me, right then as Shank headed for the bathroom and Britz got himself another Diet Coke – God knows why I thought of it then – exactly how Shank knew Billy was in Brooklyn.

I waited. Shank returned from the bathroom still zipping his pants.

"So old man Farone, John Sr, your ex-partner, called to tell you his grandkid Billy was coming back to the city? Isn't that right, Shank?"

"He don't talk so good anymore, far as I know. Poor bastard stroked out, in a wheelchair. Fuck knows what he's saying, just drools into the phone."

But old man Farone had called out, "Everything OK out there, Billy boy?" as we left his house in Florida. His voice was thick and the words blurry, but he could talk all right. Shank was bullshitting me. The old man could talk, so long as someone put the call through for him.

I leaned into Shank's ugly face and said, very quietly, "Just stop following us."

"Or?"

"Try me," I said.

From where I sat in the freezing cafe, I could see a couple of guys hanging around on the street near my car.

I wasn't getting anywhere with Shank. I wanted him locked up. I knew it was him who put the dolls in the Chinatown fridge, but it wasn't enough. Maybe I could shake his smug demeanor, I thought; maybe I could get him for assaulting a cop. I was willing to let him take a slug at me for that.

I leaned over the table. "You and your pals still like little girls?"

Shank's face blew up like he just ate something poisonous.

"What the fuck you talking about?"

"I know, and I could let everyone else know, how people said you and old man Farone liked feeling up little girls, how you put your hands under little girls' dresses, you kept pictures, you protected each other. Maybe you did other stuff with them. You were a rookie when you and old man Farone first became partners. He taught you, right, and you got him whatever he needed," I said close up to Shank's face. "You got him whatever he needed. You tell your priest about that? You want me to remind people that it happened to May Luca who was murdered? You heard there's a little girl got killed recently over in Jersey? You heard that, Stan?"

Shank lurched towards me. Britz put up a tiny manicured hand to try to stop him. Nothing could have stopped Shank, who was surprisingly fast on his feet and had me by the throat, his hands like hams.

"You're a fucking asshole," he screamed. "That was Farone, not me, you hear? I never did that stuff."

"So how come you never see your kid, Debbie? Your own kid, you never see her, isn't that because she stays away from you?" I remembered the toy stroller at the Shank house and I took a gamble. "You even keep toys for Debbie's kid, your own granddaughter, who never comes. Isn't that right? I bet

Debbie wouldn't let her little girl near you, but you just keep hoping and they never show."

He gripped my neck and I gasped for air and thought I was going to pass out, then he let go and pushed me, and I fell backwards into my chair. It tipped over. I was on the floor, my legs in the air, and I felt like a fool because what I wanted was to get out my gun and beat the shit out of him. I got up.

"You want to know the truth?" Shank said.

I waited.

He was purple and I thought he might have a heart attack, but he grabbed Britz's Diet Coke and slugged it down.

"The truth is, your fucking nephew killed Heshey, and he deserves whatever. That's the truth and you don't tell the truth about it, you and that prick, Sonny Lippert. You just fixed things up with some judge."

I wanted to get him good and mad; if he got crazy, he might talk, or attack me; one way or the other, he'd give me something to use against him.

"What eats you, Shank, is that your own son, who was damaged goods, died, and Billy is alive and well."

From his back pocket, Shank took a knife. I saw the blade glint in the dull light.

"I could kill you, you know," said Shank. "I could carve you up. I made up my mind I wasn't going to do him, the kid, your nephew, or whatever he is."

"I don't believe you."

"I'm a Catholic and the priest told me, don't kill nobody, and killing kids is worst, you go to hell forever and they got devils down there stick you in the eyes and the balls for the rest of your life," said Shank who clearly believed it and was terrified. "Farone told me from Florida, keep an eye on my grandson, keep an eye on Billy boy, just make sure no one else gets to him, that he's safe, so that's what I done, you hear? The old man, he was my partner, and he's stroked out, and I done what he asked me." He lunged at me "I didn't make no promises about you."

The air on my arms was so cold, the hairs stood up and seemed to freeze like icicles, and my skin was raw and rough as paper.

"Let's talk about the toys you sell off the back of a truck, dolls for little girls, say."

"You don't got nothing, do you?" Shank was two inches from my face. "Or maybe you got some prints on some toy dollies, is that it?"

I didn't say anything.

"Who's going to indict me because I sold a couple hundred dolls that fell off the back of a truck, like they say, so to speak, and some of the same type ended up at a toy store off Fifth fucking Avenue and another one on Madison, and some ended up in Chinatown, you think anyone's going to indict me for that?" Shank said. "There's hundreds. I sold hundreds of them. A big item for little kids. So someone got hold of a few and stuck 'em on ice. Yeah yeah, I heard about it. So fucking what? Now get the fuck out of here."

On the street, I pushed past Shank's guys who were standing too close to my car. Sammy Britz came after me.

"You shouldn't push Shank like that," he said, still holding his can of Diet Coke. "He has a temper."

"Fuck you. You told him I came to see you, you owe me now."

"In that case, here's something else," said Britz flicking imaginary dust off his little lapels.

"Yeah?"

"You gonna try to pin the dolls on Shank?"

"I have to go."

"We're even now, right, detective?"

"No."

I could see Britz doing his accounts in his head.

"Shank told me when he was keeping an eye on your nephew, he noticed the kid was always holding a cell phone, like he was taking pictures with it, never took his eye off it, that anything you can use? I mean tell me, 'cause I don't like to end the week with owing people, you know? So does that make us good, detective, does that even us up?"

Britz was more anxious than I even remembered him being, and I let him hang around for a few minutes while I patted my pockets for a pack of cigarettes, fiddled with the door of my car, enjoying the pinched, scared look on his violent little face.

"So?"

"So I'm thinking, we're even." Britz worked on the Diet Coke he held, and even when the can was empty he sucked on it like a baby sucking on its mother's tit, like he couldn't get enough. "You know, Detective Cohen, Shank told you like it is."

"Like what is?" I said.

"Whatever he does is for his brother, Heshey," Britz said.

"He never gave a rat's ass about Heshey, who was only his half brother, the kid from his father's second wife, the Russian Jew he hated," I said. "Come on, Sammy, you want your accounts evened up, don't you?"

I opened my car door, and made to get in.

Britz leaned down, dropped the Coke can in the gutter, and stamped on it, smashing it up like the little plane on Coney Island beach.

"You really got to him when you mentioned the daughter and the grandkid."

"So?"

"Yeah, well, the husband, Debbie's husband, Shank's son-in-law, it was him didn't want their daughter anywhere near Shank or his pals. Debbie Shank didn't say nothing about it, just went along with her husband."

"Go on."

"Your hand's shaking," Britz said. "You mentioned you went out to Staten Island recently, isn't that right?"

Did I? I couldn't remember. I kept my mouth shut.

"So Debbie and her family, they lived over there for a while, came back from Italy, moved into a place on Staten Island, out by the mall near Fresh Kills," said Britz.

"Why would I care?"

"Debbie's husband got nervous about Shank and they took the kid and moved some place upstate. Catskills, I think. Town of Accord. Cut themselves off from both families, Shank, her husband's family, too," said Britz. "His mother was dead, his father remarried. Another Russki, the second wife."

"What's the husband's name?"

"Frank Laporello," said Britz. "So are we even now?"

At Vera Gorbachev's house there had been a tricyle in the yard. When I had asked if they had children, her and Al Laporello, she had said, "Not now." Even then I had thought it was strange.

The house where May Luca had lived was shut up. There was a FOR RENT sign in the front yard, which was full of weeds. A filthy shriveled pink balloon clung to the low fence around the yard, and the remains of some rosary beads, and I remembered the night after May was murdered how people came with flowers and balloons and stuffed animals and candles, and stood for hours, praying, weeping, lighting candles, in the street. It had seemed an open and shut case: May's body dumped at a nearby marina, a local crackhead who ran from the cops and got shot dead.

Now Sonny Lippert was working the case of another dead girl whose name I didn't know, who lived somewhere near here, and there was evidence that the same perverted bastard who killed May had killed Jane Doe. Had killed others also, years earlier, cold cases that had been shelved.

I was already thinking about Stan Shank for the killer. His desperation to set Billy up, the fact that Billy and May Luca had been friends long ago, maybe it was Shank all along. Maybe he had wanted May Luca dead because his pal, old man Farone, had felt her up and she had talked; maybe it was Shank who killed the little girl in Jersey to set up Billy.

Vera Gorbachev had called me because her husband, Al Laporello, had disappeared, and Laporello's son was married to Stan Shank's daughter.

Where did I fit in? Was I in so deep I was dragging Billy down with me?

"Who is it?" Rhonda Fisher yelled through the door of Sonny's apartment when I got there.

There was the sound of locks turning, a chain removed, the door opened, and Rhonda said, "Hi, Artie, come on in. Sonny's asleep." In the background John Coltrane played "My Favorite Things." Sonny had a fancy Bose system and the sound was great.

"You don't look so hot." Rhonda kissed my cheek, invited me into the kitchen, and offered me a cold beer that I drank down in a couple of gulps.

Before Lippert let Rhonda into his life, there was nothing in the kitchen except a jar of stale Medaglio d'Oro instant espresso and bottles of Scotch; now there was food and some red mugs on the draining board and a bunch of yellow roses on a round table. Rhonda wasn't living there, but she came around a lot and fixed things for Sonny.

Neatly stacked next to the roses was a pile of newspapers, copies of the *New York Review of Books* and the *London Literary Review*, which Sonny read religiously and discussed with me, or tried to. Once, during a long discourse on Charles Dickens and Darwin and if they ever met each other in London, I fell asleep over dinner.

"Sit," said Rhonda, who had lost a few pounds – she told me she was into Pilates – and looked great. She was wearing a pair of white shorts and a red and white striped shirt, a pair of gold Italian earrings Sonny had given her, and she leaned against the stove, sipping tomato juice, glancing up once in a while at the portable TV on a shelf where a Yankees game was on.

"You look good," I said, still standing. "The place looks good."

"Thanks, babe, but tell me what you need," said Rhonda. "And sit down. You're making me twitchy."

"He OK?"

"Sonny? He's taking a nap, but yeah, he's OK. I just wish he'd give it up, this thing is getting to him."

"The dolls?"

"The dolls, the girl that got killed in Jersey, everything that goes down with children, he can't stand it, he gets drawn back in. Should I wake him up?"

"I came to see you."

"You want me to fix you something to eat?" Rhonda said.

"I need to know about your cousin, or whatever she is, on Staten Island. Vera Gorbachev. You asked Sonny to get me to go talk to her, what did she say exactly?"

"Didn't she tell you?"

"You tell me. Please."

"She's not my cousin," said Rhonda. "Or maybe she's a cousin but like really distant. Vera Gorbachev, I almost laughed out loud when I heard the name. So, anyway, I had heard way back from some of my mother's family when they got to Brighton Beach, you know, like in the 70s or 80s when they all started coming, and I didn't do fuck all. I wasn't interested in a bunch of Russkis I had no relationship to, and I went once and it depressed the hell out of me, all those Russians talking about how they missed Russia, you know?"

"Do I ever."

"So I didn't do anything more except I sent some money and

I felt kind of bad, in a not very important way. I planned on seeing them again," Rhonda said. "You plan on seeing people, and you don't. And then they move on, or they get old and then die."

"No other reason?"

"I was busy. I was young, I was waiting for Sonny to like me," said Rhonda. "It took me hours to get ready for work every morning so he'd notice me. I didn't care about a bunch of immigrants, and anyhow I had already made it out of Brooklyn and into the city, what did I want to go back there for?" said Rhonda. "When this Vera Gorbachev moved over to Staten Island she called to tell me. I visited her once, I think I brought some smoked fish, chubs, I think, and I didn't go back. I felt bad afterwards. Jesus, the Yankees really suck this season overall, in spite of the last few days," said Rhonda, a rabid Yankees fan, as she looked up at the TV.

"So your cousin, or whatever she is, calls you out of the blue. When?"

"It must have been like, a week ago, ten days, something like that. Around then," said Rhonda.

"Go on, so Gorbachev calls."

"Yeah, she calls and says her husband disappeared. Someone came in the house and tried to rob them in the middle of the night, and the husband, what was his name, Al Leporello, something like that, chased the asshole down the street and then disappeared. She was a little hysterical, so I asked Sonny and he asked you."

"Laporello," Sonny said, wandering into the kitchen. "Laporello, honey, Leporello is a character in *Don Giovanni*, an opera by Mozart, libretto by Lorenzo da Ponte. Did you know da Ponte was the first professor of Italian up at Columbia University?"

"I know what that is, asshole, I know about Mozart," Rhonda said, kissing him.

In dark green shorts and a white polo shirt, Lippert sat down, looked at the TV, then back at me.

"What's going on?" he said.

"Artie wanted to know how come Vera Gorbachev called me," Rhonda said.

"Yeah, go on." Sonny took Rhonda's hand and saw that I noticed him doing it.

"Fuck you," he said under his breath, but he was smiling.

Rhonda shifted her chair closer to Sonny's, and said, "So Vera calls me, and she says, I need some help. I don't know anyone who speaks Russian out here."

"Did Vera know that Sonny was connected to a Russian speaker?"

"Yes," Rhonda said. "I could tell she knew about you, she didn't say it by name, but who the hell else could it be, she said, your husband's guy, the Russian who works for him regular."

"Why didn't you tell me?"

"Like I said, it didn't seem important. I just asked Sonny if you would give her an hour, no big deal. I felt guilty. I should have called to say so. I put it off on you, Artie, and I'm sorry."

Rhonda started taking platters of food out of the fridge and I sat on the edge of a kitchen chair. Couldn't get comfortable. Pain from the beating I took still ran around my body.

Sonny's new interest in food meant he practically rubbed his hands together watching Rhonda fix the food. She sliced bagels into three perfect slices – she said she had read Mel Brooks sliced his bagels in three and it was better like that – and toasted them. She fixed sandwiches from tongue, which Sonny loved, handed one to me and another to Sonny and made one for herself.

"Listen to me." I leaned over the table towards Lippert. "Listen to me. I need help. I need to know who wanted me in the Laporello thing. Just help me, OK?"

"Yes, like I said, I'm sure they knew it was you," Rhonda said. "There's nobody else Sonny knows well that speaks good Russian. She must have known, but loads of people know you two are friends."

For years Lippert told people he had invented me, that he talent-spotted me when I was a rookie and noticed I could speak some languages, and had an education. He told people and I hated it, him making out like I was his creature. Worse, he made me understand that I owed him something, some kind of fealty. I probably did, and maybe that's what rubbed me the wrong way. I got over it, though. Everyone knew we were tied together. Even Vera Gorbachev knew.

"Vera Gorbachev needed a Russian speaker so bad that she called you, a distant relative she hardly knows at all, right, and she asks you to ask your big-deal husband to send one of his guys she knows is a Russian speaker, which means me, right?"

"Yeah, go on," Rhonda said.

"How the hell did she tell you all this in English? You speak Russian, Rhonda?"

"I don't speak Russian."

"How did she talk to you?"

"She knew enough English."

"You got the feeling she knew more than she let on?"

"Yeah, now I think of it," Rhonda said. "Her accent was heavy but she could talk English pretty good. Jeez, you're right, Artie. She's been here a long time, she had a job, I mean, how the hell did she manage?"

"It didn't bother you at the time?"

"I figured she wanted someone she could really communicate with, or maybe she was lonely for somebody from home. I don't know, Artie. I didn't think about it a lot."

Sonny said, "Let's go on the balcony for a smoke."

"I don't have much time."

I followed Sonny into the other room. Rhonda stayed where she was in front of the TV set, watching the game.

We stood on Sonny's balcony and smoked and looked at the river.

"You were making Rhonda feel pretty lousy," Sonny said. "It was like you were interrogating her, man."

"I had to know why Vera Gorbachev got Rhonda to get you to send me over to see her. I had to know if it was accidental or not."

"Go on," Sonny said.

"You still think there's a connection between your dead girl, and those old cases? Including May Luca?"

"You want me to run the details by you? It's DNA stuff, we got some stuff off the little girl that died in Jersey – her name is Ruthie Kelly, little Irish kid – that looks like a match for some of what we found on May Luca. I didn't bother you with the details, shit like that, because I wasn't asking you to work it, only to help me on the dolls thing and maybe ask Billy if he remembered May Luca."

"I don't need the details, I believe you." I said. "I'll ask Billy tonight. You remember Stan Shank?"

"Heshey Shank's brother?"

"Half brother."

I told Lippert what I knew about Stan Shank.

"I like that," said Sonny. "I like that it fits. Fuck. I like Shank's prints being on the dolls. Ruthie Kelly had her doll with her when she was murdered; I showed you that, right? I'm already checking it against the dolls in Chinatown. I'm impressed, man."

"Thanks."

"Maybe it's time you came back to work for me," he said, getting up.

"I have to go, Sonny."

"Billy Farone still with you?"

"Why?"

"I'm just thinking, while Shank is still out there, is Billy safe?"

"It's what I've been thinking."

"Artie, man, I'm beginning to think you have to take the boy back to Florida. Keep him safe. Shank sounds like he could be some kind of serial nut."

"Then pick him up."

"I'm trying, man, I'm on it," said Sonny. "But keep it in mind, what I just told you."

"How soon you think you can pick Shank up?"

"Next forty-eight hours, I'm hoping." Sonny already had his phone in his hand. "I want the bastard fast."

"Shank likes big fishing knives," I said. "That help at all?"

Sonny sat up. "Yeah, man, you fucking bet it helps. Let me get on the phone."

I didn't have forty-eight hours. It was Friday night. Stanley Shank was out hunting Billy, or finding new ways to set him up. Maxine was coming home Sunday. I couldn't keep Billy locked up in my loft. Even if Johnny and Genia made it back before that, Genia was so febrile I didn't know how she'd cope with her kid.

Billy would hate me. It would be a betrayal. I knew I might have to trick him to get him on a plane. I didn't want him thinking about May Luca, I didn't want him sinking into the past. Most of all, I wanted him safe and I couldn't take care of him that way in New York now.

25

"Hold it. Hey!" A kid wearing a greasy yellow slicker held up his hand as soon as I got out of my car. He pulled at his scruffy goatee. "Just wait right there." Behind him movie extras were attacking a table piled with food like locusts.

My block was jammed. From the number of vehicles stretching around the corner and the gangs of people, you could tell it was a big movie. Some of the crew were holding golf umbrellas. Didn't notice they were making the street impassable. Didn't care. Monster lights almost a story high lit up the dark night, sky the color of damp slate. Screens made of white and silver fabric reflected the light and the rain, which came down in slanted sheets, made it feel apocalyptic.

Vehicles with dressing rooms lined the side of the street opposite my building. A generator in a truck whirred noisily and it would go on all night. More trucks spilled rigging equipment. Fat teamsters sat around eating Danish and apple turnovers between meals. Thick coils of electric wire snaked along the curb. Extras crowded in doorways, trying to keep dry.

I looked up at my building. There were lights on in my

windows. Again I tried crossing the street when a second kid tried to stop me.

"We're filming," he said. Like most film sets, the self-importance was heavy as the humidity.

I kept myself from pushing the kid out of my way. I showed him my badge and told him to move. I wasn't in the mood for his attitude.

"Which show you working on?" said the kid who couldn't conceive of life outside movies. Lucky for him that, before I answered, a cop in uniform came over and asked if I needed anything. Then I noticed that Mike Rizzi's coffee shop was shut up tight as a drum, the metal gate pulled down over the door and I wondered what time he left.

In my building I hit the elevator button. Come on. Come on!

Rizzi was supposed to keep an eye on Billy and he had gone home. I couldn't wait. I bolted for the stairs, took them two at a time up four flights. There were scratches on the wood frame of my door but I couldn't tell for sure if they were new or not; one of the lights in the hall was out and it was hard to see. I unlocked the door. My key jammed like it always did when I was in a hurry. Come on!

"Billy?"

He didn't answer.

"You there, Billy?"

The lights were on. The TV was on.

"I'm over here, Artie," Billy said, getting up from the floor and standing and yawning. "I didn't hear you come in. The TV was too loud. I was watching the news."

On the screen was a picture of the suicide bombers in London; the youngest had been only eighteen. On the floor where Billy had been sitting was the framed picture of my father, which I kept on my desk.

"Did you eat?"

"I found some cookies and a piece of cheese," Billy said, sitting down again in front of the TV.

I sat next to him. "I need to talk to you."

Billy picked up the photograph of my father he had taken from my desk.

"What was he like?" Billy said.

"My dad?"

"Yes."

"You look a lot like him," I said. "You really do."

"Like you," he said. "We all look like each other," Billy said. "Like real family. Tell me some stuff about him, Artie. I want to know."

"Let's talk about that later," I said. "Tell me what's been going on."

Billy's attention slipped away. He turned towards the TV.

"Can I just finish watching this?" he said. "Is that OK?" He leaned his head against my shoulder briefly, then, as if embarrassed, pulled his knees up under him and rested his chin on them, gazing at the television. I didn't mention the scratches on the front door. I couldn't find a way to tell him we had to leave New York.

Sitting with his back to my old couch, surrounded by his books and some newspapers and photographs, a couple of empty Soda cans and an empty package of Malomars, a box of Ritz crackers, a plate with cheese rinds, he looked as if he had made a nest for himself.

I couldn't tell him and I couldn't tell anyone else, except his parents, and I wasn't even sure about them. Johnny Farone was a good sweet man who loved his kid, no question, but the Farone family was tied up with the Shanks and maybe, through them, with Al Laporello on Staten Island.

I got up and turned out the lights except for a lamp on the table beside the couch, and sat down again.

"Why did you do that?"

"Easier to watch TV," I said.

Truth was I felt it made us less of a target, my lights being off. Crazy stuff was running through my head as I listened for unfamiliar noises in the building. With the movie people in the street yelling to each other and their generators grinding, it was hard to tell where sounds came from.

I felt trapped. The building seemed surrounded. My paranoia made me hot. Sooner or later, I'd have to get us out. At least we were together, Billy and me.

Inside the building all I heard was the bass turned up loud on some crap heavy metal music from downstairs, and a dog somewhere, and the clank of an air conditioner and a toilet running.

Billy put on a sports show, a gabfest, a bunch of ex-athletes dishing about current players taking steroids. I got up again, and wandered into the other room. The place I loved felt like a prison.

It was the only place I had ever owned in my life. Before it, before I saved up the down payment, I had lived in rentals around Chinatown, and one in Brooklyn. When I was growing up in Moscow, we lived in a cramped two-room apartment near the Arbat. We were lucky: it was central and it had a bathroom, but it wasn't ours.

So who owned your family apartment in Moscow, a friend once asked, which made me laugh. No one, I'd say. The State owned it, I'd say to uncomprehending friends. It didn't matter. The whole Commie enterprise had disappeared. It was off the map. All gone. Communism was a theme park for tourists: in Beijing people bought painted statuettes of Mao and his wife drinking tea; in Germany, people lined up for vintage clothing and furniture made by old East German companies; revolutionary posters from Cuba or the USSR sold at auction for big bucks. I went to the kitchen and got some Percoset.

"Artie?"

In the living room I sat down next to Billy again.

"What's going to happen?" he said.

"It'll be OK."

"Don't leave me again."

"I won't. Maybe I shouldn't have brought you here, there's always some shit going down in my life," I said to him. "It's nothing to do with you," I added, but he knew I was lying. "Did anything happen while I was out?"

"That guy, Mr Rizzi, he must have been up here three times, and he kept calling. As soon as he went out, he called, and it was nice, but it was like driving me crazy, so I said I was fine and I'd just call him to check in, then he said he had to go home, and I said it was fine. I didn't know why he was so worried, but he left his phone behind and these things. I tried to get to him, but his place was locked up." Billy held up Mike's phone and some crumpled latex gloves, the kind Mike wore when he dished up food.

"What else?"

"I so don't want to go back to my mom and dad. I want to be with you and I know there's no room for me when Maxine comes home with her daughters," said Billy, sounding desperate. "What am I going to do? I don't want to be a baby about it, but where will I go?"

"Tell me what's been going on."

He got up and wandered around the room.

"Come sit with me," I said.

Billy sat on the edge of the couch.

"There were like phone calls," he said. "You told me to write everything down. That was right wasn't it?"

"Yes."

"Lily called and that was like so nice, I really like her a lot, and we talked about some of the books she gave me, and it was so cool just being on the phone with her, and we talked about stuff."

"What kind of stuff?"

"Lily said she would come over if I wanted."

"What else did you talk about?"

"You," he said. "We just talked about how great you are, and stuff. And also Mr Sverdloff."

"Tolya called?"

"Yes."

"Did he say where they were?"

"He said they were back in the city from East Hampton, and he made me say hello in Russian to Luda, the little girl," said Billy. "She really talks a lot."

"You don't like her?"

"I do like her. I told you I liked her, I just feel kind of impatient some of the time, I so try not to, Artie, but when she says oh, where's Artemy, where is he, I want to see him, blah blah blah, and I felt bad I couldn't tell her. I couldn't help her. Also, speaking Russian to her makes me feel kind of dumb because she can talk it better than me, and she's only a little kid, so I get jealous of how good she is. Am I stupid or what?"

"Well she doesn't speak any English, so you're kind of even," I said. "What else?"

"Some old guy called. Sounded old. Called and knew my name, and said I should go away forever and never come back, that no one wanted me because I was a sicko, that's what he said, go away, and it scared me, how he knew who I was."

"He used your name?"

He nodded. "Both names. He said Billy Farone."

"Why didn't you call me?"

"I was getting ready to when you came home. I'm glad you're home."

"Anything else?"

"Somebody buzzed downstairs, and I answered and there was no one. I just sat here."

"I'm sorry."

"Artie?"

"What?"

"Please, please don't make me go home to my parents."

I wondered if Billy had somehow blocked it out that he had to go back to Florida in ten days.

"You want to say why you hate it so much at home?"

"I don't feel happy there," said Billy. "No one is happy there. My dad is so fat and he falls asleep at the table with his mouth hanging open, and he keeps watching me all the time. I know he loves me but it's too much, it's like he has to love me to make up for the fact other people think I'm a freak, and then his crazy mom comes by and brings this stupid priest to talk to me, and I heard someone talking about exorcists.

"Did you know they teach exorcism at the Vatican college, I mean, it's like the Middle Ages, and all I want is for them to leave me alone so I can read and maybe feed my fish or something, and my mother, I mean she loves me and all, but she can't stand my dad. She never says she feels, like, grateful, which is sort of worse." Billy flapped his arms as if he was trying to find a place to put them. Then he crossed them over his chest. "Listen, I know I have to go back to Florida, but I still have ten more days, and I just want to be with you. Artie?"

"What's that?"

"It's about my dad, about Johnny, and I don't know if I should ask you."

"Go on."

"Just a feeling," Billy said. "I met this friend of my mom's a couple of times, and I saw how he was looking at me, and he brought me books. I heard my mom on the phone whispering to him once. People think kids don't know, they think they're being such good parents, like they go in another room to talk about the kids and stuff, and of course even little kids know what's going on and I'm fourteen."

"What are you saying?"

"I think this other guy might be my real father," said Billy, voice uncertain, as if he didn't know it was OK even to ask.

"Do you know his name?"

"I think it's Mr Zeitsev. Please tell me. I have to know."

"You have to ask your mom. The thing is, Johnny loves you and to him you are his son."

"That's not an answer."

"I'm not sure," I said.

"You think Johnny knows?"

"I don't know, Billy. Listen, I have to tell you something. You want me to be straight with you, right? You said that before, right?"

"Yes," Billy said, but again he wandered aimlessly around the apartment, glancing out of the window, as if he didn't want to hear the truth.

"I have to take you back to Florida early." I said it as fast as I could, like ripping a Band-Aid, and I could see the shock on his face. Then I was sorry I'd told him. I wished I'd just taken him to the airport and made him get on the plane with me.

Billy turned away from me.

"Billy?"

For a while he was silent, his back to me, and I knew he was crying. I didn't know what to do. I was scared as hell even to take him out of my building. I couldn't protect him and there was no one else.

"I know they think you're a great kid and you'll probably get out much sooner than you think, and maybe we can fix something, maybe then you can come back and live with us, I mean me and Maxine and the girls, I know they'd like it, we could fix something like that."

He turned to me, eyes dry now, and said, "Please don't lie to me, Artie."

"I mean it."

"Yes, I understand."

"I'm telling you how it is. I'm treating you like you said you wanted, like a grown-up."

"It doesn't matter."

"It does to me. It matters a whole lot to me."

"How early?" he said.

"What?"

"When do we have to go?"

"Soon. I'm sorry." I couldn't stand telling him how soon, not yet.

"There's just one thing."

"Anything."

"Promise?"

I hesitated. I had to keep whatever promise I made.

"Yeah, I promise."

Billy smiled at me. "Can we have one more day together? Is that crazy?"

"What do you mean?"

"Tomorrow. Can we go fishing like we planned and make a picnic and just like hang? The weather forecast says it's going to be really nice, and it's Saturday, can we do that? I wish we could have just one day."

"We'll do that, we'll have a great day together, we will. Let's get everything ready, then you should get some sleep."

I was on my knees in the closet in my room, digging under magazines coated with dust, an old bicycle pump, fossilized winter boots, stiff with ancient frost, and some weights I had never used and probably never would, but I couldn't find the fishing stuff and right then the phone rang and it was Lippert.

I crawled out of the closet, listening to Lippert's shaking voice. We found another baby, he said. Dead. In another freezer. Real, he said. A real infant.

Dead?

He said yeah, it was dead.

I told Billy I had to go out for a while. I told him to go to sleep in my room. It faced the back of the building. No one could see in from the street. You couldn't see much anyhow because my place was on the fourth floor, but it made me feel better. It was quieter in back I said softly to Billy, who didn't argue. I could see he was scared and trying to hide it. I said I'd be back soon.

When he was in bed, I sat with him for a while until he fell asleep, then I locked the windows, and took my gun, and did something I hated doing: I took the keys I'd given Billy out of his jacket and locked him in. I didn't want him going out in case Shank or one of his goons was watching my place.

By the time I got to the ground floor, I could hear the sirens. My throat was dry; trying to get it clear I coughed, but it didn't help. I made my way past the film crew and knocked against a table piled with candy bars that flew off into the gutter.

I remembered Billy's cell phone when I was already on the street. I was afraid to go back, afraid to wake up Billy. I'd have to get it later, but I wanted the phone bad because it might show me who had been following us, not just Shank but his cronies. Sammy Britz had reported Shank told him Billy was never without the phone, always taking pictures with it.

26

It was the size of the body bag that was so horrible. One of the cops on the scene said the rash of child crime around the country meant manufacturers had stepped up production, turning out pint-size black body bags that you could use for children, or for certain other kinds of remains; I didn't ask what.

As bad as the little body bags, and what gave me a chill on this dank humid evening, was the fact that the baby was found in Mike Rizzi's freezer out back of his coffee shop, in the alleyway where he had constructed a makeshift shed.

The rain was letting up. I was standing near the curb, watching a cop holding the body bag when I spotted Sonny Lippert. He was talking to Bingo, the homeless guy who worked my block. I went over to them. Bingo told me that he'd found the baby. He'd told the story to other cops and to Sonny Lippert, but he wanted to tell me.

There were cops everywhere, some trying to shut down the movie set where crew people were whining about the loss of time. Others were putting up orange cones with yellow tape slung between them to secure the scene. Bystanders gawked.

A woman picked up her rat-like dog in her arms, as if the dog was in danger. There were a lot of those tiny dogs around these days and women carried them like expensive handbags.

"What time?" I said to Lippert.

"Tell him," he said to Bingo.

"Around an hour ago, man," he said. "I guess. Don't got my Patek Philippe on me tonight."

"He's OK," I said to Lippert. "I know Bingo. Is she dead?"

"Looked dead to me, God rest her," Bingo said. "I was there when they broke the lock on that there freezer."

It was a fluke that he had found her. Bingo was a black guy who always said he named himself for *Bingo Long and the All Stars*, which was his favorite movie. He was a regular on the block. He was a drunk, but he was cheerful. He carried your groceries before he asked you for a buck. Told me he had played the sax long time ago, and he announced to tourists that he was not just a panhandler but was soliciting contributions to the "United Negro Pastrami Fund".

Mike Rizzi gave Bingo food and people gave him money and whenever he disappeared for a while, a couple of older ladies who lived in my building worried about him. One of them had asked if he needed a place to stay once, but he said he had a room with an aunt somewhere in Jersey. "I just like to drink," Bingo always said.

He wasn't drunk now. He led me a couple of steps to the alley and Lippert went with us. I pushed my way into the narrow space. Six of us were crammed in, Bingo, Lippert, me, two cops, someone from the Medical Examiner's office.

Bingo had come into the alley here, he said, like he sometimes did when it rained. The tin shed protected you from the rain, and you could climb up on the humpback old-fashioned freezer and catch forty winks, or smoke, or do the crossword puzzle.

He said he had heard the baby cry, or thought he did, or

maybe he thought it after he saw her. Soon as he did, Bingo started yelling like crazy until a cop showed up and broke the lock on the freezer.

Maybe it was a premonition. When the cop opened the freezer, Bingo told me, underneath the boxes of pies and the plastic-wrapped lumps of meat, was the frozen baby girl, wrapped in a pink blanket and a sheet of tin foil. The face was visible.

I said to Sonny, "Where's the baby now?"

"They're taking her to the hospital, man, but she's dead."

I pushed my way through the crowd in the alley and made it to the ambulance that was getting ready to drive off. I pestered the driver. I had to see. Later I was sorry I had looked.

The baby was tiny, very wrinkled, like an old woman, one of those ancient people they sometimes found in an arctic wasteland. I couldn't look at her, couldn't look away.

I went back to the alley and said to Lippert, "You think she was already dead, you think Bingo only thought he heard her?"

"I don't know," Sonny Lippert said.

"No, man," Bingo said. "I heard her. You wouldn't last long in the fucking deep freeze, would you? But I heard her cry."

Rizzi kept blueberries for his pies in the freezer, along with other reserves, a side of bacon, frozen pancake mix he got suckered into buying wholesale. I didn't know how often Rizzi used any of it. On a hot summer day once, I found him out there sitting on the freezer having a smoke.

The wall where I was leaning was damp. I could feel the heat from the others, smell Lippert's breath, hear my own heart pumping adrenalin, and taste the horror that hung in the alley.

Someone from the ME's office came over and told Sonny Lippert the baby had not been frozen long, far as he could tell. It was possible that Bingo had heard some kind of noise, but maybe it was only been the thump and grind of the elderly freezer.

"You're saying it's really possible she was alive when some bastard stuck her in there?" Lippert asked.

"I don't know," he said, and then someone pushed me out of the way back into the street while two other cops went in.

I got a cigarette out of my pocket and called Mike Rizzi. He was already on his way.

Lippert was holding two phones in one hand, and had another clipped to his belt. Around us the crowd of officials grew bigger.

"You want to talk, Artie, man? You want me to help you?" Lippert's voice was soft, almost gentle. His raincoat hung open over the green shorts I'd seen him in earlier and his bare feet were stuck in a pair of loafers, same expensive loafers he'd worn on the beach in Coney Island, little loafers, small as a boy's.

"Help me with what?"

I didn't want to talk. I wanted to go back to Billy, I was on the street a block and a half away from my loft where a dead baby girl had been carted off in an ambulance. The area was crawling with law enforcement.

My neighborhood, my turf, the place I had lived for twelve, almost thirteen years, where I knew everyone and where I belonged. Being here had made me feel like a New Yorker instead of an immigrant.

I was a sucker for community and I went to block meetings, dragged friends to street fairs where we ate greasy calzone to raise money to plant trees and other shit. I complained when local shops shut down and Starbucks opened up. The Englishman with dreadlocks at the bike store on Lafayette, best bike store in town, checked my bike for free because I liked making bike talk, and he didn't get that many cops, and the Korean dry cleaners I used were as courteous as some ancient noble clan.

Some of the time I drank at a little bar a few blocks away where a furious bartender thought he should be a film director. And there was Mike Rizzi, of course, and his pies. It was the life in this piece of lower Manhattan that kept me sane.

The image of the tiny, nut-like, frozen face of the baby girl stayed in front of my eyes; it looked less real than the face on one of the dolls.

"Where did the baby come from?" I said to Lippert. "You're thinking Shank, right, but where did he get her?"

"They're checking hospitals, orphanages, daycare centers, also anyone who called in a baby that got snatched. People still leave babies alone and then they say, I only turned my head for one second. Fucking people," said Lippert. "Come on, man, let's get away from this, there's plenty of people on it, nothing you can do, let's sit down somewhere. You want to go up to your place?"

There was a Chinese take-out on the corner that stayed open late.

"We can sit there," I said. "I want to stay around until Mike Rizzi gets here."

"Who?"

"Mike Rizzi, you met him, the guy that owns the coffee shop. He's a friend."

"You always got friends, Artie, you always got a lot of friends, maybe too many," Lippert said, but this time he wasn't sarcastic. Usually, he meant I was a sucker for people who were nice to me, but not this time. He took my arm.

"I feel for you, man. Listen, your friend who owns the coffee shop, Rizzi, tell him to get a good lawyer. His prints will be all over the freezer."

"Mike's a good guy."

"Probably he is, but he'll need someone. Let's sit down," Lippert said and we went into the take-out.

Inside under fluorescent lighting was a single table. We sat. Behind the counter, a Chinese guy slept, his head against the wall.

There were no customers, only Sonny and me, sitting with a couple sodas in front of us. From where we sat we could watch the street, people moving up and back, cop cars parked everywhere, lights flashing, people hanging out of their loft windows, dog walkers stopping. I tried not to think about the baby's face before they zipped up the bag, but it was all I could see.

"You think there's really a chance the baby was alive, Sonny?"

He looked down at his soda can, then up at me. "Probably not," he said. "Probably not, man. You seem restless."

"I'm tired," I said. "I'm really tired, Sonny. Maybe I'll go home."

"I'm sorry about Billy, but you knew he had to go back to Florida, right? You knew it wasn't good, him being with you, didn't you, Artie?"

I didn't answer.

"You think it was always like this, the way things happen with kids, man?" said Sonny. "I don't remember anymore. I don't remember so much shit from when I was a kid but maybe it was because no one ever talked about it, they kept it in the family when someone whipped a kid and almost killed him, because it was OK to hit children. You read Dickens, like I told you to?"

"Yes."

"How come people treat children like garbage, man? I don't get it. They kill themselves to get one, and then they get divorced and they use the kid like a fucking domestic football," said Sonny. "It's like the whole fucking society went nuclear, boom, and the fallout is the little kids who are just trash. Garbage. I don't know." He leaned over the Formica table.

"Artie, man, I have to ask you this. You know the poor bastard got kicked to death in Chinatown?"

"What?" I was surprised he wasn't asking about the baby.

"Maybe you didn't hear, a guy kicked to death, lay bleeding in Chinatown?"

"Maybe I heard something on the news," I said.

"He was a kid, fourteen maybe, small for his age. You want to tell me exactly where Billy was during that time?"

"With me."

"All the time?"

I didn't say anything. We sat for a while in silence, and I could hear everything out of sync, my heart, my watch, the snores of the Chinese guy behind the counter who was still asleep. From outside came the insistent sound of a car alarm.

"Artie, you and me, we go way back now," said Sonny. "I helped you all I could with Billy after we found him with Heshey Shank out in Breezy Point, right, I helped you fix it so he went to Florida instead of Spofford or some other fucking terrifying juvie place. It was us, me, you, poor dead Sid McKay, we made deals with the prosecutors and Sid manipulated the media so the way the story came out the kid was practically a hero. Billy the Kid, wasn't that what they called him? Said he was kidnapped and defended himself?" Sonny stopped.

"I don't know why the fuck they let him out even for a few weeks, but they did, and I don't want you in this again," he added.

"Yeah, so you say."

"Artie, for God's sake. They're bringing kids up on adult charges at eleven, twelve. You know how many kids under fifteen, sixteen are doing life in prison in this country? I'm not saying it's right, but that's where we're at, kids who don't get a decent lawyer or say whatever the prosecutor wants, and they go away for fucking life and people say you're lucky it wasn't the death penalty, kiddo. We kept Billy out of all of that. So you take him back to Florida because it's the best deal he ever got in his life."

"Go on."

"I think you're fucked up about him. You're in denial. I was pretty fucking surprised when I saw you on the beach with him Tuesday."

"Yeah, you sure let him know."

"Artie, for chrissake, get real. The boy killed a man."

"I'm taking him back to Florida, but it's to keep him safe from Shank."

"Whatever. Tomorrow night I'm going to call the facility, you hear? Make sure he's in Florida." Lippert's eyes glazed over some and I could see he'd had a couple of drinks before he came out. "Artie, I'm asking you, stay away from the Farone boy. I know you're attached."

"He was twelve years old when it happened, Sonny."

"He was plenty smart. He pulled off something a grown-up couldn't have done. He was smart and he was bad."

"He's better."

"Yeah, and Heshey Shank is still dead. Look, man, it was me helped you fix it all up so Billy didn't get a needle in his arm, it was me talked to the judge and got him adjudicated to the place in Florida," said Sonny. "I did that for you. But it doesn't mean I think he's a saint suddenly. It doesn't mean I don't think he's capable of some other shit."

"Maybe they let him out because he is better. He's a kid, kids change. Maybe he was sick. Maybe he didn't do what we thought."

"You're dreaming, man, you are. You want me to spell it out for you?"

I got up. "I have to go."

"You're in fucking denial, man. If I hear one single thing about that boy that makes me suspicious I'm going to be in touch with the facility in Florida, or if I don't hear he's heading back on time, I'm also calling. So do me a favor, take the boy to his parents and then take him back to Florida."

I lied. "Yeah," I said. "Yeah. OK, I'll do that."

"I have to ask you. You don't have to answer me, man," he said, "but you have to think about it. What Billy has, whatever his craziness is, I've seen kids a lot like him sometimes get threatened if someone gets in their way. There anyone around who gets attention from you when he's around?" Sonny got up. "I have to go, but think about if there's anyone Billy could see as competition."

"It has all the marks of something Shank would do," I said to Sonny when we were out on the street. "He told me he sells bootleg dolls, his prints were on at least one of the dolls in the warehouse in Chinatown. You have it all wrong, Sonny. He's trying to set Billy up; he wants him dead or locked up for good. He does this religious thing about not hurting Billy because he's a Christian, and the truth is he never gave a rat's ass for Heshey, but it gives him someplace to put his rage."

"What about May Luca, and now the little girl, Ruthie Kelly, who was killed over in Jersey, you're saying Shank did that, too?" said Sonny.

"Why the hell not? He's an animal. Him and old man Farone liked little girls, maybe a little girl got to talking about how the old men felt them up or maybe raped them."

"OK, so we get Shank for the dolls, and maybe even for Ruthie, Kelly and May Luca, so for argument's fucking sake, let's say I like him for that, and so does the DNA. What about this? What about the baby girl in the freezer?"

"You don't think Shank could do it? I have to go," I said.

Sonny got hold of my sleeve.

"Listen to me. Maybe you forgot that Billy Farone made that poor retarded Heshey Shank, a guy that wouldn't hurt a flea,

run away with him," said Sonny. "You recall? You want me to
go into the details, how Billy fixed it all up, how he organized
it, how he highjacked Heshey, or kidnapped him, whatever
you want to call it, and left a trail making us believe it was the
other way around, that Heshey abducted Billy? How he put
everyone on the wrong track, namely you, Artie, man. And
then he took Shank out to Breezy Point and carved him up.
Slow. You remember? Carved little pieces out of him, hung
fishing nets around him, and left him to die, and it took what,
two days for Shank to die like that, tangled up in nets. Billy
sitting right nearby. You remember we found him sitting there
like nothing at all happened?"

I didn't answer him.

"One more thing, Artie, man."

"What's that?"

"I had Stan Shank picked up earlier today."

27

In my loft, Billy was still asleep. I closed the bedroom door, went into the kitchen and put on a single light so I wouldn't wake him. It was one in the morning. Outside in the street, I heard news crews arrive, greedy for the story of the dead baby in a freezer they could get on the early morning shows if they hustled. I drank some Scotch from the bottle. Tried to flush the image of the baby out of my head.

No exact time had been attached to the baby's death, not yet. Even if Shank had been picked up, maybe he had killed the baby first. It wasn't impossible, and there were always Shank's pals. The little baby in the freezer would have been a great way to set Billy up. Shank would have known.

Billy's duffel bag was near the front door, his jacket hanging over it. I rummaged around in it. I couldn't find his phone.

I went into the bedroom and without waking him found the phone on the floor. I picked it up and went back to the kitchen. I needed another drink before I looked at the pictures. Didn't know what I was going to find. Didn't want to find anything.

It took me a couple of minutes to get the hang of it, but it was easy even by my technologically crappy standards. I found the stored images.

There were pictures of Stan Shank in the maroon Town car that Billy had probably taken when Shank was following us. There were pictures of the Farone house, including Billy's empty room and his empty fish tank. Pictures of people out on Staten Island, the Provones, Vera Gorbachev, even the young cop reading a comic book outside Gorbachev's house.

Everywhere Billy had been he had taken pictures, and he had saved them carefully as if he was building up some kind of archive of his time in New York.

There were no pictures from Florida, none of the school, or his grandfather, no friends, nothing. Maybe he had erased it from his mind. I found another picture. It looked like it had somehow been taken underwater, a fisheye view of the water and fish. I didn't know if you could use a camera phone under water.

I tried to make some connection between the pictures but there wasn't any, except a lot of them were of me. I hadn't noticed Billy taking the pictures.

There were pictures of the party at the toy store, and my stomach turned over at what I saw in one of them. I started looking for my car keys.

The phone rang. I found my keys and I was out of the building and in my car in seconds, not stopping for a cop, not stopping for traffic lights, my head killing me, from noise, from Percoset, from things I had seen and didn't want to think about. I made it over to Tolya Sverdloff's place in five minutes flat. Lily was already there.

"Where's Luda?" I said before I was all the way through the door and all I could see were Valentina and Lily sitting together on a red leather sofa holding glasses, and looking like they'd already had plenty to drink.

Val had a bottle of rum clutched in one hand. Lily was holding her other hand, and whispering to her like she was a little girl. Val's face was wet. In spite of everything, or because of it, I was out of my mind glad to see Lily.

The TV was on, local news already showing a reporter near the alleyway where the baby was found.

Staring at the TV, Val sucked some rum straight out of the bottle, and I could see the picture of a pirate on the label when she put it to her lips.

She placed it on the floor, picked at her hair, and twisted a piece of it around her finger, then plucked out a single strand. The skin on her face was tight and the circles under her eyes were purple with fatigue and wet from crying. She kept hold of Lily's hands as if she'd sink without the support.

Tolya, who leaned over the back of the couch as if to protect the two women, talked into a phone, his voice furious.

"How did you know?" he said to me. "You saw it on TV? I was trying to get you."

"Know what?"

"About Luda."

"I just felt worried about her," I said. "I don't know anything. What should I know?"

"She's gone," Lily said. "Tolya called me, and I got here as soon as I could. She's just gone. We left you messages. We called and Billy answered, and we told him. Didn't he tell you?"

"He said he talked to Luda."

"That was earlier," Lily said. "Much earlier. We called again. I told him, please tell Artie to call. I said it was urgent."

"How gone?" I said. "Tolya? What's going on? I need you to tell me what happened." I was talking in Russian very fast, but Tolya didn't even look at me, just waved his hand in my direction to tell me to shut up while he was on the phone.

"My dad's got a bunch of his guys on it, he says he doesn't trust the cops, it's no different from Russia," Val said.

"What else?"

"I didn't bring Luda into the country with all the right papers. You won't report that will you?" Val's beautiful face was pinched with fear.

"Don't be ridiculous." I put my arms around her. "What would I report, anyway? You're American."

"But Luda isn't." said Val. "I got sick of waiting, I mean Luda's ten, she was nine then, and she was so excited. I took her to the US embassy in Moscow and they wanted to know about her family and I said she was pretty much an orphan and they asked her all these stupid questions, and finally I lost my cool and I said, what the fuck kind of terrorist did they think Luda was? It didn't really go down well and they more or less told me they'd never give her a visa. I pulled some strings. I asked daddy to spend some money on it, I asked him to get some friends to smooth things out," Val said, and burst into tears.

"Oh, God, what did I do? It was a vacation, Artie." Val said. "I was bringing the kid here for a vacation, and all I got from the shitty US embassy in Moscow was some kind of runaround, so now I'm scared if we call the cops, they'll find her and just ship her back to some crappy orphanage in Russia. You should see what those places are like."

"You have to tell me where she's gone," I said.

Val got up suddenly and wandered around the living room. Wearing a long-sleeved T-shirt that came down to her knees, nothing else, her hair pulled back in a knot, she was on the verge of hysterics.

I put out my hand. She turned away. Lily followed her, and put her arm around Val. Val looked at her gratefully and kept talking, unable to stop.

"It was bad after the thing at the toy store. For Luda, I mean.

The baby dolls, you know, she had never seen anything like that, but what was worse for her were the dolls they made that looked like her. You remember? It made her cry, just the idea, and then later – I think you were outside smoking – she saw a row of them and they all looked like her, and she freaked."

"I remember," I said.

"We found out that Luda had a twin who was killed in some terrorist subway bombing in Moscow. When she saw the doll, she thought it was her sister. We also found out it was Billy who got her to pose and told the people at the toy store to make up the dolls."

"He probably didn't know," I said. "He probably just thought it would be fun for her. He liked her. He told me he likes her a lot and he feels for her."

Lily looked at me and didn't say anything.

"I didn't hear what Billy said to Luda," Val said. "But she calmed down, that was Wednesday, I guess, we got her calmed down and we went out to East Hampton and she was happier. Why isn't there anything on TV about Luda? Why don't they find her?"

I said, "Let me call Sonny Lippert. He knows everyone who works on child crime."

Tolya reached out and grabbed my arm, and said to me, "No!" and then into his phone, "Just do it," speaking in crude Russian.

He snapped the phone shut. He picked up a cigar that was burning in an ashtray and said to me in English, but with the hood's accent he used when he was angry or to mock me, "Is all shit. Policeman don't do nothing for Luda, who is also in their eyes illegal. How can little child be illegal? What that mean? Bastards," Tolya let out a stream of Russian curses.

"All they talk is terrorists, but they can't do anything. America," he snarled. "Wait until real disaster hits country that does not even believe in global warming, and there's refugees from floods inside this country."

"She's illegal, Tolya," I said. "I can help fix that if you let me. I know people who work immigration. Please, don't let your guys make a mistake; muscle isn't going to work here. Please."

"No. I find her."

"What happened?"

His body seemed to fold up; like a wounded animal, Tolya seemed to lose his bulk, his scale, vigor. He sank into a chair.

"We get back from East Hampton today, maybe late afternoon, early evening. Val goes out to do shopping, and then I hear Luda on phone and afterwards she is very quiet, calm, and asks me to make some food, says she's hungry, everything normal. Says she'll watch cartoons. I go into kitchen to make some food for her, and I come out, she's gone. Fucking gone, Artyom. Just walks out, or maybe someone kidnaps. Just gone."

"Will you let me help?"

Tolya said softly, "No, Artyom. Not this time."

"I'm sorry."

"Just go do what you have to do."

I took the stairs down from Tolya's. Steps clattered behind me. It was Lily, her sandals clacking on the concrete. On the second-floor landing, she caught up with me, put her arms around me and said, "Do you know anything about Luda? Artie?"

"No."

"I'll be there for you whatever," said Lily. "I mean that. I'm not running away from you anymore," she said. "But if you know anything, you have to help find Luda. She's already had a miserable life. Valentina is falling apart. She thinks it's her fault. Please, if you have to tell someone, tell me, and I'll go find her."

I leaned against Lily and for a minute it felt as if she was holding me up; maybe she was.

"I don't know where Luda is."

"Do you think Billy might know anything about it?" Lily said. "They talked a lot. You said he liked her."

"He did like her. Does like her. Sure, I'll talk to him, of course, but what could he have had to do with it?"

Lily made me sit down next to her on the stairs.

"I have to go."

"Sit with me for one minute. You have cigarettes?"

It had always seemed conspiratorial, the two of us smoking together away from other people, and I got out a pack and gave her one, and we sat without saying anything.

"Do you know that I dream about you a lot," Lily said.

I was pretty startled. "Me too."

"You do?"

I nodded.

Lily said, "I don't want you to hurt anyone. I just need us to see each other, or talk, even if we just talk, and I wanted to say that now, before you leave."

"Leave? Where am I going?"

"Do you want to tell me?"

"It'll be OK," I said. "I'm going to call Sonny Lippert about Luda. Tolya doesn't want that, but I have to. It's the only way."

"Wait a few hours," said Lily. "You promised him. How's Billy doing?"

"He'll be fine," I said. "You like him, you thought he was a good kid, right? Lily?"

"I didn't get to know him that well," she said. "I liked him, though. Yeah, I did."

I got up. "I have to go."

She followed me to the lobby, and kissed me, and said, "I love you, you know."

*

I didn't tell anyone where we were going, Billy and me. I couldn't tell Lily or Tolya or Sonny Lippert. I couldn't trust anyone until I got us both onto a plane and back to Florida. We'd get a flight out tonight. I'd keep my promise to Billy and take him fishing. It was what he would remember.

It was late, almost morning when I got home from Tolya's. I didn't have a chance to put Billy's phone back before he woke up. Maybe I didn't want to. I kept it in my jacket pocket.

He smiled dozily, and said, "Is it a nice day? Can we go fishing?"

"It's great. It's going to be a nice day," I said. "Good forecast," I added. "Come on, get dressed."

"I can't find my phone," said Billy.

"It'll turn up."

"I need it."

"I can get you another phone."

"I want my own cell phone," he said.

"Then go look around, but hurry up."

Five minutes later when he had searched the loft, Billy said, "I can't find it."

"We have to go."

"All right," he said, still unhappy. "OK. Where are we going?" Billy was in jeans and a T-shirt and now he pulled on a green sweater. I didn't know if he was furious about the cell phone or if he had accepted it. His face was blank.

"It'll be a surprise," I said. "Grab your stuff."

"What for?"

"We're going to spend the day fishing and we're going to stay over out on Staten Island together. I thought that would be nice, I know a place where we can stay."

"Wow," he said. "Oh, cool. Thanks. Do I still have to go back to Florida early?"

"We'll talk about it later."

I picked up a small carry-on where I'd put a few things that I figured I'd need in Florida – I wanted to go down and be back before Maxine got home Sunday – and I said we should be quiet leaving my loft because it was early and people were still sleeping.

Baseball cap on his head, his knapsack in his hand, Billy was near the door, standing almost to attention. Maybe he knew we weren't coming back. He smiled tentatively at me as if he was trying to respond correctly to the situation.

Billy learned fast, his teachers had said; an uncanny ability to learn whatever you showed him made him a terrific student. Once in a while, just for a split second now and then, I had wondered if he only imitated emotion.

Now, Billy looked at me, a blank look on his face as if he didn't recognize me for a second, and then he smiled as if it was something he put on and took off; perplexed, he seemed to be a tourist in his own emotions, looking for the right landmark.

The street was empty, though I could still hear the buzz from the next block over near the alleyway where the baby had been found. TV crews, I figured. And cops.

"What's up?" Billy said.

"Probably some junkie or a fight or something," I said, holding the car door. "Get in."

There was no traffic, and as the first light came up over the city, the blue light of a perfect summer day, I drove through the empty streets. Billy put his head against the back of the seat and smiled.

"So where's the mystery place?" he said.

"Staten Island," I said. "Isn't that where you wanted to go? Isn't it? You said that."

"Just us? We're not going to visit people?"

"Just us."

"Promise? I mean where will we stay and all?"

"Hank Provone has a house, way out opposite Jersey, he rents it out but there's no one in it now. He gave me the keys."

"How come?"

"Nothing, I just mean when I knew you'd want to fish. I thought it would be special."

Billy turned and got on his knees and reached into the back seat where he unzipped his suitcase and dug into the pocket for something. My phone rang. I didn't answer immediately, but it kept ringing and I saw it was Sonny Lippert's private number. I answered.

"What?"

"I might have some good news for you, man."

"Yeah?"

"It looks possible for Shank," Sonny said.

"What looks good?"

"It looks maybe possible he killed the little girl, Ruthie Kelly, who lived in Sheepshead Bay. Maybe May Luca too. We got some initial results."

"That's great. Great," I said, thinking: Shank was guilty. Shank had done it all.

"I mean possible, man. There're still a lot of things to consider, OK, so don't celebrate, you know? We got more tests to do, we need evidence, we can't get this to a Grand Jury yet. Hold your horses, man. Where are you?"

"I was asleep," I lied. "At home."

"Yeah, but not alone, right? You got that squirrely sound."

I hung up.

"Smile, Artie," said Billy returning to his seat with a little camera in his hands. He pointed it at me.

"What?"

"I'm taking your picture. I can't find my phone, but I have my camera. I want to keep some pictures of you. I want to remember," said Billy.

Part Five

Saturday July 9

28

And then we were alone. Just us. Me and Billy, very early Saturday morning going to Staten Island on the ferry. Billy had asked me if we could take the ferry instead of the bridge. I didn't like the idea because more people would see us, but it was early and probably OK and it was what Billy wanted.

The news on the car radio was still about London – the suicide bombers, the missing people, grieving parents and friends and children. I hadn't heard from Johnny Farone to say which flight he and Genia were getting. Saturday, he had said. It was Saturday now. Billy had stopped asking me about his parents.

Otherwise, he seemed fine. I didn't mention Luda's disappearance. There wasn't much I could do about it, and once word got out the whole city would go looking for her – she was a pretty little white girl with a sad story. I had called Sonny Lippert in spite of promising Tolya I wouldn't call. All that I could do was take care of Billy now.

I drove onto the ferry. The rain was over, clouds gone. The sun coming up was reflected orange and gold in skyscraper windows. Not so long ago a Staten Island ferry captain had gone AWOL and his boat crashed and people were smashed up, maimed, killed. Today, the scene was benign, gilded, beautiful.

"Let's go out," said Billy, so we left the car, bought some coffee and walked up to the top deck.

Leaning against the railing, we watched the city recede, the skyline, the Statue of Liberty, the slight dark blue chop on the water, the clear sky. The air was soft.

For a while we stood like that, not talking, Billy working his way through a couple of donuts he had taken from my place, his upper lip smeared with chocolate. The coffee in my hand was warm, and from time to time, Billy passed me pieces of donut, and I popped them in my mouth and made faces because the frosting was too sweet for me; it made Billy laugh.

"You OK?"

"I'm so good." Billy was perched on a bench, looking out at the city, as it grew smaller. "It's so incredible. New York is the most awesome place in the world, isn't it, Artie?"

I told him I thought it definitely was and then he was silent, and I drank my coffee. I looked at my cell phone to see if there were any messages.

"It's pretty early for people to call," said Billy.

"I was thinking maybe your parents," I said. It was a lie.

I didn't want Billy knowing I'd put in a call to Andy Swiller, the doctor I met when I picked him up in Florida. I'd liked Swiller and trusted him as much as you could trust anyone who locked up kids.

Maybe Sonny was right and I was in denial about Billy. Anyway, I didn't tell him I made reservations on a flight to Florida for that night. Only way to keep Billy safe, I kept thinking. But who from? Far as I knew, Shank was locked up on Riker's.

In my pocket I had the keys to Hank's rental property over by Fresh Kills. It would be empty for a couple of weeks, Hank had said. A beach was close by, some creeks too, where you could fish, a small boat tied up to the dock out back of the house. A quiet street, Hank had said. Not many neighbors.

I looked over at Billy who was tossing donut crumbs into the water. Maybe he could see fish below the surface.

Tuesday, four days earlier, we'd been on the beach at Coney Island. Went over to Brighton Beach where we had supper and walked around, then I had dropped Billy at the Farones' house where I left him for a while when I met Sonny Lippert.

What time had Stan Shank started following us in his maroon car? What time did I leave Billy at his parents' house that night, what time did I get back there and when did Shank call? How long was Billy alone?

I tried to work out where Shank had been when the boy on a skateboard was murdered, beaten, slashed and left near a garbage can over in Midwood. Reported as a gang crime. What time did it happen? Was it dark already? Had it been dark when I got to the Farones' house?

I was pretty sure it had been dark, but I couldn't remember turning on the lights when I went into the house. Couldn't remember if Billy had put the outdoor lights on when he went for a swim. Maybe he swam in the dark. I remembered: there had been a light on. I had watched him from the kitchen window.

"Artie?"

"What?"

"I said your name twice and you didn't answer," said Billy.

"I was just drifting," I said. "Thinking."

"What about?"

"Nothing."

A sharp breeze whipped against the boat and against my face. I zipped up my jacket. Billy looked up at me from his seat on the ferry bench and smiled. He really was a handsome boy.

But what kind of knife did the Midwood gang use on the

little boy on the skateboard? Someone had beat him over the head, but there had been knife marks too.

The ferry maneuvered into position to move into the slip; the boat's wake frothed up like egg whites.

"Shouldn't we get the car now, Artie?" Billy said. "Isn't it time?

I followed Billy down the stairs to the lower deck. A few cars were in front of us. While the ferry bumped the last few yards to the slip, we leaned against the hood of my car and shared a cigarette. The boat thumped against the wood of the pier. I tossed the cigarette butt overboard into the scummy water.

Stuff that had happened over the last three or four days, kept running in my head, like your tongue working at food stuck between your teeth. Billy had denied he'd been out of the apartment Tuesday night while I was drinking champagne with Tolya.

Tuesday night. Swore he didn't go out, and Jorge, the doorman at Battery Park City had also said he didn't think Billy went out. Wasn't sure. Jorge had gone on a dinner break. There had been something in the apartment when I got back, though: the way magazines on a table near the front door seemed to have shifted; a different smell. The next morning Billy brought me orange juice, but now I recalled there hadn't been any juice in the fridge. I'd forgotten to buy it.

Did Billy go out? Did he pretend he was in all night when he had really wandered over to Chinatown? But the boy in Chinatown kicked to death, that came later, didn't it?

Other gaps occurred to me. And the way Billy had begged for some time on his own. He wanted me to trust him so bad. Even Tolya had said the kid needed some freedom. There were the dolls. There was the frozen baby with the nut-like face. I didn't want to think about her.

Where the hell was Luda? I was afraid to ask Billy if he knew where she was. Afraid he would lie. Afraid he would tell the truth. Afraid, and this was the thing I really believed most, that Billy had nothing at all to do with any of it and, if I asked, he would resent me for the rest of his life.

I unlocked the car, Billy slid into the passenger seat and I got behind the wheel. I reached for the radio, but Billy put his hand on mine and said not to put it on, it was so peaceful without the noise, and then he popped the last piece of donut into my mouth, said he had been saving it for me. He crumpled up the donut bag, scrunching it into a tighter and tighter little ball, and tossed it from hand to hand, looking out of the window, humming, glancing at me, smiling, but restless.

"What's wrong?" I said.

"Nothing's wrong," he said. "Should I get out the map? Should I navigate? I brought the map."

"Sure."

Billy looked at the map he got out of his knapsack while I drove through the little town of St George.

"What's the address?" said Billy.

I told him. Intent on the map, he peered at it, tracing the roads with his finger, reciting the route first to himself, then to me.

"You find it?"

"I'm still looking," he said. "I have to make sure that we get the best route. Otherwise, we could meander around for a long time."

"Meander," I said. "I like that word."

I kept driving, past the rows of neat suburban houses, people still asleep inside except for one where an elderly man sat on the porch in his electric-blue pajamas, reading a newspaper.

Flags flapped in the breeze at strip malls, nail salons, Italian food joints. RV parks were filled with mobile homes.

In one park with a scabby baseball field, a lone boy hit balls listlessly.

I was lost again. Couldn't get the hang of the way the island worked. I pulled over to the side of the road, and peered over Billy's shoulder at the map he was reading. He told me where to go.

We drove. It was Saturday, nice weather, people hauling fishing poles up towards the boardwalk that ran parallel to the beach.

In a sort of campground just off the road were pickup trucks and vans that contained dogs, some of them in cages. A sign announced that it was Dog Day on Staten Island. A big trailer had a sign out front that advertised dog grooming. Kids in yellow T-shirts handed around samples of doggie treats to the dog owners. People sat on deckchairs in the camping ground, their dogs around them, and talked to other people surrounded by their dogs.

"What, Artie? You look weird," Billy said. "We're OK now, we're on the right road."

In the rear-view mirror, I saw a green Jaguar behind me. I kept driving steadily, not hitting the gas or looking over my shoulder. Then the Jag pulled up, passed. The driver, alone in the car, was a trim good-looking woman with prematurely white hair who wore a sun visor. On the seat next to her was a fancy white leather bag of golf clubs. "Dykes on spikes," someone had cracked about women golfers. Who was it? I couldn't remember.

Sure, Billy had been on his own for a while on Wednesday morning, the time I'd left him at Tolya Sverdloff's so I could take a run at Vera Gorbachev's case. Billy told me he'd left Tolya's to get ice cream. Mint chocolate chip. When I got home I found him in front of my building eating it. Told me he'd already eaten a Cherry Garcia cone from Ben and Jerry's and looked a little worried in case I said it was too much, the Cherry Garcia and the mint chocolate chip. Same thing that night after the party at the toy store. All he did was leave and go home to my loft. Billy was a city kid and he could get around. Knew the subways. Knew how to get a cab.

"Got it," Billy pointed to the map. "I found a really good way to get there."

"What?"

He tapped the map. "Make that right over there," he said.

"Billy, listen I have to tell you something."

"Sure. I know something's been bugging you. Go on."

"Luda's disappeared."

He put the map down and half turned towards me. "What do you mean, disappeared? I talked to her yesterday."

"I went over to Tolya's while you were asleep. She disappeared. She walked out of the apartment or someone took her, and she's gone. She's just gone. You know anything at all about it? She say anything to you?"

"No. Course not. I would have told you." Billy looked surprised and maybe a little hurt. "Course I would."

"You're sure?"

"Sure. I really liked her. I felt she was like a younger sister. Oh, shit, Artie, that really sucks," he said and I saw he was on the verge of tears. "We should go back to the city," said Billy. "We should go back and help them find her. Where are you going? That's not the right way at all."

We didn't go back. We kept going. I told Billy there was nothing we could do about Luda. I knew I was driving in circles but I didn't want to stop, didn't want to get to the house where we were going. I felt like I was losing my mind.

Up around the north-eastern edge of Staten Island I could see the Bayonne Bridge that linked it with New Jersey. In the car, Billy moved closer to me, for comfort or as a gesture of affection – I couldn't tell.

"You have any gum, Artie?" he said. "I need something, mints, gum, something, I'm really trying not to smoke, I mean if I keep smoking, by the time I'm your age, I'll have been smoking for like over thirty years. I'll be dead, and also second-hand smoke is shitty for other people, so I'm trying." He reached into the pocket of my jacket. "I used to think it was cool when I was a kid, but it's not cool."

I told him to get his hand out of my pocket and made it sound like I was kidding around when I pushed him away. It didn't take Billy ten seconds, though, to find his missing cell phone.

29

For a while, Billy just held his phone and stared at it and didn't say anything. I told him I was sorry; I said I'd found it and meant to give it to him but the words were hollow and we both knew it.

The image of the frozen baby in the freezer, buried between plastic bags of blueberries, came up from nowhere. I couldn't get rid of it no matter where I put my attention, the road, the scenery; like floaters, those strange spots that sometimes drift into your vision, and you can't get rid of, the baby stayed in front of my eyes.

Billy's silence unnerved me. He sat, body rigid, straining against the seat belt. He didn't ask me if he could drive, even though there weren't many cars on the road and usually, if the roads were empty, I let him. He didn't put his feet on the dashboard like he sometimes did. All I could see was his profile. He didn't look at me at all.

When I started to apologize again, he finally turned his head slightly, looked at me and made it clear he didn't want to talk. Unsure about the road I was on, I reached for the map and asked for his help. Billy passed the map over silently.

Taking the dolls out of the toy store would have been easy for Billy. Kids everywhere. Luda screaming. Parents arriving to take their children home. No big deal for Billy to take the dolls, leave the store, get a cab or take the subway.

For all I knew, he had stashed them at my place – under the bed even – that night before he put them in the fridge in the Chinatown warehouse, if that's what he did. His prints weren't on them, but so what? Then I thought about the latex gloves in my loft. Billy said Mike Rizzi had forgotten them.

Billy's expressionless face, rigid limbs, his refusing to talk, made me suspicious. The suspicions hit hard and made me feel cold.

"You're shivering," he said.

"I'm fine. Thanks. What about you?"

He shifted on the seat slightly, so that he half faced me while I drove.

"It's mine," said Billy "The cell phone is mine and I would have given it to you if you wanted, I'd give you anything of mine you wanted, but you just took it while I was asleep."

"You knew?"

"How could I not? It was there, and then it wasn't. No one else was in the loft."

"Why didn't you say something?"

"I think you're going the wrong way, Artie. Give me the map back, OK? I think you should turn left up at that corner."

"How come you didn't say anything about the phone if you knew I had it?"

"How come you didn't? I wanted you to say something. I wanted to trust you."

"I'm sorry."

"Me too. Did you look at the pictures I took with the phone?"

"Yes."

"Left, left and then right at the next corner. Artie, go left!"

"You want to talk about the pictures?"

"Not really," Billy said. "I'm just looking forward to our day together," he added formally, like an adult accepting an invitation. "Did we bring enough stuff? Do we need bait? Are we OK on everything?" He reached into the pocket of his jeans, got out his red Swiss Army knife and, one at a time, checked the blades.

"What are you doing?"

"I just wanted to check that everything's in OK shape," he said. "What did you think I was doing? Shipshape, isn't that the right expression?"

In the suburban streets now we passed a few kids out on skateboards and bikes. In driveways people climbed into their SUVs and vans and backed out, probably heading for the beach or the supermarket.

It was still very early, but it was Saturday. People out doing regular stuff, they looked like figures in a TV commercial, ordinary but unreal and apart from us, Billy and me.

I turned the radio on, and Billy hit the buttons for some country station he liked. I wanted news. He stopped me putting it on.

Was he afraid for me to hear it? I needed to know what was happening, needed to know about Luda, and when I saw a gas station, I pulled in. I didn't want Billy to hear the call.

I climbed out of the car and Billy followed.

"What did you talk about on the phone with Luda?" I said. "Remind me."

"I told you," said Billy. "You're getting old, Artie, you don't remember." He laughed amiably when he said it. The anger had gone. He punched me lightly on the arm. "You're the best," he said affectionately.

"So tell me again."

"I don't really remember that much. Luda was just like talking in Russian and I told her some funny jokes and stories,

I think. She kept saying I have to talk to Uncle Artie, I said you were out, so she started crying. I felt bad for her so I made nice."

"You want to get me some coffee," I said to Billy. "Get us some kind of snacks?"

"Sure, Artie."

Billy ambled toward the store attached to the gas station.

I called Sonny Lippert. The phone was busy. Tolya's phones were busy. I kept hitting the buttons on my phone. No one answered. Nothing.

Billy returned with cartons of coffee, and after we were back in the car, I said, "I feel so bad about Luda. Val wanted me to be her American godfather."

Sonny Lippert had asked me if there was anyone Billy could be jealous of, someone I cared about. I was testing Billy. If he was jealous of Luda, if he thought she had some kind of hold on me, maybe he'd open up.

"I know that," said Billy. "She told me. She says to me, oh, I love Artemy I want him to be my American godfather, and I said, wow, that'd be nice because then we'd be related too, her and me, in a way." Billy drank some of his coffee and got gum and candy out of his pocket. "I always wanted a little sister," he said. "So I got Juicy Fruit," he added. "I got spice drops. And some red Twizzlers. You want something? You can have all the white spice drops, if you want, I mean sour pineapple flavor, yuck, but I'd give you the reds, too."

Eager to please, Billy rubbed his eyes with one hand, and offered candy. I took some gum.

Near the Bayonne Bridge that connected Staten Island to New Jersey, oil terminals rose on the horizon. On the Jersey side was where the big container ships now docked, and Bayonne and the area around it had expanded – tough working-class towns.

The Kill Van Kull separated New Jersey and Staten Island,

and around here on the island were ramshackle houses, a few cheesy new condos, woods, creeks. For this part of Staten Island up in the north, you couldn't see the rest of the city at all. It made me feel I was a million miles from home. Kill Van Kull. Lots of Dutch names, I thought, drifting, tired from not sleeping.

"There's an island around here," Billy said, "with a bird sanctuary. We could go. I'd like that. What do you think? You think we could do that?"

"I don't think there's any boats anymore that go. I think those were from old times, those islands. Some of those islands were for quarantine, diseases, maybe smallpox, that kind of thing."

"Who would stop us?"

"So, about Luda, what do you think, I mean would you mind if I was like a sort of godfather for her?"

"Didn't we just talk about this? Sure," Billy said casually. "That's OK. I'm good with that, like I already said. It's fine."

Out of the corner of my eye I could see him, but he was relaxed, head back against the seat, feet on the dashboard, a kid having a good time. He ate the spice drops out of a bag, selecting the green ones first, placing them on his tongue, one at a time, and then swallowing.

"You're not chewing those things?"

"I'm chewing, I'm chewing." He laughed.

Why couldn't I just ask him straight out about Luda and everything else? But if I asked, I thought for the second time, it was the same as accusing him. I'd lose him. It was bad enough he didn't know I was taking him back to Florida that night.

For sure Billy had been at my loft when Luda walked out of Tolya's. Had I been there with him? I worked out the times again. There was no way he could have gone and snatched her, and anyhow, here he was sitting beside me. I breathed out. I looked for some cigarettes.

"Here." Billy handed me a pack.

Billy rolled down his window and leaned out.

"God, what's that smell," he said. "What is that? Fuck! I thought they closed the garbage dumps. Sorry, I'm not supposed to say fuck."

I opened my own window and took a whiff.

"It's methane," I said.

"Where are we?"

"Fresh Kills. That's what it's called. Used to be this was the city garbage dump," I said. "They covered it over with some kind of plastic, wrapped it up, put landfill on top, and dirt and stuff, so they could grow grass and trees."

"You're not wise in the ways of the wild, Artie, are you?" Billy was giggling. "I mean nature's not your thing."

"Yeah, well, they had to put in pipes so the gas from all that packed-in garbage could escape, otherwise the whole thing would just explode."

"Like boom!" Billy said. "Wow, that's weird, all that crap just festering away under the grass, getting ready to push up through some golf course. Totally, completely weird. Can we take a look? I could do a science report on it. Festering is a good word, right?"

"There's nothing to look at, unless you want to drive up to the old sanitation plant, I mean what for?"

"Can we?" Billy said. "I want to. Please?"

When we found the road that led to the sanitation plant, I stopped and we got out of the car.

After a few hundred feet, the road turned into dirt; there was a fence with a locked gate and a sign warning people to keep out. In the distance, you could see some of the chimneys from the old plants. The insidious stink of methane got to me.

I said, "Let's get out of here."

Billy had his face up against the gate, curious, interested.

"Come on."

"You want to fish, come on, let's get moving." I was irritated.

Billy dawdled some more. He looked through the fence, he bent down to examine some pebbles, he kicked an empty soda can with the toe of his sneaker.

He was halfway up the path to the old recycling plant. I got out my phone. The reception was lousy out here, but I got through to Tolya who told me Luda was still missing. He was furious I'd called the case in to Sonny Lippert. Told me there were now so many cops on the case Luda was good as dead. Tolya said when the cops came in on a kidnap, the kid always turned up dead. I told him he'd more or less said that already.

I listened while Tolya yelled at me in Russian. I told him Luda would turn up. I didn't believe my own words. He was angry and hurt because I didn't keep a promise. I hung up and saw that Billy was watching me; he didn't say anything, though.

Billy stuffed his hands in his pockets and sauntered slowly towards me, kicking the dirt, ambling around, behaving like a teenager. What bugged me was it felt Billy was putting it on. It was as if he had learned an act, to prove to me he was just a regular guy. I had a sour taste in my mouth.

Out here in Fresh Kills, I felt cut off. Nobody was around, only me and Billy, and him wandering around what used to be a garbage dump, the methane leaking, stinking up everything, getting in my throat and making me gag.

Watching Billy while I waited for him, I started thinking again. Stuff that I had discarded, things I'd pushed down pretty deep, pressed up.

On the road all morning, I had started trying to fit together the pieces. Started trying to account for Billy's time – days, hours. I let the poison in.

I got into the car and turned the radio to 1010; stories about the dead baby in the freezer were followed by news about the dead girl, Ruthie Kelly, who got killed in Jersey and had lived in Brooklyn.

Ten minutes later, Billy was still kicking stones around. He was Genia's son. My father was his grandfather. If I didn't take care of him, who would? I tried to keep myself focused on this. I got out of the car to get some air, but it didn't help.

At the toy store Wednesday night, Billy had scared Luda plenty. Somehow he knew seeing dolls that looked like her would shake her up good. Maybe he did it for the hell of it. Maybe it was his idea of a joke. He talked Russian to her, a nice American boy who talked to her in Russian, a good-looking boy who was almost family. Billy was my father's grandson.

It never ended, this Russian thing. Tolya had warned me over and over that it would never go away. It was part of who I was, my history, but I had refused to believe him until now.

I had made myself into an American, a New Yorker; I didn't have an accent. I buried the whole fucking past as best I could. But when I looked at Billy – he was poking around a grassy knoll near one of the methane pipes – I couldn't escape. I looked at Billy, I saw my father.

When I'd stopped being a little boy, I found out some of the things my father had done in the KGB. He never told me. I asked around. At home I overheard my mother in the other room yelling at my father. As a teenager, I tried hard not to like him. Tried not to love him. It didn't work.

He was my father and he remained tall and handsome and sweet and funny, the guy who brought me chocolate candies wrapped in gold paper and, later on, the jazz records you couldn't get in Moscow unless you had connections. My first Miles Davis. My first Stan Getz and Ella and Charlie Parker albums.

But my father was always a true believer. Those days, he still believed in socialism, in the system, in the greatness of the project. He told me about Yuri Gagarin, and Tupolev, and the USSR space program. About his own time as a very young guy still in his teens, fighting the Germans in the Great Patriotic War.

Some of the time, he asked me about school and friends and what I was reading; he knew I sneaked books that were more or less forbidden. My mother bought me black-market editions of paperbacks in English – westerns, mysteries, stuff like that. My father never yelled at me, he never threatened.

I had a friend at school named Mikhail – we called him Misha Three because there were three Mikhails, all of them Mishas to their friends – who came from a working-class family where the father was a factory worker, a real Stakhanavite who won prizes for productivity.

When Misha Three turned fourteen, he told his father he hated the USSR and he was going to defect, a fantasy that kept him going. His father said that if he tried, he would report Misha to the KGB. A year later, Misha went on a school trip to Poland and jumped out of the window of some crummy building in Warsaw. The father had to go get the body. My father wasn't like that. He never threatened.

There had been a day once when I played hooky and he found out. It was spring and a bunch of us just took off for the river.

My father was waiting for me when I got home. I must have been about twelve. We sat at the kitchen table, and I stared at the poster of Paris my mother kept taped to the wall, and my father made tea for both of us, and offered me a spoonful of cherry jam from the jar. My mother wasn't there; maybe she was working; maybe she was shopping, eternally hopeful she would find some French shoes.

What I remembered after all these years was the session

with my father at the kitchen table and how the tea got cold, and the jam congealed in it; drinking it anyway, I stuck my fingers in to reach the sodden lump of cherry jam at the bottom of the glass. Restless, my foot tapping against the linoleum on the kitchen floor, I held the tea. My father told me to sit still. I couldn't look at him and he told me my inability to look at him made me seem shifty.

He didn't sound angry. He was polite and soft-spoken that afternoon and only a little aloof, but there was a chill in his voice and his eyes. Right then I realized that it was probably the way he behaved during interrogations. I started sweating. By the time you were interrogated by a senior KGB officer, it meant you had done something bad; bad things would happen to you afterwards. Kids I knew whispered about it; people talked about the KGB, if they mentioned it at all, in hushed voices.

My father went on and on, asking me questions, gazing at me with those chilly blue eyes, until my mother came home and made him stop.

Later, when I was in New York and I became a cop, I discovered I was as good as my father with suspects. I had inherited not only the eyes, but some of his ability to make people talk. I hated that. I tried to lose it. In Billy, I could see him, my father; and myself.

Waiting for Billy near the garbage dump, I was hot and I pulled off my jacket, and threw it onto the back seat of my car. From across the dirt road, Billy was waving at me, and throwing pebbles, and fiddling with his red Swiss Army knife, and I called out to him to hurry up.

He took his time, then skipped over and climbed in the car. I got in. Billy straightened his T-shirt. He ran his hands through his hair, fastened his seat belt and locked the car door. It seemed to take forever.

I turned the key in the ignition, hit the gas, and by now Billy was changing the stations on the radio constantly, unable to settle on any of them, and I lost it.

I slammed on the brakes. I undid my seat belt, and turned to Billy and said in the same low hard tone I used with suspects, "Just stop playing games. I know you talked to Luda on the phone yesterday, I know you made her cry in the toy store, tell me what you talked about. Where is she?" I leaned into him, my face almost in his. He shrank away. He shuddered as if I were literally shaking him.

"You knew she was missing, didn't you, Billy?" I said. "It was something you said to her on the phone that made Luda walk out of the apartment, wasn't it? She's a little kid. She doesn't speak English. Now tell me where the fucking hell she is."

"I don't know," said Billy, holding back tears. "I swear to God, I don't know. She didn't say anything, but my Russian isn't that good, maybe I didn't understand. Maybe she didn't understand me. Don't. Please, Artie, don't yell at me. I didn't do anything. I know people think I'm bad, and I know I did something horrible once, but I promise. I didn't hurt Luda and I don't know where she is. I know everyone thinks I'm bad, but I'm not anymore. You have to believe me. Otherwise I feel I'm in some kind of horrible maze and I can't get out and no one can hear me."

30

Hank Provone's rental property turned out to be one of those double-wide mobile homes you didn't see that much around New York. I'd seen plenty of them out west when I went to Montana, but not in the city.

Still, it looked pretty solid, and it was set up on concrete blocks and newly painted, white with yellow around the windows. New gravel covered the little driveway, and there was a yard out back with some chairs and a table.

In front was a garden planted with yellow and white flowers, even a fountain with a stone mermaid, a drizzle of water coming out of her mouth. By now I was so edgy I felt like a guy walking a high wire, trying to balance in the middle while I figured out where to put my foot next.

As soon as I pulled into the little street and stopped on the gravel drive, Billy was out of the car, looking around.

The house opposite Hank's had a FOR RENT sign stuck in the front lawn. The house next door, where there was an overturned garbage can near the front door, looked shut up. You didn't get the feeling that there was anyone much around.

"The yard out back leads right down to the water," Billy

yelled. "It's so great. Come see, Artie, we could even fish right here, there's a little dock and everything. It's completely neat."

Carrying our bags out of the car, along with a sack of groceries I brought from home, I went into the house and set them down and picked up a few bills lying on the floor. When I opened the windows, the breeze that came in smelled a little bit salty. I put some food – bread, cheese, ham, fruit, eggs, milk, soda, beer – in the refrigerator and waited for Billy to come inside.

When I asked him in the car what he had said to Luda, he'd just looked at me like I was beating up on him. When he begged me to believe him, I'd felt like crying. I believed him. I had to. But once I had started thinking about Billy and Luda, I couldn't stop.

So now I waited inside the kitchen watching Billy through the window. Finally, I went out and sat on the front steps.

Without a word, Billy came back from the water, and went past me into the house where I followed him. He started fooling with the fishing gear and bait and other stuff. The way the light fell through the window, Billy was half in shade, leaning against a table with a blue bowl of wax fruit on it. He picked up a fake green apple.

"Tell me now," I said softly.

"I kind of don't think that Luda really understood what I said to her," said Billy. "My Russian isn't so hot, like I told you."

"Bullshit."

Billy, who seemed not to have heard me, said, "I'm so glad it's just us here, Artie, I really am. I wanted it to be just you and me, for us to have some time together, not anyone else."

"We've been together all week."

"I mean just us. All week there's been other people all the time. I wanted you to myself."

Had he manipulated me? Did he plan it, getting me to bring him out here, just us alone? It was crazy. All the kid wanted was my attention.

"I'm thirsty," he said.

"I put sodas in the fridge."

He went and got a can of Sprite, popped it and drank half of it in one gulp. Then he belched loud, and giggled.

"I'm sorry about that," he said. "It was so good. You want one?"

"I want to know about Luda."

"I felt sorry for her," Billy said. "I was with her that morning at your friend's, Mr Sverdloff's – Tolya, right? He said I should call him Tolya – and also at the toy store, and I felt bad, Artie. She didn't speak English. The girls who came to the party were horrible little New York girls. They were ten, but they were like little grown-ups, always posing and talking about clothes and stuff, and Luda had no idea how to join in and she seemed so like lonely, so I stuck around with her for a while, and I told her we could get some dolls made up that would keep her company. She asked me about America and I told her it could be really hard if you didn't speak the language, and if you were like foreign, and I said did she miss people back in Russia, and she started crying."

"She didn't want the dolls."

"Not at first. Later. You weren't there. I think you were on the sidewalk with Lily smoking or something."

"Go on."

"I tried to like make Luda feel better. I said it was OK if she wanted to go back to Russia. That's what she was asking me about on the phone yesterday, she wanted to know if she was safe here because she heard so much about terrorists maybe it wasn't any different from Russia. I said I could help her because she was probably illegal. I heard Valentina say, I thought I did anyway, or someone said, that Luda didn't really

310

have all her papers. I told her I'd help her. I said, I can help you. I wanted to. That's why I said it."

I was betting Billy had scared Luda bad. Maybe she walked out of the apartment to try to get home to Russia – I knew about children who left home intending to walk huge distances to some kind of perceived safety – or maybe to meet Billy. He had said he'd help her.

"Did you say you'd meet up with her? Is that why she left? Did you tell her you'd help her, which was nice, it was OK, nobody would blame you, but were you going to meet her?"

Billy shook her head. "I didn't say that. I promise. I just told her what I thought and said she could call me or whatever, and she said, what about Artemy? Will Artemy help me? Will he be there? I told her you would be there soon, and both of us, we would take care of her. Artie, I don't want to talk about this stuff anymore," said Billy. "Let's go out and at least look at the water. There's this dock down there. I'll carry your stuff for you, if you want."

"I'll follow you."

"Why?"

"I just will. Go ahead."

Looking over his shoulder, Billy went down the path. As soon as he was out of view, I was going to call Tolya.

My phone wasn't in my jeans or my jacket, not in my carry-on bag, or anywhere in the house. Not in the car either. I felt panicky, and went back in the house and picked up the phone on the kitchen counter. There was no dial tone. Maybe Hank hadn't reconnected it after the last tenants left.

I ran down the path to where Billy was standing at the edge of the water, flicking the fishing pole out as far as he could with a graceful gesture of his hand and wrist. He reeled in the line, took the fly at the end of it and examined it. It had bronze and bright red feathers.

"You have your phone?" I said.

He turned around, and looked at me. "I dropped it in the water," he said. "It was an accident."

"Where's my phone?"

He shrugged.

"I can't find my phone," I said. "Where is it?"

He looked at the water.

"You dropped mine, too? You threw my phone into the water?"

"I just wanted us to be together without you always calling all those people you know," Billy said. "You know so many people, Artie, and there's never really like time for us, me and you, just time like you told me about you and your dad when you would go fishing outside Moscow and nothing could get in the way. "You told me about the river where you went and the big cheese sandwiches and thick black bread and the Russian ice cream that tasted a little bit sour, like vanilla yogurt, and how you would sit on the banks during the summer, and sometimes go for swims, and there was no one else, and no cell phones, and it was all I wanted. Honest," said Billy, smiling at me before he turned back to the fly he was examining.

31

I didn't have a phone. I didn't have a weapon with me either, because I had left it at home. I didn't want Billy around guns. There were too many cases of kids playing around with guns that went off and someone getting hurt or dead.

Working on the tangles in some fishing line, Billy sat cross-legged out on the crumbling little dock, blue water behind him, sun on his face.

Again I watched him through the kitchen window of the house. From the fridge, I got a beer – it felt cold enough – and drank it. For a while I tried to work out if someone had cut the landline or it was just out of order or – it's what I'd thought first – Hank Provone turned it off between tenants. Maybe I was just paranoid.

The day got hotter. In the bedroom I found the air conditioner, turned it on and left the door to the main room open. I picked up the bills I'd left on the kitchen table and looked through them.

What I should have done was drag Billy away from the dock and into the car and back to the city. Instead I looked for a phone bill. I felt like I was coming unglued, and sweat ran in thick streams down my back.

Maybe I was crazy. There had been times like this before when crap was coming down on me from every side, when I was working on cases that made me drink too much and I wasn't sure if I was completely sane.

When I got like that, I could get things wrong. Paranoia, denial, fatigue, booze, a missed clue, a lazy-ass appraisal of some evidence. I wasn't some kind of detective hero, just a regular asshole and sometimes I blew it. If I was wrong this time and I accused Billy of something he didn't do, it would ruin the rest of his life. It would stick to him forever.

He said he just wanted us to be together. The four days he'd been with me in the city, there were people around all the time. I hadn't planned it that way, it's just how things went. I felt dizzy. All Billy wanted was my time. Now we were alone and he was happy.

On the window sill, next to a couple of pots with some kind of herbs in them, was a radio. I turned it on and I saw that the soil in the pots was damp. It was weird. I wondered if Hank Provone had been out here to water his plants and check on his property. Maybe Billy, but what the hell would Billy have been doing here at all, much less watering the basil? How did he get here, if he was here? Stop it! I thought: STOP IT!

I drank my beer to the bottom and tossed the bottle in the garbage can under the sink, and then ripped open the phone bill I found.

My T-shirt was wet with sweat, the air con not really working well. I went outside and around to the rear of the house where the sun was hot but there was a breeze off the water. I sat in one of the dark green metal chairs, and looked at the phone bill.

Dated three days earlier – it must have just arrived – the bill didn't show a disconnect charge. Hank could have called the phone company after the bill was sent. Or not. It didn't mean anything.

From the house, which was behind me, I could hear the radio playing something by Sting, and I could see Billy on the dock, and everything suddenly felt surreal and I was paralyzed. I couldn't figure out what the hell to do, so I sat there in a rusty green garden chair on metal rockers, my sneakers in front of me on the green grass that needed cutting, staring at some high yellowish grass and reeds that led down to the water. Billy was intent on his fishing gear: there was no sound except the radio, and me breathing. I could hear my heart pump, my breath going in and out.

I looked at the second hand on my watch, decided to wait until it passed twelve twice before I did anything. Right then I should have somehow made myself get up; I should have but I couldn't move.

"Where are you going?"

From my chair, I saw Billy turn swiftly, still holding his fishing rod, like he forgot something all of a sudden. Tall, dark hair long over his forehead, his eyes almost hidden by it, Billy made for my old red Caddy that was baking in the sun. I knew what he was going to do and I got up slowly, like somebody in a bad dream.

He got to the car ahead of me. I knew what he wanted. I knew he was going for the car keys. If he threw them in the water, we would be here together, just us. It made him seem nuts. There was no reason to throw the keys away. We were only on Staten Island, we were in New York City and I could turn and walk away and leave him and go get help. He knew that I wouldn't.

Before I got to the car, I heard the horn. Billy was in the driver's seat, leaning on the horn, honking, making a little tune of the honks. He was leaning out of the window, honking and smiling. He didn't take the keys out of the ignition. He wasn't going to throw them away. I had been crazy.

"You want to take a ride?" Billy said, calling me over. "You want to go get a slice or a sandwich or burger or something, because I'm hungry, and we could see if we can find a place where there's a better fishing situation. Artie? I don't think there's a lot of fish out here. I was looking at the water, I tried to read it, but it didn't look that fine to me."

I had been wrong about Billy. Maybe he had simply dropped the phones in the water by accident. Sometimes his hands flapped around. I had noticed a couple of times that in spite of being a generally graceful kid with pretty good coordination, he sometimes resembled a sloppy teenager whose limbs went in different directions, his hands flapping as if they were attached to his arms by strings, like a puppet's.

So I got in the car, and he asked me again if we could go eat somewhere and if he could drive a little bit and I said sure, why not, partly because I was hoping we could get to a place with a phone. I made conversation about fishing. I thought about how big he was now, almost as big as me.

Was I sizing him up in case I had to fight him and force the information about Luda out of him?

He drove. There wasn't much traffic over this side of the island, though I knew the marinas and beaches would be filling up. After a while, I said, "You want to go to the beach? Take a swim or something? You want to see if we can find a boat to take us out, over to Perth Amboy where the good fishing is, I mean I once went over there to Jersey and it's fantastic."

I was faking it and I thought that he knew, but I kept talking, spinning fantasies about a trip I'd taken in a fishing boat off Jersey just opposite Staten Island, and the guys on it, and the good times, and the great catch. Blue fish. Stripers. Couldn't remember. Wrong season. Billy knew.

He kept driving.

Looking ahead, watching him only from the corner of an eye, I was smoking, my window open all the way down so I could rest my elbow on it and the breeze took the smoke away. The sky was pure blue and the sun was hot on my arm. I thought: who is this boy?

When Billy was born, back then I hardly knew Genia, but she had asked me to be his godfather. I told her right away that I didn't know anything about being a godfather or religion, for that matter, but she said she wanted someone of her own, someone Russian. Please, Artemy, she had said to me, please do this. I have no one else in America, so you'll come, OK?

I was broke. Genia took me shopping. We went to Brooks Brothers, which was Gen's idea about how real Americans dressed, and we chose a nice gray suit and she paid for it and I bought a white button-down shirt and a red knitted silk tie, and we went over to the Plaza and had tea in the Palm Court.

After tea and cakes, we drank Manhattan cocktails, which Genia ordered. Because of the name, she had said. It was one of the good times we'd had together. We had laughed about the baptism; we didn't believe, not her or me; we had been raised good atheists in the Soviet Union. "Opium of the people," Gen giggled and ordered another cocktail.

Johnny Farone had a big Catholic family. Genia went along with the christening, the whole works. I showed up. All I knew about it was from the great scene in *The Godfather* where the baptism is cut in with a lot of bloody murders.

My Brooks Brothers suit made me look like a guy from Wall Street in the church in Brooklyn. I read out the responses, including stuff about Jesus Christ and the devil.

In the long frilly christening dress Genia got for him, Billy was one of those angelic babies, blond curls, blue eyes. Genia – I remembered she wore a bronze-colored suit – held him, and the godparents stood around in a circle all dressed up. I tried not to smile when I said the part about renouncing the devil, or maybe it was Satan they called him.

Afterwards there was a big party at Gargulio's near Coney Island with a lot of Italians and a lot of Russians. Johnny was one of the few outsiders the Russkis trusted.

A woman in a purple velvet dress with a low neck got up and sang a Russian song a cappella and it haunted me for weeks afterwards, just the sound of her voice.

So I went. I said stuff I didn't believe in a church where I didn't belong. When Billy was eight or nine, we started fishing together. I began caring about him.

He was smart as hell, but intense and obsessed with fishing and fish, his fish in the tank at home, even fish he saw in a market or in a pail near one of the fishing boats. He was pretty much a loner in those days. To Billy, other kids were boring, though he was friendly for a while with May Luca at the Catholic school they both attended.

Whatever had been wrong with him, I always figured he'd grow out of it. Anyhow, you didn't offload a kid because he didn't come out the way you wanted. So he was different, so what? Then he hurt Heshey Shank. Killed him. Say it, I thought to myself: Billy killed Heshey.

I tried to replay it, the time I found him with Heshey Shank's body out at the beach club on Breezy Point. As if he could read my mind, Billy interrupted.

"Let's stop there," said Billy pointing out a silver-colored diner with a pink neon clock out front. "You can call someone there if you want, tell them they should come and take me away."

"Nobody's going to come and take you away. Don't be ridiculous."

"Then let's go get something to eat. I like desperately want a cheeseburger," he said. "With fried onions."

"What made you think I'd call someone to come take you?"

"Because I lied about Luda," said Billy.

We sat opposite each other in a red leatherette booth. The waitress was Russian. Billy ordered his burger and fries in Russian, which impressed her. I recognized her as one of the women sitting under the dryer at Queen of Hearts beauty salon. I didn't know if she recognized me.

I ordered a cheeseburger too, and we both got Cokes.

"Can I have some onion rings?" Billy said. "And fries?"

"Sure."

"Cool."

The place was almost empty. A couple of fat young white guys sat in their red booth at the far end of the diner slumped low in their seats. Looked like they were eating off their hangovers from the night before.

For a few minutes, waiting for our food, Billy read a newspaper he found on the table. The waitress appeared with the burgers, and stood talking Russian to Billy a while. She told him about growing up in a village near Saratov, and what it was like, and he listened intently. Then one of the fat young guys called her over to bring more coffee.

"So, listen Artie, go use the phone if you need to," Billy said finally. "I'm really sorry about losing our cell phones, I really am, it was like a giant idiotic mistake, I had grease on my hands or something and they just slipped. So there's a payphone over by the wall there. Don't worry, I can just eat my lunch." He bit into his burger and the cheese squished out around the sides.

I looked at my plate.

"What did you mean you lied about Luda?"

"I didn't lie just about Luda." His mouth was full. He put down the burger on his plate, picked up the ketchup and squirted it on the meat. He swallowed and picked up the burger again, then added pickles to it.

"Stop fucking eating and tell me what you mean, you didn't lie just about Luda."

"Luda was extra," Billy said. "It wasn't exactly part of my plan at first."

32

Billy had planned the whole thing as soon as the bad dreams started. In the dreams, he saw that only Artie could save him, literally saw the letters of Artie's name hanging in front of him, and him, Billy, reaching out for them and needing to get with Artie as soon as he could. Sometimes the letters were made of ice and they melted and dripped away when he touched them. Sometimes he was at home in Brooklyn and his mother told him not to write the letters on the wall.

In Florida he learned that kids who were good sometimes got a few days out of the institution. First you got yourself out of the hospital section, which was what they called it, though it was really a prison ward with locked doors. After that you had a chance. You did well in your therapy. You took your meds if you were on anything. You aced your classes. You didn't try running away. You showed up for sports and looked enthusiastic and didn't headbutt the other kids.

Compared to the crazies and losers who made up most of the population, it was easy for Billy. He became a star. He knew that most of the others were poor and dumb. Ninety percent of them were from economically deprived backgrounds, as they called it, which made Billy laugh because most of them were just stupid fuck-ups.

Billy knew he was smart. He knew how to talk to grown-ups. The doctors and teachers liked him. They could talk to him. They gave him books, which he read. He got invited to eat with some of the younger teachers, him and one or two other boys, the ones who didn't eat like pigs.

The honchos who ran the place looked at him as a possible success story. Told him how one of the kids had actually gone to Princeton. He told them he'd like to go to Princeton. He told them he knew that Albert Einstein had taught at Princeton and that F. Scott Fitzgerald had attended Princeton and he, Billy, had read *The Great Gatsby*. Also, there was that movie with Russell Crowe about the guy at Princeton who could see numbers or something.

The grown-ups made Billy a pet because, as he knew, there wasn't a whole lot of choice. What other boy could they shoot the shit with about what was on the news? What other kid told them he hated violent video games, and preferred reading books and newspapers? It made them feel successful, the way he improved, got better, took things in.

Billy also discovered he had a talent for mimicry and he made the other kids laugh by imitating the teachers. He steered a skillful course through the institution.

After a while, he realized the same talent he used to mimic teachers could be used to imitate anyone. He watched TV shows about nice families and normal people; most of the TV shows they were allowed were about more or less happy families. Billy saw he could turn himself into a perfect specimen. It didn't matter what you felt; it was how you acted. Wasn't it? It seemed to him that it was all that mattered because that was how people judged you.

Billy told himself he was working his passage home. He'd read the phrase somewhere in a novel about sailors, some sailor who got stuck in a foreign place and had to take a job on a lousy ship to work his passage home.

Sitting in the diner on Staten Island, leaning forward in the red booth, Billy told me all of this, his hands clasped together lightly on the edge of the table.

It wasn't that he felt he got a raw deal in Florida; he just didn't want to be there. Wanting something was what mattered. Why should he be there if he didn't want to be? So he worked and got good grades and behaved and planned for the time he could get away.

To pass the days, when he wasn't in class or reading or watching the TV shows, or playing baseball – he was developing a good arm – he liked the old classic movies, westerns like *High Noon*, or war movies like *Bridge On the River Kwai* where there were really interesting feats and the good guys foiled the enemy. He looked at DVDs of old movies, like *The Great Escape*.

He loved the escape stuff, men in jails who tunneled out with spoons or rolled under barbed wire and made it safe. He knew it was make-believe. Billy knew that. You didn't escape like that.

There was one doctor he got really close to. Andy Swiller, the young guy I'd met, was from Brooklyn; like Billy, he was a Yankees fan. Billy let Swiller think he was special for him. There was another doctor, too, who was much more gullible than Swiller and after two years and four months, he recommended Billy be allowed to go home for a few days. Swiller was reluctant, but Billy got him to agree.

Usually they let the kids out for a few days but because Billy lived so far away they gave him two weeks. He fixed it so that I would pick him up instead of his mother. Billy had heard about the trip to London from Johnny, who would tell you anything because he was an idiot. Billy knew Genia wouldn't come pick him up a few days before a trip so he asked for me to come. Can Artie come? All he had to do was ask.

When he heard about the bombings in London, part of him hoped his parents were dead. If they were dead, it meant he could be with me. We could be together all the time, Billy said.

"What about Luda? What did you mean you lied?" I said again and again, but it was as if he didn't hear me, just kept talking, determined to finish his story in a certain order.

"Then what about the old man," I said. "What about your grandfather? I thought you were friendly with John Sr."

"Yeah," Billy said. "When I was little, he was OK, I liked him."

"And after?"

"After, when I knew Johnny wasn't my real father and the old man wasn't my grandpa, it was different. Weird, it was grandpa's idea in the first place for me to go home on vacation. He put it in my head. I didn't trust him anymore, and he stopped liking me because I wasn't really his own grandkid," Billy said. "He didn't like me anymore. I could tell."

Billy repeated himself, outlining carefully what he had done. The calm boy sitting opposite me in a diner on Staten Island was filled up with rage. It was invisible. Billy could hide his emotions, but I knew. He glanced at the phone, then at me. Waited for me to go call someone. Call a cop. Or Florida. Get rid of him. I sat where I was.

"Luda?"

"Yeah. I lied to you. I'm sorry," said Billy. "Before you got home yesterday – I think you said you were over at your friend's, Mr Lippert's – I called Luda. They just got back from East Hampton. I asked her to meet me. I did that, I told her she was in trouble with the police, I already told you that part. I knew what would make her come out and meet me."

"How did you know?"

He picked up half an onion ring that remained on his plate and examined it, then put it back.

"I knew from my mom that people from Russia are scared of the cops, so I told Luda the cops would be looking for her because she was illegal."

"Was that why she kept asking for me?" I said, watching the two fat guys pay their check and waddle out of the diner.

"Maybe she thought you could protect her," Billy said. "Right from Wednesday morning when we went to Tolya's house, she wanted to be around you."

"What about the dolls?"

"I wanted to warn her."

"About what?"

"About what could happen to her if she got caught," Billy said.

"Go on."

"I took the baby dolls from the toy store, I thought it would be a kind of like good warning. I heard Mr Lippert talk about the little girl that was killed in Jersey, and that she had her doll with her and they cut off the doll's foot, which gave me the idea."

"You listened in on the phone?"

"I don't remember. Maybe you mentioned it or something."

"You got the dolls out of the toy store that night? Wednesday night?"

"Yeah. We were having such a good time at the ball game that day, you and me, and then we had to go to Luda's stupid party. It was easy just to take some of those dolls. Things aren't that hard, Artie, if you give them like some thought. Right? I mean it's sort of what they teach us at school. Just think things through. I put them in a shopping bag and left the store, and I sort of expected an alarm to go off because they had those store tags, but nothing happened," Billy said. "I had this idea I could scare Luda with them, you know?"

"You were going to show her a doll with its foot cut off?"

"I wasn't sure. Something like that. I didn't have time. I got a little nervous."

In Chinatown, Billy found a warehouse with the door unlocked. He put the dolls into the fridge. Pretty easy stuff, he said. But after that, he couldn't get Luda to come see, which was frustrating – that was the word from his vocabulary book. He made a call to the cops using a fake Russian accent. He found Sonny Lippert's number on my desk. He called the local precinct. It was all kind of fun, he said. Like a puzzle.

But afterwards, he started worrying, mostly about the fat guy from Brooklyn – he meant Stan Shank – who was following him.

"What were you going to do with Luda?"

Billy looked up, his blue eyes soft now, and said, "I wasn't going to hurt Luda or anything, I didn't want to hurt her, you know, I just wanted her to go away. I need to smoke," he added. "Can we go outside, please?"

I put some money on the table, and followed him into the parking lot.

"Do you want to call someone?" said Billy for the third time, voice not threatening or challenging, just wondering what I would do.

"Why don't you finish your story?"

"I think I'd like to go back to the house with you, Artie, if that would be OK," Billy said, digging in his pocket for a cigarette, and not finding one.

I passed him a pack I had, he extracted a cigarette, lit up and handed the pack back. I took one.

"I was kind of hurt when you stole my phone, you know, Artie, it was like you didn't trust me, or whatever," said Billy. "I'm OK with that now."

I inhaled as much nicotine as I could, sucking the drug deep in my lungs because I figured it would calm me down. I felt sick. From the moment Billy knew he could get away from the facility in Florida, he had worked on his plan.

Maybe the plan went wrong when Billy told his grandfather he was going to New York. Maybe the old man told his friend Stan Shank. Maybe Vera Gorbachev, whose stepson Frank Laporello was married to Debbie, Shank's daughter, was involved. Gorbachev had worked on Rhonda Fisher's guilt so she asked Sonny Lippert to send me over there. I had been chasing my own tail. It scared me, the whole thing, how one favor, Sonny asking me to visit Vera, led to so much horror. A little thing. The kind of thing you did every day. What if I'd never gone at all?

"I'm sleepy," Billy said now. "Can we just go back to the house a while? I'd like to take a nap, Artie." He tossed his cigarette out onto the ground of the parking lot.

"Where is Luda?"

"I don't know," Billy said. "Honest. I don't know. I just asked her to come and meet me, and she said OK, and I said where to go, I told her how to take a taxi and what to tell them, and then I didn't see her. She didn't show up."

"Didn't you think she could get lost? Or scared? Or something bad could happen?"

Billy got in the car, put his head back against the seat and closed his eyes. He didn't wait to see if I got out of the car to use a phone. He seemed to trust me. I got in.

"I just didn't want her to take you away from me," Billy said.

There was no place left for us to go. Billy fell asleep in the car. I drove away from the diner, back to the house because there was no other place I could think of. If we crossed Staten Island, one of the Russians might see us, someone connected to Vera or the beauty salon; I didn't know if Sonny was still holding Stanley Shank. Sonny wouldn't let me off the hook either, not this time.

Johnny and Genia were probably home or on their way, but Genia didn't want her own kid. And Luda was still missing. I wasn't sure now I could even get Billy to the airport. For all I knew Lippert might have put the word out to pick him up. But if I got him on a plane, and to Florida, then what?

At best, Billy would be locked up in the hospital ward. I couldn't send him there. Anyway I knew he wouldn't go to Florida. He had never meant to go back. I couldn't keep him here for long, I couldn't take him home.

Maxine was coming back the next day to our apartment over by the river, and I'd be there waiting. Somehow, I'd be there.

The onions we ate at the diner made me feel so sick, I was sweating and light-headed and I felt dehydrated, like there was no water in me at all, like I was dried out, dried up.

Around me, there was more traffic. People packed in cars and vans, some with boat stuff on the roof, kids inside giggling or hitting each other, all of them on their way to beaches or barbecues. In the street, a kid reeled around on a skateboard. The sun was high and hot. You could hear music from people's backyards. My mouth was dry as dust.

I was on my own on this huge island, part domesticated, part wild, with its rows and rows and rows of bungalows and mobile homes, semi-detached houses, condos and mansions, the lawns mown, or scruffy, the strip malls baking in the summer heat, and the swamps and creeps, garbage dumps, bird sanctuaries, oceans, bays, ports, docks.

In the most isolated part of New York, there was plenty of wide-open space where you could lose yourself, but I felt trapped. Billy had wanted it that way. He fixed it up to get me here with him where we'd be alone.

I drove until I got back to the house, and thought about calling Hank Provone. I could talk to Hank. Hank would never refuse, but if I called him it meant putting him in deep.

In front of the mobile home and not thinking, I slammed on the brakes and it jolted Billy awake. He rubbed his eyes, yawned, got out of the car, and stumbled inside where, like a little kid, he fell onto the bed in the bedroom and went back to sleep.

I left the bedroom door open, and sat at the kitchen table. Billy wasn't going to hurt me. Even if he could, he wouldn't hurt me. He knew I wouldn't leave him or turn him in.

In the little house near the water, we were alone and a while later he came out of the bedroom and sat with me at the kitchen table and told me straight out that it wasn't him who beat up the kid in Brooklyn with a skateboard on Tuesday. I asked him about the homeless boy in Chinatown, but Billy told me no, that wasn't him either.

I couldn't ask about the baby in the freezer, not then, not yet, maybe not ever, because if he had done it, if he had killed the baby and put her in the freezer – if he had put her there before she was dead – what would I do?

I couldn't just throw Billy away. I wouldn't let them lock him up again. If you loved someone, you took care of them. Wasn't that all that mattered?

I loved him, and I held onto that, taking a last deep drag on my cigarette. Billy was bent slightly forward, whistling to himself, tunelessly like he sometimes did. He looked up at me and grinned because he knew he couldn't carry a tune and neither could I. We had agreed we were both shitty singers. We laughed about it again now. Then Billy yawned and said he was going to get some more sleep. Somehow he never got enough sleep. Growing fast, maybe, he said. He ruffled my hair as if he was the grown-up and then went to the bedroom.

I started making plans for where I could take Billy if I couldn't get back to the city safe, and he wouldn't go back to the school in Florida. Then I heard the sound of car tires on the gravel in front of the house.

33

"Where's the boy? Where's Billy?" said Hank Provone who got out of his car, followed by Tolya Sverdloff climbing down from his Hummer.

They were a crazy-looking posse. In a giant pair of red and green flowered swim trunks still wet from a dip in the ocean, his belly hanging over them, a pink towel around his neck, Hank wore thick white socks and big white sneakers. I wondered if he had an ankle holster with a weapon under the bulky socks.

Sverdloff looked like he hadn't slept for a long time. Heavy bags hung under his eyes and his shoulders seemed to slump under his own weight.

"Billy's inside asleep," I said to Hank.

"I'm sorry, Artie. I had to bring Tolya because of the little Russian girl," Hank said. "He told me and I had to bring him."

"Sure," I said.

I expected Sverdloff's fury, but he just put his hand on my shoulder.

"Are you OK?"

"I don't know."

"We found Luda."

"She's dead."

"No," Hank said. "She's not. She's not dead. Sit down," he said and I stumbled onto a plastic lawn chair then got up and sat on a redwood bench that put me between Tolya and the front door of the house.

"Tell me why you're here," I said to Tolya.

"I came to see Billy. To help you," he said. "Do you want to go get him?"

"You can't help me this way."

Hank said, "I tried calling you on your cell and the landline out here, I couldn't get any answer."

"I thought you disconnected the phone."

"No," he said. "Lily Hanes called me, she said she knew we had seen each other recently. I told her I thought you could be here. Do you want me to stay, Artie?" Hank said. "I'll do what you want me to, whatever you need."

"One thing."

"Yeah, anything."

I dug in my pocket for a scrap of paper with Vera Gorbachev's address on it and gave it to Hank.

"Try to find out how this woman is connected to a guy named Stan Shank or his family in Brooklyn, ex-cop."

Hank looked at it. "Gorbachev?"

"No relation."

He nodded. "You know how to get hold of me," Hank said.

"Yeah. Of course. Thank you. Hey, Hank?"

"Yeah, Artie?"

"Yesterday, how come you left my place? You took Billy there and left before I got back."

"Lily came over," Hank said.

"I don't mean that, I know you didn't leave Billy alone, but what made you need to go?"

"Don't ask me, Artie. Just say I wasn't comfortable around

the boy. So, you need me, just call." He turned and got into his car and pulled away.

"What about Luda?" I said to Tolya, when Hank had gone.

"Valentina is with her," Tolya said. "Lily also. Artyom, what made you come to my place last night? You knew, didn't you? You knew something happened to Luda."

It was a picture in Billy's phone that had made me run to Tolya's late the night before. The picture showed Luda posing at the toy store with one of the dolls that looked like her. On her face was a look of pure terror.

"Lily's with Luda where?"

"St Vincent's," Tolya said.

"God, what happened?"

"It's not completely clear, Luda doesn't want to talk, but it seems she left the house last night because the kid — Billy — got on the phone with her and scared her about her being not exactly legal here, and said he would help her if she met him. He told her to take a taxi. Luda just left the house and tried to get a cab but she didn't have any money. She's ten, Artyom, and she's lived most of her life in a fucking Russian orphanage and now she's on the New York streets wearing shorts and flip-flops and it's dark and she doesn't have any money."

"Let's walk," I said. "Just up to the water. I want to smoke."

"Where is he?"

"He's asleep, I told you. He's not going anywhere," I said, but I went and got the keys out of the car.

There was a rough plank bench near the water, and we sat on it.

"She cut someone, Artyom. This is almost worst part."

"Who?"

"Luda."

"Christ, tell me."

"When she goes out, she takes only one thing, a knife from

the kitchen. This is how Russian children are after a whole life in orphanage."

"How did you know she took it?"

"I left it on the cutting board in kitchen, I was slicing a lemon, I left the room, when I came back, the knife was gone. I knew exactly what knife as soon as I heard what happened. Maybe I knew even before."

"What made you think about it?"

"I could see this fury in her, I saw it, and I heard it," said Tolya. "I could read in her the things she never talked about, the orphanage, the kids who died from radiation poisoning after Chernobyl, the kids held hostage and killed by terrorists at the Moscow theater and in Beslan. Her own twin sister. All they have left is rage, and they feed on it, and they will grow up only to think about revenge."

"It's what Billy said."

"He knew. He understood her." Tolya lifted himself heavily off the bench. "We have to take Billy."

"Linda took the knife for protection?"

Tolya pulled the cigar case out of his shirt pocket and lit up a skinny little cigar. "I don't know if it was for protection or to somehow hurt Billy, or just because she was so afraid."

"I see."

"Luda was alone on the streets most of the night, and there was a boy, and she cut him," said Tolya.

A cop had found Luda curled up on the sidewalk in the doorway of a shop in the Village that sold Russian antiques and books. She said she read the sign on the awning and felt comforted by the Cyrillic letters and was waiting for someone to come. She didn't speak much, not to the cop who couldn't understand her.

She still had the knife. The cop saw there was blood on it and on her hand. He didn't know what to do with her because she was so small – he thought she was seven or eight – so he picked her up and put her in the patrol car and took her to St Vincent's, which was a couple of blocks away.

He called into his station house and found out that a woman who lived on Thirteenth Street reported a crazy little girl had attacked her son with a knife, a girl who didn't speak English. Her son had gone out very early, before it was light, carrying a basketball on his way to practice before a game. He came home bleeding and his mother took him to St Vincent's, where they sewed him up and let him go. The police were notified.

In another part of the hospital Luda lay on a bed, not speaking. There was no one who spoke Russian. She had on pink shorts and shirt and the red flip-flops. Her legs were bruised and no one could tell if it was from fighting with the boy with the basketball or from stumbling up the curbs.

Eventually a Russian nurse from Washington Heights arrived, and before she put her bag down – it was a huge fake Vuitton bag that she used to carry her lunch in, she said, hastily – she was taken to Luda.

The nurse – her American name was Michelle, she said – stayed with Luda until she sat up, drank some milk and started talking. She was a good listener. She sat on the edge of Luda's bed, and Luda talked to her. Luda told her Valentina's name but Val wasn't listed and neither was Tolya. It took hours to find them, but then Val arrived at the hospital with Lily.

Somehow, Luda had met up with Billy. After she left Tolya's place, wearing her shorts, carrying a shopping bag from the toy store where she kept the knife, she started walking. Somewhere, she didn't remember where, she heard people on the street talking Russian. She asked for directions. They asked her if she wanted a ride and she said yes. It was raining.

Luda knew you weren't supposed to go in strangers' cars, but the people looked OK, a nice young man and woman, and Luda had her knife, so she went. They took her to Billy, who was waiting for her on the corner of Broadway near my loft. The nice man and woman waited until Luda got out of the car, and when they saw Billy put his arms around her, drove off.

Billy complimented Luda on the way she had come by herself and said he had something to show her. He took her hand. She yanked it away. She was scared of him, but he promised to help her and she thought this meant she wouldn't have to go back to Russia.

"I just have to show you something," he said in Russian. "I have to show you what happens in America to people who break the law."

It was Friday evening just before I got back from Sonny's. People were in a hurry. The film crew was milling around. Everyone was preoccupied, and if anyone saw the two kids, they barely paid attention to a boy and his little sister.

Clutching her shopping bag, Luda followed Billy into the alley where he opened the humpback freezer. He showed it to her. He showed her the dead baby girl. He told her it was what happened to bad kids. It was how it was, he said, and she looked and then she ran. She ran as fast as she could, not turning around, not knowing where she was going, just ran.

For hours she sat in the doorway of the Russian antique shop. Maybe she fell asleep. Much later, early in the morning, in fact, a boy with a basketball stopped to see if she was OK, and when she saw him, she thought it was Billy and she ran at him and cut his hand with her knife.

"How do you know she was telling the truth?" I said to Tolya. "Maybe she was screwed up about what was happening, maybe she saw the story about the dead baby on TV and constructed her story."

"She was gone out of the apartment before it was on TV,"

Tolya said. "Her English isn't good enough for TV, but she was already gone."

"Maybe Billy just heard about it and told her to scare her. Does anyone know who the baby in the freezer was? Is there anything on it? You talked to Lippert?"

"Yes. There was a report of a baby taken from a carriage outside some Korean deli downtown. Canal Street area. Woman went in to get cigarettes and left her in the baby carriage for a second. A lot of people were around. A second, she said. She left her baby for a second and then she was gone," Tolya said. "Artyom, it was Billy. He showed Luda the infant in that freezer before anyone knew the baby was in there. You have to know that."

"How do you know Luda wasn't just scared? She could say anything."

"Billy didn't want her getting between you and him, I saw that the first day. You were the only thing he had, and she was there, and he saw that you paid attention to her." Tolya hesitated. "He has no conscience, Artie. He doesn't have some disease, or fucked-up genes, he has no conscience. I told you once I thought he was like this country, beautiful and brilliant but unaware of anyone else."

"You're wrong," I said. "You're wrong."

"I don't know how this happens in someone," said Tolya. "But I can see this in him."

I thought about my nephew, the good-looking boy with the hair falling in his face, and the way he laughed and how the laces of his sneakers trailed all over the ground.

"Where's the proof? Except for Luda's story, where's the evidence?" I was desperate. I didn't want to know. Go away, I thought, but I didn't say anything, just waited for Tolya to finish.

"Luda had a picture of it," Tolya said. "Luda had a little cell phone she got at the toy store Wednesday night, we set it up so she could call us, or take pictures or just have fun with it.

She was there. Luda was there in the alleyway, looking in the freezer and Billy was there, and she took a picture. The time is marked on it. I have a copy if you need to see."

34

Billy was gone when we went back inside the house. He had slipped out while Tolya and I were sitting on the bench, talking. I'd pretty much known if I turned my back, he'd go, and Tolya knew, too. I let Billy go because I didn't want to believe what he had done, and I didn't know what to do.

My car was still in the driveway. I knew he couldn't have gone far. I glanced out of the window of the house at the water. For a second it crossed my mind that maybe Billy just walked in, let the water into his mouth and nose, sucked it up, drifted down slowly. But it would have been tough for him to get to the water without me seeing him. Billy's stuff was still in the bedroom.

I went out into the yard.

"He's not here," I said to Tolya.

"Do you know where he is?"

"I'll look," I said.

"I'll go with you."

"I think I have to do this myself. It will be OK, Tolya, I promise. I'll do what I have to. I can manage, I swear. Trust me, OK? Go home to Luda and Val."

"And to Lily, who is so nice to all of us," Tolya said. "She helps my Valentina, she helps Luda. Val loves her. She is so good for us."

"And me," I said.

"All of us. I think if she didn't belong to you, I would try to marry her," said Tolya.

"Yes." I started for my car, and then I said to him, "Tolya, you keep a weapon with you? You told me once you had one."

"You really want to know?" He tried to smile.

"I want you to give it to me, please."

He went to his car, opened the passenger door, leaned in got out a gun and gave it to me. I took it, put it in my waistband, put my jacket on so the gun didn't show.

"You'll be OK?" Tolya said.

"Yeah, I'm fine. I just feel naked without a gun, you know, I'm a cop, right?"

"Sure," he said.

I patted him on the arm because I didn't know what else to do, and then I got into my car, and backed out of the drive, watching Tolya who just stood there, hunched over a little, a cigar in his hand, looking at me.

About half a mile from the house, in the woods near the water, I found Billy sitting on the ground, hidden from the road. He told me that he had tripped and caught his foot in some weeds.

"I knew you'd come, Artie," he said. "I waited for you."

I squatted down near him and untangled his foot. I had to take one of his sneakers off first because the long laces were caught in the undergrowth.

"OK?"

Billy rubbed his foot. "Yeah," he said. "I think I heard something snap, maybe one of those little bones, you know?" He looked up at the sky. The sun was going. "We didn't get in much fishing."

"No." I sat, still holding his sneaker.

"I can't go back to Florida," said Billy. "You know that, right, like I just can't do it, Artie."

I didn't tell him that Florida probably wasn't an option anymore. I didn't tell him he'd be tried as an adult this time and locked up for the rest of his life if he was lucky. There would be no friendly shrinks, or appreciative teachers, or hospital wards where clouds were painted on the sky-blue walls.

"I understand," I said.

I got out some cigarettes and gave him one, and for a while – it must have been a minute or two at least – we smoked together sitting on the ground in the woods, Billy leaning a little against me, but not complaining about his ankle.

"You think my mom and dad are back by now? From London?"

"Probably. They said they'd be back today."

"Oh."

"The girl is OK? Luda, I mean? They found her and everything?"

"Yes."

"Good."

There was a noise behind me, and I turned fast, but it was only a dog.

"How come you're wearing a gun?" Billy said.

"What?"

"Under your jacket. Your jacket opened and I saw it."

"I'm a cop," I said. "I always wear one."

"You didn't have it before."

"No."

"Artie? I think I might need your help to get back to the house, I mean my ankle kinds of hurts."

"I have the car," I said. "It's up on the road."

"Should we go?"

"In a minute. It's nice here. Let's just sit for a minute, OK?"

"OK." Billy looked like a young teenager instead of a half-grown man. "I was wanting to ask you about the little plane that crashed on the beach. Did anyone ever find out what happened?"

"I'm not sure," I said. "Sometimes stuff is just accidental, you know, and there's no reason."

"Right," said Billy. "Like magic."

I handed Billy his other shoe and he tried to put it on, but his foot hurt too much. Holding the sneaker, he tried to get up and then fell backwards. I helped him. On the way back to the car, he leaned on me, hobbling on the one foot, keeping the other one off the ground.

We got to the car, and he leaned against the hood, breathing hard from the effort.

"Is there something you want to ask me?" said Billy, and for the first time I realized how sweet his voice was; the actual sound of it was sweet.

"What do you want me to know?"

"I need you to know everything about me, Artie. I need you to feel OK about me no matter what."

I couldn't speak.

"You can ask me anything, you know, I mean I could tell you anything, and you wouldn't get mad, right?" Billy said.

"Yes."

"So ask," he said.

"Did you do it?"

"Do what?"

"The baby." I'd have traded an arm or a leg or ten years of my life not to have to ask, much more for not having to hear the answer. "The freezer. Out back at Mike Rizzi's coffee shop."

"Yeah," he said. "Yes."

When we pulled up at the house, Tolya was still waiting. He was sitting in the chair on the front lawn, the butt of a cigar in his mouth, and as soon as I hit the brakes, he got up and waved. I got out of the car.

Leaning on me, Billy got out of my car, and Tolya put out his hand and Billy shook it. We sat down in the three chairs on the front lawn. Tolya and Billy talked a little bit about fishing and Tolya described how he had once gone way out to sea on a fishing boat off the coast of Cuba, and another time for salmon in Alaska. He told Billy that there were some great places in Russia for fishing; he painted him a picture of it, the wild places, the virgin lakes, the big rivers; Tolya said that maybe they could take a trip, him and Billy.

Summer was best, Tolya said, standing up on the ragged lawn and pretending to cast a line into a river. He could show Billy where he grew up and where I grew up. We could all go fishing.

Billy said he'd like that.

"You have your things with you?" Tolya asked.

"Sure," Billy said. "I brought most of my things with me here."

"We can buy whatever else you need," said Tolya.

"Maybe you should get packed," I said.

"I am packed," Billy said to me, "I'd like to see where you went fishing with your dad, Artie, with my grandfather. To that river you told me about." His face was alive with anticipation. "We could all go."

Tolya nodded. I stuffed my hands into my pockets to keep them from shaking too much. No words seemed to come out of my mouth when I opened it, and I had to turn my back to Billy so he wouldn't see my face.

"Great," Billy said. "It's great, Artie, right?"

I turned around and, not looking at his face, noticed that the laces from the one sneaker he wore were trailing across the lawn.

"Yeah," I said. "Go on, get your stuff."

Smiling, he hobbled across to the house.

I said to Tolya, "I can't do it."

"I know," he said. "That's what I'm here for."

"Don't tell me, OK, not now."

"Yes," he said.

I gave Tolya back his gun.

While Billy was still inside packing – I could hear him there, whistling something that had no tune – I got into my car and slowly, trying not to make much noise, backed out of the drive. I hoped Billy would come out of the house so I could see him before I left; I hoped like hell he wouldn't.

He didn't come out. When I got to the main road, I turned the car around and, trying not to look back over my shoulder, hit the gas and headed back to the city.

Red Hook

Reggie Nadelson

It's a late summer Sunday in downtown New York City, and Artie Cohen is getting married. Watching the sun rising over the East River, he's content.

A message comes in from an old friend, Sid McKay, asking Artie to come out to Red Hook in Brooklyn. It's his wedding day, but Artie owes Sid, so he goes. On arriving he finds a dead man spread-eagled in the water off the old docks. When Sid eventually shows up, he's scared, edgy and evasive, Artie suspects he's holding something back.

Even at his own wedding party, later that day, Artie can't stop thinking about Sid. Why has the death of a vagrant spooked him so much? It's not his case, but the more he digs, the more it drags him in, implicating – and threatening – his closest friends . . .

'It's rare that crime writing should so passionately and precisely examine its own time. Its also reassuring to find a writer who is so magnificently up to the job.'
Literary Review, Book of The Month

'Artie Cohen is the detective New York deserves: smart, wounded, emotional, haunted, and not as tough as he thinks. Reggie Nadelson's Cohen books get better and better'
Salman Rushdie

arrow books

arrow books